KRUSO

For Charlotta

LUTZ SEILER

TRANSLATED BY
TESS LEWIS

SCRIBE
Melbourne • London

Scribe Publications
18–20 Edward St, Brunswick, Victoria 3056, Australia
2 John Street, Clerkenwell, London, WC1N 2ES, United Kingdom

Originally published in German as *Kruso* by Suhrkamp Verlag Berlin in 2014
First published in English by Scribe in 2017

Typeset in Garamond Premier Pro by the publisher
Printed and bound in the UK by CPI Group (UK) Ltd, Croydon CR0 4YY

Scribe Publications is committed to the sustainable use of natural resources
and the use of paper products made responsibly from those resources.

Supported using public funding by

ARTS COUNCIL
ENGLAND

This book has been selected to receive financial assistance from English
PEN's PEN Translates programme, supported by Arts Council England.
English PEN exists to promote literature and our understanding of it,
to uphold writers' freedoms around the world, to campaign against
the persecution and imprisonment of writers for stating their views, and to
promote the friendly co-operation of writers and the free exchange of ideas.
www.englishpen.org

 GOETHE
INSTITUT

The translation of this work was supported by a grant from the Goethe-
Institut which is funded by the German Ministry of Foreign Affairs.

9781925321845 (Australian edition)
9781911344001 (UK edition)
9781925307955 (e-book)

CiP entries for this title are available from the National Library of Australia
and the British Library.

scribepublications.com.au
scribepublications.co.uk

But to return to my new companion. I was greatly delighted with him.

DANIEL DEFOE, *ROBINSON CRUSOE*

SMALL, UNFAMILIAR MOON

From the moment he took off, Ed had been in a state of exaggerated alertness that kept him from sleeping on the train. Outside the Ostbahnhof, renamed Hauptbahnhof on the new timetable, there were two lamps, one diagonally opposite on the post office and another over the main entrance where a delivery van waited, its motor idling. The night's emptiness contradicted Ed's idea of Berlin — but what did he know about Berlin anyway? He went back into the ticket hall and retreated to one of the broad windowsills. It was so quiet in the hall that, from his spot by the window, he could hear the rattle of the delivery van out front as it drove away.

He dreamt of a desert. On the horizon, a camel was approaching. It was floating in the air, and four or five Bedouins held onto it with more than a little difficulty. The Bedouins wore sunglasses, and paid no attention to him.

When Ed opened his eyes, he saw a man's face, shiny with lotion, so close that at first he couldn't take it all in. The man was old, and his lips were pursed as if he were about to whistle — or had just given someone a kiss. Ed recoiled and the man raised his arms.

'Oh, I do beg your pardon, I'm very sorry, I just ... I really don't want to disturb you, young man.'

Ed rubbed his forehead, which felt damp to the touch, and gathered up his things. The old man smelled of Florena skin cream, and his brown hair was swept back in a stiff, shiny pompadour.

'It's just that I'm in the middle of a move,' the man warbled, 'a major move, and now it's already night, midnight, much too late, stupidly, and I've still got one armoire left — a very good, very large armoire — out on the footpath.'

As Ed rose to his feet, the man pointed to the station exit. 'It's very close, not far at all, where I live, don't worry, just four, five minutes from here, please, thank you, young man.'

For a moment, Ed took his request seriously. The old man's hand plucked at the extra-long sleeve of Ed's jumper as if he wanted to lead him. 'Do come, please!' As he spoke, the man began ruffling the wool upwards, imperceptibly, with circular motions no larger than the radius of his fingertips, soft as gelatine, until Ed felt a gentle, elliptical caress on his pulse. 'You know you'd like to come with me ...'

Ed rammed the old man aside, much too roughly, almost knocking him down.

'There's no harm in asking!' the old man screeched, but it was more of a hiss, almost inaudible. Even his lurching seemed put-on, like a short, rehearsed dance. The old man's hair had slipped down to the nape of his neck, and Ed could not figure out at first how that was possible; he was appalled at the sight of the bare cranium floating like a small, unfamiliar moon in the semi-darkness of the ticket hall.

'I'm sorry, I ... have no time right now,' Ed said, then repeated, 'No time.' As he hastily crossed the hall, he noticed there were timid figures in every corner trying to draw Ed's attention with tiny gestures — yet, at the same time, they seemed anxious to hide their presence. One raised a brown Dederon shopping bag and pointed at it, nodding at Ed. The expression on his face was as warm-hearted as Santa Claus's on Christmas Eve.

The station's Mitropa restaurant smelled of scorched fat. A faint humming noise came from the neon lights in the display case, empty but for a couple of bowls of solyanka on a hot plate. A few oily sausages and chunks of pickled cucumber protruded like rocks from the pale grey membrane that had formed on the soup's surface, bobbing slightly in the relentless stream of heat, like the workings of some inner organ — or the throbbing pulse of life just before it ends, Ed thought. He instinctively put his hand to his forehead: maybe he really had jumped, and all this was his final second.

The transit police entered the dining area. The short, semi-circular visors on their peaked caps gleamed, as did the cornflower blue of their uniforms. With them was a dog, which kept its head lowered as if ashamed of its role. 'Ticket, please. Identification, please.' Those unable to show any travel documents had to leave the restaurant immediately. A shuffling of feet, a scraping of chairs, and a few acquiescent drinkers staggered out without a word, as if their duty had been to wait for this last order. By two a.m., the Mitropa had lost almost all of its guests.

Ed knew it was one of those things that was simply not done, but he got up and grabbed one of the half-empty glasses. Still standing, he drained it in one gulp. Satisfied, he returned to his table. It's the first step, Ed thought; being on the road is doing me good. He cradled his head in his arms, in the musty smell of old leather, and fell asleep in an instant. The Bedouins were still busy with the camel, but they were not all pulling in one direction; instead, they tugged from all sides. They did not seem to be remotely in agreement.

The raised Dederon bag — Ed had not understood what it was supposed to mean, but, then again, it was the first time he had spent the night in a train station. Although he was by now almost certain that there had never been any armoire, Ed pictured the old man's furniture in the middle of the street and felt sorry — not for the old man, actually, but for the associations that would stick with him from now on: the smell of Florena cream and a small, hairless moon. He imagined the old man groping his way back to the armoire, opening the doors, and crawling inside to sleep, and for a moment Ed felt the movement the old man made to curl up and turn away from the world with such intensity that he would have liked to curl up with him.

'Your ticket, please.'

They were checking him a second time. Maybe because of the length of his hair or because of his clothes: the heavy leather jacket Ed had inherited from his uncle, a motorcycle jacket from the Fifties, an impressive coat with an enormous collar, soft lining, and big leather buttons, one that connoisseurs traded as a Thälmann jacket — the term was not used in a derogatory way, quite the contrary, it was used mythologically, if anything — perhaps because the working-class leader wore a very similar jacket in all the historical footage of him. Ed remembered the strangely jolting masses, and Thälmann on the podium, his upper body jerking back and forth, his twitching fist held high. Ed couldn't help it; every time he saw the old footage, his tears began to flow ...

Awkwardly, he pulled out the small, creased piece of paper. Under the heading DEUTSCHE REICHSBAHN, the destination, date, price, and distance in kilometres were printed in thinly outlined boxes. His train left at three twenty-eight a.m.

'Why are you headed to the Baltic Sea?'

'Visiting a friend,' Ed repeated. 'On holiday,' he added because this time the transit officer did not answer. At least he had spoken in a confident tone (a Thälmann-tone), although his 'on holiday' immediately struck him as inadequate and implausible, almost inept.

'Holiday, holiday,' the transit officer repeated.

He spoke as if giving dictation, and at once the boxy grey two-way radio attached to the left side of his chest with a leather strap began to crackle softly.

'Holiday, holiday.'

Evidently, the word was sufficient; it contained everything anyone needed to know about Ed. Everything about his weaknesses and dishonesty. Everything about G., his fear and his unhappiness, everything about his twenty wooden poems from thirteen attempts at writing over a hundred years, and everything about the actual reasons for his trip, which even Ed himself had not fully understood until now. He saw the control centre, the transit-police office, somewhere high above the iron structure of the June night, a cornflower-blue capsule, glassed-in and neatly lined with linoleum, criss-crossing the endless space of his guilty conscience.

Ed was very tired now, and for the first time in his life he had the feeling he was on the run.

TRAKL

Only three weeks had passed since Dr Z. had asked if it might not be agreeable to Ed (he used this expression) to write his final thesis on the Expressionist poet Georg Trakl. 'Perhaps it will even lend itself to a more substantial work,' Z. had added, proud of his offer's attractiveness, which apparently had no other requirements. Furthermore, there was not the slightest overtone in his voice, not one of the displays of pity that had rendered Ed speechless more than once in the past.

For Dr Z., Ed was, first and foremost, the student who could recite by heart whichever text was being discussed. Even when Ed retreated to the back of the classroom and hid behind the curtain of his dark, shoulder-length hair, he eventually spoke at one point or another, hastily and at length and in well-formulated sentences.

For two nights, Ed barely slept so he could read everything on Trakl that was available in the Institute library. The Trakl literature was shelved in the last in a series of access rooms, where, as a rule, he was alone and undisturbed. A small desk stood under a window with a view of the shapeless, cobweb-shrouded hut in the tiny garden where the caretaker of the German Studies Institute would retreat during the day. He probably even lived there — any number of rumours about the man were making the rounds.

The books stood on one of the highest shelves, almost directly beneath the ceiling; you needed a ladder. Ed climbed up without first sliding the ladder closer to *T* and *Tr*. He awkwardly leaned sideways and pulled one book after another from the shelf. The ladder started to wobble; its steel hooks stuttered a warning against the rails on which they were hung. This didn't make Ed any more cautious, quite the contrary. He leaned his torso even further towards Trakl, then further still, and yet a fraction more. It was the moment he had felt it the first time.

That evening, when he was sitting at his desk, he recited the poems softly to himself. The sound of each word became associated with the image of a vast, cool landscape that completely captivated Ed; white, brown, blue, an utter mystery. The writing and life of Georg Trakl — pharmacy student, military pharmacist, morphine addict, and opium-eater. Next to Ed, on an armchair he kept covered with a sheet, Matthew lay sleeping. Now and then, the cat would swivel an ear in Ed's direction. Occasionally, its ear would twitch repeatedly and vigorously as if the chair were electrified.

Matthew — G. had chosen the name. She had found the cat, tiny, mewling, a bit of fluff hardly bigger than a tennis ball, in a light well in the courtyard. She had crouched near the well for two or three hours until she finally lured the kitten out and carried it upstairs. To this day, Ed had no idea why G. had chosen that name, and he never would find out unless the cat were to tell him at some point.

Ed had declined all offers of help. He attended his seminars and took the exams that Professor H., the Department Head, would have gladly exempted him from: the sympathetic bend of his large skull, the benevolently wavy hair, white and lustrous, and the hand on Ed's arm when H. took him aside in the Institute stairwell, but, above all, the velvety voice to which Ed longed to abandon himself ... But knowledge was not Ed's problem. Nor were exams.

Everything Ed read at the time imprinted itself in him, almost automatically and literally, word for word, every poem and every commentary, whatever he cast his eyes on when he sat alone at home or at his desk in the last room of the library, gazing at the caretaker's hut. His existence without G. — it was almost a kind of hypnosis. When he resurfaced some time later, what he had read still buzzed in his head. Studying was a drug that calmed him. He read, he wrote, he cited and recited, and at some point the expressions of condolences dwindled, the offers of help trailed off, the concerned glances subsided. And yet, Ed had never spoken with anyone about G. or about his situation. He only spoke when he was at home: he prattled on endlessly to himself and, of course, he spoke to Matthew.

After his first days with Trakl, Ed had attended only Dr Z.'s lectures. Poetry of the Baroque, of the Romantic period, Expressionism. According to the curriculum, this was not allowed. There were attendance lists and entries in one's transcript. Facts that even Dr Z. could not avoid in the long run. To some extent, Ed still seemed to be protected. His fellow students rarely tried to take the floor when he was speaking. They preferred to listen to him, intimidated and impressed at the same time, as if Ed were some exotic creature from the zoo of human unhappiness, surrounded by a moat of timorous esteem.

After four years in the same course of studies, they all had the relevant images in mind: G. and Ed hand in hand every morning in the Institute car park; G. and Ed's long, tender, untiring embrace as the lecture room slowly filled; G. and Ed and their evening scenes in the Café Corso (initially about nothing, then about *everything*); and then, late at night, the effusive reconciliations, out on the street, at the tram stop. But only after the last tram was gone and they had to run to get home, three stations to Rannischer Platz and, from there, another stretch on foot to their door; as the tram rounded the last curve on its final run through the city and the infernal screeching and whining of the steel chassis pervaded the night like a harbinger of the Final Judgement.

Ed, that's what G. had called him, and sometimes Edge or Eddie.

Now and then (more and more frequently), Ed would climb the ladder to feel it. He called it *the stuff of pilots*. First, the hooks' stuttering beat. Then the beguiling surge, a shudder that reached his very core, his loins — after which, the tension eased. He closed his eyes and breathed deeply. He was a pilot in his space capsule, floating in the air on silken strings.

Lilacs had bloomed for a few days in the dooryard of the caretaker's hut. An elderberry bush swelled from under the threshold. The spider webs in the doorframe were torn, and the loose ends dangled in the wind. The man must be at home, Ed thought. Sometimes Ed saw him slinking through the overgrown garden, or standing motionless as if he were listening for something. When he went into his hut, he did so very gingerly, with arms outstretched. Nevertheless, clinking resounded from his very first step; a sea of bottles covered the floor.

According to one of the rumours, the caretaker had been a university professor and had even worked abroad, in 'non-socialist economic territory' no less. Now he belonged to the class of outcasts who lived their own lives — the garden and the hut belonged to another world. Ed tried to imagine what the man ate for breakfast. He simply could not picture it, but then the image of a small camembert came to him (the 'Rügener Bade Junge' brand), which the caretaker divided into four small, bite-sized pieces on a worn wooden cutting board. The man pricked the triangular pieces of cheese onto the point of his knife and slipped them into his mouth, one after the other. Hard for others to imagine that loners ever eat anything, Ed thought. For Ed, however, the caretaker was the only truly real person in that period of his life, as lonely and forlorn as he was. For a brief, bewildering moment, it wasn't clear if Ed would have preferred to consign himself to the custodian's care rather than remain under Dr Z.'s wing.

The Institute library closed at seven p.m. As soon as he got home, Ed would feed Matthew. He gave him bread, a slice of cold cuts, and some milk. It had been G.'s job. As reliably as Ed cared for Matthew, he still did not understand that cats don't need milk but water to survive. That's why he was puzzled when the animal dug around the lemon geranium in the hydroponic pot as soon as he left the room. Ed stood as if rooted in the kitchen and listened to the noise. The clicking of the little pebbles as they rained out of the pot onto the cupboard and from there onto the floorboards. He couldn't do anything but listen. He couldn't believe that these things were part of his life — that he was the one to whom all this was happening.

MATTHEW

Then, on the evening before Ed's twenty-fourth birthday, Matthew disappeared. Ed was up half the night reading for Dr Z.'s seminar on Barthold Heinrich Brockes: 'As I walked back and forth / In this tree's shadow ...' At some point, he fell asleep at his desk.

In the morning, he went to the Institute, crossing Rannischer Platz and continuing on to the Markt Platz, then along Barfüsserstrasse towards the university. In the dark, narrow street was the Merseburger Hof restaurant, where Ed always stopped to drink a cup of coffee before his lectures. The greasy print on the back of the menu (perhaps an excerpt from an older chronicle) revealed that Barfüsserstrasse, the Street of the Discalced, used to be called 'Bei den Brüdern', Friars' Way, then 'Bei den geringeren Brüdern', Lesser Brothers' Way, and finally 'Bei den Barfüssern', Barefoot Brothers' Way — a strange descent that inspired in Ed a feeling of solidarity with the street.

In the afternoon, Matthew was still missing and Ed began to call him. First down in the courtyard, then from the apartment window, but the faint, reproachful cry with which the cat usually answered did not come.

'Matthew!'

The smell of the courtyard: it was like inhaling an old, already-mildewed heartache. A sorrow made of mould and coal that lived in the row of rundown sheds across the way; a sorrow constantly exuded by the things that had been trapped in the sheds and were now buried forever. The house was mostly occupied by *Bunesians*, workers at the Buna Chemical plant that lay south of the city. Bunesians — Ed remembered that the workers referred to themselves that way. They used the word matter-of-factly and not without a hint of pride, the way you emphasise the fact that you belong to a tribe whose history is well known, a clan into which you are born and which you can be sure will exist for a long, long time.

'Matthew!'

Ed stood at the open window for a while and listened to the rats. He thought, 'birthday, my birthday,' and began calling again: 'Matthew!' He had turned the light out so he couldn't be seen. Across the way, on the hill that rose above the trees, was the long, flat brick building of the nursing home. Since he'd started calling, the barracks' windows had filled with people. He saw the faded colours of the shirts and cardigans, and the grey pates gleaming in the neon light — the elderly were interested in everything that happened in the courtyard, especially at night. It often took a few seconds before they turned their ceiling lights off again. Ed looked at the lavender afterglow of the neon, and imagined them standing there in the darkness, pressing together, with those further away from the window exhaling their putrid breath onto the napes of those standing in front. Maybe one of them had seen Matthew? And they were now debating softly (softly at first, then louder, then more quietly again so as not to alarm the staff) whether and how they should send their secret messages.

Two days later, he was still calling. In the beginning, he'd found his loud calls unpleasant, but now he couldn't stop. Every hour, he called down into the courtyard for a time, mechanically, almost unconsciously, his face chilled by the night air, becoming a mask that grew all the way to the ends of his hair.

The sense of sympathy in the house had been exhausted. Windows were thrown open and slammed shut; there was cursing, in the Halle dialect or that of the Bunesians. Neighbours rang his doorbell or pounded on his door.

'Matthew! Sausage, tasty milk!'

'You know where you can shove your sausage, you punk, then maybe we could get some sleep!'

The June night was cool, but Ed left the window open. Without noticing, he had begun to lean over the windowsill, which was built up with an iron bar for security; he leaned only slightly at first, then further and further out. As if it were a gymnastics apparatus, he grasped the rusty bar with both hands and extended his upper body slowly towards the courtyard:

'Matthew!'

The volume of his voice increased; it grew clearer and stronger, a dark, cleanly resounding 'ew':

'Matth — ew!'

Inside, somewhere far behind him, the tips of his toes skittered over the linoleum, and, round about the tip of his spine, *the stuff of pilots* began to flow with a completely unexpected and unparalleled intensity. He stiffened with a pleasant sense of desire. No, it was much more than that; it was a wave of lust that made him go rigid, from head to toe —

'Matth — — ew!'

His body was swimming or floating. He relished the warm, velvety hue underlying the echo; all foreignness had disappeared. Once more, cautiously, he drew a breath and began to call, immediately striking the tone that bound the courtyard, the darkness, and the surrounding world of Halle an der Saale to a single soft, swaying oneness into which he was inclined to plunge. Now, finally, he was completely prepared to —

'Matthew!'

Ed shot back into the room as if he had been struck. He managed to take only two steps before he doubled up and fell to the floor. It was Matthew, Matthew's cry. An indignant, offended mewing or squealing, the noise of an unoiled hinge, a door between the here and now and the hereafter that was slammed shut with a bang, flinging him back from his fall — second, third, fourth floor. He started to faint; he had to inhale deeply and exhale again, inconspicuously, as if he weren't really breathing, as if he actually weren't breathing at all anymore.

After a while, he was able to take his hands from his face. His gaze fell on the open window.

The cat was very quiet.

It wasn't there at all.

As he fell asleep, G. bent over him. She was very close to him and pointed a finger at her half-closed mouth. She stretched her lips wide and pressed the tip of her small, gleaming tongue behind her front teeth, which were set at a slight slant to each other, like the blades of a snowplough: 'Matthew, try saying Ma-tth-hew.'

He tried to get out of it, and asked if all English-language teachers had the same small snowploughs in their mouths into which their tongues could nestle so perfectly.

G. shook her head and stuck her index finger in his mouth.

'Edgar Bendler, is that your name? Edgar Bendler, twenty-four years old? What is it you're missing then, Ed? You think your handicap is inborn? Then try to say *thanks*.'

'Thanks.'

'Try to say *both of us*.'

'Both of us.'

The finger in his mouth moved and made everything clear to him. Everything he was missing.

'And now, one more time, *both of us*, and then please go on as long as you can.'

'Both, both ...'

As stiff as a small black sphinx, Matthew sat next to the bed to watch for a while as Ed penetrated slowly, very slowly into G., the way she liked best, millimetre by millimetre.

WOLFSTRASSE

Strictly speaking, Ed's residence at 18 Wolfstrasse, in the brick building turned grey by the daily emissions of the two large chemical plants, was not quite legal. He was subletting his place from a subtenant, and so was a kind of sub-subtenant. There had surely been other subleases in the at least one hundred years long rental history of this building, arrangements loosely bound through informal, often merely handwritten, contracts and inventory lists, or verbal agreements about the use of the cellar, and binding agreements concerning the use of the toilets, none of which a single soul could recall. Over the years, entire genealogical trees of subtenant relations had expanded far beyond the housing authorities and their procedures of *central allocation*, and yet, after just two generations of subtenants, previous occupants were lost from view. Soon only their names were remembered, names that collected on mailboxes and doors, like the faded and scratched crests of distant cities on a well-travelled suitcase. Yes, that's how it is, Ed thought to himself: you travel the world in apartments like *ageing baggage*.

The entire day, he had wandered, half-conscious, through the city.

Fear still thundered in his head, and he felt a sense of shame that was somehow connected to the question of whether he had jumped or not.

He was still standing in front of his door with its small flock of plastic and brass nameplates crowded together on the grey-painted wood surface. He thought of his grandfather's walking stick, covered from the handle to the tip with gleaming silver and gold badges of foreign places. Later, the stick had served as a cane. As a child, before he had begun school — that is, at the time of his grandfather's great expeditions — it was pure joy for Ed to run his finger over the small shiny-metal plates from the tip of the stick to the handle and back again, over and over, back and forth. He could feel the coolness of the crests and as he stroked the foreign places; he spelled them out as best he could, and his grandfather corrected him.

'A-a-sh-chn. Aschn!'

'M-mm-me-met-tss, Mee-tz.'

'Ss-ss-sht-ssshhtuuu, sshtuutt, shtutt ...'

'C-C-Co-o-op-en, Coopeen ...'

Aachen or Copenhagen, the words resounded for places that seemed to lie in a kind of faraway realm, or at least in strange, distant lands, and their existence was doubtful at best. Peculiarly, Ed still found them dubious, although he knew better. In the end, the badges had made the familiar figure of his grandfather seem strange, and set the old man at a certain distance, in a prehistoric era — its connection with the present could no longer be established. It was the same with Stengel, Kolpacki, Augenlos, and Rust — the names on Ed's door that were still legible. His own name was on a label above the doorknob. The name underneath was neatly crossed out, but for him was still visible, even in complete darkness, even without the nameplate or the door. He had written his own name in pencil at the time he moved in and had carefully glued on the paper label, which had in the meantime begun to warp and turn yellow at the edges.

'My well-travelled door,' Ed whispered and turned his key in the lock.

On the one hand, there was the omnipotence of the officials and the sharp tool of the *Central Housing Authority*; on the other hand, no one in the building knew where Stengel, Kolpacki, Augenlos, and Rust could have gone or even if they were still alive — Ed began to feel this was a good omen.

He opened the kitchen cupboard and looked over his meagre stores. He threw most of them away. Following an inspiration, he unscrewed the oven damper. He grabbed the notebook with his seminar notes from the previous weeks, stuck it in the oven, and set it on fire. It burned well. He took another notebook and then another, grabbing them at random. The room soon grew warm, the fire-clay bricks made clicking sounds. He pulled the grey marbled folder with his first attempts at writing off the shelf and laid it on the baking tray. After a while, he put it back and opened the window. It was an experiment.

He spent the whole day cleaning up his apartment, sorting books, notebooks, and papers, and putting everything in some kind of order, as if they were his literary remains. Of course, he also noticed he was attached to certain things, 'but only because you want to leave,' Ed whispered. It did him good now and then to stick a twig of a softly uttered half-sentence in the embers, so that the feeble hearth of his presence didn't completely expire.

Matthew was missing.

Matthew.

The next morning, Ed removed the ash pan from the oven and carried it to the bucket covered with a cloth so the fine, flaky black ash would not drift about, as his father had taught him. Ed had been a latchkey child since his tenth birthday, and therefore responsible for heating the tile stove when he came home alone from school in the early afternoon. Along with cleaning the cellar and drying the dishes, stoking the oven was one of his 'little chores' — his mother's expression. She used diminutives for almost everything related to him: 'little chores', 'little hobbies', 'you and your little friend'. Such things lurked in Ed's mind (and he felt the heat of confusion warm his forehead) when he decided not to tell anyone of his plans. Edgar Bendler had decided to disappear — a sentence that could have come from a novel.

He knelt down and swept around the oven. He mopped the floor until it glowed a dull reddish brown. The blunted edges of the doorsill and the bare, worn patches turned black. The black patches had questions for him. Why hadn't he jumped? What else had he lost here? Hmm? Hmm? Ed tried not to bump into anything, and set the bucket down carefully. He already felt like an interloper, a stranger in an old, former life, a man without a country. He heard steps outside the door and held his breath. He tiptoed into the kitchen, took the bottle of Megalac out of the cupboard, and drank. It was a kind of liquid calcium that coated his mucous membranes; since early adolescence, he had simply had too much stomach acid.

It was late afternoon before he could begin packing his bag. He chose a few books and added the oversized brown notebook he had sporadically used as a kind of journal. It was bulky and impractical, but it was a gift from G. He carried Matthew's blanket and his smelly litter box down to the courtyard. A broken window, a moment's hesitation, then he tossed it all into the darkness of the sorrowful shed.

In a shoebox filled with postcards and street maps, he found an old map of the Baltic coast. Someone had underlined the names of several places using a ruler and traced the coastline with blue ink. 'It's possible, very possible, that you did this, Ed,' Ed murmured. As a matter of fact, he couldn't say how the map had ended up among his things; maybe it had been his father's.

In farewell, he wanted to play some music: soft, very soft music. He stood mindlessly in front of the stove for a time, until he realised he could not play the record on the burner, that the burner wasn't a turntable.

Finally, before Ed left his apartment on Wolfstrasse, he unscrewed the fuses in the fuse box and set them in a row on the meter: an expensive automatic fuse with a switch, and two older, discoloured ceramic fuses. He concentrated on the blank counter for a few seconds. Because of the faint, hypnotic fluting on the small disc, it was hard to tell if it was actually immobile. Ed remembered the time, when he was thirteen or fourteen, that his mother had sent him into the stairwell to change the fuses by himself for the first time. The noises of the house and their muffled echo, the voices from the neighbour's apartment, a cough from upstairs, the clattering of dishes — that world was aeons away when he put aside the old fuse and accepted his fear as a form of boundless temptation. He watched himself as he slowly, but irresistibly, stretched out his index finger, and began to stick it in the empty, gleaming fuse socket. It was the first time he had experienced it so clearly and distinctly: under the surface of life, to a certain extent *behind life*, there reigned a perpetual allure, a proposition without equal. It took a firm resolve to turn away, and that is exactly what Ed did that day.

He put his key under the mat; the door on his mailbox, he simply pushed closed: the Bunesians could be depended on in case of an emergency.

THE STATION HOTEL

He smelled the sea even before he got off the train. From his childhood (memories of their only trip to the Baltic Sea), he remembered the Hotel am Bahnhof. It lay directly across from the station, a big, beautiful attraction with oriels built as round towers, and weather vanes in which the numerals of the years crumbled.

He let a few cars pass and hesitated. It wouldn't be wise, he thought, especially as far as money was concerned. On the other hand, there was no point in arriving on the island in the afternoon, since there probably wouldn't be enough time left to find a place to stay — if he could find one at all. He had about 150 marks on him; if he were careful, he could make it last for three, maybe even four weeks. He had left ninety marks in his bank account for rent transfers, enough until September. If he were lucky, no one would take exception to his disappearance. He could have fallen ill. Summer holidays would begin in three weeks. He had written his parents a card. They believed he was in Poland, in Katowice, for the so-called International Student Summer, as he had been the year before.

The reception desk was built unusually high and looked as if it had been swept clean, no papers, no keys; but what did Ed know about hotels? At the very last moment, the heads of three women appeared, rising like the pistons of a four-stroke motor in which the fourth spark plug has failed to ignite. Impossible to discern from exactly which depths the receptionists had suddenly surfaced; maybe the high shelf of the desk was connected to a back room, or maybe over the years the women had simply got used to staying under cover as long as possible, quiet and still, behind their dark veneered barrier.

'Good afternoon, I ...'

His voice sounded weary. Alone in the compartment, he had once again been unable to sleep. A military patrol, probably some kind of advance border security, had confiscated his map of the Baltic coast. The train had stopped for a long time in Anklam: the patrol must have got on there. He regretted that nothing more intelligent had occurred to him than claiming that it wasn't *actually* his own map ... As a result, he had no way of knowing why particular places were underlined and particular sections of the coast line were traced in ink ... His voice had suddenly failed, and in its place was the murmuring in his brain — Brockes, Eichendorff, and, as always, Trakl, who echoed most relentlessly with his verses of foliage and brown — that made Ed grab his head. A sudden move: in reflex, one of the soldiers raised his machine gun.

In the end, Ed could consider himself lucky that they left him alone. 'Odd duck,' the Kalashnikov-wielding soldier murmured out in the corridor. Ed's forehead was covered with sweat. Fields flashed by, black grass along the railroad embankment.

'Do you have a reservation?'

Ed was taking a room for the first time in his life. The amazing thing was, it was working. They gave him a long form on dull paper and asked for identification. As he lifted his elbows onto the high surface of the desk with some effort and filled out the form with a stiff wrist, the receptionists took turns leafing through his pass booklet. For one absurd instant, Ed feared his secret departure might have automatically been registered in one of the very last, empty pages in his pass, under 'Visa and Travel'. *Unauthorised displacement* — from the days of his military, he remembered this fateful stamp that incurred a wide variety of penalties.

'I beg your pardon, this is my first time,' Ed said.

'What?' asked the concierge.

Ed raised his head and tried to smile, but his attempt to bridge the gap fell flat. He was given a key from which a varnished wooden cube dangled on a short string. He closed his fist around the cube and knew his room number. The number was neatly burnt into the wood. He briefly pictured the hotel caretaker in his basement workroom, bent over an endless row of little blocks sawed to the proper size and sanded, onto which he placed the glowing rod of his soldering iron — number after number, room by room. Ed had once been a labourer, too, and part of him was still at home in workshops, in the caves of the *working class*, those side rooms of the world, in which things asserted their definite, tangible outlines.

'Second floor, stairs on the left, young man.'

The word *Moccastube* shimmered above a brass-studded door next to the staircase. On the first landing, Ed looked back again; two of the three women's heads had disappeared, while the third woman was speaking on the telephone and following him with her eyes.

When he woke, it was already after four in the afternoon. A wardrobe stood at the foot of the double bed. In the corner, a television stood on a chrome-plated stand. Above the toilet hung a cast-iron flushing tank, coated with a film of condensation. The tank must have dated from a much earlier era. The lever for the flushing mechanism imitated two leaping dolphins. While the animals sedately returned to their initial position, an endless stream of water gushed out. Ed liked the sound of the water, and felt like the dolphins were his friends.

That you could go into a hotel, ask for a room, and get one (rather straightforwardly) had to be counted as one of the few wonders of the world that had survived — 'for a' that an' a' that,' Ed gurgled into the stream of water from the showerhead. Over time, you simply forgot that such things still existed; fundamentally, you didn't believe in them anymore, yes, you forgot what life could be good for. Ed's thoughts ran along those lines. He wanted to masturbate, but couldn't muster enough concentration.

To the right of the hotel was a lake with a fountain that regularly rose into the sky, collapsed in on itself, and disappeared for several seconds. A couple in a pedal boat glided slowly up to the water feature. Ed was suddenly overcome with *a good feeling* as he crossed the road towards the lake. All this was the beginning of something. Someone who'd been through a fair amount showed himself capable of ... With that, his sentence ended. It was clear to him that his departure was overdue. He felt the pain, as if he were only now awakening from anaesthesia, millimetre by millimetre.

A cobblestone street that turned off to the left was named An den Bleichen. He passed a few run-down villas with conservatories, courtyards, and garages. He walked up to the nameplate near the door of one to have a look at the house's travel itinerary until now. The small, brave lighted doorbell plate also preserved the legibility of some of the names that had been pasted for some time, perhaps for years now. As he passed, Ed tried to capture their rhythm: Schiele, Dahme, Glambeck, Krieger ... His muttering formed a bridge across the lake, and his steps on the wood were a kind of metronome. 'All-of-those-who-died-al-ready ...' whispered Ed, and he automatically covered his face with his hands, 'see everything in a new way?' The old city wall appeared, then an archway and a café called 'Torschliesserhaus', The Gatekeeper's House.

He crossed the old city to the port and checked the ferry departure times. In the kiosk of the White Fleet, he bought a crossing for the following day. The sight of the boat put him in a euphoric mood. The steps to the dock, of light-grey cement, and then: the sea.

To eat cheaply, Ed returned to the train station. He felt rested, and gauged his chances. A hide-out in the sea, hidden sea, Hiddensee … He knew the stories. Continuous whispers washed around the island.

Ed chewed deliberately and drank his coffee in tiny sips. First, it wouldn't be easy getting onto one of the boats. Then it would be almost impossible to find a place to stay, but another goal was not conceivable *inside the border*. Certainly, he had heard the experts who claimed that Hiddensee actually lay outside the border, that it was exterritorial, an island of the blessed, of dreamers and idealists, of failures and rejects. Others called it the Capri of the North, booked-up for decades.

In Halle, Ed had met a historian who'd worked winters as a waiter in the Offenbach Stuben, a wine restaurant where he and G. had occasionally sat at the bar. Every spring, at the opening of the season, the historian (that's what everyone called him, after all) returned to the island. 'At last, at last!' he liked to call out to his customers, who nodded indulgently when he started in on one of his eulogies, which he usually began by addressing his audience in the Offenbach Stuben with 'Dear friends!' 'The island, dear friends, has all I need, all I've ever searched for. As soon as it surfaces on the horizon, seen from the deck of the steamboat, its slender, delicate form, its fine outline, and behind it, the mainland's last grey cockscomb, Stralsund with its towers, the entire hinterland with its filth, you know what I mean, dear friends, the island appears and suddenly you forget it all, because now, before you, something new is beginning, yes, dear friends, right there on the steamboat!' the man rhapsodised. Grey-haired and in his mid-forties, he had left his position at the university — voluntarily, it was said — and was therefore all the more deeply immersed in dreams. As many of the country's thinkers did, he wore a beard like Marx's. 'Freedom, dear friends, is essentially a matter of writing one's own laws within the framework of existing laws, of being simultaneously the object and the subject of legislation, that is an essential characteristic of life up there, in the north.' That's how the historian of the Offenbach Stuben summed it up, holding a tray as round as a bass drum and full of bottles in front of his chest.

For Ed, the most important piece of information was that places could suddenly free-up even in season. From one day to the next, waiters were needed, or dishwashers, kitchen-help. There were seasonal workers who disappeared overnight for a wide variety of reasons. Usually, those telling such stories would stop abruptly at that point and throw a glance at the listener — and then, depending on the situation, would continue in one of the possible or impossible directions: 'Of course, there are people who give up and return to the mainland, who just aren't cut out for it.' Or: 'You know, an exit visa is suddenly authorised, in the middle of the summer ...' Or: 'Sure, it's hard to believe, fifty kilometres, but there have always been strong swimmers ...' After every conversation, Hiddensee seemed like a narrow strip of land of mythical splendour, the last, the only place, an island that was constantly floating away, always outside the field of vision — you'd have to hurry if you wanted to reach it.

After eating, Ed returned to the hotel. Someone had been through his things, but nothing was missing. He stood at the window and looked across at the train station. In bed, he began to call for Matthew — a regression. But he only called quietly, and really just to hear his voice again before going to sleep. No, he had not jumped.

THE ISLAND

Most often he was turned down immediately. Someone passing would call out: 'We're all full!' A few heads were raised when Ed whispered 'thank you' and left as quickly as he could, clutching the sweaty straps of his fake leather bag in his fist.

He had landed on the northern end and walked south, about six kilometres, which he then covered again in the opposite direction. The island was so narrow at some points that you could see the water on either side. To the left, the sea was silver; to the right of the land, a dark-blue glass, almost black. The clouds seemed to drift lower than usual, and Ed mused for a while on their curiously elongated shapes. While the horizon expanded, the distance between it and the sky shrank, one dimension displacing the other. At the end of the day, when he had just begun to lose hope, the question left him all but indifferent: 'Would you happen to have any work for me? However, I'd also need a room.'

In a guesthouse called Norderende, he was offered one mark forty an hour for all manner of jobs, as they put it, 'but without accommodation'. A few discarded roofed beach chairs stood a short distance away. Ed liked their canopies' faded blue. It was the colour of idleness, of July, of sun on one's face. While the surly waiter exchanged a few words with him (Ed's first conversation on the island), two employees scurried past, their heads lowered, as if worried about losing their jobs. Ed paused for a moment between the garbage bins and the beverage crates. Without being aware of it, he had adopted a beggar's humble demeanour.

As Ed walked away, one of the employees called to him through the almost closed door of the storage shed, so that Ed could not understand the man clearly. All that he caught was the word 'hermit' and then 'Crusoe, Crusoe —' as if the man were delivering a secret message. It was far more likely that the man wanted to mock him with the old story of the shipwreck.

Night was falling and lights were going on in the houses. The weight of his bag made Ed walk a bit crookedly. The straps were much too narrow and cut into his shoulder; the imitation leather had turned brittle. Ed wondered if it would have been better to have left the bag somewhere, or, even better, to have hidden it in a sea buckthorn bush on the way. He had surely phrased his request for work wrongly, wrongly and stupidly, as if he himself weren't part of the same society. Here, one simply *had* work; no one needed to go around asking for a job, especially not the way he did, going from house to house with a ratty bag on his shoulder. Work was like a pass: you had to be able to show it. Not having work was against the law and a punishable offence. Ed sensed that, the way he had asked it, the question couldn't even be answered; in fact, it was like a provocation. And as he plodded along with his much-too-heavy bag, he reformulated it:

'Might you possibly need additional help this season?'

He had found the right words.

On his way through Kloster, the northernmost village on the island, he met a few holiday-makers. He asked them unceremoniously for a place to stay. They laughed as if he had cracked a hilarious joke and wished him 'all the luck in the world'. He passed a row of beautiful old wood houses. A man his father's age scolded from his balcony and repeatedly thrust his beer bottle jerkily in the air. He was obviously drunk enough to recognise *someone from who-knows-where* at first sight.

'Do you need another pair of hands in your kitchen? I happen to have some time at the moment.'

From the bartender in the Offenbach (Ed was always on the lookout for the Karl-Marx-type beard), he knew that sleeping on the beach was risky. Something about the border patrols. They would find him with one of their long torchlights; they would shine a light in his face right in the middle of a dream and ask him about his escape plans. Without a permit or accommodation, any stay in the border area was forbidden. The inspectors on the ferry had not been particularly interested: they assumed that passengers on the early ferry were day tourists. What was important was to have some kind of story to tell if asked, a name, an address of any kind. The Naturalist writer Gerhart Hauptmann had claimed that everyone on the island was named Schluck or Jau — in fact, those were the only two families on the island: Schluck and Jau. Ed found the two names suspect. They didn't sound convincing, they sounded made-up. Yes, that was possible in fiction, but not in real life. In the Stralsund port, he had looked in the telephone book and chosen the name Weidner. He wrote down on a piece of notepaper he kept on him, folded up tight: *the Weidner family, Kloster, number 42.*

'Do you happen to need any help in your restaurant establishment?'

A sentence made of wood.

And they could probably see that he just wanted to get away, simply disappear, that he was, fundamentally, a failure, washed-up, a wreck, only twenty-four years old and already a complete wreck.

The beach was out of the question, as were the rest of the shelters along the shoreline. His fears were childish: someone might step on his head by mistake when he was asleep. The water might rise suddenly and drown him. There might be rats in the bunker.

As darkness fell, Ed reached the northern tip of the island. He had crossed all three villages twice: Neuendorf, Vitte, and Kloster. In the port (it was strange to arrive once again at the place he had landed that afternoon, though it seemed years earlier to him), he saw on a signboard that the area behind the town was called Bessiner Haken and was a bird sanctuary.

A night under the stars was now going to be part of his life, Ed was convinced of this, and it was right that things should start off this way, despite his fears. At the edge of the village, he saw a weathered signpost with the inscription: 'Radiation Institute'. On a distant hill, behind poplar trees, he could see the outline of a large building. He passed a large barn, and several fences coated with waste oil. The reeds lining the path rustled. They were taller than he was and blocked his view of the water; the evening cries of some kind of goose resounded in the air. The last house, its thatched roof covered with moss. The vegetable garden reminded Ed of his grandmother's garden: potatoes, kohlrabi, and asters. The path, carelessly paved with slabs of concrete, petered out in a swamp.

The first raised hide looked rather like a cabin, a tree house, an extremely good hideout, but unfortunately it was locked. The second, smaller raised hide was open, and swayed so much that Ed wondered if it was even used anymore. With an effort, he heaved his bag up. He tried to arrange things as quietly as he could. He gathered some wood to provisionally barricade the entrance to the tower and the top of ladder. When he dragged a few rotten branches to the top of the ladder, a beam of light hit him. He threw himself to the floor, knocking his head on a bench. He lay without moving. He breathed heavily, he could smell the wood, his forehead burned. The hide's tight floor space did not leave him enough room to stretch out his feet. He thought of *Klondike Fever*, of the man in the snowy wasteland who managed at the very last second to light a fire with his last match, but then ... After a time, the beam of light returned. Ed got up slowly and greeted the lighthouse like an old friend he had lost sight of temporarily.

'And would you happen to need more help?'

The beacon fitfully fanned out and narrowed in turn — that probably meant 'no'. Strange how the prismatic finger of light would shoot out in sections, only to freeze in the next instant, as if it had hit something and that was more important than continuing to revolve endlessly in a circle.

'I mean, just some help for this season?' Ed murmured.

He had given up his plan to return to the small town and eat in one of the inns. He hadn't even been to the beach yet. But just the fact that he was here, on the island ... He kept listening in the dark to the sounds of the jungle around him, then he pulled on his sweater and put on his jacket. He spread the rest of his things as best he could out on the wooden floor of the hide. It was cold that night.

ZUM KLAUSNER

13 June. Ed's raised hide was still submerged in darkness when a deafening noise broke out. The birds in the sanctuary woke and clamoured for the day, their din filled with reluctance and continual, protracted complaint. Ed left his quarters well before sunrise and trotted inland, his face full of insect bites, his forehead on fire.

His first task would be to explore the area and, above all, to find a better hideaway or at least to sniff out a place he could safely hide his bag and his things (his heavy Thälmann jacket, his sweater). Apart from the myths and legends he had heard on the mainland, Ed didn't know much about the island, either about its geography or the cycles of surveillance and border patrols. At first, it all seemed easy to survey: meadows, grasslands, and a few streets, partly paved with slabs of concrete. This was no landscape for hideouts. In contrast, the woods and the highlands to the north were inviting.

The following night, Ed crept into one of the high inlets at the base of the coastline. His cave resembled a broad and recent rift; the bluff had opened itself for him. There were no mosquitos, but water dripped from the loam onto the back of his neck. The sea was black and almost silent, except for the regularly recurring sizzling sound in the pebbles between the rocks on the shore — as if someone were pouring water onto a glowing hotplate. There were a multitude of noises in his cave that Ed couldn't identify. Something rustled above him and something rustled *within the loam*. And, sometimes, there was a sound of breathing or soft groaning. A few verses rose, murmurs from the hoard of lines he had learned by heart, verses comparing the little lapping Baltic waves to the whispers of the dead. These insinuations annoyed Ed; if he were serious about his departure (and fresh start), he would have to fight against them, which is why he tried again to form his own thoughts.

He closed his eyes and, after a while, pictured the Man of the Baltic Waves. He was tall and stooped: it was the caretaker at the Institute. He scooped water from the sea and poured it over his fire pit on the beach. The water turned to steam, smoke rose, and the man himself grew thinner and more transparent each time. At last, all that remained was his face. The face smiled at Ed from the sand, exposing its rotten teeth, a mess of mussels, tar, and algae; it said, 'My presence is spent.'

In the morning, Ed's things were drenched and a thin delta had formed on the beach. The spring water turned the loam into shining blocks that were perfect for walking on. The water pooled here and there. Kneeling properly at first (like an animal with its hindquarters raised and head reaching forwards) and then lying flat on the ground, Ed tried to drink. Although no one would be on the beach before sunrise, Ed felt he was being watched. With one hand, he pushed his hair back towards his nape; with the other, he pushed against the stones that wanted to press in between his ribs. 'Nature's no picnic, no, indeed,' Ed murmured; he imitated his father's voice and couldn't help snickering. He had made it through the second night.

The spring water tasted of soap and smelled fermented. He followed the delta back to the crevice that lay right next to where he had been sleeping. An animal was watching him. It was a fox. He was protecting the source and had probably been tracking Ed for a long time.

'You gave me a start, you rascal,' Ed whispered. The fox said nothing and did not move. It rested its head on its front paws, like a dog; its gaze was directed out towards the sea. An uprooted sea buckthorn bush threw a shadow over its fur, which looked very fresh and alive.

'You've got a nice spot here, you old rascal, nice and hidden. No mosquitos, fresh water ... You're a clever one, aren't you?'

Ed spread his things out to dry on the rocks, but he felt uneasy and gathered them up again. He was hungry and had a bad taste in his mouth. The rolls he had bought in Kloster from the baker named Kasten had turned to mush. He squeezed a few of them, and out dripped a semen-like liquid. He chewed slowly and swallowed. The energy of his departure was used up, and he felt a tightness behind his eyes. It was not an ache, but a reminder of fingernails bitten to the quick. The inflamed nail beds and the frayed, ragged plaster — G.'s fingernails. He wondered how long he could keep this up. How long his strength would last. When would he have to turn back?

'There'd be no point, you old rascal.'

The high, gaunt coastline — he had never seen anything like it. There were outcrops and overhangs and a kind of glacier landscape, with huge meandering tongues of loam and clay heading out to the sea. Some sections were overgrown, some bare, cracked, and rutted, and there were grey, loamy walls from which, now and then, the head of a cyclops would protrude and look contemptuously down at Ed. But Ed hardly ever looked up. He wasn't interested in cyclopses or whatever these rock formations resembled. He strode along the stony beach, his head lowered, and tried to keep the small fire of his monologue burning with encouragements and sound arguments. With his own words.

Some distance further north, the coastal shrubbery suddenly opened up to reveal a flight of stairs. The cement blocks that were supposed to anchor the steel construction into the beach hung in the air about a metre from the ground. When Ed stepped onto the lowest step, there was a high, clear metallic sound. 'The way the steel panels of sinking ships begin to sing,' Ed whispered and stopped. The rusty iron seesawed threateningly. In the end, Ed counted almost three hundred steps (every third step rotten or broken), spread over various intervals and gaps up to the top of the fifty- or sixty-metre-high cliff.

A light-coloured building, its gables trimmed with wood, shimmered through the pine trees. At first sight, it looked like a Mississippi steamboat, a beached paddle steamer that had tried to reach the sea by going through the forest. A few smaller log cabins were anchored around it like lifeboats encircling the mother ship.

Ed kept his eyes firmly on the image so that it couldn't evaporate: from the ship, a stone-flagged terrace with tables and beer garden chairs extended almost to the edge of the bluff. The outer rows of tables were covered, and looked like mangers for forest animals. Something was written in looping handwriting on the slate board near the front door, but Ed was still too far away to read it. To the left of the door, over a sash window in the wooden covered porch that formed part of the steamship's paddlewheel case, hung a small, stiff flag with the word 'ice-cream'. A handmade sign was screwed on to the front of the porch: ZUM KLAUSNER. The Hermit Inn.

The 'Z' was elaborately embellished, and Ed briefly imagined the sign-painter; he saw him being assigned the job, saw him noting down the name of the ship and the date of its christening. Ed sensed to the nth degree the trouble this first letter must have given the sign-painter, and a sense of futility washed over him for a moment.

To make sure the building had three dimensions, Ed slowly circled it. It was a ship built in the style of a forest dwelling. The gables had turned moss green, and saltpetre deposits bloomed on the foundation. Behind the first house was a second, somewhat-more-modern one. Between the two was a courtyard, and behind them a forest. The site consisted roughly of three concentric circles. In the innermost circle were the courtyard, the two main buildings, and another smaller terrace, populated by a horde of cast-iron coffee-house chairs, their white paint stained with rust. In the second circle were two log cabins with two sheds and a wood yard with a chopping block. To the north, the courtyard opened out onto a clearing, a sloping meadow that was covered with pine-tree roots and that rose gently towards the edge of the forest and onto a path, which no doubt led to the lighthouse, Ed's old friend. A playground had been set up in the middle of the clearing with a mushroom-shaped jungle gym, a teeter-totter, a sandbox, and a concrete ping-pong table. Ed was surprised for a moment that the kind of playground found all over the country had made it into this fairytale place high above the surf. A small palisade marked the third, outermost circle, or, more exactly, a kind of deer fence made of deadwood, carefully woven between the nearest tree trunks at the forest's edge. The entire compound was surrounded by a thick growth of pine and beech trees.

Ed strolled across the clearing towards the coast, and looked out to sea. A soft, sweet current flowed through the morning damp, a captivating mixture of forest and sea. It was foggy, and you could breathe in the milky, washed out horizon if you inhaled deeply enough; it's like being here and out there at the same time, Ed thought.

A man lay motionless on the hill above the playground, dead or asleep. When Ed approached, the man heard him; he jumped heavenwards. Maybe a prayer, Ed thought, but it sounded as if it came from a snake, a kind of hissing, and at some point he understood it.

'Piss-ant, piss off, piss off ...'

It was, in fact, only six o'clock in the morning. Ed sat down at one of the manger-tables and decided to wait. He was shivering, he was hungry, and he had hardly slept the past few nights. His leather Thälmann jacket was completely soaked, heavier than any armour. But the bench, the table, and the little roof offered solace — as if he had been gone for a week and was just coming in from the wilderness. He opened his bag to let the moisture escape. He pulled out a few things and several books and laid them out to dry.

The windows of the porch, behind which must have been the restaurant, were covered with coarse, net-like curtains that moved noticeably several times after seven o'clock. Ed tried to sit up straight and look relaxed at the same time. The wind was blowing in off the sea. The door opened, and its two wings were fastened with hooks to the porch wall. The man who opened it paid no attention to Ed. He had a glowing white shirt. For a moment, Ed saw his oval, wire-rimmed glasses and a big, bushy black moustache. The man went up to the slate board and erased the previous day's braised steak and wrote with chalk in the dark, still-damp spot the words 'ox-tail soup'.

'Rimbaud!'

Someone had called and Ed had jumped up, ready to recite. He did it automatically, he couldn't help it; in the very first moment, in any case, the verse hoard rumbled in his head: *The Drunken Boat* in Paul Zech's free adaptation ... 'Rimbaud!' someone called again from inside the Klausner, and Ed understood that they meant the moustachioed waiter.

Almost an hour went by before another, shorter man appeared in the doorway and looked at Ed for a while without moving. His face remained in the shadows. Something in his posture made it clear he was not going to cross the threshold. After a time, he lifted his hand in an indefinable gesture, only halfway, as if he were waving hello or waving Ed away. Ed stood up and, although he was a few tables away from the door, the man began to speak as loud as if two-score or more people were gathered on the terrace, by whom he wanted to be understood clearly from the very first words.

'My name is Krombach, Werner Krombach, manager of the company vacation home, Zum Klausner.'

'My name is Edgar Bendler,' Ed answered hurriedly. He called it out to the back of the manager, who had turned to rush away and

now picked up his pace in response. They crossed the dining room.
The man looked athletic, stocky; the shining egg of a small, carefully
groomed bald spot extended to the back of his head, while the hair
on the sides was grey and cut short. Only half-aware, Ed took in the
counter and the cast-iron cash register. They entered a tiny office. The
manager deftly squeezed past his desk, took up position, and offered
Ed his hand.

'Please have a seat, Mr Bendler.'

Nothing in his appearance betrayed the slightest mistrust or
contempt. He took Ed's passport, opened it up, and leafed through
it, wiping his high forehead several times as he did so, as if what he
was seeing in it were simply too much. The man finally asked him if
he was *healthy*.

On Krombach's desk stood an antediluvian typewriter, a
Torpedo, and next to it a grey telephone and a photograph of him
standing before the entrance of an enormous, shining, copper-plated
building. It was the legendary Palace Hotel — built by the Swedes.
Whenever and wherever it was mentioned in this country, there was
always someone who whispered to the group, 'by the Swedes ...' The
photograph showed the manager surrounded by an entire regiment
of women and men in hotel or wait-staff uniforms, only Krombach
wore almost the same outfit that he had on that very day: a light-pink
summer shirt with burgundy cufflinks, a light-weight, light-brown
checked jacket, and a scarf around his neck, probably silk. The only
thing missing was a tie.

'No ailments at all?' Ed looked up, and Krombach gave him a
serious, penetrating look.

Maybe he simply didn't understand the question properly. Ed
had no idea what Krombach was getting at and so, to be on the safe
side, didn't answer. He had decided to be suitable for each and every
occasion. Where had Ed come from and what had he done previously
— Krombach's questions were asked casually and in passing, as if
they were part of some routine that didn't particularly interest him.

Ed's professional experience included being trained as a mason, and he mentioned this. 'Skilled tradesman, then,' Krombach corrected him. 'Plastering, masonry construction, concrete and formwork, etc., then your studies, German literature and history, teacher training, I assume, the usual path, and then the usual?'

Before Ed could answer, Krombach spoke about the island and his *restaurant*. His voice changed; it grew soft and distracted. 'We have a special location up here, special conditions, in every respect, but you're surely aware of this, I believe, Mr Bendler, or else you wouldn't be here. First, the flow conditions. The constant breaking off and slow drift of the coastline on which this restaurant was built, almost eighty years ago now, on the stones of the old hermitage, the foundations the hermits left us ...'

As the manager changed topics from the gradual, inexorable disappearance of the island into the expanse of the Baltic Sea to the history of Zum Klausner, he seemed to forget that Ed was sitting before him. He talked for a long time about a man named Ettersberg or Ettenburg, whom he spoke of warmly as the *Ur-hermit*, a man in a long cassock 'always moving between gymnastics apparatuses and Tusculum editions of the classics, shower baths and shelves of books ...'

Ed absent-mindedly relished the soporific music in Krombach's talk. The manager obviously enjoyed using nautical expressions; his co-workers were part of the 'crew', and now and then he was called 'the captain'. 'So you noticed then? Chunk after chunk is breaking off the coast and sliding into that beautiful gorge, true natural drama, and at some point the Klausner, too, *our ark*, will be sent on its way one night, maybe even in the next storm or the one after that, it will sail out to sea, and with it, its passengers and crew, then we'll really depend on it, you understand?'

The office was, in fact, nothing more than a cubbyhole, and the ceiling sloped sharply behind Krombach's back so that the room, at the end, was no more than a good metre high. A day bed was set up in that space and covered with a counterpane. To Ed's left was a wardrobe. In its open, upper section were piled metal boxes with Dannemann Brasil cigarillos; on the shelf underneath were twenty or thirty small dark bottles. Ed couldn't make out their labels. A porthole dominated the wall over the wardrobe with a view of the light-brown striped wallpaper. Only then did Ed notice: the office had no windows. To judge by the sounds, the office was built under a staircase that led to the upper floor. Without a doubt, it was a place usually reserved for storerooms or broom closets. Next to the porthole hung a row of small square display cases with complicated sailing knots that looked like hearts that had turned grey behind the glass, their twists like eternal puzzles —

'... and Iphigenia?' the manager asked. Ed stammered, but his memory hoard sprang to attention, his little survival dynamo.

'Exactly, that play, precisely!'

Ed nodded every time the manager's eyes met his. He had trouble following the monologue, which must have been Krombach's hobbyhorse harangue. Perhaps he had repeated these sentences too often already. Despite their unusual subjects, there was something second-hand about them, but also something warming, cozy, and so the cubbyhole suited them. Four days after his leap (no, he hadn't jumped), it seemed to Ed that sitting in this tiny office and listening to the manager was *only good*. Yes, he had wanted to be gone, to disappear, to be on his own, but he didn't want to be alone anymore. Krombach's soft, murmuring voice was enough. Ed felt snug. This also had something to do with the smell that filled the cubbyhole, the smell of an earlier time, sharp and biting; it seemed to emanate from Krombach himself, from the smooth skin that stretched over his skull as if freshly oiled, but it might also be coming from the bottles in the wardrobe ...

'Very well. Why are you here, Mr Bendler?'

I leaned too far out the window, flashed through Ed's mind. Only with great effort did he manage to say his prepared sentence, but accidently in the old, ineffective way: 'I'm looking for work, however, I'd also need a room.'

Krombach took a deep breath, swivelled in his chair with his profile to Ed and looked at the grey hearts.

'Don't worry. In this chair, no one has ever had to apologise *for that*, on the contrary, it is, to a certain extent a requirement. Believe me, my crew includes all sorts of people who have trod all sorts of paths, but all those paths led to this office, and not one of them has been badly treated just because the mainland spit them out. All sorts of paths, but in the end it's the same everywhere. Everyone has seen it, everyone knows, sooner or later there comes a time. The island took us in. We found our place here and among us *esskays*, we're here for each other, when push comes to shove. In this crew, however,' his hand waved in a wide arc over his desk and almost brushed the cubbyhole's walls, 'it's about more than that, and we are all of one mind on this ...'

The manager swivelled back to face Ed, and stuck his finger in the telephone dial. He kept his eyes fixed on Ed, as if he were waiting for Ed to give him his number.

Without a doubt, this was the time for Ed to add something of his own. Something that showed he could fulfil all the (for the most part, unspoken) requirements, a statement about his life until now, about his own past, that did not, in fact, have anything to do with trouble or being spat out, but rather with a trolley car.

The manager's finger twitched in the dial, impatiently — a small rattling noise.

'So, you're healthy?'

'Yes, yes, I think so, at least, as far as I know ...' The question embarrassed him.

'Healthy, but no certificate of health?'

'Certificate of health?' Ed had never heard of the necessity of having such a document.

'Healthy, but no proof of residency or registration form?'

'No, I wanted ...'

'Healthy and freed from the past, like the rest of us up here?'

Krombach laughed softly and threw a quick glance at the greying hearts; he seemed to be on especially close terms with them. His sudden straightforwardness made Ed uncomfortable.

'I mean, no real serious illness in the past, right?'

'No. I broke my arm once, my left wrist, it was complicated. I fell while climbing, I was nine years old and was supposed to go to summer camp, but that morning ...'

Krombach looked at him blankly and silently, and Ed stopped talking.

'No one knows you're here?'

'No,' Ed answered quickly. He noted that Krombach had addressed him informally, and took it as a sign of progress.

'You didn't tell anyone, did you?'

'No.'

'You came alone?'

'Yes.'

'How long could you stay?'

'The summer ... ?' Ed had briefly pictured his diary in front of him with the registration date for the autumn semester — he almost felt ashamed. He heard the clattering of dishes from outside. To judge by the footsteps and the voices, breakfast was being cleared; it sounded crude and provoking. Strangeness wafted towards him, the fear before entering into the unknown.

'For the summer, then. Maybe autumn, too?'

'Yes, maybe.'

'Maybe, hunh? We had difficulties here during last year's season, "problems" would not be an exaggeration. We lost people, in various ways, our last ice-cream seller, for example ...' Krombach's breathing was strained.

'Why did you sneak up here?'

'Sneak?'

'You came from the back, over the bluffs, that's a long, arduous path, two hours along the rocky beach, with luggage!'

'I ...'

'It's fine.' The manager suddenly looked exhausted. He bent Ed's pass with its damaged plastic cover back against the binding, until the paper was about to tear. Then he just let the passbook drop from the tips of his fingers into a bureau drawer Ed could not see.

'You'll stay until Crusoe gets back. Get a hang of the work and then we'll see. Lodging, free board. You'll get two marks seventy an hour. How do you feel about washing dishes? According to one's aptitudes, as they say. Everything else ... everything else will come later.'

Ed nodded and lowered his gaze. Krombach's loafer was resting on the grate cover of a portable heater. Suddenly Ed recognised the smell; it was the cologne his father used every morning, every evening — Exlepäng.

THE ROOM

The room Ed moved into that morning looked lived in. A toothbrush with a crust of dried toothpaste lay on the sink. A pair of glasses stood in the toothbrush mug. The bed linens were not fresh. The sheets were crumpled in bulging wrinkles, a greyish ridge of folds that gave off a sour smell ... Ed leaned over the bed and listened; there was a hellish song of curving, very light, very far away. G. waved, the train made its final run, a few verses rumbled in his brain.

At first, it was hard for Ed to grasp the Klausner's layout, its internal coherences, and the various connections between one room and the next. The number and configuration of the rooms remained a mystery to him for a long time; it basically didn't seem possible for them all to fit into the two-storey building that looked rather modest on the postcards made from real photographs printed by the nationally owned postcard publisher Bild und Heimat (twenty-five pfennigs a piece at the counter) — it was, at any rate, no ship, no Mississippi steamboat. It was more of a mountain hut with wood-panelled gables and extensions on all sides instead of paddlewheels. Nevertheless, in Ed's mind's eye, all the rooms faced the sea. This was perhaps due to the fact that, day and night, the Klausner was bathed on all sides by the roar of the waves; one's sense of sight was constantly flooded, sharpened, transformed by one's sense of hearing. Trapped by sound, one's thoughts adapted to the noise of the surf, the movement of the tides.

Krombach had first led Ed to the back of the house. The door was low and narrow. A separate entrance, behind which a flight of steps rose abruptly, the stairs up to the rooms. It reminded Ed of the servants' staircase in his childhood home, and so he looked around for bellpulls like the ones that had run from his grandparents' bedroom to the servants' quarters. The rooms had stood empty for decades, but his grandfather took care of the mechanism nonetheless and liked to operate it every once in a while, especially to show Ed. As a child, Ed was certain the servants would hear it, that the ringing of the small, rusted bells at the end of the pulls would somehow *summon up* the long dead servants again; as soon as the light was turned off, a bony shuffling would sound in the corridor, then the rap of bare bones on the bedroom door, and finally the call, 'Yes, Master, yes?'

There was no need for a key, Krombach had explained: the door was left unlocked at night, too, unlocked at all times, and that, incidentally, was one of the important things for the Klausner and for its atmosphere. Ed once again had the feeling he had not understood something, that he'd missed some particular meaning or proviso, perhaps, hidden in the words 'esskay' or 'Crusoe'.

There was a spring that made the door swing shut behind them as they climbed the stairs. Krombach opened the door to Ed's room, and they were immediately swamped by a stream of stale air, sweetish, oily air you could feel on your skin. The manager swore softly, crossed the room in two strides, tore open the curtains, and opened the window. For a moment, light flooded in; a silver glittering that calmed to a clean shade of blue. Outside the window lay the sea's body, overwhelming and auspicious.

'One of our best,' Krombach said.

It was one of the gable rooms, right at the top of the stairs. From the landing, the corridor stretched out into the depths of the attic floor with further doors to the left and right. There was a wardrobe to the right of the door, and behind it a sink, wide, bulky, with two grey plastic taps. Under the window, a night table with a lamp. No table, no chair. The bed under the sloping roof.

'Bed linens are at the end of the corridor, with Monika. And in the morning, you will report to Chef Mike, eight o'clock, in the kitchen,' Krombach instructed Ed softly, and disappeared.

Ed only learned days later that Monika, or Mona as she was also called, was Krombach's daughter. Her perfume started in the last third of the corridor, at the very end of which was the door to her small apartment. Among themselves, the staff referred to her as 'the little invisible one'. She held the position of chambermaid, but hardly ever cleaned the rooms. Instead, she washed everything that needed laundering and transferred her lovely smell to the bedsheets, dishcloths, and tablecloths, which is why people often thought she was close by.

Ed's door also could not be locked, but he thought no more about it. He was sure there was no better place for him to be this summer (and perhaps all autumn and winter, too); only then did he remember his bag.

A small group of holiday-makers had gathered on the terrace. They were drinking coffee or beer, and looking out over the sea. Someone had turned Ed's books over and pushed them out a bit into the sunlight to dry. Nothing was missing. A large breakfast had been set down at his place: mortadella, a chunk of cheese, and a blob of fruit preserves that appeared to be glowing from within. Ed looked around. The waiter who had been called Rimbaud nodded at him. Ed was missing a cup of coffee, but he didn't dare ask for some. When he returned to his room, he found fresh bedsheets on the pillow — the old ones had disappeared. He called out a soft 'thank you' into the corridor, and listened. He tried to imagine what Monika looked like.

He pictured a tiny woman with black hair, a braid, maybe. As soon as he made his bed, Ed sank on to it and fell asleep.

The Bedouins were now pulling so hard at the animal (bulges of camel skin in their hands) that it stretched out flat, wide, like the desert's horizon. It was a way of using the animal as a flying carpet. 'The Bedouins had readied camel,' the narrator whispered. 'A blast of sand hit their sunglasses, but that was only the beginning of a long journey.'

It was evening when Ed awoke. The wallpaper above his head was peeling away like burned skin. The entire slope of the roof was covered with the remains of smashed insects. Some spots had small streaks of blood, like the tail of a comet. Sometimes the blood had just spattered around the spot, like a tiny explosion. Ed thought of his first room, with the moon over his bed, along with stars and the sandman who cycled over the hills of a dark blue night on a beautiful and clean Diamant bicycle with his bag of sand laced up tight. Ed, himself, had later only had a Mifa bicycle, a so-called folding bicycle, which you could fold up and fit in the boot of your car or some other small space. Everything in his childhood had been *practical*. 'How practical!' was the highest compliment: a folding bike, a folding bed (which you could fold up during the day against the wall, where it turned into a kind of closet), and clothing of almost unlimited durability.

Despite the dirt and the smell, Ed felt secure in his new abode. A room like this might have disheartened others, Ed thought, but for me it's exactly right. He felt a kind of joyful anticipation, but also a fear of failure.

The bed frame consisted of a heavy case covered with light wood veneer. The mattress had a hollow, in which Ed could feel his predecessor's sleep — he didn't find this uncomfortable. Only the pillow was unusable, a solid lump. He would use his sweater as a substitute, as he had on the previous nights. Ed was proud of those nights. He stood up and threw the stony pillow towards the wardrobe; dust rose in the air.

When he opened the wardrobe door, it began to melt from the inside in dark waves. Initially, it was like a dream, but Ed immediately began pounding on the door — hammering hard, almost splintering the thin wood. At some point, it passed, and he stopped, breathless, his heart racing. On the soul of his shoe was one single strike. Half an insect, the tail end, to be precise, was squashed, while the front end still struggled to get away. Of the nearly fifty cockroaches, he had only got one. Just one, Ed thought.

THE ONION

15 June. Ed was unfamiliar with the work, and went about it clumsily. But no one came to demonstrate or explain anything to him as he delved, bucket by bucket, into the onions' mystery. On probation, Ed thought, in this place, on this island. He tried to picture the movement of his mothers' hands, the way she wielded, as fast as lightning, *little pointy*, as she called the razor-sharp knife with a bleached wood handle, its blade ground down to just a few millimetres; he tried to imitate her — she was his mother — as best he could, her posture, her movements.

His spot was outside, behind the Klausner, at one of the manger-tables. He sat right under the spider-web- and grease-encrusted windows of the dishwashing station. The dishwashing station was an elongated grey plastered extension, with a back door that opened onto a small, square ramp. Now and again, Ed heard voices from within and a kind of singsong he couldn't interpret; there was an almost uninterrupted clattering of plates interspersed by a dull underwater rumbling, cutlery, no doubt, being rolled around on the bottom of some sink. When it was quiet, they may have been watching him, the motionless outline of his stiff back, a no longer exactly young adventurer in knee-length cut-off jeans and a red undershirt cut wide at the armpits, and maybe the sight of him amused them. Ed's hair was held back by a fraying bandanna that constantly slipped down; the sun stung his face. No one had explained to him that it would be better to sit in the shade, in any rate not in the courtyard, but under one of the pine trees near the shore where there was always enough breeze to help your eyes. Regardless, he would never have dared leave the courtyard on his own initiative. He wanted to be part of the crew without being relegated to some outpost. Most of all, he wanted to show that he knew how to work with stamina and discipline. Seven buckets on the first day.

'So, I'm Chef Mike,' the heavyset man in the black-and-white-chequered clown pants had said to Ed. Beads of sweat coated his broad, bald head and glittered like jewels. A dishtowel was tucked into the strip of fabric that held his stained chef's jacket closed over his belly, and he used it periodically to wipe his forehead and the back of his neck. The towel was so large that he didn't even have to take it from his belt. It dangled between his legs like an enormous member, and he occasionally draped it over his shoulder. The few times that Chef Mike spoke, gave orders, or cursed, he was difficult to understand because he used the pauses to wipe his face with his tail. Ed had never met anyone for whom the expression 'a workhorse' was more fitting. Almost ashamed at the good opportunity to hand off an unpleasant task, Chef Mike carried the onions out of the cold storage into the courtyard and set one bucket after another down on the ramp. The expression 'penal labour' occurred to Ed, but he didn't feel offended. He didn't feel anything at all.

At times, a warm breeze blew in to the courtyard from the shore — it was enough. But when the air was still, tears inevitably filled his eyes. It was an endless, inexorable weeping that began somewhere behind his eyeballs and compelled him to furrow his brow. Ed stretched his chin towards the heavens like a helpless animal, or he tilted his head to the side, but that didn't help. In the beginning, he would still wipe his face with the back of his hand, but then he gave up; he let his tears flow. Flecks of light and swarms of floating spots settled onto the landscape, swirling like snowflakes. It was the first time he had cried since that day.

That morning, around eleven, the delivery arrived. The coachman Mäcki approached the Klausner. Mäcki, a short, stocky islander with hair like a hedgehog that had probably played a part in his getting his nickname, used the narrow concrete paved road that led from the port to the military barracks in broad, sweeping curves over the hilly landscape; a hundred metres before the base, a forest road forked off to the Klausner. At first, there was the dull thump of hooves, but then, in the courtyard, the rubber-wheeled cart floated in almost soundlessly. Mäcki never had to tie up his horse. He had a cast iron anchor behind the coach box, which he shoved into the sand wherever he wanted to stop. Ed, who wanted to show that he was someone who *saw* work ('now that is someone who can see work' was his father's praise for people who 'didn't need to have everything explained to them'), helped the coachman unload. When they were done, Mäcki disappeared through the dishwashing station into the kitchen without a thank-you or a goodbye.

After three days, Ed was sure enough of himself. His back hurt, but the peeling proceeded almost of its own accord. Apart from a few holiday-makers who crossed the courtyard obliviously on their way to the dining room (guests lodged in the building behind the Klausner), no one was near when the tears flowed from his eyes. No one except for the coachman's horse, which now and again quietly turned its soft black nostrils towards Ed, so close that he could feel the horse's warm breath on his face, reddened by the constant wiping and rubbing. With its shaggy appearance and its rolling gait (thick hair and short legs; the fringes hung down to the heavy, unbelievably broad hooves), the horse looked like a bear. It was a kind of bear-horse, who watched Ed weeping and when Ed raised his eyes. He also wept to the trees on

the bluffs, those wind-evading cripples on the cliff that looked warped
even when his eyes weren't brimming with tears — or as if they were
ducking away from something flying furiously at them from the sea
that very instant.

Slowly, space returned behind his eyes. He felt a pleasant emptiness
in his head. He was amazed at the satisfaction the work gave him. He
did not have to think or talk about anything, only enjoy the sun and
the sea's blurry presence. Looking at the horizon, the expanse he had
crossed to get here seemed much greater, the distance he had travelled
much longer; the sea stretched time out and the wind cooled his
cheeks.

With the exception of Krombach and Chef Mike, Ed had not spoken
with anyone since his arrival. The bedrooms were all on the same
floor, off the same corridor, and they shared one toilet, so there were
encounters, but these didn't lead to any conversations. The Klausner's
crew remained under cover, as if Ed should learn as little as possible
about the ship he wanted to sign on to until a final decision had been
reached. Ed liked thinking in Krombach's nautical terms. You just
needed to change a few words and it all turned into a fairytale, hardly
any less adventurous than a journey on the *Ghost* or the *Hispaniola*.
Curiously, the thought soothed him. *Fifteen men on a dead man's
chest ...* Why couldn't he just continue his life from this point, where
it had ended in his childhood? Barely ten years ago. Why shouldn't he
— in a certain, more intellectual way — pick up where the four-part
series on Crusoe and *The Sea-Wolf* had ended, back then? Before he
had read and reread his way through *Treasure Island* and the stories of
Alexander Selkirk and Peter Serrano, about Mosquito-William and
The River Pirates of the Mississippi, along with all the other legends of
his childhood, for the last time, and lugged the books tightly bound
in bundles (he remembered the cheap, fraying string) to the junk
shop. Once again he felt ashamed — although he hardly needed to be

embarrassed about it, since junk shops were, without a doubt, among the highest authorities in the land in those days: 'Bottles and glasses for Angela Davis' or 'Rags for Luis Corvalán'. Second-hand goods and international solidarity went together, were inextricably bound. The phrase 'forever united' wafted through Ed's mind, empties and America, rags and Chile, a bundle of old issues of the *People's Watch* in the fight for Unidad Popular, and a crate of empty pickle jars against racism ... With the second-hand shop as his guide, Ed freed himself from literature. In any case, it was certain that his future (some cold, woodcut-like construct) lay in building, that he would go into building and begin an apprenticeship as a skilled construction worker. Ever since the eighth grade and a half-hour appointment in the career-guidance centre at the foot of the women's prison in Gera, his future had been considered decided. He remembered how, sitting next to his mother and infinitely relieved, he had managed to conclude the conversation satisfactorily (feigning interest, he had followed all the suggestions and then 'decided'), and when he left the guidance centre, his gaze had fallen on the women's prison that towered above the slope in warning. And now, from his spot in the Klausner's courtyard, with a little pointy in his hand and a bucket of onions between his legs, once again it struck him as very puzzling that after only a few years (years on construction sites, in site huts), he had found his way back to books, just not to Selkirk and Mosquito-William, not to the adventures of his childhood, the Mississippi river pirates ... A slight vertigo came over Ed, and fresh tears streamed down his cheeks.

Every day, Chef Mike's assistant brought Ed food in the courtyard. His name was Rolf. Rolf balanced his way down the ramp, set the tray on the table, and disappeared again immediately without a word. He wore a stiff, roomy chef's jacket; it resembled a casing into which he could retreat when necessary, like a tortoise into its shell.

Ed's breakfast came right after the workday started, but he had to wait for lunch; it mostly came well after two o'clock. Usually, meat

and potatoes with mixed vegetables. Ed often felt undeniable hunger
before noon. At some point, he would take an onion and eat it like
an apple, without stopping. Onions had been the only thing (aside
from blood sausage) that Ed would not eat, or only reluctantly —
now he liked the taste. And suddenly, he seemed to have got over his
sensitive stomach as well. From then on, every day at noon on the dot,
Ed would take one of the large onions he had peeled, and later a slice
of brown bread filched from the breadbaskets intended for guests on
company holiday. It was a kind of second breakfast; the first habit of
his very own.

THE JOURNAL

When Ed sat up in bed in the morning, he saw the sea, and that was enough. Even so, he could not relate this happiness directly to himself. It remained inaccessible in some way, either in his chest or in the sight of the sea, even with the lights of the ocean liner on it, or it was hidden in the twilight that did not actually exist; there was only the golden light that slowly crept up the stained walls and flooded the room, and then, after sunset, the long finger of the search light that groped over the surface of the water and glowed each time it hit the crest of a wave as if there were something there.

Ed stared out as if hypnotised, and expected the sound of a motor and with it a bare arm trying to fend off misfortune with desperate gestures.

The sphere of light from the searchlight was rooted somewhere in the forest behind the Klausner. Sometimes, the finger rose up and pointed further out, over the open water. Ed pictured those who lived on the land opposite as they sat at dinner, shielding their eyes with their hands so as not to be blinded. During the day, when the view was clear, you could see Møn, the chalk cliffs of Møns Klint, which belonged to the Kingdom of Denmark, but of course the light could not cover the fifty kilometres and, in truth, the distance to the other shore was almost infinite. For that very reason, Ed was tempted to picture these people to himself, fantastic inhabitants of a distant planet sitting down to their evening meal ... 'It's a dream,' Ed whispered into the light of the rapidly sinking sun, and the new happiness suited him, if in a muted, obscure way.

One disadvantage of his room was its proximity to the stairway and the corridor. Around midnight, a racket set in, voices and slamming doors in the servants' quarters, all of it introduced by the whine of the spring being stretched, a noise he found painful because it reminded him of Matthew and his soft, hurt cry just before Ed jumped (hadn't jumped). Then steps, the sound of feet, exhausted breathing at the top of the stairs. Now and then, Ed had the feeling someone had stopped outside his door to listen. But that was ridiculous, and over time he got used to the commotion. He decided to pay it no attention. 'It's the island life, all that hustle and bustle out there. You don't know the first thing about it,' he whispered into the darkness. His voice was completely calm, his reflection motionless in the open casement window. He bowed his head as if he wanted to dive deeper into the eternal roar. But before the *stuff of pilots* began to flow, Ed took a step back. He turned on the light on his bedside table and pulled his small diary out of his travel bag, which he didn't store in the wardrobe, because of the cockroaches. His eyes burned. As soon as he closed them, a tiny fire blazed. *Don't rub them, I shouldn't have rubbed them,* Ed thought.

19 JUNE

Onions again, but everything's already much better. Need to get sunscreen, eye-drops maybe. What are esskays? Who is Crusoe? Don't have anything in writing. Should I ask K.?

Writing calmed Ed down. Each day had only five lines. Room for 'Appointments and Notes'. He flipped to the previous page and wrote:

18 JUNE

The guy with the piss-off prayer is the ice-cream man here, bad lot. Better be careful. Dragged me out of the bar lounge. Looks like Rilke, long face, bulging eyes, and a moustache, like almost everyone else here.

Ed thought over whether it made sense to use the five lines for that entry. Definitely not if he wanted to keep a journal recording only the most important events. On the other hand, this was the one person he had really met here since Krombach, aside from Chef Mike. Halfway through the lounge, the ice-cream man had grabbed Ed's shirt from behind and pushed him right back out the front door in front of all the guests. Evidently, the customer toilet was taboo during opening hours. Just using the front door probably counted as an affront, Ed thought, and felt the slight again. He had been so surprised that he'd let himself be led away without any resistance — like a child; he had even apologised. He hadn't wanted to go up to the staff floor, so that he wouldn't give the impression he was sneaking off to his room during working hours. That was all. 'Go shit in the goddamn sea,' the ice-cream man had said. He wore a black velvet vest with gleaming silver buttons. Maybe he took himself for some kind of torero. Ed leafed back another page:

17 JUNE

The chef's assistant doesn't say a word, maybe mute. I'm silent too. Got my peace and quiet. The room is a gift, there's enough to eat. Battling the onions, complete onion-frenzy!

Sometimes his entries sounded like postcards from summer camp, but that didn't matter. As soon as Ed wrote something of his own, with his own words, he wielded his pen against the verse hoard murmuring in his head like a planer levelling a heap, Ed thought, or cutting right through a heap. Yes, it was, in fact, more of a drilling; he wrote and drilled for something, in search of G. perhaps, or of himself, or a wide open space, a bright, windy bay where he walked along the sandy beach for hours, his mind quieted and his temples cooled, his feet washed in the fringes of the sea ...

The sound of a radio came from the floor below, voices, sometimes music, but very sporadic, wavering, interrupted by a coughing or scratching sound. Before midnight, Haydn, beautiful and mysterious in the radio's tremulous sound, but then the din on the landing became too loud.

Ed pulled on his clothes and slipped outside. He went down the stairs to the courtyard without making a sound and marched across the clearing and into the forest; the darkness soothed his eyes. The light was on in the dishwashing station. Someone must have forgotten to turn it off or it was left on all night. Not that unusual, Ed thought. There were houses in which one light or other was left on every night in the huge kitchen, strange really, maybe some kind of ritual, a navigation light for desolation. Ed would have liked to destroy all these lamps, to shoot them out in favour of wholesome, protective darkness — a short, sharp cry twitched in the night. Through the smeared windowpanes in the dishwashing station, he could see shapes, shadows, silhouettes. Ed scooted a bit higher up the slope. A few of the shapes almost reached the ceiling. Then they ducked and disappeared. Ed tried to make out more, but his eyes were watering again. Someone was busy with the large shapes, rubbing his hands along their outlines, up and down. He caressed them, sometimes with long, slow movements, then again with short, quick ones. Maybe to measure their size, Ed thought and felt a flood of shame. His mother had sat next to him when the tailor had pushed the tape measure and his fingers holding the tape measure into his crotch; he was thirteen years old and it was all perfectly normal. Even the shapes in the dishwashing station gradually shrank to their usual size. One had already gone out into the courtyard and was walking towards him. Ed wiped his eyes — a ghost with long, wet hair? A woman? Wrapped in a sheet? The shape flitted across the courtyard and went up the staff staircase. Matthew's cry, the slam of the door, then another and yet another ghost; then peace returned. The desolation receded and wholesome darkness took the Klausner's dishwashing station under its protection. Ed saw a man cross the courtyard and plunge onto the path that led down to the sea.

KRUSO

As he spoke, the man held his forehead gently out to the bear-horse —
as if he had greeted the horse rather than Ed. He slapped the horse's
flank roughly with a firm hand, as only those who are familiar with
animals do. Ed wiped the tears from his face. The man bent down
slowly towards him, and Ed saw he was smiling.

'Alexander Krusowitsch, most people say Kruso, a few friends
call me Losh, from Alexander, that is from Alyosha, Alosha — Losh.'
Smiling, he took the little pointy from Ed's hand and led him like a
blind man up the ramp into the Klausner. Ed felt the light pressure on
his forearm distinctly. Since G. (that is, for more than a year), he was
no longer used to sustained touch; more precisely, he was no longer
equal to it, which is why he felt almost lost when the man let him go.

'Thanks,' Ed said, looking at the ground. He couldn't manage to
say any more, and what was he thanking the man for?

People did not think Krusowitsch was Russian, German-Russian,
or Russian-German. He had longish black hair he pulled back in a
ponytail when washing dishes. Because of a curl above his forehead,
the hair billowed at the roots when tied back, like a limp black

cockscomb. The comical aspect of this deformation was offset by the seriousness of his gaze; in any case, no one felt there was anything comical about Krusowitsch when they were facing him. His nose was chiselled and narrow, his face a soft, elongated, almost perfect oval with large cheeks, almost straight eyebrows, and a dark complexion — Krusowitsch looked more like a Venezuelan or a Colombian about to pull out his pan flute and play a song in tune with his defiant-melancholy charm.

The dishwashing station was a narrow, tiled extension with a dimly lit passage leading to the bar lounge and a swinging door to the kitchen. 'Our backroom,' Kruso said. It sounded important, as if he were trying to convey something else as well. Under the high windows were two large brown stone sinks as well as two smaller sinks made of steel. The water poured from two short rubber hoses fastened onto the taps with wire. The sinks stood next to each other in pairs (one stone sink, one metal sink), with metal tables between them. On the opposite wall were rusty shelves filled with pots, ladles, and dishes. The floor was slippery with a film of grease. The formerly reddish-brown tiles had reconciled themselves to the dirt and taken on a grey cast. A few of the tiles were broken, a few missing; the holes in the pattern had been filled with cement. A muted light fell through the windowpanes.

'Here we work with our hands, our bare hands,' Kruso announced emphatically and stretched his open hand towards Ed, as if he wanted to prove an all-encompassing innocence. But it was simply the beginning of his first session of instruction, Kruso's first lesson. Ed saw a tangle of lines, long, thick, branching stories waiting to be read and understood, along with broad, squarish fingernails ...

'Show me your hands!'

Ed complied hesitantly.

'Stay like that,' Kruso said then grabbed a soft-drink bottle from the windowsill and sprinkled some thick, whitish liquid onto the backs of Ed's hands. 'These aren't a student's hands,' Kruso declared, and jabbed his fingers between Ed's. He kneaded Ed's bones so hard that Ed was a hair's breadth from crying out. But his mouth seemed sewn shut. Nothing and no one could have made him utter a sound.

'Cum, pure cum, the waiters say. And Rimbaud claims that over the years there's never any less of it ...' Kruso smiled at him gravely. In conclusion, Kruso raised his right hand as if he wanted to swear an oath, but he simply pressed his thumb and index finger together. 'The precision grip, you know. Thumb and forefinger suddenly meet and the ape's transformation into man begins, long before the first word ...' Without further ado, he went up to one of the sinks and plunged his arms into the water up to his elbows. His hands swirled in a brew covered with yellow foam, and accomplished some task that he did not need to see to finish.

While working, Kruso, who was a head taller than Ed, wore a black undershirt with the armholes and neckline cut wide open. When Kruso leaned forward, it stuck out away from his torso. The hair on his chest was very thick and his skin was tanned. A towel was wrapped around his waist like an apron. Water gleamed on his moccasins.

The stone sinks for coarse cleaning (pots, pans, mixing bowls) and the metal sinks for lunch dishes were on *his side* — 'your side,' Kruso explained trustingly to Ed without the slightest trace of irony. Ed's side was next to the passage to the dining room, a slightly sloping corridor, through which the waiters carried the dishes in and piled them up, often at a full run. Kruso called it the approach lane, with rules that had to be followed.

On Kruso's side was the sink for cutlery that must *soak* for as long as possible, so that then, with no intermediate step, in other words, in one single process, the cutlery could be cleaned and polished. 'Otherwise, even you couldn't manage it,' Kruso said and smiled at him again. Why on earth would he try, Ed wondered, but before he had formulated the question in his mind, he felt the warmth of trust and affection spread through his chest.

Because a normal dishtowel quickly became completely soaked and stained during the single-step process, bed linens were used instead, enormous century-old sheets and coverlets from the Klausner's early days. The sheets' ends were tossed over one's shoulder or tied around one's waist, just as Ed had seen that night in the courtyard. So cutlery sink duty was called 'going Roman'. Romans, as Kruso pointed out, had never been liked much — only Cavallo thought Romans were 'the tops'. Cavallo was one of the three waiters, that much Ed had understood so far.

Kruso stayed at Ed's side for a while, so he could explain the process better. Ed, Kruso's student, stood next to him and tried to pay attention to everything. The master fished around the bottom of the sink for a second, special brush he wanted to show Ed. In his eagerness, Ed also plunged his hands into the sink. Fast as lightning, Kruso grabbed his hand and held it tight under water for a moment — evidently a reflex or a sudden cramp, a fleeting epileptic fit. Ed apologised at once.

While Alexander Krusowitsch explained the Klausner's various workstations (bar room, kitchen, beer garden, dishwashing station, dormitory, and dining room for the company vacation guests) and mentioned this or that name (it was impossible for Ed to remember everything), he pulled an entire stack of lunch plates out of the water with one hand. A single turn of his powerful wrist was enough to set the plates on a large, rust-covered wire rack.

Kruso stared at the wire rack as if he had just noticed it. 'We need to make more of those, more and maybe better ones.' He sounded both exhausted and determined. 'We have to take care of ourselves. Of ourselves and the pilgrims, we have to keep the entire business going for ourselves and for them. It's our daily bread.' Ed would have liked to agree, but that would have been ridiculous. He knew nothing about draining racks and how they are made and he had absolutely no idea whom Kruso might have meant by 'the pilgrims'.

He had met Kruso the day before on the beach. Ed had screwed up his courage and talked to the manager. His question was when the man on whom the final decision about his employment depended was going to return. Krombach had answered that once a year, always at this time of year, Kruso circled the island, 'even the reedy and marshy areas — he walks through the brush, at least thirty kilometres, no problem for someone who practically grew up on a military obstacle course.' Ed had the sense that Krombach did not want to say much more. Nevertheless, the manager lingered next to him for a moment, looking out over the water, perhaps simply not to end the conversation too abruptly. 'It's a kind of memorial march, in his sister's honour. That is, we never know exactly when he'll get back.'

'Do you have any more questions, Edgar?' It was the first time that Kruso had addressed him by name. Ed felt the warmth in his chest again. 'No. That is, which toilet can I use, I mean, during working hours?'

'I know, I know,' Kruso murmured.

He carefully took the soft drink bottle from the windowsill. 'René is ...' Kruso took a deep breath. 'Please don't take it seriously. We all stick together here.' He shook a little blob of the strange cream into his hand and left Ed behind.

For the first few hours, Ed washed and scrubbed without looking up. The strips of fat cut from the meat, the food scraps mixed together, the paper napkins full of snot or blood, the ferry tickets, the pamphlets, the chewing gum, the knotted up hairbands (with a few hairs clinging to them), the cigarette butts, the vomit, the sunscreen, all the garbage on the plates that came in to the dishwashing station from the terrace, all of it was now part of his job. He looked at the bite marks in the meat: big bites, little bites, some tiny, as if made by rodents rather than humans. He looked around — he was alone. He grabbed a potato with a woman's red-rimmed bite mark, threw it in the air, caught it and crushed it in his fist. As he did, he bared his teeth and spat the remains of an imaginary 'Sea-Wolf' cigar in the bin. As Kruso had shown him, he put the good scraps in various bowls and scraped the rest from the dishes into the garbage bin with a greasy piece of cardboard.

Sometimes, it was hard to decide which scraps could be considered *good*. Kruso had said something incomprehensible on the subject and had not given many concrete examples. He had started talking about the pilgrims again and about their soup, possibly their *sacred* soup or maybe their *hasty* soup or both together. In the desolate echoes that filled the dishwashing station, it was all a giant soup. Now and then, there were lunch plates that came back almost untouched, with entire schnitzels, cabbage rolls, potatoes, vegetables. Then it was easy.

Before long Ed's back ached. When he was sure no one was watching, he raised his hands out of the water and stretched. Some of the yellowish brew trickled into his armpits when he did so. When he stood on tiptoe, he could touch the ceiling with the brush for scrubbing the pots. The backroom, in the backroom — didn't that mean to be on the best path?

At first, Ed was almost dazzled by the appearance of the three waiters. He didn't know much about gastronomy and found it astonishing that men in white shirts and black suits, men in tails, so to speak, would appear here, in the dishwashing station, right next to the garbage bin (Kruso called it the pig slop bin). It all seemed like a kind of circus or absurdist theatre where the spectators could join in; he had heard the music and the lions' roar, and had snuck away, and now he was watching the show, his heart thumping in his chest. A vagabond hoping to escape his misery on the road, Ed thought, and for a moment keenly felt the shabbiness of his dishwater-drenched garb. He discreetly scratched himself. The greasy steam over the sinks clogged his pores.

From noon on, Ed was inundated with dishes. Because there were never enough clean plates to cover the lunch shift, he simultaneously had to wash, dry, and place the plates into a specially made hatch to the kitchen. He worked fast but could hardly manage on his own. The waiters ran, but it was fundamentally all too much for them as well. Even so, the waiter they called Rimbaud went above and beyond, and scraped the plates he brought in himself and then tossed them into Ed's sink for coarse cleaning. He did it with great verve and surprising deftness: the plates nosedived past Ed's whirling hands and, a few centimetres before impact, executed a turn that could hardly be believed before finally settling on the bottom of the sink as evenly and supply as dreaming flounders. With that technique, Ed could keep both hands in the water and wash at a much higher tempo. He noticed that Rimbaud, too, observed the rule about good and less-good scraps, and the bowls gradually filled.

'Plates, you dogs, I need plates, plates — spiders and spoonbills!' It was Chef Mike, his strident, raspy voice from the kitchen. When they were almost out of silverware and his Roman had slipped and fallen on the greasy floor and Ed didn't know where to begin, Kruso reappeared.

He stayed at Ed's side for a whole hour without a break. Ed admired the calm symmetry of Kruso's movements. Kruso worked in a different and — Ed could find no better term for it — a *locally unusual* way. Everything he did emphasised his seriousness. It was not so much his stamina or speed, it was more a kind of rhythm and inner tension — as if his entire existence were part of something greater or as if his work washing dishes were simply an expression of something else, something all his own, that had to be handled with care.

Rimbaud joked with Kruso, but Ed didn't understand either of them. Even the short waiter (his name was Chris) had increased the pace of his odd, woodcut-like hobble, which may have been caused by his bowlegs. His greasy, curly black hair moved mechanically forward and back — his hair hobbled along with him.

They were quickly gaining ground, and the calls for plates from the kitchen trailed off. Rimbaud stood at Kruso's side, speaking to him quietly. They were both looking in a book at the photograph of a man, as far as Ed could tell. The book was wrapped in brown paper, and, if Ed were not mistaken, it had come from the basin Kruso called 'our nest', a blue-green plastic basin filled with dishcloths. Rimbaud leafed through the book and began to read aloud. He recited into Kruso's ear. He stood stiffly, leaning forward slightly, as immobile as a drawing. When he finished, Kruso hugged him to his chest. In the middle of the embrace, a scream rang out in the hallway behind Ed — with a powerful leap, Kruso dove past him to catch a slowly but inexorably toppling mountain of plates. The hobbling Chris had loaded his right arm past his shoulder and almost up onto his head with dirty dishes. Everyone laughed. Rimbaud clapped the book shut and slipped it back into the nest between the cloths. Ed heard Chris calling him 'onion' behind his back, but maybe he was mistaken. The dishwashing-station echo chamber swallowed every word. For two people to be able to talk, they had to stand close to each other. Still, there was a lot that Ed did not understand, as if some of the crew were speaking a foreign language. The term 'allocate' or 'exonerate', for example, kept surfacing — whatever they meant remained a mystery to Ed.

I will learn, Ed thought.

For the first time since he had made his break, he felt forlorn. He scraped the streaks of vegetable remains into the bin and let the plate slide into his sink. Once again, a few verses from *The Drunken Boat* echoed in his mind; the murmur of the hoard.

Shortly before the end of the shift, mute Rolf came in and carried the bowl with the good scraps into the kitchen. A small pile of coffee sets slipped from Ed's hands and shattered. No one said a word. Chef Mike pushed open the swinging door to the kitchen and handed him a hand broom and a dustpan. A cloud of steam billowed over the floor. Ed had ducked immediately to pick up the biggest shards. He sensed Kruso's silhouette behind him, then felt a hand on the back of his neck, fleetingly, the way you touch a child doing homework.

TO THE SEA

Captivated by the sight of topographies that seemed to roam under the water's surface, Ed almost tripped. The descent to the beach led over several tableaux of loam and sand bound by flights of steps which, going by their construction, must have dated from different centuries and were in a terrible state. With each step, a new panorama was revealed. The sight of the sea! Ed felt the promise. And he longed for nothing else, a kind of beyond, vast, perfect, overpowering.

Halfway down the bluff, the view to the north opened up, onto the uppermost section of coastline. There, in the scrub on the cliff, lay the army compound of the observation company. 'No heavy armaments,' according to legends from the mainland. Others whispered of an *extremely* precise cannon with an almost unimaginable range.

Ed was the only one who took advantage of the midday break to go down to the water. At that time, life in the house was at a standstill. After the chaos of the lunch shift with boatloads of day tourists, sleep settled over the clearing. It reminded Ed of the midday nap time of his primary-school years, when they took the mats from the back wall of the classroom after lunch and fell into heavy dreams as if on command. Rimbaud collapsed onto the battered chaise longue in the dining room, placed to extend the so-called reading corner with its small round table full of magazines, the TV guide *FF-Dabei*, the magazine *You and Your Garden*, and the monthly *Good Advice*. He let his feet in his run-down waiter's shoes dangle over the backrest, and covered his face with a newspaper, *Ostsee-Zeitung*, which was delivered daily on the post boat. The locals called all the ferries that ran between the islands 'post boats'. Ships from the mainland that docked at the island were called 'steamers'. 'Are you coming by post boat or by steamer?' was one of the first, crucial questions ... Now and again, Rimbaud stretched out on the grassy embankment on the edge of the forest, not far from the spot where the path to the lighthouse began. On some days, Ed could see all three waiters lying next to each other, their white shirts unbuttoned, immobile, as if shot down in a bloodbath from the era of Prohibition — three dead friends with arms akimbo on one of the Romans' sheets.

'What did you do all those years?'

'I went to sleep early.'

Only Kruso never rested. And he never seemed tired. He often worked in the cellar under the dishwashing station, which housed the boiler to heat the water as well as a workshop. Or he gathered dead wood and carried it to the splitting block. With his apron made from a red-checked dishcloth, his bare torso, and hair in a plait, Kruso actually looked like an American Indian making necessary arrangements with resolution, yes, with strength and elegance, though Ed could not say what the arrangements were for. It was surely something important.

Every day they *made wood*, as Kruso called it, cutting driftwood or deadwood into oven-sized pieces with the axe. Once in a while, he worked on his barrier, which enclosed the Klausner in a half-circle, for which he skilfully wove together the lower quality, thin underbrush branches, using the trunks of the smaller, densely growing spruce trees as pickets. He called the fence the 'outer palisade', although it was not clear where the 'inner palisade' was meant to be. The palisade was a natural barrier that turned green over time and seemed to grow of its own accord.

When Kruso was splitting wood, the water in the sinks trembled. Once, Ed had watched him split wood, almost transfixed by the rhythm of the axe and the smooth, powerful movement of his flawless body. Logs were diligently reduced to smaller pieces. Ed knew he couldn't be seen through the dirt-encrusted window of the dishwashing station, but Kruso had suddenly stopped chopping and waved. Moments later, he was standing at Ed's side, the axe still in his hand. Smiling gravely (that irritating combination of two expressions in his large, oval face), Kruso once again took Ed by the arm and led him around the courtyard.

'The garden has to be protected, the wild boars root everything up with their snouts,' he said, pointing at an enclosure near the edge of the forest, where, with a fair amount of good will, a few vegetable beds could be made out. Half-buried schnapps bottles encircled the plantings. It looked to Ed like the garden of a drunk who longed to be reconciled with the world.

Kruso knelt down and laid his hand on the vegetable bed.

'The only reason they come here is that they catch the scent of freedom — they're like humans.'

For a moment, he looked into Ed's eyes.

'Last year, they destroyed the entire garden, all the mushrooms and the sacred herbs. The dose was too high, of course. After that, the pigs felt completely free, free from all constraints. They swam around the island a few times and set off a Battle Stations alarm. Have you ever seen pigs swim, Ed? Father, mother, baby, they move through the water all in a row, much faster than you'd think possible, their snouts sticking high up out of the water. And that's how they were shot down, father, mother, baby — bam, bam, bam. The soldiers thought what they were supposed to think: fugitives, seasoned border violators, who don't react to shouts or even warning shots. For a while, the sand down there was red. It took hours before they recognised their mistake and dragged the cadavers from the water. Naturally, Chef Mike tried to scrounge up some fresh meat for the Klausner, but there was nothing doing, fugitives are treated as fugitives: there's no such thing and therefore there are no corpses — they simply don't exist.'

Kruso looked at the ground. His lips were bloodless, his eyes almost closed. This man was a stranger to Ed, but Ed also felt they were close. And yet, not truly close — it was more the kind of closeness one longs for.

Kruso plucked something from the garden bed. Ed couldn't tell the difference between herbs and weeds. He tried to make sense of the story and wanted to ask Kruso about the herbs.

'The wild pigs had too much freedom in their blood, you understand, Ed? This freedom ...' He gestured at the herb garden and at the Klausner, and fell silent.

Because the beach was rocky at the foot of the stairs, Ed headed north to the first promontory where there were a few sandy stretches. He had brought along the bulky notebook with G.'s dedication on the cover. He hid it in his towel. He treasured the thought that he could find himself somehow during this break, that he could breathe in the sea, think things over, but he was much too exhausted. So he just sat there and looked out into the distance. Despite the cream, his hands seemed waterlogged, the skin porous, pale, and wrinkled. The hands of a drowned corpse, Ed thought. His fingernails wiggled in the nail beds as if loose, and, if he'd wanted to, he could have pulled them easily from his flesh. He turned his palms towards the sun, rested his hands in his lap, and looked out over the water.

At least his eyes felt better. In the putrid, soapy haze of the dishwashing station, the contours of the fear that still throbbed in the marrow of his bones had softened (hadn't jumped!). Ed's exhaustion reminded him of his stint as an apprentice on the construction site, of the nearly forgotten exhaustion of his younger years (he referred to them that way again, as if he had grown old since then), and he felt a kind of homesickness for the work. A physical, almost inborn longing he hadn't thought of in a long time or, rather, hadn't completely shaken off. His studies had made him vague and arbitrary. When he was working, he became like himself again: work returned him tangibly to his own likeness. Werther's 'weariness' came droning from his verse hoard, whereupon Ed started throwing stones into the water. He wondered if he'd passed the test, if he was now the Klausner's dishwasher.

He gathered driftwood on the way back. Roots, pieces of boards, perhaps the remains of ships. In the end, he carried a considerable bundle in front of his chest. On the stairs up the bluffs, the mussel- and algae-covered wood almost slipped from his grasp, but he wouldn't let it: he was determined to pass this test no matter what. The stairs were steep and sweat ran into his eyes. He imagined Kruso noticing him. His grave smile. Seeing Ed, the savage, who caught on quickly and proved himself useful from the very first day. When Ed got to the woodlot, he let the bundle fall with as much noise as possible. In his life's confusion, he had found himself an incomparable teacher.

THE BREAKFAST

21 June. Breakfast was the only time the Klausner's crew all gathered together, and Ed quickly understood that it was impossible not to be punctual. Every morning at seven, the table was fully set. Twelve plates, five on each side, one on each end. Ed's *acceptance* lasted only a few minutes — no wonder he would picture it again so often.

After Kruso and Chef Mike took their seats, Ed chose a place on the far side of the table, the one nearest the wall. It was a good choice. He had, in fact, chosen the place where his predecessor, a man named Speiche, had sat. Speiche was still mentioned now and again in conversation, but only when they wanted to make fun of someone who had obviously *not passed* at the Klausner and was 'unsuitable above and beyond that as well'. That's how Kruso put it, as if, Ed assumed, he were referring to a binding set of rules, a codex for the esskays.

Ed, in the meantime, had understood that 'esskay' was simply the acronym 'SK' for *Saisonkraft*, seasonal worker. SK reminded Ed of the term EK for *Entlassungskandidaten*, discharge candidates in the army, and he reasoned that, just as at the time of his military service there had been an EK culture — a conglomeration of crude to deadly jokes combined with an implicit desire for submission (all in all, a kind of martial anticipation of the day of 'freedom', of their discharge) — there surely must also be an SK culture, with its own, entirely different set of rules. In that case, it would serve him well to master this codex as quickly as he could. And Ed recalled a particular soldier who, like himself, had been what they called a 'fresh one', a 'smooth one', that is, a soldier in his first six months of service. For a game called 'Turtle', the EKs had strapped steel helmets onto the soldier's elbows and knees and then hurtled him along the linoleum floor of the corridor in their barracks, which was smooth as glass since the soldier himself had waxed and polished it for hours on end. His trajectory was tremendous — all the way to the wall at the end of the corridor, against which the soldier broke his neck.

Kruso never laughed at the jokes about the vanished dishwasher being a flunky or a work-shirking loser. Speiche, the Orphan Child ... At first, Ed thought the nickname was a rude joke. He found out later that his predecessor actually had been an orphan who had left the orphanage as soon as he came of age and gone straight to the island. No one seemed particularly interested in where Speiche, alone and without any family, could have vanished to so suddenly. The thought that here, on the doorstep of disappearance, no one asks where others might be headed, flitted pointlessly through Ed's mind. There actually did seem to be cases of emigration in other establishments on the island, establishments with better terms and conditions. The Wieseneck Pension or the Dornbusch Apartments offered higher hourly wages as well as a premium on days off. There was even talk of a 'weekend bonus', and in the Island Bar the waiters were required to polish the silverware or to pay the dishwasher an extra five marks to do it for them, or at least that's what he'd been told by mute Rolf, who could, in fact, speak, if the topic was money. But in the end, for Ed, it wasn't about money. It never had been.

Speiche had not only left behind his sour smell, his toothbrush, his glasses, and the cockroaches in the room. He had also left a bag at the bottom of the wardrobe, with a warm, hand-knitted sweater and a pair of leather shoes. With their thin, flat soles, these shoes — called hitchhikers — were in high demand and difficult to find, which made it all the stranger that he'd left them behind. Maybe Speiche would appear some day to reclaim his belongings, Ed thought, and so did not touch the bag.

The breakfast table, the so-called personnel table (or *perso-table* for short), was in the back third of the bar room, in a niche with a door to Krombach's cubbyhole. Once everyone was seated, the door opened and Krombach walked behind his chair in a cloud of Exlepäng. He rubbed his hands as if everything had succeeded, at least for the moment. Kruso then rose quickly and carried the steaming, brown-grained metal coffeepot from the counter to the table, where he served Krombach, himself, and Chef Mike before setting the pot down in the middle of the table. Ed saw that Kruso concentrated intently on each of his movements, adopting an attitude that suited the particular pride he displayed washing dishes or chopping wood. Both Krombach and Chef Mike thanked Kruso with discreet gestures that looked bashful to Ed, but maybe he was mistaken.

Krombach murmured a few trivial remarks about the weather the previous night, the currents, the swell, and the wind that morning, as if they were about to set out fishing. Then he bemoaned another collapse on the coastline 'between Signalmasthuk and Toter Kerl'; he must have been down by the water right at the time. Then silence fell over the table — perhaps a moment of silence for the steady dwindling of the island. The silence was pleasant. For a time, there were only breakfast sounds and the scornful cries of seagulls out over the cliff. The French doors to the terrace were open wide, and the sea breeze flowed in and washed away the smell of the previous evening. Ed closed his eyes for a second and pictured the bear-horse's head; no more tears.

There were rolls, bread, liverwurst, Teewurst, spreadable wedge

cheese, some salami, sliced cheese, and a trembling, glutinous slab of
mixed-fruit jam on a plate — 'two perso-platters for a twelve-man
perso-breakfast' in the words of Chef Mike, who brought his own
extra-large cup to the table. Ed hacked at jam. After a few minutes,
the manager began gently scattering his assignments among the
group in a barely audible voice. All their knives froze in the air for
a moment, and Ed could feel the tension. 'One thing I don't want
to forget ...' Krombach murmured; it concerned the gas cylinders
and the ramshackle line to the valve. Kruso had the answer. Basically,
Krombach spoke only to Krusowitsch or Chef Mike. Kruso stroked
his muscular arms pensively and lowered his head, holding it slightly
aslant. It was only June, but his skin was already deeply tanned, the
complexion of a Sioux. Ed studied his large, slightly hooked nose.
Now and again, Kruso shook his head a little; it was an expression of
his unflagging attention, certainly not one of denial.

Chef Mike took notes on a scrap of old wrapping paper he had
torn off in a shapeless piece the size of his palm. He revised the kitchen
order list for the next few days with a grease pencil. He broke into
a sweat, and the list became illegible. Evidently, the Klausner's cook
considered it his natural obligation to find a solution for all shortages
of provisions. He sat at the far end of the table, opposite the manager.
The two men's sentences sped back and forth between the lines of
esskays as if up and down a narrow alley.

'Sailors, I'd like you to meet Edgar Bendler.'

The manager rose from his chair. Ed was touched to hear his name
pronounced out loud like this — complete, forceful, in a positive,
almost cheerful tone. It was like a rare show of tenderness, and for a
moment the bad feeling that he was simply there representing another
person disappeared. Yes, it seemed he could now assume that he was
the one sitting at the table and that he had arrived in the heart of the
Klausner high above the sea and was indeed a member of this still
incomprehensible group.

'In a difficult situation and after a few nights of wandering about ...'

A short speech followed in which Krombach introduced Ed with a half-invented, half-true description of his 'background to date'. Around the table, not a single expression changed. With the flat of his open hand, the manager finally gestured towards each single place at the table, although first at the one empty chair to his right:

'My daughter, Monika — who is excused today.'

His hand gestured towards the floor above before making the round of the table. 'Chris, Mirko, and Rimbaud from the wait staff: excellent waiters, in fact, I'd call them *unbeatable*. Speed and stamina, cleverness and wisdom, as well as gastronomic and philosophical knowledge are perfectly united in them.' Krombach smiled. There wasn't the slightest trace of irony or cynicism in his smooth, shining face. 'Mirko has a doctorate in sociology and comes, like you do, Edgar, from Halle an der Saale. We call him Cavallo. And here, of the same academic rank, his friend Rimbaud, our philosopher — I've almost forgotten what your real name is, my friend, what your real name used to be, I mean ...' His hand paused briefly in its round. 'Kruso you've already met, Patron of our Island, one could say, and Chef Mike, from Samtens on Rügen Island, you worked with him on your first day, about which I've heard only good things. Rolf, our hardworking ship's cook. And there, on your left, are Karo and Rick, that is Karola and Richard, our counter-couple, who really are married! The two of them and I have a shared past, if I may put it that way, a capital past, isn't that right, we could even call it a palatial past! In any case, Rick is the one to ask if you have any questions. He is Head Bartender and Head of the Wait Staff. And to your right is René, our ice-cream man, my son-in-law.'

Only the last part of the manager's introduction struck Ed as forced. The back and forth motion of his soft white hand, raised to head height, and its movement in a half-circle from chair to chair reminded Ed of a benediction. Before the introductions were completed, the ice-cream man had turned away in disgust, which is why Ed had kept his head down at first, to avoid looking René in the eye.

'Let's not forget that we are all castaways in some sense ...' The manager raised both hands as if he wanted to include the entire globe in his blessing. His voice fell again. Then it looked like he was thrusting his hands through an invisible wall or into water or through something that had come between him and the rest of the world.

Ed was nervous. Krombach's oratorical efforts embarrassed him: they were excessive for a dishwasher, a *newcomer* at that, and he had trouble concentrating on Krombach's sermon. In the corner, above Chef Mike's sweaty walrus pate, were hung photographs of the personnel from previous years. Some had the date written on the frame in felt-tip pen: 1984, 1976, 1968. In one of the photographs, the one from 1968, every one of the men and women was holding a beer mug to his or her mouth. The shot looked obscene and made a deep impression on Ed. A second group of pictures, hung diagonally opposite from those of previous staffs, were framed photographs of famous guests, of whom Ed recognised only Billy Wilder and Thomas Mann immediately, then he noticed Lotte Lenya. Next to her was a tiny reproduction of Leonardo's *Last Supper*. Under it was a stylised portrait of King Hedin from the *Edda*, as far as Ed could tell. The picture showed two men in battle, holding each other tightly, though it was impossible to tell if they were fighting for love or to the death or both. The caption read 'Hedin on Hiddensee'. Celebrities and personnel were placed in such a way that they were practically looking each other in the eye. But over it all, hung just under the ceiling and like an icon on the top of an altar, ruled the photograph of Alexander Ettenburg in a monk's cassock, accompanied by a donkey and a cat. (Krombach continued, 'we recognise as the Ur-hermit's legacy ...' — from this point on, Ed knew the speech.) The most recent photograph was not framed, just pinned up on the wall, a shot taken at the opening of the season in April. Ed spotted the man who had to be Speiche. He was tall and remarkably slender. His crooked smile offered a glimpse of a gap between his front teeth. Ed initially recognised him by his glasses; why had he left his glasses behind?

'... and this island was our salvation when we'd been spat out, not by the sea or a fish, but by the land ...' While Krombach went on about 'the Klausner's further duties' and called it once again 'our ark' (apparently the staff had decided to keep the hotel open at least until Christmas Eve and maybe even for the entire winter and to 'stay up here amongst ourselves' as Krombach put it, as if it were a matter of keeping a family together through difficult times), Ed daydreamed about being part of the obscene crew of 1968. He glanced furtively at Kruso to gauge if he had been a 68er.

Kruso's expression was now stone-faced, and he looked as if he were praying. Chef Mike wiped the sweat from his brow and kneaded the small towel into a pyramid. The waiter Krombach called Cavallo was breathing heavily and looking nervously out into the courtyard. The fan on the ceiling made a soft sound. Flakes of dirt stuck to the nicotine-yellow appliances, which were remnants from the 1920s, fixtures by Emil Hirsekorns, a Berlin dealer in fine wares, 'the finest wares', Krombach had emphasised in his summary of the house's history, at least his account had sounded so when it reached Ed's ears, or rather, when it flowed past Ed's ears. The scraping of the fans removed the Klausner to more southern climes, yet ones that could still lie somewhat to the north or west, somewhere on the open sea. The constant whirling strengthened the drift; the fans lifted the perso-table and its breakfast crew out of the room, then further still, even more distant from mainland and country than they already seemed ...

When Ed surfaced from his daydream, he saw Krombach holding his hand of benediction out towards him, diagonally across the table. Ed leapt up and grabbed the hand in surprise, therefore rather too hastily. And Krombach shook it longer than was perhaps necessary. As Ed had been taught since he was a small child, he looked the manager in the eye while shaking his hand. Krombach looked at him, too, but Ed didn't feel Krombach's eyes on him. He saw only the skin that surrounded his eyes, gleaming as always with freshly applied cream, and then watery blue buttons with black spots in the centre. It seemed as if exhaustion or some illness had blunted the manager's vision or as if sight no longer came out of his eyes properly. The manager had spoken so thoughtfully and seriously, just like a real captain. Still, those facing him had no sense they were being looked at. He seemed instead to be looking at nothing in particular or at everything — everything that concerned him and Ed and Kruso, even that which was still to come. Yes, Krombach was looking right through him. He could see that Ed did not meet the unspoken requirements, that he was fundamentally unsuitable.

'All hands on deck!' They all raised their coffee cups. Breakfast was over. 'Cheers! Bon appétit!' René banged his cup on the table and burped. Krombach turned without further ado and disappeared into his cubbyhole. Ed was part of the crew.

THE CHRISTMAS PINE

Sometime in the night, the roar fell silent. The surf was still. The forest was still. The foghorn blew.

'At the sound of the beep ...'

Ed groped his way to the servants' staircase. The sky was clear, an unfathomable vault. The pine trees were waiting for him. They were his friends; he could talk to them. Every twenty seconds, the beams from the lighthouse stroked their branches.

There was one large, solitary tree very far forward, almost at the edge of the cliff — for an instant, it was completely illuminated, as if it had been caught. The esskays called the tree 'our Christmas pine' or just the 'pine of light'. Three days earlier, they had gathered around its trunk and toasted the horizon — merry Christmas and best wishes for the coming season. It was one of their customs. The reason they gave for it was that they wanted to celebrate with their nearest and dearest, with their 'family'. In winter, they'd all be alone again, without each other. They'd also sung 'Silent Night' and 'Oh, You Joyful'. 'My third Christmas on the island,' said Rimbaud, standing next to Ed on the terrace. A few esskays had dressed up; a couple of them wore candles on their heads. They celebrated the holiday on the summer solstice. Afterwards, they all went to eat at the Karl Krull, where duck and red cabbage were served. It all resembled some kind of provocation, 'but that's not how it's meant,' Rimbaud explained.

Rimbaud lived in the bee house, a small hut in the forest, a side building not far from the Klausner. There he had his own realm, and he received a few guests. On alternating weeks, they were the beekeeper who brought fresh queens to the island and a man Rimbaud called the book dealer. In a special frame backpack that sat on his back like a coal carrier's basket, the book dealer (he was a sales rep for an art-book publisher) carried his wares into the Dornbusch highland, expensive prints, rare editions, but also valuable titles from other, inaccessible publishers. Rimbaud paid for them with overnight stays.

Ed shivered. He still had one hand on the Christmas pine. In the lighthouse's beam, its trunk shimmered like the hide of a prehistoric beast. He went up to the very edge of the cliff and listened to the sounds far below. A soft, subtle sizzling. Water was being pushed through the pebbles and then drawn back out again — the Baltic Sea's heavy, asthmatic breathing. He leaned forward slightly. The temptation to let himself fall was still in him, perhaps it always had been. Ed realised that you always had to defend your life against things that were constantly happening to you on the one hand, and on the other against your own self and the desire to simply give up.

Among the staff, his favourites were Kruso, Chef Mike, and the counter-couple. Karola and Rick had welcomed him warmly from the start. The waiters formed a circle of their own. Chris seemed harmless and good-natured, but with Cavallo and Rimbaud things were different; he could sense their irritability. Rimbaud gave the impression of being well-groomed, with an almost old-fashioned concern for cultivating a masculine aura. He was the only one on whom the waiter's tailcoat really sat well. A few silver strands gleamed in his thick, helmet-like mane of hair, as evenly distributed as if they had been carefully painted in.

The guests often mixed up Cavallo and Rimbaud. Because there was no resemblance between them, this could only be explained by the fact they both had moustaches. Still, Cavallo's moustache was much thinner, essentially just a fine line above his upper lip; Rimbaud's, in contrast, was a thick, meticulously trimmed tuft on which he liked to lay his little finger while speaking or reciting. Nevertheless, customers regularly asked if they weren't brothers 'given the resemblance ...' It was like confusing Dalí with Nietzsche. Of course, these guests only wanted to be friendly and open (or to crown their holiday by having a conversation with one of the waiters in the legendary cliff-side restaurant on Hiddensee, something that would make a good story back home), but from that point on they got no more service, either from Cavallo or from Rimbaud. Under the circumstances, it was a good thing there was still Chris.

Apart from that, Cavallo and Rimbaud were, in fact, good friends. During their shift, they played chess. Their board was always set up on the waiters' small break table, right in front of the counter. If there was no time to sit at the break table, they would call out their moves to each other over the guests' heads. To Ed, they were like old Tatars, who could play entire games while riding alongside each other over the steppe for hours, without chess pieces, simply by calling out their moves. Now and again, Ed saw René, the ice-cream man, at the break table, but he never played, only guarded the board. The ice-cream man talked a lot, cracked jokes, and laughed hollowly into his vat.

Despite everything, Cavallo and Rimbaud often argued, either about philosophy or politics, occasionally about women. 'It's just about winning the day's battle,' Rick explained while preparing the drinks for their orders.

In front of a central pillar, the cash register dominated the room. Whenever Rimbaud approached the unusually high stand, he studied the picture of his namesake and whispered the question, 'Fame, when will you come?'

The picture was a bad reproduction of an early photograph torn out of a newspaper and pasted onto cardboard. On the day of his first shift, Rimbaud had placed the picture next to the cash register and so earned his nickname. Ed had been prepared to take the alleged entreaties as just one more of the many stories about Rimbaud, but then he had seen for himself — Rimbaud's raised head, the movement of his moustache.

'Fame, when will you come?'

WHY DO THE MOON AND THE MAN SLIDE?

Even before noon, the terrace was awash with guests. Every morning, four boatloads of day tourists surged from the port up to the Dornbusch highland, as if there were nowhere else to go. The clearing and the surrounding woods up to the cliff edge were also filled with holiday-makers ready to pounce. A few tried to place orders from the edge of the terrace, and before long a few of the most brazen were standing between the tables, right in the waiters' paths. They looked down at the tables around them and discussed the dishes, their hands stretched out to point at the food, almost touching it; or they tried to drive the seated guests away with hostile muttering. The waiters yelled 'Careful!' and 'Look out!' but even their sternest commands worked only for a short time, and sooner or later Krombach came out to patrol the beer garden. In a placating manner, he would lead the most impatient back to the edge of the terrace as if guiding them out of a labyrinth. He held them by the arm, sometimes walking them all the way to the bluff, up to the cliff edge — to rush them right over the edge, Ed thought, which would have been one solution and would have given the term 'rush hour' a new meaning ...

In fact, the rush brought out the best in everyone, and Ed soon began to understand what lay behind the elevated terminology of crew and staff. Krombach, who otherwise never left his office, would pull a short length of grey rope from his trouser pocket and begin to demonstrate sailors' knots, holding his hands high. He tied various heart-shaped knots and raised them in the air to applause. The fact that someone was offering a demonstration immediately attracted attention, especially because it all seemed unplanned, spontaneous, without supervision or entry fee, and therefore amounted to a rare and exotic event, something you could only experience here, on this island.

Ed never found out what Krombach was trying to make evident with his knot-tying. The grey hearts seemed to have the same hypnotic effect on the tourists as they did on him. After four or five hearts, the manager took a bow. Then he pulled more short pieces of rope from his trouser pockets and handed them out to the bystanders, who accepted them incredulously, as if receiving something extraordinarily precious. A few of them immediately began knotting the short ends, or at least they tried to, and for a while creating hearts of their own seemed more desirable than schnitzel or *steak au four*.

Rimbaud and Cavallo soon fell into a continuous trot. Chris tried to maintain a walking pace but still had to move as quickly as possible and so fell into his characteristic hobble. The dishes now arrived at the sink in tall, swaying, food-encrusted stacks, and had to be washed, dried, and set out for use again immediately — there were simply never enough available. Chef Mike's pale walrus skull appeared above the swinging door to the kitchen at regular intervals. His floods of verbal abuse weren't mean-spirited or aggressive; instead, they were daily rush-hour arias of unsurpassable drama and urgency about missing plates, knives, and bowls and the inevitable consequences of these conditions: utter collapse, death. When the aria sounded, the time for niceties was past. Entire stacks of unscraped dishes were unceremoniously tossed into the sink, and the greasy scraps of schnitzel, potatoes, salad, or meatballs were swept from the surface of the water and onto the floor with a backhand stroke. With a bit of practice, Ed could clear the water with two or three strokes in quick succession. In a matter of seconds, his sink was cleared. He merely had to be careful not to dirty the cleaned dishes, and it was no small disadvantage that they then, until evening, had to wade through a revolting morass of trodden refuse, a swamp of leftovers that made obscene noises under the soles of their shoes, which is why Ed soon began gliding over the tiles as if on skis. Kruso regularly mopped and dried the waiters' approach paths so they wouldn't slip — even then, when hardly anyone knew whether they were coming or going, Kruso kept control, acting responsibly and thoughtfully. Ed could have embraced him for it.

The Klausner's thermometer read forty-three degrees Celsius. They worked like madmen but still always lagged behind. The sun bored through the window, and the dishwater exuded a corrosive mugginess. By the litre, they downed the tea Karola prepared at the bar and brought into the dishwashing station in a large brown earthenware pitcher. The pitcher's usual spot was behind Ed in the opening to a dumb waiter that probably once went down to the cellar or up to the servants' quarters, but was now used only for storage. Since there was no time to pour, Ed drank right from the spout. In his rush, the lukewarm tea spilled over the rim of the pitcher onto his face, which made no difference since he was bare chested and the drying towel around his hips was already soaked with dishwater and sweat. He was a galley slave. He felt naked — even his privates were damp, and itched between his legs.

After an hour of rushing, Cavallo first began to whinny, leaping in small but unbridled hops, like a child pretending to gallop. He also gave light puffs and snorts that made his thin moustache vibrate. This performance was hard to square with Cavallo's usual manner (his complete reserve). 'Romacavalli,' Rimbaud brayed through the

Klausner, spurring them on. 'Avanti, avanti, dilettanti!' Ed marvelled at the way Rimbaud, his arms spread wide, twirled as if on tiptoe. Ed admired the way he ran the till with one hand, sorted receipts, then stood still for seconds at a time deciphering something on the tiny slips while reaching (with an arm that seemed to extend longer and longer) for the large tray full of beer and soda, lifting it from the counter in one fluid motion as if endowed with telescopic strength. He did all this while keeping an eye on the serving counter and making imperceptible gestures at Chris as he swept passed with his hobbling gait.

'Fame, when will you come?'

As the noon rush peaked, Rimbaud began reciting quotations with scatological or pornographic references that stood in complete contrast to his elegant demeanour and expressed, Ed thought, an indefinable hatred, an unfathomable contempt for everything in life, even for life itself, which Ed was sure Rimbaud could never have intended. Yet the euphoric, essentially combative tone of his voice spoke another language. Ed understood Rimbaud's dirty jokes as an expression of the difficult synthesis of philosopher and head waiter this member of the crew — by far the most well-read of the lot — fulfilled as best and as proudly as he could every day. Sometimes Rimbaud suddenly started speaking French: 'mon plongeur, mon ami', and when he rushed past Krombach's door on his way to the dishwashing station, he would berate the manager loudly, 'Chef du personnel — une catastrophe!' After his sortie onto the terrace, the manager remained unseen.

Ed toiled and sweated away what remained of his thoughts and feelings. He worked his way to the solid foundation of true exhaustion, and, for those few hours, he felt purified, redeemed from himself and his unhappiness. He was nothing more or less than a dishwasher who held the fort tolerably well in the surrounding chaos.

The first time he heard it, Ed thought Kruso was explaining something, offering more of his instructions, which were always worth paying attention to. Ed's ears had grown accustomed to the echo chamber that was the dishwashing station, but he still understood only individual words that were repeated, the words 'man' and 'sea'.

'What?' Ed hollered into the rush hour, too forcefully, perhaps, since Kruso immediately stopped moving his hands. The water slapped against the sides of the sink.

'Past the high reeds, past the low meadow, the canoe slides to the sea.'

It seemed to be a kind of magic spell because silence immediately fell over the room; even the kitchen radio fell silent. Kruso kept his head lowered, and Ed assumed the conversation was over before it had started. He plunged his hands into his sink to grab a plate when the chorus rose:

'Past the high reeds, past the low meadow, the canoe slides to the sea. With the sliding moon, the canoe slides to the sea ...'

Ed registered the presence of Rimbaud and Cavallo behind him, singing, panting, heavily laden. Their outstretched arms loaded with dirty dishes, they seemed like extras in an absurdist play. Then, behind them in the semi-darkness, Karola's wonderful dusky singing voice:

'So to the sea they are companions, the canoe, the moon, and the man ...'

Now Kruso merely whispered, so the basses sounded that much stronger, the voices of Chef Mike and Rolf:

'Why do the moon and the man slide together so submissively to sea, so submissively to sea!'

Before Ed realised what was happening, the waiters' plates crashed into his sink. Chris pushed past everyone, yelling 'So submissively to sea!' and hugged Kruso, who remained almost completely unmoved, which did not seem either dismissive or unnatural. It suited the dignity of the poem they had recited together, apparently a kind of hymn of the Klausner, 'our sacred song' as Kruso often explained later.

Like Krombach's knotted hearts or Cavallo's whinnying, the
chorus about the man and the sea was a part of the rush-hour ritual
and its delirium: it was its climax. In the minutes that followed, Chef
Mike bellowed his '*finito*' from the kitchen, the end of *à la carte*
orders. The menus were collected quickly: a few were torn right out
of the hands of some particularly disappointed guests. Only two or
three dishes remained available, mostly solyanka, jägerschnitzel, and
roulade. The announcement of the back-up menu was left to Chris,
the most popular waiter among the guests due to his boyish, affable
manner. Our best man on the wait staff, Rimbaud, warbled and
pursed his lips. Rimbaud and Cavallo liked to make fun of Chris,
who had come to the island the year before, from Magdeburg, from
his previous life as an electrician, as an *electrical* as he himself put it.

After Chris had hobbled back and forth like a dervish for two
hours (his greasy, black curls covering the nape of his neck like
a sluggishly bouncing blanket), he stepped outside and took up
position on the terrace steps like a royal herald. He waited until the
din had subsided and all eyes were turned toward him. Then he called
out 'solyanka', and those who wanted to order solyanka learned to
answer loudly and clearly with 'here' and to stand up at the same time
— 'so I can keep an overview', as Chris would explain, logically and
understandably. There was a similar procedure for serving the dishes.
Chris often stormed out onto the terrace carrying six or seven plates
on his arms and called 'schnitzel'. Those who had ordered it rose and
yelled 'here', often unnecessarily loud in the hopes of being among the
first served. A few played it to the hilt and called out 'Here, Sir!' or
clicked their heels, whereupon Chris would slide one plate or bowl
after another onto the table while bellowing responses like 'Drop and
give me twenty!' or 'Fall out for squat thrusts!' and throwing his head
back with an expression that swung between contempt and insanity.
Of course, it was all just a game.

Nevertheless, some of the salutes were given with a serious
expression, as if there actually were some higher power emanating

from Chris, or as if he elicited from the guests something a few of them could not keep in check. There were guests who dropped into push-up position or extended their arms abruptly and, with their jumping jacks, scared away the scavenging birds hiding in the surrounding bushes. A few guests simply knew no bounds (as Ed's mother would have put it); they obviously were not enjoying their holiday or were at the mercy of their utterly unfulfilled existences. Chris didn't care. At the end of the rush, he left them to their fates. The kitchen closed at one thirty. The gate to the terrace was locked at two p.m. on the dot.

After surviving the rush, Rimbaud and Cavallo threw off their jackets and shirts, bent over the dish sinks, and splashed their armpits with handfuls of cold water. When Ed stepped out onto the ramp to rinse the dishwashing vapours from his irritated lungs with fresh air; he felt encrusted, like a fossil not yet completely petrified. Whereas the skin on his face stretched like old leather, the skin on his hands disintegrated, pale shreds fraying around his fingertips. He felt unsteady on his feet, slightly dizzy from the syrupy detergent that barely produced any foam but emitted caustic fumes that upset his stomach.

During the common meal at the staff table, Ed had a hard time separating the image of the stringy pork schnitzel on his plate from those he had just seen, carved up, chewed up, spat out, trodden flat, or swimming in the soapy water that filled his sink. In fact, he would have been satisfied with his daily onion. He didn't need more than that. He was tired and didn't want to move anymore, just lie down, stretch out, and sleep, but he held fast to his walks down to the sea.

Before setting off, Ed lingered for a moment with the others at the table in the courtyard; at some point, he decided to eat something after all, then had a cigarette. He'd started smoking again — everyone smoked and hardly anyone spoke. He felt the same weighty satisfaction that had done him so much good on the construction sites in the years before he began his studies, before he started getting lost in the history of language, its labyrinthine constructions of syntax, morphology, orthography, and lexicology, the whole *idiotic merry-go-round*, as the students called their first-year exams in these subjects, their voices full of loathing and respect. This was before their preliminary examination, consisting of sentences from Musil or Kleist, which caused more than a few to despair and fail.

Ed enjoyed the satisfaction of the afternoon break. It was a kind of honour: for at this moment they were all united in their pride, a genuine pride that came perhaps less from the nature of their work (slave labour) as from the sense of having achieved the impossible, yes, of having withstood a storm. Nothing gave them as clear a sense of solidarity as the high-season rushes with their commotion and excessive demands. They belonged to a crew that would defend their ship to the very last, that much was certain, with every ounce of their ingenuity, gastronomic bravado, and the skills they had gained from their academic or artistic backgrounds. By achieving the impossible in their violent, chaotic campaign, they obviously fulfilled the honour code Kruso had mentioned, the code that united the esskays. Assisted by a special kind of lunacy, an essence of gastronomy and poetry, they kept their ark afloat, day after day. And saved the lurching island.

THE AMPHIBIAN

At three on the dot, Ed returned from the beach up the stairs on the bluff. As he climbed, sweat streamed from every pore; his body overheated from the sun. There was no shade on the beach. As always, he walked in a small arc, half in the woods, so he would be seen as little as possible when he passed the terrace, now filling with the first café guests.

'Why else, why else, why else on earth are you here?' he babbled softly to himself as he crouched, naked, on the greasy floor in the dishwashing station and let the wonderfully cool water run over his head and back. He stared at the row of vats: his silhouette was mirrored in the steel of the sink, in which the cutlery was still soaking — only then did he notice the feet. Feet and legs, protruding from under the basin, as immobile as a dead man's limbs. Following the slope of the floor, the water Ed had cooled himself with flowed directly and inexorably straight towards them. Mortified, Ed apologised, that is, he stammered something at the feet, at Kruso's feet, which Ed, in the meantime, thought he recognised. The basin's drain ended about a hand's breadth above the tiles and the water flowed in free fall onto the grate of the drain in the floor. To keep from having to wade through a putrid swill of old wash water while they worked, it was necessary to clear the constantly growing swamp of food scraps from the grates. Kruso called it 'pulling the weeds', a task that was even less popular than 'going Roman'. Ed could not understand why Kruso was lying so still under the basin. Maybe Kruso hadn't even noticed him and there was still a chance to escape unseen, Ed thought. Then came a crash. A second later, the man who belonged to the legs was standing in front of Ed, as naked as he was, a bushman, powerful and gleaming with streaks of moisture. In his right hand, he held his machete, a large kitchen knife. In his left hand, he held up the drain grate, from which dangled a metre-long clump of slime. A trickle of blood ran down his arm; a disgusting stench filled the room.

'It's already old, four months, maybe, that's why it took some patience,' Kruso explained, and looked at the plait of slime as if it were a living creature he had been hunting for a while. The creature was tapered towards its tail and ended in a thin grey rivulet. Kruso behaved like — how could Ed put it — a warrior. He was a warrior, a primeval hunter, a chiselled figure, impressively tall, hirsute.

'You're bleeding,' Ed said, relieved to have found something to say.

Kruso tossed the knife; there was a light splash and water spattered Ed's face. The hunting knife spun towards the aluminium mass of forks and knives covering the bottom of the sink, shimmering dully like a treasure no one on earth was ready to raise. Then Kruso extended his bloody arm over the sink and looked Ed in the eye. It was a scout's look, a look from another, earlier time when there were men who still lived in tents with Indians or planned ambushes as a member of an outlaw gang. It was a severe, secretive look, a confiding look.

The cut wasn't deep. While Ed carefully cleaned Kruso's arm and wiped the blood from his skin and hair, cold drops of slime from the plait dripped between his toes, but he did not move. Ed was almost spellbound by the matter-of-factness with which Kruso expected his help. Something about this did him good, more deeply than he could understand. It had nothing to do with their being naked, nor, naturally, with the sight of Kruso's genitals. It seemed to have more to do with what Kruso relied on him for, with the fact that he could *use* Ed for something.

The plait creature must have been heavy; it trembled lightly at the end of Kruso's raised arm. Kruso's arm trembled. The thing looked like an amphibian, or rather an enormous tadpole that was about to turn into a toad so it could break through the grate with its slimy hunched back and bite their calves while they worked.

'The spade is next to the cellar door,' Kruso said. This time his voice was too close and the sentence a hiss, so Ed had to rearrange the words and recall them one by one.

'The spade,' Kruso repeated, his large teeth bared as if he were trying to articulate more clearly. But it sounded no different than if he had said 'coffee' or 'saucer'. Kruso was no savage; he was the opposite of a brute, naked in the dishwashing station, with an unknown animal on a hook. Kruso was patient.

'Next-to-the-cellar-door,' Ed repeated, and quickly wrapped a dishcloth around his hips.

They buried the amphibian near the edge of the property, but still on the grounds, in the area Kruso called his herb bed. Kruso, wrapped in one of the old, pinkish sheets, said it was the best spot for growing mushrooms in the world, 'four varieties and eight different kinds of herbs'. Then he launched into his instructions: how to knock the amphibian off the grate with a branch; how to slam the grate against the tree — a particular tree, Ed could see from the injuries to the bark — until the last bits stuck in it have squirted out; and so on.

For the first time, Ed noticed traces of a dialect in Kruso's speech. It was partly a kind of Swabian, essentially an archaic mixture of different pronunciations. Kruso rarely spoke that way, only when he forgot to pay attention.

Ed made an effort. As he dug, the dishcloth kept slipping off his hips. He shifted the cloth to the leg stretched out in the forest grass and kept working without interruption. He himself didn't know why it had to be this way. He felt shame, but, at the moment, there was something more important. With bare feet, it was painful and almost impossible to force the blade into the sandy soil. Ed tried pushing with his heel and exerting pressure with sharp jabs; he knew how to use a spade. Even Kruso, who ripped up roots and pushed the sand aside with his hands, could not miss how hard it was. But for now, the only thing that mattered was to do what was necessary and not to show any weakness while he was at it. Ed's penis was illuminated by the sun; his testicles imitated the digging motion in a way he found ridiculous.

In the end, Kruso placed the amphibian into the hollow. Only then did Ed notice the myriad long, apparently human hairs that ran through the creature like veins, similar to the web of blood vessels on the surface of a newly exposed organ. There were blond hairs that shone white in afternoon sun, but also black and red hairs. Ed hesitated, as if he were being forced to bury a living being, a live creature (as his mother put it), but Kruso said 'spade' and Ed poured the sandy dirt onto the amphibian.

There was a moment of silence, into which the roar of the surf swelled. Slowly at first, then lightning fast, deafening — a grey jet plane sped over the Dornbusch highland at low altitude. 'This is where the cycle of freedom comes full circle,' Kruso announced as if he were starting a eulogy, his voice enveloped in the thunder. 'We lead the metabolic process of man and nature back to the roots of an earlier community.' In his pink sheet, he looked like the Ur-hermit in the photograph in the breakfast niche: only the cat and the donkey were missing. But still, Ed was there, and he bent quickly to pluck his apron from the ground, as quickly and discreetly as possible.

On the way back to the Klausner, Kruso spoke of a megalithic tomb on the Dornbusch and of hearths, three thousand years old, but still recognisable, up on the Swantiberg, the sacred mountain.

A king's throne ... He easily adapted his steps to the length of his sheet, and his pace had the dignity befitting a tribune, whereas Ed found he had to keep rearranging his sheet — his hips simply gave the cloth no purchase.

'The Black Hole,' Kruso explained, and climbed down an outdoor staircase near the Klausner's foundation. Ed lost sight of him at first, then a light bulb flared in a porcelain socket mounted between two cast-iron boilers. The lamp's glass was covered with coal dust; its beam of light illuminated a pile of broken briquettes. 'There's no light switch at the door, you have to cross the darkness to here, in front of the boiler.' A soft laugh rang out, but maybe Ed's ears deceived him. The MiG's thunder was still ringing in his ears. He shivered.

Across from the boiler stood a row of large, broken-down closets. 'Our supply stores,' Kruso called, 'and here, the archive!' He pressed a pair of checked trousers into Ed's chest, thin and with a cloth belt, just like the ones mute Rolf and Chef Mike wore. Ed would rather not have tried on the trousers in front of Kruso, but he did. If he had any ability, then it was this: he could sense what was expected of him; he could perceive how the world others lived in was constituted. At such times, he had moments of utter clarity when he *understood*, and he could behave accordingly when he wished. Maybe it was a kind of compensation — for the fact that he was missing a particular trait, something that brought people closer, that bound them together.

The first pair was much too large, and, in the second and third pairs as well, Ed looked like a dwarf in a clown's clothes. These steps were called fittings and dressings. Friday was given his goatskin. After they found the right pair of pants, Kruso draped a long white chef's coat over Ed's shoulders. Ed felt Kruso's eyes on him, the pleasure.

'I'd like to ask you something.'

The clothes smelled of mould and had soot on the hems. Ed was not sure he wanted to wear them, yet he sensed the honour — for faithful service, or what should one call it? He had goosebumps under the jacket.

'It's very important for our duty here. The question is whether you want to take responsibility for one of the boilers. Lighting it early, at six in the morning, our caretaker forgets too often. You know how hard it is with cold water in the dishwashing station, basically impossible ...'

While Kruso explained the boiler and the set-up of the Black Hole, Ed pictured the caretaker of the German Studies Institute in his garden hut, the ground covered with bottles, and he pictured the caretaker of the Station Hotel in the basement cauterising numbers onto wooden blocks, and he saw Ebeling, the Klausner's caretaker (he had not met him yet), lying in bed drunk in the house on the island he shared with his mother. And for a moment, Ed saw himself, too: as in a gym class, all the caretakers were lined up according to height, and he was the last in line, and above his head was written '6 A.M.'

Over the following days, the cellar became his cave, his hide-out, quiet and isolated. In one corner, where old dining room furniture had been piled, he found a tiny table and a barstool. He had carried them outside, scrubbed off the mould, and left them in the sun for two days. The table fit well under the window in his room, although one drawback was that it smelled of misery (mildew and coal). Ed shortened the barstool's legs with a saw; the tabletop was still too low.

After the furnace was fired up (the wood had to be burning well before he could lay the damp coal on it), Ed made his round. One of the cabinets was filled with small bars of hotel soap, wrapped in once-white paper with 'Palace Hotel' in elegant, copperplate writing. Then the metal cabinet with files and account books. Behind the metal cabinet that was almost rusted through but immoveable, there was a niche. Through a gap as wide as an arm, you could see discarded lumber, prehistoric gymnastics apparatuses, rotting burlap, and a zinc tub. 'Alexander Ettenburg called this tub his incinerator, his crematorium,' Kruso had explained, as if it would be useful for Ed's work. 'There used to be an urn that went with it. The Ur-hermit had prepared everything. He was a man of nature, well ahead of his time. He named all the places here, the Svantovit Gorge, Flag Mountain, the Zeppelin Stone. In the end, the old man wanted nothing more than to be buried on the island, but they sprinkled his ashes over the sea. The island people didn't want any foreigners in their land, and that's still true today, with a few exceptions. Great men like Hauptmann or nameless drowned bodies.'

When he finished his round, Ed lit the cellar candle. In a corner hung with plastic sheeting, there was a small, square shaft into which wooden steps led. He set the candle on the ground and started pulling snails off the walls. He was amazed how tenaciously they stuck to mould-darkened cement. Every morning, there were new black and brown specimens — there was no explanation for it. He picked them until his hands were full, then he climbed the stairs and tossed them into the fire.

Ed discovered that the shaft had originally been a shower, and used his time in the cellar reconditioning it — he scraped the ancient sludge out of the drain and knocked the scale from the showerhead. The water was rusty and foul-smelling at first, but got better after a while. The fixtures squeaked and creaked pitifully, but they worked. For a while, Ed stood knee-deep in water, until a fill-level sensor started a pump. When he had lit the furnace and the water in the tank had been warmed, he could take a shower, an incomparable luxury. Aside from the onion, it was the only other thing of his very own.

The snails glowed in the fire. They straightened out to their full length one last time, like newborns, before suddenly collapsing in on themselves with a short whistling sound, as if air were escaping from their bodies. 'God knows how they keep coming back,' Ed whispered into the furnace. A brief whistling from the embers, then he began loading the briquettes, piece by piece.

VIOLA

Today Rimbaud showed me a book and read out loud from it. It's called The Theatre of Cruelty, a book from the West. Every week there's a new title in the nest, sometimes several. Probably gets them from the book dealer. I'm allowed to use the nest, even by myself, when I have the time. They're all a community here.

Every day at noon, Ed ate his onion. Along with his silence, his onion ritual (as if it were even necessary) gave him an image of being a moderately odd duck, who was unlikely to cause trouble and whose hiring, yes, could hardly have been a mistake. In a certain sense, the onion established his position in the Klausner. Soon Ed was seen as an island of calm amid the galloping and reciting representatives of the wait staff, the irascible ice-cream man with his constantly rattling ice cubes, and Rick at the counter, who, with his stories and bits of wisdom, ran a kind of life-philosophy bar. Ed at his sink, in contrast, was a model of concentration and discretion. That was an obvious reason why he was close to Kruso, a Friday at Robinson's side. There was no need for anyone to wonder much why the two were increasingly seen together, although as a rule it was simply Kruso's daily briefing for Ed as the new dishwasher and boiler-man. Ed marvelled at the changes, and once again he wondered how it could all be happening to him. Now and then, he was overcome with a bashful joy that was reluctant to ally itself too closely to him, and sometimes, very suddenly, G. appeared to him — he had no control over that.

Why did it do him so much good to talk so little?

He hadn't intended it, but then Ed realised that silence was the core feature of his flight — that's what he had come to call it. He simply had to keep to himself, but he also knew he shouldn't be alone at this time ... In his mind, he had accidentally formulated it the other way around, and yet that's exactly what he had meant: I'd like a place in this world that keeps me apart from everything. Later, he had walked along the beach and had spoken the sentence out over the water, like a plea, but the waves were too high, the sea too loud, and the wind pushed the words right back in his mouth.

His reserve helped him avoid giving any signs of weakness or inexperience. He said, 'Hello' or 'Yes' and 'Exactly'. He could use 'exactly' for any situation. 'Exactly' was the best possible answer if anyone presumed to joke with him or wanted to ridicule him, which happened often at the beginning and then less and less. Whatever happened to Ed was simply redoubled by his 'exactly', and, in this doubling, it was relieved of its weight and robbed of its magnitude. In this way, everything could be quickly accepted or deflected. He needed no defence, no trench. Everything that happened to him in this foreign place was nothing more than *exactly that*. 'Exactly' was the briefest and best description of the island. The island 'exactly' lay in the middle of his silence, impregnable.

From the dishwashing station, Ed had discovered it at some point
— a radio that Chef Mike called 'my Viola'. It was a Violetta-brand
valve radio, a dark wooden box on an inaccessibly high shelf above
the refrigerators, right under the kitchen ceiling. Apparently, it could
no longer be turned off. The shelf was supported by raw steel brackets
and seemed more solid than the Klausner's foundation walls. The
cover on the speakers was coated with a hard layer of age-old grease,
out of which flashed the flickering green lens of a magic eye. The silver
of its name glittered above it like eyeliner in an old woman's make-up.
Viola winked at Ed. She winked at his back as he bent over the sink.
Sometimes, she disappeared completely in the haze. In the layers of
echoes that filled the kitchen, the radio's voice was irritatingly difficult
to place, and seemed to come right out of the ghostly swirls that
rose from the cooking pots. Viola, Chef Mike explained, belonged
to his predecessor, who had drowned when out for a night swim in
the summer of 1985. The station had already been set and the radio
turned on when he and Rolf took over the Klausner's kitchen not
long after. As far as Chef Mike was concerned, there was nothing
more to say about it.

Ed was troubled by the thought that the radio had outlived its
owner — without falling silent. In a certain way, it could be seen as
the voice of the drowned former cook that had poured out for years
over the pots and pans in the Klausner without interruption, covering
the dishes he prepared in an endless stream. For an absurd moment,
it appeared to Ed like an act of resistance, perhaps evidence of some
injustice long past, surfacing like a hand reaching out of a grave again
and again. Ed fantasised as the acrid fumes of the detergent went to
his head and he channelled plate after plate through the stone sink for
coarse cleaning. He worked hard to maintain his rhythm; he did not
want to be slower than Kruso.

The control dial was missing, and the ivory-coloured buttons
that recalled an overbite were broken. Mangled as she was, Viola
could only receive one West German station, but did so with the

relentlessness attributed to soldiers wounded in battle who fight on
and on despite their injuries. What Viola made of these broadcasts
with her shaky reception, her sudden silences or obstinate humming,
her rasping, gurgling, and coughing (her bronchial sounds were
particularly bad) coalesced into a kind of undertone in the Klausner.
Her constant broadcasting was like the house's breathing, varying
but continual, like the crash of the breakers and for the most part
ignored ... 'Droning on and on, just droning ...' as Chef Mike said.

In the dishwashing station, they could not hear much from Viola,
often just a low roar with overtones. The time signal was the most
distinct sound. Twelve o'clock. At the last pip, Ed lifted his hands
out of the water. He pushed the swinging door to the kitchen open
a crack and asked for an onion. Eventually, mute Rolf went over to
prepare him a plate and set it on the shelf behind the swinging door
on the right so that Ed only had to reach out and grab it: a large,
gleaming onion sliced in half with a slice of brown bread. Ed paused
for a moment, his back pushing against one wing of the swinging
door, and before he could shout his thanks into the kitchen (he
peered through the haze to catch sight of Rolf or Chef Mike), a few of
Viola's sentences reached him. Ed felt drawn to the monotony of her
half-hourly stories, with contents that hardly changed for days. At the
end, the weather, water conditions, wind speed. There were missing-
person announcements and emergency broadcasts for motorists. Not
even a storm advisory warranted a change in intonation. 'Federal
Minister of Economic Affairs Haussmann has repeated his advisory
to reduce working hours. The people of the Federal Republic are to
be relieved of low-altitude flights. And now the detailed news report.'

To show Kruso that the onion would not interrupt his work, Ed
ate it right at the sink like an apple, taking a bite now and then. In the
beginning, Ed would wash his hands before each bite, but now that
he had gradually become one with the dishwashing station and its
toxic essences, he no longer took the trouble.

Except for Viola, the refrigeration units, the coffee machine, and

an electric potato peeler that could only be used by the caretaker who
was rarely there, there was no machinery in the Klausner aside from
Krombach's grey telephone. Nevertheless, there were windows that
could be opened a crack and, if possible, wide-open doors. The wind
blew in from the sea through the front entrance, swept the dining
room and kitchen clean, and wafted out the back door. As a result,
Ed and Kruso were enveloped for hours in a warm, greasy current,
a mix of vapours, a combination of tobacco, smoke, human smells,
and alcohol fumes, musty and stifling. 'Smoked, we're being smoked,'
Kruso swore, 'when the savages come, they'll smell us first. We have
to take precautions and wash thoroughly every evening. Wash and
groom ourselves, put on moisturiser. Always be vigilant. Expand the
caves, create more hideouts. Ed, *the expectation of evil is more bitter
than suffering it!*' The echo chamber that was the dishwashing station
distorted his words, so Ed misunderstood them. It didn't sound like
Kruso was joking. He basically never did, especially not when talking
about his namesake's legendary story.

At the end of the shift, the ice-cream man shoved his empty buckets
between Ed's legs.
    'My tidy friend!'
    'Exactly.'
    'That's *exactly* what I mean.'
    'Exactly.'
    'Don't get cheeky, Onion.'
    The buckets stank. René's cold, nasal tone of voice stuck to
their insides. Ed scrubbed it away. René's big-city arrogance (he was
from Berlin, too) made an impression that was both asinine and
intimidating. There was something in his intonation, something that
seemed indomitable and that you did not hear in the Thuringian
or Saxon dialects. His white shirt looked freshly ironed; he always
smelled good, Ed thought. René wore real jeans and a comb sticking

out of his back pocket. It was plastic and had a wide, lightly curved handle. Occasionally, in the middle of a conversation or even at the breakfast table, he would pull it out and comb his wavy hair.

Ed dried the buckets carefully and put them back in the hutch under the ice-cream counter. Then he crept up to his room. He had learned early on that there was a hall that led from the dining room directly to the stairs; you didn't have to circle the entire building to reach the stairs. In the depths of the small corridor between the dining room and the staircase, the second door was barely visible, although it usually stood open and connected the kitchen, bar, and dining room with the upper floor like a duct.

This outer corridor complied with an old regulation that Krombach repeated whenever he hired new crew members. It all went back to complaints made by senior-level guests on their company holidays who were outraged when unhygienic, unattractive characters would suddenly appear next to their tables and, with a cloud of sweat, smoke, and alcohol, spoil the candlelit holiday existence the guests had dreamt of for so long and worked for so hard. Krombach was just a tenant and didn't want any trouble with the so-called parent company. In any case, the manager made sure his crew did not come into close contact with the holiday guests, those official representatives of the working classes.

That night, Ed experienced the *beneficial isolation* that was mentioned now and again in the calmest possible voice with the most soothing words, which hid the fact that no one actually knew if there was such a thing. He listened to the tattered melodies floating up from Viola. He dozed to the crashing of the waves or stared into the darkness over the water and saw the bear-horse. It was completely calm. He could look the animal fixedly in the eye.

It was as if he had only started to think during that first afternoon in the courtyard of the Klausner with a horse in front of him and an onion in his hand. To think thoughts he knew had actually originated with him. It was thought beyond the powers of perception and somewhere deep within, beneath his memory hoard. The horse's moist, velvety nostrils, the sound of its breathing, the stillness in its eyes. Ed was twenty-four years old. He had lost G. For the first time in his life, he could feel how he was starting to think. When he rubbed his face with the palm of his hand, he could smell the daily special. His skin was greasy, and shone.

THE ENDDORN HOTEL

A slight wind rose. Little lapping Baltic waves followed in quick succession; a short-winded sea. Sand martins flashed by, crisscrossing above Ed's head as if they wanted to chase him away. He lay on the beach, on his back, lost in contemplation of the fist-sized caves sprinkled across the steep coast on the northern end of the island. They were high up, right under the cliff's edge, in ten or fifteen levels on top of each other, and reminded Ed of the desert Indians' cave dwellings he had seen in a Western or in an adventure movie. The birds appeared in their caves at intervals, then shot back out.

'A giant cuckoo clock, old gaffer,' Ed whispered, 'can you hear the ticking in the clay? With their open beaks, they catch mosquitoes like seconds. In flight, they digest time into a pap, and then at home they vomit it all up and stuff the mouths of their tiny sprogs — stuffed only with a brew of time, they learn how to fly, old rascal, did you know that?'

Ed liked spinning yarns even if his fox was out of earshot. Still, it was his first free day, his first day off since he had arrived at the Klausner, and he had decided to walk around the northern tip of the island.

Days off: there had been no instructions or explanations given, and why should there? No one thought of him, no one wanted anything from him. For Ed, they were an intermediate goal, a small triumph. 'You made it this far,' he whispered to the swallow-filled sky, and started on his way.

Like a beached whale helplessly pushing its mouth into the waves and trying desperately to return to the water, the Dornbusch highland rose from the sea — a large, slowly crumbling animal. The storm tide constantly excised huge blocks from its Ice Age body — sandstone, shale, and Uppsala granite — from which its earlier home and the ten thousand years since its arrival could be deciphered. Its Scandinavian body was fraying, and little by little its corpse was returning to the sea. The current washed marl and clay back onto the north-east of the island and began rounding out the coastline. The area called the Bessin, whose shape led many to compare the island's contour with a seahorse (and so to take the island even more deeply into their hearts), had become bloated over the last few decades — the seahorse grew extra muzzles, and its head expanded to monstrous proportions.

After only a half-kilometre, the way was blocked. Part of the bluff had recently broken off and slid into the sea. Holding his bundle of things over his head, Ed made his way awkwardly around the landslide. The ground was stony; he could hardly stay upright. The water was above his waist. At one point, he thought he heard someone laughing, but it seemed to come from over the water. Apparently, there were no tourists on this part of the island. There was just one man sunbathing, probably younger than Ed. He was naked and lay half-hidden in one of the small bays. When Ed looked back again, the man was already tightening his belt over his jacket. He pulled his machine gun from an alcove and waved at Ed.

Fine gravel cushioned with algae covered the beach. The larger stones lay near the water, skulls with algae for hair, carefully and endlessly combed by the waves. There were extensive rockfalls, enormous slabs, and deep fissures along the coast. There were small, fresh glacier tongues of finest clay into which one could sink knee-deep. At the first step, they stretched like rubber under your foot, then suddenly gave way and swallowed your ankles — deep, gluey clay. Once you had sunk into the clay, there was nothing more pleasant than stomping around in it and feeling the slime ooze between your toes ... Here and there, the loam and clay had washed up and formed gleaming terraces, small tableaux as smooth as glass, taut and out of reach. There were huge adder stones and poppy flowers scattered over the loam. The water was turquoise along the shore and grey further out. The sun rose and the horizon grew more distinct. The realisation that someone was looking down at him from the top of the cliff, fifty or sixty metres above him, was an unpleasant sensation for Ed. He lowered his eyes and tried to walk more quickly, which was difficult with the stones.

Where the bluff began to level out, Ed happened on the remains of the bunker Kruso often mentioned. There was a gap that opened onto the depths between two concrete slabs that had been torn from their bracings, from which the sound of the surf rose like an oracle. It smelled of vomit. Behind the bunker rose the tourists' sandcastles, elaborately constructed and inscribed with small black stones — arrival and departure dates, and names, Köhler, Müller, Schmidt. Some of the castles had roofs of driftwood and some had flags. They reminded Ed of dugouts or command centres in one moment, and in the next of birthday cakes decorated with all sorts of small objects, tin cans, old shoes, washed-up rubbish. Ed supposed the guards at the doors of these cakes wore aprons, grilling aprons, but were otherwise naked. In general, everyone seemed to be naked on the northern end of the island, so Ed turned eastward. Suddenly, he recognised his raised hide in the distance. Although no more than three weeks had passed, he was moved at the sight of the place where he'd spent his first night — 'where I landed,' Ed whispered to himself.

The bird sanctuary was overgrown with thick underbrush, but a path led out onto the spit. He pushed his way forward and entered

complete absence. A noise — Ed automatically stepped to the side
and ducked. He was not alarmed; he had no fear. He noted that as
he crouched, a fresh shade of green filled his field of vision. The green
moved and whispered 'grass' as softly as if it were caressing the inner
dome of his skull.

'That this is the wilderness and this our creeping away into it, is
something all of you out there will never understand,' Ed murmured.
He had put another fine log on the bonfire of his monologue. He
thought, 'Places where there is no one but me.' Crouching, he
listened to his heart's hard beat and felt the familiar longing for a
hiding place. And he realised this longing had increased and was now
much stronger than it had been in his childhood.

When Ed stood up, a swarm of birds shot into the sky, and for a
moment he was not of this world.

In the courtyard of the Hotel Enddorn, one of the few buildings
in the village of Grieben, Ed ordered coffee and cake. In the shade of
willow tree, he sat on one of the rickety chairs scattered randomly
throughout the garden. As if something about him gave away the
fact that he was a seasonal worker, he was received more warmly and
above all served more quickly than the day tourists at his table. And
even the day tourists treated him respectfully. His coffeepot was filled
to the brim, almost three cups' worth. At one point, the innkeeper
stood in the doorway and called something to the waitress and then
greeted Ed briefly — the innkeeper, no less! For a second, Ed was
conscious of the unspoken requirements. Nonetheless, there was no
doubt: he now belonged to the island, everyone could tell. He was an
esskay on his day off.

On the side facing the street, the Enddorn — a smaller ship than
the Klausner — had a barracks-like extension. The door swung open
once, and a gust of stale air swept over the tables. Ed glimpsed an
iron bed frame, a pile of sleeping bags and maps on the floor. Only a
moment later did Ed notice it was Kruso who had walked out of the
Enddorn's extension. Ed wanted to call out to him. He shot to his

feet, raised his arm, but could not make a sound.

Kruso's upright gait was not athletic but not without power, as if he were propelled by some imbalance, Ed thought; a blow, perhaps, had struck his core and pushed him forward and now he was trying to regain his balance by rapidly thrusting his legs out in front, his hips rigid, his feet skimming the ground ... Suddenly Ed felt a pang that Kruso had simply left without looking to the right or left. It was absurd, and Ed had to admit that there was *more* to it. Kruso touched something inside him that was lacking, something missing, an old emptiness that gnawed at him, a longing for — he didn't know for what; it had no name. At first, Ed had found the way Krusowitsch had taken him on as an employee disconcerting — Kruso was direct, open, sincere, and yet much of what he said was puzzling. But ultimately, it was up to Ed to figure out, little by little, how things worked on the island. Despite the wretched conditions in the dishwashing station, which Rimbaud said were fit for galley slaves, Ed enjoyed working at Kruso's side, enjoyed his presence even though the man also seemed so unapproachable. The work was something they accomplished together: it had an intimacy that nothing could supersede. Kruso assigned him tasks. He had brought clarity to Ed's days, along with an irrefutable feeling that Ed, too, could rise above his hazy, muddled existence.

The waitress at the Enddorn did not want a tip. Instead, she asked if he were planning to go to the *waiters' beach* that night.

'Yeah, maybe,' Ed replied, hearing the term for the first time. The waitress was almost two heads taller than he and had a sturdy build. Ed found her round face astonishing, as if he had not seen a face for a very long time. When he rose, she took a step towards him and laid her cheek against his — 'We don't pay each other here, just so you know for next time,' she whispered, her lips brushing his ear. It wasn't a hug, yet Ed had distinctly felt her soft skin and her warmth.

In front of the hill that rose from the landscape like a skull, a few horses stood as still as stones. With their hindquarters to the wind, they waited for the earth mother to come and make them fruitful. The bodden shone in the afternoon sun, and the port was calm. No tourists, just a boy in front of the board with the ferry schedule. For a while, he read the ships' arrivals and departures out loud to himself, then he turned to the dock and shouted them out over the water. He did this fervently, with a kind of desperation, as if the boats could not possibly come in to port without him, as if the boats might forget the island. The boy wore a sailor's jacket and a flat cap, and moved oddly. He ran so close to the edge of the dock that Ed had to look away.

A framed poem hung in the case outside the Gerhart Hauptmann House. Next to it, a watercolour by Ivo Hauptmann. The surf was stronger than it had been in the morning. A few butterflies fluttered above the stones as if they were having trouble finding a place to land. 'Where are you, gaffer?' Ed muttered as he looked for the spring in the delta. He was afraid he wouldn't be able to find his friend again. Nests of tiny creatures adhered to the algae. Ivory-coloured spiders and cuckoo wasps. Ed saw hordes of chiggers pass like miniscule white cockroaches, shimmering with damp. Squalls of fine sand swept in: Ed could see them come in from far off; they flew like silk scarves in the sun, barely brushing the ground.

The cave was undamaged. His fox still seemed watchful somehow. Its coat appeared intact, but seemed to have lost some of its lustre, and its head had begun to grey, at least around the temples, if that can be said of a fox. All in all, the animal had shrunk slightly, its body was a bit shrivelled, 'but otherwise completely unchanged,' Ed murmured into the gap in the coastline.

'What did you expect?' the fox countered. 'Fresh salt air, the cool loam all around, and solitude in freedom, the calm, and especially the sound of the surf — the surf is pure balm, you know what I mean. It's just the wretched damp, it gets into your bones, and on top of that, the sewage, the effluence from the Klausner. Pestilence seeps past every day ...'

'Oh, gaffer,' Ed murmured.

The fox fell silent. As Ed followed the delta, he felt a small, surprising contentment. He held back his hair and drank from the spring. It tasted of lye. Repetition gave him confidence; he felt he was taking possession of a place, the very first place of his own.

'You can do it, gaffer,' Ed whispered, 'one step at a time, that's the only way, you know?'

At night in his room, he heard the cries of the seagulls that flew inland from the sea and then out again — the screams had no particular rhythm, and the birds sounded like nervous dogs that had started barking for some reason and took a long time to calm down again. Ed stood at the window. The air was filled with the sound of panting dogs. He pulled out his diary to jot down his five-line diary entry, but the verse hoard murmured continuously in his head, and he could no longer come up with any words of his own. He lay in his bed and listened to the silence as it expanded its territory. Well before the Klausner's midnight clamour set in, Ed had disappeared into his dream.

THE CASTAWAYS I

There was no light in the hallway. Past the turn towards Kruso's room began Monika's lovely fragrance, exactly what Ed imagined the smell of oranges to be. He had only met the little invisible one once. But then again, he had only ever eaten oranges once in his life, when he was a child, in 1971, when all of a sudden *southern fruits* were available in stores on account of changes in the power structure — 'due to the transition' as his father explained at the time. There had been no further transitions since then, and too much time had passed for Ed to remember exactly what oranges smelled like.

Monika's door at the end of the hallway was the only one with a doorbell. The button glowed orange, and its little thread of light flickered. It seemed alive but imprisoned (and pleading for help), so Ed found it hard to look away. He took a deep breath, inhaling the scent of the transition. He tried to imagine how René and Monika could have become a couple, and what bound them. Sex? What else could it be? René was an animal in bed, which made him self-confident, loud, and malicious.

'Come in, already!' The door was not latched.

Kruso stood at the open window, leaning out over a cumbersome metal stand, a kind of tripod welded together from rusty, ridged steel rods. A battered pair of binoculars were fastened on top. Ed stood in the doorway, but Kruso waved him over.

That evening, Ed saw Alexander Krusowitsch's room for the first time. It wasn't much bigger than his own, but it was at the front of the building, over the terrace. From here, it was possible to see the entire property: the first steps of the stairs on the bluff, half of the Svantovit Gorge along with the path to the barracks, and, above all, the sea that swelled along the horizon — 'shallow as a dog's palate', Ed thought or heard whispered from his verse hoard. The tripod with the binoculars stood directly behind the curtains that reached to the floor and swayed slightly in the wind. They were the same coarse curtains that looked like fishing nets and also hung in the bar and the dining room, and they seemed, in fact, to give off an odour of the sea, a smell of fish and seaweed.

'Do you recognise the spot?' Kruso stepped carefully to the side and pushed Ed in front of the tripod. Ed saw algae, a section of the beach, a few small, silent waves. Then he recognised the delta and the hollow he had drunk from on the day he had arrived.

'Good, good, now you've got it.' Kruso laughed but only briefly. His laughter stuck in his throat and so perhaps was just a sigh. To avoid looking at him, Ed kept peering through the binoculars (he was disconcerted, what should he have said?). 'Move a little,' Kruso said softly, and touched the top of Ed's head with his fingertips gently but firmly, the way hairdressers do when they want to move a customer's head into a certain position without speaking. At the same time, he swung the binoculars slowly to the right. Roots, grass, pine trees, then barbed wire appeared, a double barbed-wire fence, blurred, then more distinct. Ed saw a grey steel frame, a tower built of steel with a cabin on a platform; next to it, a searchlight, antennae, and a radio. A soldier stood with his elbows propped on the railing, staring at the sea through binoculars. He was in uniform. A double-

barrelled field gun stood to the right of the tower, covered with a
tarpaulin. At the foot of the tower, the outline of a freshly tarred
bunker was visible, and behind it two barracks and a garage, in front
of which were parked a multicar and a motorcycle. Next to it were
three kennels in a row. Kruso adjusted the position of the lenses right
above Ed's nose. Enquiringly, Ed turned his head slightly, but Kruso
turned it back. Ed felt Kruso's breath on the back of his neck. A man
stepped onto the neatly raked strip of sand between the fences of
barbed wire. Two dogs immediately lunged at him. The sound of
their barking could not be heard, only the roar of the surf. The surf
roared with teeth bared.

'There — there's someone there ...' Ed whispered and shrank
back. He had broken into a sweat, and he felt the familiar burning
sensation under his eyelids. Nothing more was evident in the room's
dim light. Between the two windows stood a dresser with open books
lying crisscross on top along with newspapers, maps, pages of writing.
A command post. Kruso bent unhurriedly over the tripod.

'That's Vosskamp. After dinner, the commander plays with
the messenger dogs. He is commander of the island. The guardian
of our fate, if you like, and even if you don't. And here comes his
staff sergeant. With a bottle. That's good to know. Good for us this
evening, Ed.' Kruso fiddled with the worn binoculars as if he were
calming a dog. Ed discreetly wiped a few tears from his face. The field
glasses strained his eyes.

'Whatever has three legs can stand,' Kruso said. He was proud
of his tripod. He pointed to the two small ridged wheels between
the lenses that were marked with various colours. 'Those are the
focal settings I need. White for the observation company with their
watchtower and the radar, red for the Svantovit Gorge, blue for the
patrol boats and everything else that passes by out there. Identify the
movement, identify what's coming, and identify what's disappearing.
Identify the light signals at night. Vigilance, versatility, and above all
secrecy — those are the three things that matter, Ed.'

The terrace had begun to fill even though the Klausner was closed. Kruso opened the curtains a crack, careful not to bump the tripod. The floor paint was scraped away under the rough ends of the steel rods. Ed felt almost compelled to register this detail, yet at the same time, he didn't want to see anything, to know anything. As if the simple fact that he saw what he saw were enough to make him a traitor. I'm not meeting the unspoken requirements — the sentence and its throbbing filled his head. All this was outside his world, light-years away. Then again, what was his world? The Klausner had taken him in. He had found work and a place to stay. And Ed felt safe in Kruso's presence; the oddness of Kruso's affairs didn't need to worry him. In fact, they had nothing to do with him.

For a while, they observed the guests Kruso sometimes referred to as *our homeless*, but usually as *the castaways*. Unlike Krombach, Kruso used the term with a hidden tenderness and respect. His gaze was watchful (like an Indian's), and his attitude expressed affection and solicitude. Kruso pointed at this or that table, or at the tables without any canopies, or at the manger-like tables with their benches completely occupied and explained to Ed what he saw: drop-outs, adventurers, supplicants. He saw lovers, defectors, failures in one way or another, and 'refugees *in spe*', whom he called his problem children. He had categories, as Ed understood it, which created a certain hierarchy, levels of urgency.

'None of them really belongs to this country anymore, they've lost the ground under their feet, you understand, Ed?'

He referred to a few of the castaways by name; either he had already met them on the waiters' beach, at one of the bonfires, or another of the esskays' gatherings, or someone had told him about the new arrivals. Now and then, he paused as if he were waiting for Ed to make a suggestion or ask about someone by name.

They stood by the window the entire time, hidden by the fishnet curtains. It was not important that their upper arms brushed against each other several times. Ed felt the small hairs on Kruso's skin brush against his, faintly enough that it could count as not touching at all, when Kruso pointed down at the garden again and again and wondered aloud which ones might most urgently need 'our help', as he put it. He would hold his arm outstretched for a very long time as if he were selecting someone. He was not pointing, he was taking aim.

'The castaways are like children,' Kruso explained. 'Every evening, after the last ferry has left, they fill the beach as if there were something there that would embrace them and sing them to sleep at the end of the day. Until just before nightfall, they believe, like the grasshoppers, in an endless summer. At sundown, the beach wardens start their rounds. Once twilight sets in, volunteers come out, people from the island, and, for money or some other reason, they comb the dunes and inspect the canopied beach chairs. They even shine their flashlights into the chairs when the canopies are closed, as if someone could have crawled through the framework. Of course, some of the castaways are thin, very thin, actually ...' Kruso smiled and took a deep breath.

Ed understood the purpose of his visit. It was for another session of instruction, like the ones in the dishwashing station or when they buried the amphibian, but this time it was a critical matter, a step forward from which there was no turning back.

'They still have a bit time,' Kruso continued, 'until the first patrol, who are serious about border violations — at least that's what they call it because from their point of view it's the border that's being harmed. A few know-it-alls sneak into the forest, but no one lasts there for long. The bunkers along the shore are inspected regularly. Experienced clandestine sleepers burrow into the sand with a handkerchief protecting their faces and a section of reed to breathe through in their mouths. If you ever go for walk there at night, it can't hurt to keep them in mind ... Of course, a few make friends on the waiters' beach, but the majority of the lot, almost all of them, I mean, come to us over the concrete path or using the Capri-path along the bluffs all the way here, on the Dornbusch.'

Ed knew that people liked to call Hiddensee the Capri of the

North, but this was the first time he had heard the term 'Capri-path'. Without a word, Kruso made a gesture that included everything: the paths, the bluffs, the sea, and even themselves standing in Kruso's room at the window behind the net curtain.

'They don't know what to do next. First, the great sense of longing that only increases once they get here, and then they sit there and can neither go on nor turn back.'

'Maybe it's not just that,' Ed replied, 'some might simply have been curious and wanted to see the island. Travellers in a very small country.'

'They are pilgrims on the longest route in the world, Ed.'

'And then — they sit here?'

'Where else? It's a terrace with a view, you can look far out into the distance. On a clear day, you can see into the beyond. No one can forbid you from looking, no one can prohibit your longing, especially not at sunset.'

Ed listened to Kruso's voice, which had dropped to a barely audible whisper. A shimmering dark-red reflection filled the room, and they stepped back slightly from the curtains. It was strange to see how the previously splendid ball of fire had come to resemble a bent coin, a glowing coin that was gradually melting. 'Paid up for the night' — the phrase chugged through Ed's brain, but in the end he had understood: according to an unspoken moratorium, the Klausner's terrace served as a kind of reserve, a final refuge at the country's furthest limit, paid for with Stralsunder. Stralsunder Helles was the watery beer that couriers from the barracks carried under the cover of darkness over the dunes in their aluminium mess kits or even in their helmets. Ed himself had seen the soldiers a few times as they scurried in full uniform up the steps to the bar and followed Rick down a flight of steps behind the counter into the basement. He did not have a more concrete image of them in his mind, just a kind of thermal image that captured the humility and friendliness in their postures. They arrived silently and remained almost transparent, or at least without definite contours. They were masters of camouflage. Most noticeable were their efforts, despite their waist belts, boots, and machine guns over their shoulders, to move as casually as the holiday-makers, as if they could escape their military appearance by ambling. Kruso called them the 'island warriors' and pointed out the counter-couple's good rapport with specific soldiers: 'they've got a kind of adoptive relationship — which still doesn't change anything. Everyone has to clear the terrace by the time the midnight patrol arrives, they've simply got to be invisible. Ever since the escape last year, there are no pardons. That's what we worry about, Ed.'

The sun had disappeared. The cast-iron lanterns on the terrace were lit. A deep black stripe lay over the horizon like an imaginary continent with glowing edges. Or like a thoroughly charred piece of coal, Ed thought. The oven can now be turned off ...

Kruso touched his shoulder.

'You know,' Kruso said, 'it's your first allocation. That means you choose.'

'I choose?'

'You get to choose your own castaway.'

TRAKL DECLAIMED

Everything has its limit, Ed thought. A point up to which you were allowed to overlook things, a limit you cannot overstep.

Two steps, then across the terrace through the central alley between the tables and the mangers. Kruso went outside carrying three glasses and a chilled bottle of white wine, and Ed followed. His mouth was dry. He was thirsty.

Kruso sauntered up to a full table. The greeting from the table was especially warm, as if they had been expecting Kruso or had met him before. They gladly made room. They all seemed to belong together somehow, to belong to a family that believed their deep affinity was established primarily by the fact that they were all here, that they had made it *this far*. As if the decisive border had already been crossed in a way that had nothing to do with geography. Candles were lit and bottles uncorked; an incandescent anticipation began to spread, and at some point Ed, too, was overcome.

Some of the esskays who showed up on the terrace over the course of the evening had come long distances, as Ed gathered from the conversations. They seemed like emissaries, representatives of the

three parts of the island, and their hotels had names like Hitthim,
Dornbusch, Süderende, Enddorn, and so on, but there were also
lifeguards, bird-banders, and staff from the island cinema, esskays of
all kinds. Not one from this wide range of castes neglected to come
up to their table.

In any case, the custom seemed to be to press cheek against
cheek, a childlike greeting. No one faked the motion or turned his
or her head away, and so the esskays had to stretch their necks out,
especially when there were differences in height. They had to reach
their heads forward, as if to kiss each other, though in the end it
never came to that.

Ed noticed that Kruso used the closeness to communicate, in a
whisper, not much more than a word or a sentence. Sometimes Ed
was then given a glance. Ed began to feel a sense of pride, but after
a while the scrutinising looks dispirited him. A few of the esskays
placed bottles or a small package of food on their table, along with
greetings and good wishes. According to Kruso's almost imperceptible
directions, the package made its way over the tables until it was eagerly
and gratefully opened and its contents immediately devoured. *They're
famished, why are they so hungry,* Ed brooded, *it must be the fresh air
up here and they probably don't have any money either, they probably
don't have anything at all.* He himself had very little saved up, twenty,
maybe thirty marks, but now money wasn't at all important. He had a
room, he had found a hideout on the island, and, whatever happened,
it would be something to drink to.

Ed turned his gaze out over the sea and tried to fix on one of
the lights that glided past in slow motion ... He couldn't do it. He
breathed in the sweetness of the sun-warmed body next to him, but
where could that lead? The castaways sat pressed close together; the
tables were completely full. The bare arms, bare legs, and skin that
appeared stretched taut from too much wind and water, and the taste
of salt on lips, a pleasant mask, and in addition, the stiff strands of
hair that tickled the back of the neck. They inevitably touched, it was

natural ... Yes, something along those lines, but Ed was no longer used
to physical contact (since *it* had happened). He tried to imagine it,
held his breath, filled his glass, breathed again. More beer and wine
were brought out; drinks and food, everything belonged to everyone
once they had made it this far, to the terrace overlooking the sea in
the garden of the Klausner, to the table of the chosen.

A few castaways reached — half in jest and half defiantly — for
the bottles Kruso had set on the table. Ed recognised the label now. It
was Lindenblatt, a Hungarian wine that at the Klausner was reserved
exclusively for the crew, who were all present but scattered at various
tables. The waiters had taken off their black suits (it was a day off,
after all) and they looked smaller in plainclothes, shrunken somehow
and unfamiliar or like someone known a long time ago. There was a
raucous, obscene table to the right of the entrance, over which the
ice-cream man presided. Unfortunately, little Monika sat there, too.
She looked sad and seemed to become more and more invisible.

At Rimbaud's table to their left, books were passed gingerly
from hand to hand, as if they might break if handled roughly. No
one really opened any of the books, they just peeked in them while
leafing through the pages, or felt the pages with fingers they had
carefully wiped clean and dry on their shirts. There was one person
who sniffed at the binding with his eyes closed. The readers looked
rather ridiculous, and Ed did not want to see them at all. He only
saw the verse hoard that threatened him; in some corner of his
foggy brain, his powers of memorisation lurked with complete
insatiability. Two quick glasses later, he felt himself drawn to them,
to the readers, because they glowed. Rimbaud recited something in
a deep voice, Cavallo assisted, and then they argued, but, once again,
their arguments seemed to be a complete pleasure. Rimbaud spoke in
bon mots, almost in verse, his sentences clipped, a strange staccato, as
if engraved, without the slightest mistake although he was drinking
enormous quantities non-stop. His moustache vibrated; he turned
his head contemptuously, made asides, spat in the sand, and bared

his teeth. For a moment, he looked like the man in the book, in the photograph Kruso had held up over the sink: the oval lenses of his glasses flashed.

Cavallo, who behaved with much more reserve, said: 'Well, maybe in, say, fifteen years, you'll be ...' The rest was swallowed up in the noise. Ed liked his slightly flattened nose. Cavallo was tall, and of the Klausner's three waiters he was the one with whom Ed had had the least contact so far. Cavallo had written a dissertation that was 'more than rejected ... wrong topic, wrong subject matter, probably everything about it was wrong'. Kruso had commented and explained his Latin name: 'A strange passion for old horses, I mean for antiquity, the man *loves* antiquity and especially the old horses in ancient Rome, in a nutshell.' Ed thought that Cavallo looked Roman with his sharply defined profile, his high forehead and brown, slightly wavy hair, his complete aloofness. For Cavallo, Ed simply didn't exist.

Compared to Rimbaud, Kruso seemed rather shy, almost self-conscious. He had crossed his legs and was leaning back, as much as was possible, on the desolate beer-garden chairs, whose white veneer gave the terrace a rather colonial air. Ed noticed that Kruso never blinked. Instead, he would shut his eyes for a second as if he were listening to a tune. When he opened them again, his left eyelid stuck halfway for a second before opening fully as it had before. A magical detail that fit the complete picture of his superiority. There was no doubt that he was in charge.

Ed drank fast. What was going to happen? The castaways could drive you to drink. Ed could drown himself and the castaways in drink. The castaways seemed innocent (smelled innocent), they were jetsam, tanned wood sanded smooth. Ed thought of Vosskamp, with the messenger dogs, and understood what Kruso had been talking about with the binoculars, 'as if they knew that the island and the sea were well-disposed and ready for a crossing, wherever they might be headed ...' Maybe Ed was already drunk. But he recognised their gracefulness and in it their humility, an all-inclusive readiness that seemed humiliating, almost indecent. Ed understood that he did not belong with them, the castaways, or to the honourable guild of the esskays. But now he could put an end to that, without a doubt; this evening seemed meant for that — with *his* help, Ed thought, looking at Kruso who was pouring the white wine and speaking softly, his head bowed ... 'Sentences no one understands,' bubbled inaudibly in Ed's throat.

Yes, Ed had doubts. It was all too outlandish, shady, and he was much too nervous. Lord knows, he could leave the island again. Or not? The terrace on the bluff melted into a kind of upper deck. The ship slowly drew away from the coast, sailed slowly out to sea. The journey began ... There were four women and three men at their table. Ed was being observed. Nice. He returned the looks. The woman with short hair and bare arms, the woman with slender, delicate hands resting flat on the table (as if she wanted to caress or calm it), then the woman across from him, with her foot — between his legs? No, impossible. And then the man with a face like Jesus', and long hair. Then the other man, Peter perhaps, but now he looked like Dr Z. Then the women further down, younger and older women, younger and older men, wearing handmade jewellery, macramé necklaces with wooden beads. Ed saw armbands, headbands, braided from straw or buckskin. He saw adder stones. Some of the women wore loose batik dresses, and some wore their great-grandmother's nightgowns, a recent fashion: thin knee-length cotton dresses with Plauen Lace over their chests, amateurishly dyed purple, burgundy, or blue ... Some was speaking to him. Kruso. Ed only noticed now.

'Look at them, Ed. This guy here or that woman there ...'

Ed lowered his head; he wanted to leave.

'I know, Ed. In an hour or two, they realise and then they feel strong enough. And there are always some prepared to do anything. Whether the searchlight finds them or not, they don't care. He won't make it, he'll only swallow a lot of saltwater somewhere out there, far out, and then it's the end, and nobody's there, his last moment

completely alone — what an insult, Ed, what a goddamn insult it is
to be utterly abandoned.'

Ed was drunk. He could feel the loneliness. The conversations
formed a melody, an up-and-down sound that fit the noise of the sea
perfectly. Maybe he could just lean back, sink down, and disappear
into the dawn. Music came from the half-opened ice-cream hatch, a
tinny noise that seemed to come straight from the vats Ed scrubbed
and loathed, a hauntingly sad song, maybe from one of Chef Mike's
cassettes, playing on his Stern-Recorder, but it was simply too loud
on the terrace to understand anything. Someone was rolling a toy
over the table and humming, first gear, second gear, third, but then it
was just Kruso speaking in his ear again, pushing a glass towards him
in an endless motion as slowly as the ship on the horizon, the slow-ly-
mov-ing, slow-ly-mov-ing light. Ed hummed to the music's beat. The
gesture with the glass was completely ridiculous, but no one laughed,
everyone had grown serious, they were taking the glass seriously and
taking Ed seriously and were all looking at him.

'What do you think, Ed? What's your choice?' Kruso whispered
so softly that surely no one at the table could hear it, even Ed couldn't
hear.

Ed reached for the glass and lifted it as if he were checking the
weight of its contents, then pushed it back. He mumbled something
as he did, and the car turned into a small, red, rattling tram, without
a gearshift, without brakes, with only a crank for the power supply,
and he was the driver, he was drunk — but he was the driver! On
the long straight track before the terminal loop, he started asking the
question. Softly at first, then louder.

'Where is the ... the ... the, the, the ... ?'

He was asking about the brakes, but he had forgotten *the word*
and so he had to yell.

'Where is that ritch-ratch, the ritch-ratch you have to pull hard
several times, dammit!'

His right arm paddled in the air, his left one was trying to crank away the electrical supply, away and ritch-ratch, ritch-ratch ... Ed leapt up, the glass fell to the ground, his heart missed a beat.

Then all was quiet.

Final station.

Off the tram.

Lots of people again.

Now Ed could see clearly.

He had almost arrived too late. Dr Z. was there and the seminar had just begun. Without faltering even once, he recited Georg Trakl's poem 'The Cursed', then the poem 'Psalm' (second version). Then 'Sonya', a poem he had always particularly liked, and then 'On a Journey', again a long poem, but the attention surrounding him proved he was right to incorporate it into his presentation at this point. Of course, he could skip a few lines here and there, reluctantly, but he wanted to include 'O the Dwelling' and 'The Blue Night' ...

While giving his recitation, Ed stood as if turned to stone. He spoke in a very loud voice. He was trembling. Others joined the seminar, probably from the neighbouring classrooms, and everyone stared at him. In the middle of 'O the Dwelling', Dr Z., who now was Kruso, took him by the arm. He pulled Ed away from the table and led him across the terrace, then through the dimly lit Klausner and into the dishwashing station. Without explanation, he dunked Ed's head in the scrubbing sink. Ed recoiled, but Kruso was strong and his grip was relentless. Ed thought 'swallow' and 'completely alone'. The water was as cold as ice on his head.

Then it was over.

Kruso took Ed in his arms and said something like 'Thank you, my friend' and 'I knew it'. Then he pushed Ed through the swinging door into the kitchen, sat him on a stool under the radio, and started looking for some kind of medication. Ed was freezing. Viola was playing Haydn, a concerto, and Kruso spoke to Ed. Ed knew that Kruso was talking about the poems, maybe critiquing his recitation, but he did not understand if he should have stopped or continued reciting. 'At the sound of the last pip, the time will be eleven o'clock,' Viola said, and for a moment everything was completely quiet.

In Ed's room, the day's heat enveloped them. Ed sank onto his bed and closed his eyes. Kruso had insisted on bringing him 'home', but strangely was not ready to leave. He stood in the dark without moving. Then he sat on the bed and pulled a buckskin neck pouch out from under his shirt. He carefully fished something out — it took a while — and pressed it into Ed's hand. It was a photograph in a plastic envelope. Ed wanted to hold the gift up to his eyes, but — quick as a flash — Kruso laid his hand over it, and so, hand on hand, they paused for a moment.

'It's just so that you can sleep. I'm lending it to you. It will stay here. It will watch over you, take care of you. Look at it in the morning.'

The thin plastic sheet between their hands, withered from dishwashing, grew warm and sticky, or perhaps it was already warm in Kruso's pouch, against Kruso's chest.

'I'm sure you still have — things to do out there,' Ed whispered.

'It's just so you can sleep,' Kruso repeated, and laid the photograph on the bedside cabinet.

Lindenblatt: before Ed sank into sleep, he pictured the way Kruso, with his outstretched index finger, had repeatedly stroked the bottle's damp label, which showed a Hungarian landscape, a bit of the Puszta, some shrubbery, two knights on watch.

It was a tender gesture. What his finger was pointing at as the condensation on the bottle cooled — I don't know, Ed thought, I really don't know, I simply have no idea. The only thing that's important is that you understand the signal, and what to do then.

THE GRAIL

When he came back from the beach, a page with typewriting lay on the foot of his bed — he was being given notice, the thought shot through Ed's mind, *finito*.

It was a sheet of the old Klausner letterhead from the thirties or forties that was stacked in the Black Hole, in the so-called archive. 'Mountain Forest Hotel Zum Klausner — The Highlight of the Island,' Ed read. Under it, in script with entwined upstrokes, was a list of services offered, like 'Valet on the Steamboat' or 'Daily Postal Boat'. Beneath excessively stylised windswept trees stood three words in capital letters: Alexander Dmitriewitsch Krusowitsch.

Ed was strangely moved at the sight of the full name, as if it referred to another person, who Kruso had been keeping secret. Just as people forgot his full name, they forgot also that he was 'the son of a Russian', a fact the coachman Mäcki stressed now and again. 'You're probably Russian like him?' was Mäcki's question after he had seen Ed peeling onions a few days in a row. It had been the opening of their first and only conversation. In a sudden fit of schnapps-fuelled openness, Mäcki bemoaned the 'German-Russians' ('what all you

don't see') and warned Ed about that 'unlucky Russian' and his, as
he said, 'swimming sister' ('she swam and swam, I'm telling you'),
an endless stream of gibberish. Although it was not long before he
had stopped talking to Ed, and had turned to his bear-horse, which
looked at him calmly and sympathetically. 'Keep yer mouth shut, you
old nag.'

Under the name, without a space or a heading, began the poem
— or what Ed had to think of as *Kruso's poem*. Each of the verses
seemed scattered onto the page, offset to the left or right, and the
capital letters were coloured red on their upper edges. Ed stared at
the red, and the murmuring in his head began to swell. He did not
want to read any more poems. Ed had torn himself away from that
particular drug — that much he could claim after twenty-one good,
clear days as a dishwasher on Hiddensee.

He scanned the first line and suddenly he knew: he had recited
Trakl. On the evening of the allocation, he had started to declaim poems
by Trakl and made a fool of himself. Ed slowly sank onto the stool next
to his table, which still gave off the sorrowful smell of the black hole.
Until that moment, his excitement had suspended his memory. All
at once, everything reappeared right before his eyes. Kruso's talk, his
drinking, Dr Z.'s apparition: Ed had failed. He had recited Trakl. And
by doing so, he had distanced himself from the castaways, withdrawn
from their sweet, needy type, from their scent of sun and driftwood.
Ed grabbed his crotch and pressed it; it was a disaster.

Since the first of May over a year ago, he hadn't touched anyone,
hadn't even thought of it — it was taboo. It dishonoured the maimed
body, it injured the wounded, it touched her wounds, and that is
exactly where he penetrated, and he naturally knew it was crazy, but
it was impossible, simply impossible ...

It was already dusk when Kruso entered Ed's room again, cautiously
but without actually hesitating. His knocking signalled he was

opening the door, as if he didn't think he really needed permission and Ed felt the same way. He sat at his stinking table, leaning stiffly on the low surface, on which the photograph lay next to the small diary (ready for the daily entry) and the poem, lit by the cone of light from the lamp. A fluid movement of two, three steps and Kruso sat on Ed's bed.

'You did some work.'

'Just some reading.'

'You did some work, and I — once again, I didn't do anything right.'

'I wouldn't say that,' Ed countered, and put his hand down next to the poem. Kruso was silent, which made Ed feel embarrassed. He stared at the windswept trees on the letterhead with their extravagantly illustrated attempt to evade a storm that seemed to be blowing hard from the first line.

The poem was about a general who was departing, who had to leave his family in the middle of a feast, probably a wake. His belt buckle knocked against a half-empty glass; the poem tried to mimic the motion of the general rising from the table. In Kruso's language, the cup was a goblet, a kind of grail, if Ed understood correctly, and the belt buckle a steel band. When the band touched the grail, it made the grail vibrate, and filled it with a farewell melody. Every verse was borne by this music and thus was, to a certain extent, its *purest expression*. For the rest, Ed found the poem contrived and old-fashioned. The magniloquent style irritated him, as did the antiquated diction. He was alienated and revolted from the start. The perfect structure seemed grotesque, ridiculous. It was magnificent in a way, but a failure. Near the end, it was about the two children the general leaves behind, a brother and sister, clearly very close. Finally, the sister's image hovers like an icon over the scene. Obviously, the poem alluded to the obduracy of power (and that is how it would be read — as critical of the system, dangerous, banned), but at the same time it was filled with a strange melancholy that seemed to Ed to express the opposite: a longing for the general.

'I envy you your peace and quiet here, Ed, while I ...'

Kruso leaned back and crossed his legs as if he wanted to wait for the end of his own sentences more comfortably. His tall, lean body; his clear, Amerindian features. From the corner of his eye, Ed observed Kruso's face, or at least tried to. Ed's thoughts and feelings were partly occupied by Kruso's proximity, so that Ed could not quite grasp it. The king of the Klausner (and maybe of the entire island) had placed a typed poem, just for him, on his bed.

Kruso took a deep breath and began to apologise, in a roundabout way that was so elaborate as to be implausible, for not staying in his room the entire night. First and foremost to 'finally finish the collection'. Instead, he had only 'wandered around aimlessly'. Then he began his depiction of nocturnal life on the island: simple anecdotes of forbidden campfires, bad guitar music, sex in the dunes with the underage daughters of holiday-makers ('too sheltered, if you know what I mean'), and various amorous rivalries between the esskays and the tourists — in strangely heavy-handed prose that did not square with the admittedly old-fashioned, but genteel, almost aristocratic language of the poem that lay on the table in front of Ed.

The 'colourful life of the island' was the expression Kruso used, in a tone of barely restrained contempt. From the 'adipose, elderly juvenility of the temporary and seasonal workers' and their 'inane cheerful prattle about the sea', he moved on to their 'naivety and inability to think even a single step ahead', his gaze fixed on the door as if he were about to bolt out into night and onto the beach in order to take to task a few of 'these simpletons', as he called them.

Confused, Ed picked up the poem and opened with a few cautious questions about the paper and the typewriter. Typical questions between men accustomed to using a typewriter. Kruso woke from his tirade and apologised for the colour ribbon he had had to use ('colour ribbons are in short supply, you know ...'), which is why certain letters wore 'bloody caps'. Ed described a technique — an

admittedly complicated one — with which you could make the thin
colour ribbon used in portable typewriters wider with an iron. Kruso
nodded. They each named a few periodicals that would be suitable
for, as Ed put it, 'this kind of text', sheets of the so-called samizdats
that for years had been popping up like mushrooms in larger cities.

'I still want to wait a bit, to finish the collection first,' Kruso said. It
gradually became clear that he hadn't seriously tried to have anything
published yet and, yes, Ed was actually the first person to whom he
had revealed anything about it.

'That's what struck me *first* ...'

Ed was touched by Kruso's trust in him, and he was not certain in
which direction he should take his comments. A few phrases from his
seminars flitted through his mind, drivel about special musicality, the
inimitable sound of the grail, and so on.

'I'd like to read it,' Kruso interrupted him.

Kruso took the sheet in both hands, carefully and thoughtfully, as if its
weight were still uncertain. His back straightened and his shoulders
broadened, as if he were about to perform one of his Klausner tasks
with the seemingly untroubled concentration that expressed an
appreciation of things and was suitable for making the world as a
concrete duty intelligible to a floundering dishwasher like Ed.

Softly and in a monotone, with a slight drawl that accented
certain syllables in an exaggerated way, he declaimed line after line.
He recited the poem with the odd accent that Ed had most recently
noticed when they were burying the amphibian. At the end of each
line, there was a longish pause — an excessive pause, actually — in
which nothing was audible but the noise of the distant surf, yet so
clearly that Ed could discern single waves crashing onto the shore.
Kruso, too, listened to the sound of the breakers at the end of each
line. Then he started again, but without really moving forward —
what became clear was that everything was in suspension, caught in

the tension of his broad, hairy torso and fixed by the point of his chin, which he held slightly forward.

Three stanzas later, Ed was mesmerised by the beam of Kruso's delivery. The same exemplary force emitted by Kruso when he rinsed out the drains or carried driftwood to the woodpile now took hold of the poem and transformed it, and in the end it was the only possible ... — yes, the poem was *right*. It was perfectly in tune with Kruso himself, that is, it was said *with his words*, it had *that particular tone*. It was the only possible poem.

It was as if Ed's sense of distance had been blown away. His reservations now seemed ridiculous, and there was a sense of redemption. He momentarily felt a desire to offer something of his own in return. He began to speak, but immediately paused and remained silent, while Kruso sat next to him, sunk deep within himself; his left eyelid was half closed. Ed began again, reached awkwardly for his notebook, which seemed ludicrous given its size. He awkwardly picked up the plastic envelope with the photograph, and finally escaped his speechlessness with the question: 'Is that your sister in the picture?'

Kruso's eyelid rose fully again. He looked at the photograph. The photo: when he had first looked at it, Ed thought he was looking into G.'s eyes. But it was just a resemblance of the gaze and demeanour with which the thin girl in the grotesquely frilly dress was looking at the photographer, her head of blonde curls lightly tilted to the side, with a smile that seemed glued to the corners of her mouth. The plastic was dull and the face beneath it looked as if it were enveloped in fog. Ed recognised the straight eyebrows, the flat cheeks, Kruso's cheeks ...

'Why do you think that?'

'Because of the poem. I thought it was *about her* ... about her and you maybe, I mean ... It's truly excellent, Losh.'

The first time he had called Kruso by this nickname, it just happened of its own accord.

Because Kruso did not answer, Ed stammered something like, 'But that, for example, I don't know yet ...' and gave a pained laugh. Kruso lifted his head and looked past him into the night. Their legs almost bumped. Ed sat the entire time on the stool at his desk, a half-metre higher than his cherished guest. He talked directly to the wall; he talked to the crushed insects.

The wind rose, and a faint rumble of thunder, as if from distant cannons, crept over the bluff. Kruso rose with a jerk, and, before Ed realised what was happening, he grabbed Ed by the shoulders and leaned him backwards over the table and out the open window — yes, he had failed, failed completely, and so there was no other possibility ...

Kruso had in fact stood up and leaned out the window. He was almost leaning right over Ed, who had to lean far to the side so that Kruso wouldn't be lying on top of him.

The smell of his armpits; sweetish, as if fermented. Like old, sun-dried pine bark.

'A patrol boat.'

Kruso's face looked stony and almost white in the lamplight.

'It's sitting very high in the water.'

As if this fact were significant, Kruso grabbed his poem and went to the door.

'Thanks for yesterday, Ed, I mean — for your recitation. I wanted to ask you if you could lend me the book?'

As if someone had spoken in a dream.

'I haven't got the book with me — unfortunately.'

'I'd really be very happy if you'd write some of it down for me — I want to ask that favour. Maybe the three, four poems from yesterday?'

With that, Kruso disappeared from his room, almost without any movement. The last words had erased his figure.

'That's fine, Losh,' Ed whispered.

It was just before midnight. The clamour in the hall had set in. Ed held the photograph in his hand.

KAMIKAZE

7 JULY

Everything at work is going well, apart from René. Rimbaud put a new book in our nest. And Cavallo talked to me about Rome! As if he'd been there. Thanks to Losh, I don't have to go to the allocations anymore. He introduced me to one of the island warriors, who was just coming out of the Black Hole, his helmet full of beer. Kruso called him the 'good soldier'. It was the naked man from the beach. I recognised him right away, but of course I didn't say anything. Rick claimed he'd seen a green moon from the counter. I help him with the kegs in the cellar now and then. He's the only one who can operate the tap. I like being down there. At eight o'clock, I check the temperature in the furnace (80 degrees is ideal), and at eleven I add fuel again. Enormous waves yesterday.

Because Ed didn't write regularly, he could let some entries cover several days. Of course, as a whole, it seemed more like a report, but that's what he found helpful about it. A report of his arrival and how he gradually became part of the crew. And now? How he had made a friend. Would make one.

With his oversized notebook under his arm, and a new piece of soap, Ed balanced his way over the stones along the beach. For the past few days, he visited his fox every free evening. Of course, it was … A wave washed, chilly, over his right foot and cut short his train of thought. Ed had to smile. Perhaps for the first time since he arrived on the island … Or perhaps the first time *since then*. He had reached a state of mind in which the division of the world into categories like 'alive / lifeless' or 'speaking / mute' had lost significance. As if something becomes a being only through proximity. Just as the new friend enters the room as if through a mirror. Ed didn't know where to begin with this sentence. He found it hard to think this close to the sea. You lost your boundaries; you gladly let go. Letting go, trusting, Ed thought — you open yourself up and become part of it all.

In any case, it was his fox.

When he got to the fox's den, he first washed the grease from the Klausner off of his skin. In a spot where there was a bit of sand between the rocks, he went into the water, and the cool edge wrapped around his feet: the best moment. Then he stood up to his knees in the waves that rolled sluggishly into the cove. He soaped himself up, dove underwater, and swam out a short distance. He had hung his things on the branches of an uprooted tree that had fallen down the bluff. The entire cove was cluttered with these skeletons. Their strange contortions gave the beach the feeling of an abandoned battlefield. A few had slipped into the water, bare and gleaming like bones in the desert. Some were still sprouting. Their roots hung in the air, and yet they still somehow managed to sustain their plant existence, not as a whole, but in several branches. Ed marvelled at the fight.

'Good evening, gaffer!'

As Ed stretched out on the sand to dry in the sun, their conversation began. At first, it was about simple things: broken dishes, odd guests, Rimbaud's ecstatic scenes in the dishwashing station. Then it was about Kruso's speech, Kruso's poem. Dumb, but dangerous. Ed agreed. He opened his notebook and propped it up on a rock.

'Well, gaffer, where have you got to?'

A damp buzzing flew in Ed's face. He tumbled backwards and spat out a gold-green insect and immediately stepped on it. Without hesitating, he went back up to the den and cleared his companion's fur with a few strokes of his hand. In the meantime, its fur had turned completely grey, and its body seemed flattened, as if it wanted to disappear into the loam. The eyes in the fuzzy pelt were empty, but the ears were still pointed, and framed with a wreath of fine white fringes.

'Hello, gaffer, you old rascal,' Ed repeated with pinched lips. Then he spoke rapidly, the words almost tumbling over each other: 'You know, first there was the tram, but I don't always want to start with the tram, after all I wasn't there, will never have been there, not at the tram stop, but someone says she had been shouting for a while, "Be careful, look out, be careful" or whatever you're supposed to yell, across the tracks, and someone else says she was lying there under the tram, up to her stomach, he says, she was lying under the tram up to her stomach, you understand, her stomach, her bare legs sticking out, so warm for early May, but completely uninjured, her short skirt hadn't even ridden up, her bare legs, but another says that someone pulled the skirt back down, old rascal, straightened the skirt back down and she just lay there as if she were repairing the tram ...'

That was enough. The verse hoard rumbled; Trakl surfaced, with his rustic appearance, his large, infantile face. Ed collapsed back onto the sand, reached for his notebook, and wrote. Line after line thudded out of the rushing compendium in his mind; metaphors wedged themselves together into barricades, *chevaux de frise*, and verses marched through the devastation of his trauma like an occupying army in a giant war. At night in his room, he wrote the scribblings out neatly by hand on quad-ruled paper. In the morning, even before he had turned on the boiler, he slipped the sheets of paper under Kruso's door.

It was a kind of Kamikaze action. It had something undignified about it, and Ed felt ashamed. He carefully piled briquettes into the fire. It is the only thing he has asked of me, Ed thought, the only thing *I can do for him*. He listened to the cracking of the wood, the dampness evaporating with a hiss.

Kruso came around ten, and left half an hour before midnight at the latest. He did not wear a watch, but he always came at this time. Nothing could tempt him to stay longer. He took his poem and wished Ed a good night.

'Your table is too low.'

'I think the stool is too high.'

'Sleep well, Ed.'

'Good night, Losh.'

Cheek against cheek. The usual way.

As a three-year-old, Ed had believed that kissing was pressing your cheek against another's. Maybe that was his very first memory: his father's smell of tobacco. The black and yellow cardigan that was enormous. He had pressed his cheek against his father's; he had climbed up his father's arm, onto his shoulder, and up to his cheek. That was Ed's goal, the place of most intimate tenderness.

A KIND OF SMALL BOWER

Kruso floated silently before him like a phantom, and Ed had trouble keeping up with him. Their way led through boggy terrain into a silvery thicket that rose over their heads and was signposted as a bird sanctuary. Ed was startled by the creatures hurtling past with hectically flapping wings. He heard the noise with excessive clarity — as if the birds' fragile skeletons were shattering against the branches. He would have liked to urge the birds to fly more slowly, since there was no one walking through the thicket who wanted to hurt them, 'truly no one,' Ed whispered, upon which Kruso turned to look at him for the first time.

After all that had happened, it would have been unthinkable not to accept Losh's invitation (Losh, Ed now thought, *Losh*) to his summer cabin, which he referred to now and again as 'a kind of small bower' or as 'our outpost'. Ed saw it as one more sign of trust, and a reward for the trouble he had gone to outside his fox's den.

Kruso wore a black shirt with the sleeves cut off, and a knapsack on his back. Ed wore a plaid shirt and, for the first time, his light linen trousers. The trousers were, in fact, cut too wide, and flapped wildly around his legs. They reminded him of the sailors' trousers on the *Bounty*, or those worn by Wolf Larsen and Humphrey van Weydens, for example.

In fact, again and again, they came across the bodies of dead birds, and various feathered bits, in the underbrush, hanging in the branches as if widely scattered. It was easy to see that the birds had lost their lives in battles. They found a beak without a head, as well as bird feet that had been bitten off and now stood to one side, as if they'd been dropped and were waiting to walk again. 'Reineke, the little beast. He catches them when they're asleep with their heads under their wings,' Kruso explained. 'But he disappeared a few weeks ago, offspring, maybe, fresh little poachers.' With one swing of his knife, Kruso clipped the foot from a bird's cadaver, pulled off the ring around its leg, and held the object up to the light. 'These are good wares, Ed, the very best wares!'

The sandy path turned into a jungle. There were stinging nettles as high as their faces, buckthorn bushes arched over the path, then elderberry and reeds. The reeds looked soft, but pricked and slashed their arms. Without comment, Kruso climbed over a cordon of barbed wire. As if on command, he put down his backpack, dropped into a push-up position, and crawled through the dense underbrush.

The brush was hollowed out inside and lined with reeds, which gave off a smell of rot. For a moment, the dirt caves from Ed's childhood flashed before his eyes, the caves in Charlottenburg, in which they'd made fires with stolen matches and were almost suffocated by the smoke. 'The outpost was actually built for only one person,' Kruso explained. Both had skin impregnated with the Klausner's fumes. Smoked, Ed thought, we are being smoked ... He was thinking in Kruso's words and he was also thinking in Kruso's tone, if that was possible. They were, in fact, lying very close to each other. Because of the thorns on the branches surrounding them, they could hardly shift away.

Through a hole in the underbrush, they could survey a broad

section of the beach. Kruso stared at the glassy surface of the water for a long time. He had maintained an almost military bearing the entire time, and so Ed preferred not to break the silence. In any case, the question *Why?* never occurred to him in Kruso's presence. No one who was truly part of the island needed a 'why'.

Kruso took a small food container closed with metal clamps from a crate hidden in the reeds. He reached inside it and took out two slices of bread, a cutlet, and — an onion. He looked Ed in the eye for a second and then pressed two leaves of some herb onto his bread. Everything was cool and surprisingly fresh. While they ate, Ed was overcome with a deep sense of satisfaction and peace. Losh bent two branches aside and proudly showed Ed a small petroleum lamp. Then he reached his arm into the underbrush and pulled out a chest that held bird feathers and nuggets of amber along with a few handmade earrings — and a pair of nail scissors.

'I could never do it with my left hand, no matter how hard I tried, it just didn't work.' Hesitantly, Ed took the hand that Losh held out to him, then went finger by finger.

'Before, my mother used to do it, then my sister.'

The broad crescent moons, bleached by dishwater, dropped between the rushes. Ed thought of G., again the small, grubby band-aids around her fingernails, and the fingertips that peeked out like tiny creatures, blinded by life, so precious that he wanted to kiss them. Kruso and Ed looked at the sea for an hour or more without a word. Ed understood it as a test, a trial. And, yes, he had the calmness, absolutely. He was suited, suited in every respect. He half wondered why Losh kept his nail scissors in this secluded spot. Surely he had several pairs, Ed thought, and kept one ready at every outpost. Dusk settled slowly over their small bower.

The billiard players with photosensitive sunglasses had so overstretched the camel hide that you couldn't see the edge of the playing field. The animal's head must be somewhere, maybe hanging below the field. Somehow, the camel had turned back into the desert from which it had come. The wind moaned over the dunes. Ed heard the sound and woke.

Kruso had begun speaking very softly but right into Ed's ear, which is why Ed succumbed to a delusion at first — for a fraction of a second. He thought Kruso's voice was coming from his own body.

'In earlier times, when the monastery was closed,' Kruso whispered, 'many of the monks found it impossible to break with the island. It wasn't because of their faith or their religious denomination, many even converted. It was about the freedom that had always adhered to things here, the freedom that hung in the air, the island's ancient secret. Freedom attracts us, Ed, and it collects its helpers. The monks essentially had no choice, a paradox, but that's how it is with freedom. They moved away from home as mendicant friars, relying on alms and a roof over their heads. At first, that's all that it's about: soup, a place to sleep, a bit of water to wash with, perhaps. These monks were ready to give up their place in the order, they were dropouts, castaways, homeless — they were ready to leave everything behind, just to be *here*, understand?'

'When I was a child, I had a tree of truth,' Ed replied, and turned his head to the side. In the fervour of his speech, Kruso's tongue had brushed Ed's ear unintentionally.

'This underbrush, I mean, your summer cabin, the outpost here, reminds me of it, maybe just because of the leaves, because of the rustling leaves.' Ed hesitated for a moment; his outer ear felt cold.

'It was a tree with a raised stand, in the middle of a clearing. Years before, there had been a fire in the forest, and so the clearing was created. If you leaned far out of the window in our apartment, you could see the fire, then smoke, for days, from which the solitary tree emerged at the end; it had survived as if by a miracle. The forest was on the other side of the Elster Valley on a slope above the river. In the summer holidays, my friend Hagen — no, really, that's what he was called, that was his name — so, Hagen, he joined our class at some point, he had to repeat a year, I don't remember why, in any case that year he became my best friend. Back then, I always had a best friend, and other than him, none. First Torsten Schnöckel, then Thomas Schmalz, then Hagen Jenktner, and then Steffen Eismann ...'

Ed was surprised at how easy it was to talk about these things to Kruso. He thought about how he had not had a best friend for a long time, that he had had no one to help him, no one he could stay with after it happened.

'So, in summer holidays we often roamed through the forest, and at some point we discovered this clearing with the tree. Naturally, we climbed it, and up there, as we loafed around and kept a lookout, something happened to us, maybe because of the desolation of the burned-out area, or because the tree had been made immortal by the fire and the rustling of its leaves was able to do something to us, who knows. At any rate, everything around it was charred, and we suddenly started telling each other *the truth*. No idea which of us started it. I admitted to Hagen that I loved Heike — I had idolised Heike Burgold since first grade but never dared tell anyone, especially not her. She never learned about it, not even later, like I said, never. In return, Hagen told me his fantasies — just like that, I mean I was thirteen and he was fourteen, and he talked about sex without laughing. I've always considered my best friends stronger than I am, I was always ready to learn something from them, but this surpassed everything. Hagen had a film-star calendar in his room, one with real colour photographs. One of the pictures was of Claudia Cardinale in *Fire's Share*. Hagen described for me how she looked, in complete detail, her hair, her nose, her ears, her cleavage, but above all her lips, which were slightly parted, her unbelievably white teeth, and then he grabbed himself, but more as if he simply had to hold on to something when he said things like ...'

Kruso pressed his hand over Ed's mouth, bumping his nose painfully. Two soldiers were walking up the beach. One of them reached into a buckthorn bush and pulled a telephone receiver from the branches. At first, Ed thought he was telephoning the bush.

'Not unusual,' Kruso whispered. The soldiers sat down and smoked. The muzzles of their guns poked out over their shoulders, clearly outlined in the last light of the day.

After a short while, Kruso started moving cautiously. That he had pulled a bottle out of his backpack was something Ed had seen or felt in the darkness. But Kruso's leaping to his feet, his winding up, the flash in the branches — how could he have seen *that*?

The soldiers spun around as if they had been shot at, and one of them tore the rifle from his shoulder.

'Stop-who's-there!'

His shout was more of a screech, a pitiful sound of fear.

'Stop-or-I'll-shoot!'

'I'll-shoot.'

Now it was a cry of rage. Rage at the crack of a bottle, a glass grenade. Rage at the fright, at fear, perhaps. With rapid steps, the soldier marched towards their brush, ready to fire, before the other soldier overtook him and spun him around.

'A recruit, a smooth one, a goddamn fresh one,' Kruso whispered, still out of breath, although his voice sounded calm, as if he were commenting on an experiment.

'Heiko, hey, c'mon, man, Heiko!' the second soldier repeated without a break, stroking his comrade's machine gun, which was now pointed directly at him. Starting at the barrel, he felt his way, left hand over right, pushing the weapon slowly away as he did so. Finally, he carefully, almost tenderly, loosened the other's finger from the trigger.

'Hey, man, Heiko.'

The sea was now a softly murmuring screen. A touch of moonlight outlined their actions, all of it without music, just the constant rolling of the sea. The shrill cry of a bird twitched sporadically through the night.

'It takes so little for them to lose their composure,' Kruso whispered, 'so goddamn little. The entire system is made up only of men, Ed. I mean, those guys, there, that's *us*, in earlier times, that's us *before* freedom, understand?'

A nightmare, Ed thought. He had a headache, and there was a metallic taste in his mouth. The soldier named Heiko was still standing there, as if turned to stone halfway to their brush. The other soldier pushed Heiko's gun over his shoulder and grabbed him by the collar with both hands. Heiko. Then he let go and strode down the rocky coast with quick steps. After a few seconds, Heiko woke from his trance and started to trot in an awkward gait, as if he were shackled, his helmet banging against his waist belt. For a while, they could still hear the dull, metallic noise.

THE MAP OF TRUTH

Drive fishing with Kruso and other esskays, without weapons,
just with pots and sticks. Afterwards, there was pike-perch for
everyone, roasted on the beach in garlic and sea-buckthorn
sauce. The fish was still alive. Chef Mike says you have to grab
him by the eyes so he won't bite. Rimbaud and the counter-
couple sang battle songs, through valleys and over hills ... Rick
and his stories. He says that people like Hauptmann hurt the
island. Karola treated Cavallo's sunburn with curd cheese.
She is the medicine woman here, a pretty herb witch. Every
day, she brings us fresh tea in the dishwashing station, and
yesterday she was suddenly standing behind me. Then ice and
her fingertips along my spine, up and down — a kind of ice-
cube massage, perfect for my back pain, amazing! Since it's
been so hot, we've had even more cockroaches. I kill four or
five every morning, sometimes even more.

On the waiters' beach, they met other esskays: Tille, Spurtefix, Sylke, the tall girl with lots of freckles, Antilopé, Rimbaud's girlfriend, and Santiago from the Island Bar, who seemed to be close friends with Kruso. As a rule, everyone met naked. When burying the amphibian, Ed had already sensed it: an almost sibling-like closeness that came from this natural nudity and not from any particular cause. Ed had never experienced something like this before, a special closeness that people reached this way, a kind of casual bond — a collegial intimacy, if there was such a thing. As if nakedness were a seal, a kind of reward, Ed thought, for a collective overcoming of shame, but in any case it wasn't shamelessness. Modesty wasn't lessened at the heart of the confederation, which made it much easier to understand the esskays greeting (touching cheek against cheek). This was the first thing Ed truly understood about the island caste and the clannishness within their circle, which extended far beyond the island.

At the end of their foray, Kruso had suggested a detour on the Schwedenhagen — 'to my home', as he said with contempt. Until then, it had not occurred to Ed that Kruso might have another home than the Klausner.

A smaller path forked off towards the bodden from the concrete path. On one of the moraines, there was a light-coloured, two-storey building almost hidden by poplars. The hill, the house, and the trees that looked like cypresses from a distance reminded Ed of southern landscapes in the museums.

Radiation Institute — the sign hung crookedly behind the chain-link fence near the entrance. It was almost completely faded; only the letters remained stuck to it, or else someone had taken the trouble to repaint them. Kruso walked past the door. After a few metres, he dropped in his usual, half-military way to a push-up position and slid under the fence. They came to a tall, narrow brick building, the lower half of which was surrounded by a grass-covered bank of dirt like a protective mantle. With its steel door and skull-and-crossbones sign, it looked like an old transformer house, but without any cables.

'This is the tower,' Kruso explained.

The room had no windows, but blankets had been draped over everything as if to hide something, and they gave off the dry, sweetish smell of old wool. Kruso's steps on an old metal ladder, then silence. Ed breathed in the dust, and his mucous membranes began to swell. He slowly felt his way through the labyrinth of wool, but could not find the way up. 'Not so easy!' Kruso yelled down. He seemed very pleased.

The room hidden in the tower reminded him of a boy's room. The bare light bulb that hung from the ceiling on a wire dimly illuminated a puzzle of snapshots, typewritten pages, and drawings, along with a Che Guevara poster and a dusty brochure for a metallic-brown Volvo station wagon. The photographs were all covered with tiny black spots, as if infected with some disease. Ed thought he was going to suffocate. Kruso pulled a few bricks from the wall, and fresh sea air flowed into the room. At the same time, something moved in the corner across the room where there was a bed and an armoire. Probably a cat, Ed thought. Sleeping bags and pieces of clothing were strewn about the room.

To the right of the embrasure-like opening hung a large, childlike drawing. The rough paper, perhaps the back of a strip of wallpaper, was buckling and was pinned to the wall with small nails. Kruso pulled the wire with the bare bulb in front of the picture and fastened it to a hook hanging from the ceiling.

The drawing consisted of three overlapping fields of colour. Faint, expressionless watercolours that briefly reminded Ed of the dreary paint boxes from his school years, with the always half-fossilised paints you had to stir tediously until you lost patience, grabbed your paintbrush (there were always too few paintbrushes, yes, most often only a single one worked), and jabbed it at the round, coloured stones they called a palette, rendering the artistic tool completely useless. Ed's entire childhood had been a battle with shoddy supplies and outdated materials, a struggle full of grumbling and swearing and yet fought in complete innocence. Never in those early years did it occur to Ed that he himself was not inferior, that he was not inadequate. Who else was to blame for such misfortune?

'This is the only genuine map of our world, Ed, the *Map of Truth* you might say.'

Kruso looked at him. He paused meaningfully and gave Ed, who had been standing without moving since entering the room, a chance to look at the paper more closely. It was covered with water spotting and staining, a stylised sunset perhaps, Ed thought, a kind of Hiddensee Expressionism. Above the black section, there was a red one, and above that a yellow section. Yellow-red-black: only then did Ed recognised the upside-down flag. A light crackle — Kruso held a bottle in his hands. Very slowly, almost ceremoniously, he unscrewed the cap. From the blue label, Ed recognised the cheap brand they called Blue Strangler.

Independent of the three colours, there were lines, extremely fine lines that corresponded exactly to the edges of the water stains in some places, and Ed quickly recognised the country's borders: the outlines of Rügen, Usedom, then Darß, and very faintly, almost invisible, the slender shape of their own island, the seahorse with the sledgehammer muzzle. The animal floated upright, its swollen head turned to the east — half in black, half in red. Now it was easy to make out the outlines of the Kingdoms of Denmark and Sweden. The red between the southern and northern shores was covered with a network of barely discernible geometric links, dotted and continuous lines that intersected wildly. The whole looked like the knitting or sewing patterns Ed had once seen as a child on his aunt's living-room table. At first, it had seemed utterly incomprehensible to him — how could his aunt have anything to do with drawings like this, completely encrypted and so like a secret plan ... ?

Kruso cleared his throat. Ed had to take a deep breath to tear his eyes away from the map. He felt the bottle against his upper arm: it was cool, and he wanted to grab it, as if following an automatic gesture among drinking buddies, but Kruso held on tight and looked him in the eye.

'Please listen closely, Ed.'

With the devout and solemn look that always accompanied his instructions, Kruso pressed the bottle against Ed's chest and motioned towards the bed against the wall. The Strangler dissolved the dusty feeling in Ed's mouth, and, for some reason, he could now, sitting on the bed, see the lines on the flag much more clearly.

Kruso glanced at the map, then at Ed. Then he approached Ed again and took the bottle from his hand.

'On this island —' Kruso pointed at Hiddensee, nodded a few times and shook his head simultaneously, which made his head move in circles '— I mean, in this country —' He crossed the black section with the bottom of the bottle, which made a sound of high, cheerful gurgling '— there isn't a single real map. In this country, my friend, not only are rivers, roads, and mountains shifted until no one knows where exactly they are, no, even the coastline drifts, back and forth, like waves ...

'Don't object!' Kruso shouted with the bottle raised. 'I had them all here, geodesists, surveyors, even cartographers — through some people with security clearance, here, with the castaways and outcasts ... I've read their reports, Ed, appalling reports.' He took a swig and wiped his mouth with the back of his hand.

'It's the intervals that are never right, the falsified size of the sea, phony distances, the false horizon. From coast to coast —' Kruso tapped the bottle first on the black then on the yellow section, skipping over the red-coloured expanse of the sea '— it is absolutely not *this far*! If these maps were correct, my dear Ed, never in your life would you have seen Møn with its otherworldly chalk cliffs, that innocent white shimmer, from your lovely attic room when you sit up in bed in the morning and ask yourself what you're doing here, why you landed here, of all places ...'

'Not why,' Ed protested, but Kruso handed him the bottle with an expression of pure benevolence.

'This map, my friend, is true, as true as "amen" in church, amen.'

Ed drank and handed back the bottle.

'Møn, Møns Klint, Gedser …' Kruso lost himself in his enumeration of places marked only with tiny crosses or numbers.

'But what's with the lines?' Ed tried to ignore the slight. On the waiters' beach, he had already heard the strangest stories. A man from the district town of Plauen had placed a real flag with an emblem of a hammer, compass, and garland of rye on the ground in front of his door, and had been taken off the island and imprisoned, for years it was said … But what was such a doormat compared to the Map of Truth?

'What do these lines mean, Losh? This pattern in red between the coasts?' Ed asked again.

'Those are the routes of the dead.'

Kruso's answer came as if from far away. He was sunk in his drawing.

'Those are their routes over the sea.'

Kruso pressed his hand on the paper, on a spot that was worn away and torn, as if he wanted to cover a wound.

'At first, they keep swimming. Or they paddle a bit. Or they sit in tiny diving machines, or they hang onto motors that pull them through the surf. But they don't make it. Somewhere out there, water gets into the carburettor, or they die of exposure, or their strength fails … Some wash up over there. Some are pulled out of the sea with the day's catch. The fishermen radio the dead over the sea, and talk about them later in their bars — "another one who tried to make it, well, cheers," and so on …'

Sounds came from below. Kruso woke from his trance and took a long drink from the Strangler.

'The fishermen know the currents here. They know them exactly. They know just how long the dead can be in transit.'

Kruso slowly traced a dotted line. 'They know how long they stayed underwater and when the sea brought them up again and what they look like at that point and how they look at you with their rotten eyes ...' He seemed nervous now, and lowered his head to the embrasure.

'But no one, I repeat, no one over there knows who the dead are. That is, they're kept on ice, on the kingdom's good, cold ice, and they wait until someone comes to claim them. But no one ever comes. No one. Not ever.'

It had got louder below, and Kruso started putting the bricks back in the wall.

'How do you know all this?'

'The dead whisper to me. The dead are waiting for us, Ed. What do you say to that?'

'I had no idea, I mean ...'

'What I meant to say, Ed: it's the wrong way. Completely wrong. Or to put it differently: the maps simply don't lie *enough*! Starting with that damn, hopeful shade of light blue in the school atlases, that goddamn, deceiving light blue, it makes all the kids soft in the head. Why don't they make the sea black, Ed, like the eyes of the dead, or red like blood?' He pointed at his own map.

'Why not keep Sweden completely secret? A clever division of the pages would be enough. And what about Denmark, Scandinavia, the entire rest of the pointless world? Sure, Møn is a problem, but only because we can see Møn, get it, Ed?'

Kruso was obviously drunk. Without bothering to aim, he tossed the Strangler onto Ed's lap.

'Forget it Ed, you hear me, forgetit, getit ... But don't ever forget one thing: there is such a thing as freedom. It's right here, on the island. Because this island exists, doesn't it?'

Kruso stared at Ed with fierce determination, and Ed nodded obediently.

'And you heard its siren call, too, right? Yes, it calls, dammit, it calls like a goddamn siren ... And everyone hears something. Deliverance from a job. From a husband. From pressure. From the state. From the past, isn't that right, Ed? It sounds like a promise, and they all come here, and this is where our duty, the gravity of it all, begins. Which means: three days and they're initiated. We give each of them three or four days, each one, and with that we create a large community, a community of the initiated. And that's only the beginning. Three days here and they can go back to the mainland, no one has to escape, Ed! No one has to drown. Because then, they've got it in their heads, in their hearts, wherever ...' Kruso waved one arm in the air, and, half-turned towards the map, he pointed at different parts of his body.

'The measure of freedom.'

Ed flinched. The last sentence did not come from Kruso. A cat sat on the bed next to Ed, looking at him. Its head was enormous and round, and its paws as wide as a child's feet.

It had grown dark, and the rain was coming down in sheets. Santiago was waiting at the institute's fence; Kruso scolded him in a whisper. Ed stood to the side. His friend's state had him worried. Something had shifted. For the first time, Ed felt responsible.

The entire time, he had wanted to say: you're getting into a mess, Losh.

And you, what do you want to do with your life, Ed? What are you prepared to do?

Only then did Ed notice the castaways crouching by the embankment, motionless, drenched, like rabbits ready to jump. It was a small group, two men and two women who followed all of Kruso's instructions gratefully and unquestioningly. One after another, they crawled under the fence and disappeared into the darkness.

'I can't blame him,' Santiago explained.

'What?' Ed asked.

'They both grew up here, Kruso and his drowned sister.' Santiago touched the wet wire fence as if it were a precious object. 'They grew up here, right here on the Rommstedt hill.'

CLANDESTINE QUARTERS

Kruso's organisation — or what should it be called? Lifeguards, caretakers, waiters, bartenders, bird banders, assistant chefs, dishwashers, kitchen help — they all seemed to be connected to each other. The decision to live on the island (or at least to *estivate* here, as Cavallo put it) told them what was most important to know, and functioned like an invisible bond: whoever was here had left the country without crossing the border.

Their support for Krusowitsch initially meant nothing more than one of their cheerful givens — like skinny-dipping at the waiters' beach, midnight fires (although forbidden), or the discotheque at the Dornbusch Apartments, for which you paid two marks seventy-five (not much more than an hour's wage) to be able to dance all night long between two bars on opposite sides of the room. The bars were named after their bartenders. On the so-called sweet side of the Dornbusch (the Heinz bar), green, brown, and red liqueurs were poured non-stop; on the sour side of the room (the Heiner bar), wine, vodka, and the Strangler flowed, along with Stralsunder beer and, once in a while, a homemade sea-buckthorn brew with a 'Strangler base', as they put it. Even this 'Opposition of the Bars' (Rimbaud's phrase), which the esskays celebrated five times a week, was a concept of political significance. The Heinz bar was sweet, the Heiner bar sour, that much was certain, and life was played out between the Heinz and Heiner bars. Heinz or Heiner. No one would have seen an irreconcilable contradiction in it. There was no antagonism on the island, certainly none that couldn't be resolved. From sweet to sour, from sour to sweet, the evening swayed between the two, far beyond the Dornbusch's main room, over the fields and dunes to the beach, over the sea to the horizon, the border, invisible in the darkness.

Ten per cent land, ninety per cent sky: it was enough that they were here on the island. Certainly enough for their pride. The island ennobled their existence. Its beauty was simply indescribable and powerful. The magic of its creation. The mainland was nothing more than a backdrop that slowly blurred and faded away in the sea's continuous roar. What, then, was *the state*? Every sunset blotted out its stony image, every wave washed the grim outline of that worn hand axe from the surface of their consciousness. They were the riders of the seahorse with the sledgehammer muzzle; they were dancing over the hand axe, on their way between sour and sweet.

The esskays were not particularly interested in leading the castaways or homeless, as Kruso called them, to some new freedom. Yet they sensed Kruso's will, his strength. He gave off a sense of otherness that was charming. Above all, it was his seriousness and determination that made all the difference. Whatever he said was completely free of cynicism or irony, and his suggestions embodied the opposite of that old island habit of handling things more or less playfully. Secretly (and none of them would have wanted to admit it), their island existence was missing this substance, it lacked a duty, an idea, something higher than the daily sweet and sour.

And yet, Kruso never came off as a ringleader, though he did organise initiatives; he planned, gathered, created, and kept up ties between the circles of esskays spread out around the island.

These consisted chiefly of circles that could be easily connected to particular bars, like the group that gathered at the Island Bar, several of whom slept at the Wollner house, next to the island museum. Kruso maintained the best relations with them, including men like Santiago, Tille, Peter, and Spurtefix or women like Janina, Sylke, and Antilopé. Then there were also those esskays who saw themselves as belonging to particular campfires, where at night they grilled, drank, and regularly shouted 'Free Republic of Hiddensee', including the Enddorn fire, for example, with A.K., Ines, Torsten, Christine, and Jule. Beyond that, there was a group of older esskays who had applied for exit visas and occasionally formed their own circle at the Heiner bar. They had detached themselves and were already deeply immersed, perhaps too deeply, in a state of waiting, although Ed often had the impression that they had forgotten they were waiting, as if their lives already lay in the beyond, not just outside the country, but outside time, whose measurable passing was made irrelevant by the island and its magic, as if their state of waiting had condensed into an edenic beyond. Kruso judged it a form of self-immunisation at least partially intended to counteract the island's contagious sense of liberation — which he was in no way judging, he emphasised; on the contrary. In these circumstances, it seemed that being granted an exit visa struck one or two of them like a blow. They had drifted far out on the island and were suddenly told to resurface and paddle back to the official passage of time — often with only a few days' notice.

More open-minded were the circles of the very young esskays, some of them punks, who had decided on their eighteenth birthday to spend their lives on the island and nowhere else. Because they weren't presentable, they were never hired into *service* and almost always ended up in the dishwashing stations, where they accomplished extraordinary feats. In fact, the punks were considered the best dishwashers on the island. They were renowned for their diligence and reliability. 'They work like devils,' Kruso explained. Ata in the Norderende or Dirty in Hitthim were names everyone knew and respected. There was also an alliance between the punks and the long-hairs, who improved their situation and offered a certain protection when necessary. 'I don't care what anyone looks like, as long as they work,' the boss at the Island Bar announced.

'Hiddensee is also a gay paradise,' Kruso mentioned softly as they were standing at the Heinz bar, which, to be precise, was the Heinz-and-Uli bar on the sweet side of the Dornbusch, where Losh and now Ed got their drinks for a modest fee. Without a doubt, Heinz and Uli considered themselves a couple, which didn't seem to bother Kruso much. The Dornbusch (and not just the gays there) was the Klausner's main rival at the annual football tournament, organised by none other than Kruso. The tournament was considered the high point of the Island Day, an island-wide festival for the esskays, also supported by the locals and bar managers like Willi Schmietendorf, who ran the Dornbusch and gave the winners a keg of beer, whereas Krombach left everything up to his head dishwasher, Alexander Krusowitsch.

Through Kruso, a network of contacts and activities was formed, and this suited the esskays because it emphasised their uniqueness and gave them a sense of their special status, the peculiar and not easily understandable form of legal illegality in a country that either had declared them unfit and spat them out or to which they simply no longer felt they belonged. Rimbaud applied the idea of inner emigration to esskays, although each of them had to work hard every day for their right to stay on the island.

The majority of the esskays were unmoved by Rimbaud's talk, but they showed Kruso respect. He was the man in golden armour, and they offered him protection with their fellowship, along with a few things he asked or demanded of them, though nothing that would have caused them any real hardship. However, very few of them understood his *philosophy of freedom*. They did not feel that they were part of the resistance, and hardly any of them would have considered themselves members of a conspiracy. They were interested in the venture (its hint of the forbidden) and especially in the bacchanalian

celebrations at the allocations, the open bar on the terrace of the
Klausner, and last but not least in the unfamiliar guests who arrived
night after night — their foreignness, their charm, and their pleasant
odour, which was strangely accentuated by the odd designation Kruso
had given them: castaways.

Initially, it was only a question of the nights, of finding
accommodation for the castaways for at least three or four days in the
so-called clandestine quarters. It was an ambitious goal because their
numbers increased continuously, a pilgrimage unlike any other in the
entire country. Disoriented and reckless, the pilgrims were drawn by
the siren call of the island over the moraines and along the beaches in
search of a place to sleep, without a billet or residency permit — in
a border area.

At some point, the 'eternal soup' was added to the mix. 'They
just need something warm in their stomachs, at least once a day,'
was Kruso's simple reasoning. The 'good scraps' Ed picked from the
plates each day in the dishwashing station were cut up small, then
mixed with the freedom-granting herbs and mushrooms from the
'sacred vegetable beds' and fertilised with slime from the drain ('the
amphibian is nutritious and full of vitamins') before ending up in a
cast-iron pot, for which Chef Mike always kept a burner in reserve.
Ed had often seen how two castaways would deliver the pot of soup,
or at least what was left of it, to the ramp, where Kruso would take it
and offer them a few instructions before returning the pot to the stove
without washing it. The eternal flame, the eternal soup. For Kruso, it
was a kind of biological cycle, a closed circuit of nourishment — and
enlightenment. And this, as he put it, was all 'just the beginning'.

The three or four days on the island were an essential and primary
necessity on the road to freedom, which Kruso explained to Ed
frequently and in ever greater detail. In addition to this, there was
the *support system*. This was essentially limited to three elements: the

soup, the ablution, and the work, which naturally was voluntary and took place on the beach or at the covered tables on the terrace of the Klausner and mostly in the mornings.

At first, Ed could only associate one dim memory with the ablution — a burning sensation in his eyes and the 'Roman' who had flitted across the courtyard at night like a ghost. The work consisted primarily of making jewellery, which was astonishingly easy to sell to the tourists. There were mostly earrings (twenty marks a pair) made out of the bands from dead migratory birds, collected in the bird sanctuary. 'Sometimes you find a really old bird. I mean a cadaver that still has the old rings, from Heligoland, or rings from the Radolfzell or Rossitten bird observatories, unbelievably valuable pieces ...' Yet Kruso acquired a much greater number of rings directly from the banding station on the island, which Ed had got to know on one of their forays. The bird taggers there greeted them like old trading partners. Kruso not only acquired the rustproof material for his secret manufacturing from them, but also borrowed rare tools, fine pliers that were strange in some special way and resembled a dentist's instruments. And he let them explain their work with birds in the most minute detail, down to the finer points of drawing up the so-called tagging reports, as if that were the actual point of the visit. He had lengthy discussions with the taggers about species of birds Ed had never heard of. 'A hundred thousand rings a year, simply incredible,' he called to Ed, who was feeling nauseous from the flapping of hundreds of wings in the surrounding cages. 'Too many rings, that's why they've given up their research,' Kruso explained when they left the central tagging station. 'Hormones that trigger the migratory instinct — that was once their subject. Can you imagine, Ed? Even for a second? *That* is something we truly need to know more about. Instead, they now write up their reports. A report for every single bird!' The wire that had to be pulled through the earlobes came from another source. 'Dental wire,' Kruso whispered, as if speaking of the Hiddensee Treasure.

The profit from this small, but lucrative manufacture flowed only into the 'Esskay Fund', primarily to cover the cost of the drinks on allocation evenings. The fund was kept in Kruso's charge. The regular distribution of the pilgrims into emergency quarters, the undisputed high point and core of the organisation, resembled a celebration, which was to lack for nothing. The thought that he had recited Trakl at one of those celebrations, of all times, embarrassed Ed. He withdrew from the organisation. He was an excellent worker, that much was certain. He mastered the daily inferno of pots and cutlery, and yet he still didn't fulfil the spoken or the unspoken requirements for becoming a fully fledged member of the Klausner.

Nevertheless, Kruso had chosen him.

Finding sleeping quarters for all the castaways was, without a doubt, a difficult, fundamentally impossible task. Kruso acted as quartermaster. He divided the shelters into permanent and open-air quarters, the latter being special, as he called them 'consecrated spots' at the foot of the moraines. First and foremost were the esskays' rooms — a not inconsiderable number of sleeping accommodation spread across the entire island. The remaining system of emergency shelters and the wide distribution network was of a complexity that constantly amazed Ed. It was an expression of Kruso's strategic talent, an almost military predisposition that allowed him to see his hiding places as a system of bases and to develop his logistics accordingly. On their forays, Kruso inducted Ed in the particulars of the clandestine quarters.

- The sheepfold in the former 'Peoples' Friendship' agricultural cooperative, most recently the nationally owned farm 'Ummanz' at the foot of the Dornbusch: capacity 10–12 castaways.
- The donkey stable belonging to the theatre director Walter Felsenstein, below his villa; a small, but very sturdy building with an upper floor able to accommodate 3 people over the donkeys.
- The tower (Kruso's boyhood room on the grounds of the Radiation Institute): capacity 5–7 castaways.

- The cutter owned by the fishermen Schluck, Schlieker, Kollwitz, Krüger, Gau, and Augstein, and the freighters *Johanna* and *Hope* in the ports of Kloster and Vitte: total capacity 10–15 castaways.
- The large wooden barn belonging to the Weidner family in Grieben, which was partitioned into various stalls for bicycles, carts, and an unused horse carriage, which could serve as a pallet: capacity up to 8 castaways.
- The secret brick shed behind the former estate above the Schwedenufer, surrounded by overgrown woodland filled with rubbish. Behind the port, a narrow flight of stairs led up to it, but you had to leave the path and make your way through a section of thick undergrowth. First, you came upon the rusty skeleton of an enormous machine once used for threshing or woodworking, and then, to the left, the lodging; this stone building was considered the esskays' headquarters, and served various purposes, as Kruso put it, about which he offered no more than a few vague hints: capacity 10 castaways, more if absolutely necessary.
- The writer Gerhart Hauptmann's bed; you could climb a fence at the back of the property and, crouching, descend the small slope to the house, where one particular window was always left unlatched. The esskay who supervised the museum made sure the window was unlatched, and was also responsible for returning the bed to its appropriate museum-quality state: capacity 2 (slender) castaways.
- The tiny brick house on the path behind the Hauptmann house. It belonged to the biological station and was so small that you could only spend the night there on your feet, 'good for two people to sleep leaning against each other'. 'It's not as bad as all that,' Kruso downplayed it when he noticed Ed's incredulous look.
- The cinema tent in the small copse when the projectionist didn't already have illegal guests of his own.
- The equipment shed on the Vitte sportsgrounds, just two hundred metres from the 'Carousel', the actress Asta Nielsen's round house: capacity 4 castaways.

- The stone caves along the road between Kloster and Vitte, a rough, almost inaccessible, but very secure shelter, hidden deep between towering blocks of granite behind the so-called promenade, a dune reinforced with stone and covered with tar: capacity 3 castaways.
- The gravedigger's wooden shed, a particular favourite among castaways. A sign was nailed to the door labelled 'office'. Next to the door stood an overturned wheelbarrow missing its wheel, and a chopping block. There was a crate with masonry tools, a freshly oiled trowel, a sledgehammer, a pointed chisel, and a flat chisel. "... the ancestors' / ancient tool. / This shatters the stranger's breast ..." suddenly echoed from Ed's verse hoard. Narrow graves with crooked, weathered stones stretched up to Gerhart Hauptmann's granite cliff. Bits of grass from the last mowing hung on them, and they resembled a herd of hairy, ailing animals. Kruso touched one of the stones in passing. Only later, when Ed returned to the graveyard, was he able to decipher the inscription: 'GOVERNOR OF THIS ISLAND rests here since anno 1800 and dwells in sacred realms.' The gravedigger of Kloster was one of the few esskays with a year-round contract. His hut stood on the property's furthest edge, not far from the grave of the unknown sailor, which was overgrown with brown conifers. There was also a small white rock with steel letters, under which Kruso hid the key to the hut. 'It can't be bad for the castaways to kneel at least once in this spot, even if just to get the key.' Capacity 3–4 castaways.
- The old transformer house in the forest between the lighthouse and the Klausner. It looked like a caretaker or tollkeeper's hut at the entrance to the Dornbusch hinterland, where there was a pond surrounded by reeds and old willows to which Ed immediately felt drawn. Wood was stacked against the back wall of the transformer house. Hidden under the wood was the key, which opened the massive padlock after a fair amount of jiggling. Sleeping in the transformer house was much too dangerous, Kruso told Ed, so it served as a kind of archive, a storage area for tarpaulins, blankets,

and sleeping bags necessary for sleeping outdoors. One of the spots
specially consecrated for that purpose was nearby. 'Sleeping here is
a dream, you should try it at least once,' Kruso whispered, as if they
were already surrounded by darkness. In fact, the location of this
sleeping spot did seem marvellous — one side directly across from
the lighthouse, the other with a view of the reeds and the lights of
Rügen. As if completely hidden, you lay in a hollow that was not
visible from the barracks.

- The so-called lamp workshop, a clinker-brick building on the
lighthouse keeper's farmland, surrounded by high reeds and sheltered
by enormous, constantly rustling chestnut trees — near the bluff,
and only two hundred metres from the lighthouse. First, there
was a wooden trellis-work fence that was easy to climb over, then
a door that could be lifted from its hinges. Replacement lights for
the lighthouse were stored in the workshop, light bulbs the size of
a child's head with carbon filaments as thick as a finger, and next
to them a range of discarded reflectors, 'in which it's better not to
look at your reflection as a castaway,' unless 'the island has already
penetrated you deeply enough ...' 'A holiday from unhappiness,'
Ed whispered to himself, but Kruso heard him. 'No, not a holiday.'
His left eyelid began to twitch, and his voice became hard. 'It's
Hiddensee, Ed, you understand, *hidden*? The island is their hiding
place, the island where they can find themselves, where they can turn
inwards, that is, towards nature, to the voice of the heart, as Rousseau
put it. No one has to flee, no one has to drown. The island is the
experience. An experience that enables them to return enlightened.
An experience that makes it possible for them to live their lives
until the day that quantity turns to quality, when the measure of
freedom in their hearts suddenly transcends the constraints of the
circumstances, the moment when ... It will be a giant throbbing,
a single thunderous heartbeat.' Kruso lay his hand on one of the
large NARVA lamps. *I wouldn't be surprised if it started to glow*, Ed
thought. Capacity 4 castaways.

When Ed returned to his room on the following day, a clean, fresh brick had been placed under each leg of his table. The height was good. The wood cooled his forearms. He took out his diary and wrote.

THE ROUTE ON DAYS OFF

'You don't have to,' the voice had whispered, 'only if you want to.' It was only when he stopped moving that Ed became aware of the smooth movement that had enveloped him like sleep. The first rays of sun fell into the room, the fleeting shadows of swallows soaring and plummeting on the wall, on his bed, everywhere.

'I'm C.'

Ed listened.

He felt skin, the protruding bone of a shoulder blade, a mouth not far from his ear. He smelled the odour of someone else; it smelled good, and he embraced it.

You don't have to.

As Ed followed an imagined sequence of events he had not decided on himself and penetrated her deeply again, he realised he was not dreaming this time.

Ed heard the rushing sound of pine trees, of the surf, far below. Desire vibrated at the base of his spine.

'But if, I mean, if you did fall sleep, then ...'

'You don't have to apologise.'

That was his voice — there was no doubt. His voice, his heart, racing, his breath, his sweat. The woman lay at his side, her head on his chest. He couldn't see her face. She had a mole, high up, on her auricle, like a crumb.

'Didn't you notice me at Kruso's table?' she whispered with the usual reverence castaways expressed when mentioning Kruso's name.

'Kruso's table?'

'You don't have to pretend. I'm really honoured to have been chosen.'

'Chosen?'

'There are people who start asking about it on the ferry, they all talk about it.' She assured him that she thought them careless. At the same time, she shifted slightly, and Ed felt her pelvic bone against his thigh.

But I'm Losh's friend, Ed wanted to interject; he hadn't yet said these words. He slowly turned to the side a bit, and now he recognised her. She was the woman who had fallen asleep at their table, her head on her arms. Short, stringy hair. Unbelievable that she could sleep through the ruckus of an allocation. That was the only reason Ed had looked at her several times.

'I don't think we were at the same table.'

'I'm sorry, I just fell asleep. One night on the beach, one in the forest, I was completely worn out.'

'If you fell asleep, then how did ...' Ed fell silent. His member was touching her warm stomach. He wanted to stay this way forever. His entire life long. The woman smiled at him, and Ed saw that she was happy to have found an accommodation.

You don't have to.

Just this one, spoken sentence. An offer. Fair and friendly.

As a rule, Kruso's route around the island was determined by the hostelries' days off. He met waiters, house managers, and barkeepers, and sat with them in the empty bar rooms or often in the kitchen, while Ed waited for him at the bar, savouring the silence. He never had to pay on these occasions, and was often readily served even though the establishment was closed. A few of the esskays already knew Ed from the allocation evenings that he had recently taken part in, but just to show support for Kruso. He helped serve drinks and distribute food, and he kept an eye on the eternal soup that had to be stirred now and again. In the course of the evening, each castaway could count on a generous portion.

As if there were a friendly taboo, his Trakl debacle was never mentioned, even though the esskays often attempted to enter into conversation with him. Ed secretly admired their capacity for living, their cheerful dispositions, and their frank, open expressions. They breathed differently, Ed thought; they took longer breaths in and breathed out more slowly, as if the sea had expanded their lungs and liberated their thoughts. Every one of their movements gave the impression they were engaged in some essential activity; their lives themselves were essential, independent, filled with their own interests, and although more than once Ed had felt a longing to be part of this circle, their eyes, glowing with the sea's reflection and the island's luminosity, remained so foreign to him that he was never truly able to take up the thread of a conversation. Another obstacle was that no one asked where he had come from or what he had done on the mainland. When Ed mentioned that he (actually) was a student, the light of the sea faded from their eyes. As if everyone had always been a waiter or a dishwasher, and had never wanted anything else in life. Scarcely anyone spoke about the real reason they were here. It may not have been a rule — it simply wasn't interesting.

What Ed liked most was sitting on the verandah of the harbour hotel. In the back corner of the front porch, which seemed to be made of a few rickety window frames joined together, there was a shabby leather sofa that seemed like a relic from a long-gone era. Almost invisible in his corner, Ed had a good view of the harbour, the docking boats, the streams of tourists, and the crazy boy who ran up and down the dock shouting commands at the top of his voice as if he knew exactly what was what this season.

There was nothing better than sitting there alone, looking out over the clean, empty tables, and daydreaming. There was nothing nicer than leaning back, stretching an arm over the back of the sofa, and stroking the cool smooth leather with his hand, which was chapped from the dishwater. Nothing more pleasant than lifting a glass slowly to his mouth, breathing into it, and feeling his own breath on his face.

Ed imagined how she must have stood in his room at some point. How she would have undressed without a sound, and hesitated a moment, shivering, perhaps. Her slender body, her uncertainty as she felt around in the dark. The window open, as always. No light from the sea, just the back and forth of the surf that offered a proposal, a secret plan for all the nights to come.

Even Ed's favourite dish (a fried egg with roasted potatoes) was known among the esskays. In Kruso's wake, he had attained a certain renown on the island — Edgar Bendler, Kruso's companion. It didn't bother Ed that Losh didn't let him stay at his side for the discussions about preparations for the Island Day, for example, which was planned for the first of August and seemed to be a source of concern. The friendliness with which Ed was served was coloured by this gentle demotion. He sensed it. He was seen as one of Kruso's instruments (nevertheless with respect), still somehow ridiculous in his devotion and feeble in his overall appearance — Ed, the onion, the silent one sitting quietly in his corner, not able to carry on a decent conversation and staring fixedly out the window, as if there were something more going on out there than the inane to and fro of the day tourists, hundreds of whom grabbed the handle of the dining-room door more or less firmly, bewildered by their bad luck in landing on the island on the harbour restaurant's day off. No, Ed complied with what he called Kruso's circumspection, if, in fact, it was circumspection, and not simply benevolence and an attempt to spare a friend, in whose

head verses marched like soldiers going off to war — the daily grind
that was the lot of any GOVERNOR OF THIS ISLAND, in short,
to keep him for something else, for what was most essential ...

Ed did indulge in such fantasies on occasion. Am I not like a child
in his hiding place, Ed thought, enclosed and very quiet, but whose
heart beats faster every time the door handle moves and who feels
more forbidden with every move of the door handle?

Voices came from the kitchen, and then the sound of a metal
object skidding over the stone floor. Ed listened, as he always did,
automatically, with no intentions, and not prepared to relinquish his
cocoon of absence. C.'s face flashed before his eyes once again, her
narrow eyebrows raised, her bright, clear forehead, and her attentive,
curious gaze when she had taken Ed into her mouth and kept her eyes
fixed on his face.

Kruso!

Kruso was shouting. Ed had only heard him beside himself like
this once before, when they were drive fishing on the beach. There
was a crash, something broke, and the swinging doors to the kitchen
burst open. Someone was pushed, stumbled, dropped to his knees,
and cried, gulped back a sob — it was René, the ice-cream man.
Two esskays from the Hitthim stood behind him with their arms
spread wide, as if they were forcing an animal to its place of slaughter,
blocking the way back to its stall. After a while, René lifted his head,
and Ed saw that he was laughing, that he could barely contain himself.

'All because of that bitch, the whole ...'

One of the esskays kicked René in the kidneys, and he swallowed
his words. It was not a particularly hard kick, but Ed flinched, and
René noticed him. He turned around, bared his teeth, and padded
towards Ed like a dog. Ed froze. He slowly pulled his hand, with
which he had been trying to feel out his desire, away from the leather
of the sofa.

'The lapdog, the lapdog is here, too.'

René started making a noise, and it took Ed a few seconds to realise he was yapping. Ed sprang up and rushed outside. 'The lapdog, the lapdog ...' Ed heard René yap once more, then the barkeeper shut the door and it all disappeared.

'I'm sorry, Ed. Did you already eat your roasted potatoes?' Losh slowly rested his hand on Ed's head as if he wanted to caress him, but it was just a gesture that fit his question, and Ed immediately forgot what his friend was apologising for.

At first, Kruso had knelt between the plant beds and placed his hand (cautiously) on one of the molehills. Then he started giving instructions. Ed crouched next to him and felt a light tightness in his groin. He watched as Kruso stroked the earth several times, gently at first, the way one strokes a breast, absently, without thinking, just because of its incredible softness and smoothness, then even more gently, the way a child gives the final touches to a carefully build sandcastle — but then, almost without transition, he rammed his hand roughly into the mound.

'The holes, it's about the holes. First you expose a hole. Then you stick a bottle in it with its mouth facing north-west.'

Only then did Ed notice that the sun hung, orange, in the sky like a strange moon although it was hardly evening. The small scar above his eye began to buzz. He heard the hoof beats of his bear-horse far in the distance, and the whine of a patrol boat's diesel motor out on the sea, and he caught isolated sentences that were being spoken at the tables within the walls of the thatched houses. As if he were a part of this world for the very first time. The objects around him glowed in their crazy colours, and, eventually, blindsided by beauty, Ed pressed his ear to the ground and heard the note ...

Everything had changed overnight.

They had lugged the empty bottles from the Hitthim in mildewed backpacks. The smell reminded Ed of his earlier days practising manoeuvres, of the rubber on his gas mask that became sticky with old sweat if he forgot to put it out to dry after the exercises.

Each step was a light clinking. Backpack to backpack, walking as twins, Ed felt justified in acknowledging greetings from the locals on the way, and sometimes he returned a nod, although he knew that their pleasantries were not really directed at him — *not yet, anyway*, Ed thought, and for a moment he felt a spark of elusive brotherhood.

Ed's euphoria was transferred to his time with Kruso, and so it seemed fine, at first, not to say anything about C. He also didn't want to jeopardise his delicate position at the allocations. And he secretly hoped the mistake that had been made in the latest distribution (what else could it be but a mistake) would not be discovered for another night or two, or even just one night — one single night, Ed thought. Oh, exquisite shipwreck!

Yes, he was proud of Kruso and feared him at the same time, and these two emotions were of a pair. Kruso's absoluteness frightened him, his illusions of resistance, the 'Organisation' — sheer insanity — and on top of that, his somberness, his fanatic determination. Still, what weighed more heavily on Ed was the openness with which Losh accepted him, the blazing honesty and the respect he accorded Ed, for the very areas that were Ed's greatest weaknesses, where Ed's own insanity was rooted — *my own unhappiness* flitted through Ed's mind, and this thought almost made him feel happy. At the precise moment when his particular insanity had become clear to everyone, Losh had stood by him in a quiet, gentle way. Ed had no idea who Kruso was, but sometimes Ed felt he knew him as well as his own soul.

A third backpack was ready for them at the Wieseneck, and Losh strapped it to his chest without hesitation. A two-wheeled metal cart, filled with bottles, gleamed in the sun outside the Island Bar. They were all Blue Strangler empties, the brand Ed had got to know in the tower, in front of the 'Map of Truth'. The inn's window was only knee-high above the ground, and offered a view of the area behind the bar. Kruso went up to the window, and a man leaned out. They stood for a moment, cheek to cheek, and then the man took Kruso's hand and pressed it to his chest. Ed rushed to grab the drawbar of the cart; he pushed the vehicle over a hole in the sandy path, and the load rattled — an outcry.

'Santiago,' Kruso explained as they moved on.

'I know,' Ed replied.

The act of digging, the cool, fresh dirt. Ed had become hard just from the contact. That he could possibly feel this way ... There were a few remains, dregs, so now and again Kruso would raise a bottle to his lips before burying it. 'It's their ears, their sensitive ears, that make them crazy. It's the only way, the only language they understand.'

Glittering in the sun, the necks of the bottles looked freshly planted, the entire garden looked festive, as if decorated, glittering with glass tails.

A thin, relentless whistling.

After a while, Ed heard it. Like a kid gone wild, Kruso leapt here and there among the molehills and corrected the bottles' position as the wind grew stronger, which made the whistling sound more hollow and threatening, like the fog horn of a ship. When the wind changed direction slightly, a fantastic singing arose, like a siren's song. Almost hypnotised, with his hands in the damp earth, fingers slightly curled in a small, continuously searching motion, Ed stared at his companion, leaping hectically back and forth, gesturing wildly as he tuned his instrument, and suddenly, wondrously, laughing. Kruso laughed and leapt, leapt and laughed.

'Time to leave, you little beasts, time to go, ahoy!'

'Time to go, time to leave,' Ed echoed, and threw his hands in the air.

A ground-organ to chase away the moles had been the idea of Kruso's grandfather, a scientist who had made much greater discoveries ... This was the first time that Kruso had mentioned his family. Back then, too, they had only used Blue Strangler bottles: their shape seemed especially designed for the purposes; his grandfather had figured that out — 'wetting your whistle, as they say, get it, Ed?'

A short white-haired old woman was feeling her way along the fence. She held onto the fence with her left hand and kept her head facing slightly upward, as if she were searching for the sun — or the moon, Ed thought.

'That toots, it does,' the old woman muttered, 'it toots them moles in the noggin.'

Losh went over to her quickly and let her pat him. His neck pouch lay on her head like a small buckskin cap. He called her Mete, Mother Mete. As Kruso led the old woman through the garden, he gave Ed a sign, and Ed gathered up a few leftover Stranglers. Mother Mete wore a pair of huge light-brown plastic glasses and a cardigan, despite the day's heat. Kruso whispered something to her and she nodded.

In all, they'd buried more than fifty bottles in the garden next to the parish house in Kloster, a garden that consisted of a few plant beds, fruit trees, and a hut with a wooden floor completely covered with sleeping bags. As they wheeled away their clattering cart, Mother Mete raised her head again and gave a random wave.

'It toots, my boy, it toots.'

In the harbour, on a small, half-withered patch of grass that served as a parking lot, Kruso tilted the cart up and placed it in a row with others. Strictly speaking, it was not a row, but a wild jumble of nearly thirty or forty of these battered metal carts with labels on their undersides. Each cart had a name, and Ed automatically set them to a rhythm (one of his mnemonic devices, part of his insuppressible mechanism for increasing his hoard of verses) so that the collection of names in black, blue, or red paint flashed before his eyes as a poem:

Dornbusch, Hauptmann, Wieseneck
Enddorn,Weidner,Witt
Schluck, Mann, Schlieker
Putbrese, Blume, Gau
Kollwitz, Meding, NPA
Holstein, Kasten, Striesow
Pflugbeil, Rommstedt, Felsenstein

It only took a few changes in a few of these names grouped from a solely metrical standpoint for a shimmer of semantics to shine through: Mann-Schluck-NPA (man-gulp-National People's Army) or Kollwitz-Blume-Kasten (Kollwitz-flower-box) and so on. Kruso contemplated the rusty pile of upended carts as if he were surveying his realm. The crazy boy stood on the dock and shouted desperately at the sea. The last ferry had sailed.

'I'd like stay, through the winter, too,' Ed said.

'That will require a lot,' Kruso answered.

'I believe I can do it.'

'That you can, Ed.'

Losh took Ed in his arms, in the middle of the harbour, and Ed gladly let him, just as he let everything happen. Even if they had been naked at that moment (why was he thinking this?), it wouldn't have mattered to him.

'I knew it, Ed. I knew it.'

Ed had swept his room, even under the bed, and set a new candle in his adder stone. He didn't want to read or think. He sat at the open window and stared out, listening to the surf. His right hand gripped the stool. Thus he experienced it for the first time. He had to breathe deeply several times, and for a moment his eyes filled with tears. At midnight, Viola: 'To mark the end of the day, the national anthem.' The noise on the stairs had faded. His door had remained closed.

At some point, he heard the whistling. His eyes fell on the photograph on his table, on the face that seemed blurred, and for a long time he could not look away. A whistling and howling, all the way up to the Dornbusch highland. The wind blew over the Stranglers, the moles jumped ship, and the island set its course through the fog of his boundless, aching desire.

THREE BEARS

17 JULY

Should ask at this point if C.'s allocation to me was just a
mistake. Have to pull myself together. Chris helped me in the
dishwashing station, just like that, and Cavallo left a book in
the nest for me (Carlo Emilio Gadda), he has taken to calling
me Edgardo. Losh is making preparations for the Island
Day. He wants a huge celebration that will bring everyone
together, esskays, islanders, castaways, almost sounds like a
demonstration. It's oppressively hot, the island is like a death
ship, no wind, no waves, and even more cockroaches. With 2
shoes, killed 8 this morning, yesterday 9.

Ed took a few steps backwards, and looked down at the beach for
a while.
No one.
He didn't want anyone to take him by surprise, and under no
circumstances did he want to draw attention to the cave. He spread

the towel in which he had hidden his notebook out on the sand, and neared the face of the bluff again, but more as if he were interested in the stratifications in the clay, the writing of the ice age.

'It was — utterly unbelievable, you understand?'

'Like winning the big lottery, without having drawn a ticket.'

'Yes, yes.' The sun was beating down on the back of his neck.

'Maybe that's the solution?'

'This morning I could see G., I mean, really see her, without ... Without the terrible images, just so, eating breakfast, playing chess, on the way home. The way she would walk, turn around, and run to me as fast as she could. She had this way of jumping on me, you know, she liked doing it, and she startled me every time. I could hear her laughing.'

First the humming, then the tram.

Ed opened his notebook; the sunlight on the page was so bright he had to close his eyes.

Kruso came in the evening. In the silence, Ed formulated the question as neutrally as possible. Lust confused the words in his head, instead of *a fluke, a fuck*. It was tawdry.

'I don't think I ... thanked you properly.' Ed held the photograph in his hand.

Kruso shook his head without a word. He poured some wine; he had brought glasses and a bottle of Lindenblatt, already half-empty. Ed thought about giving him the new poem, but he had not made a clean copy yet.

'Why don't you ever talk about your sister, Losh?'

'Why me?'

The answer was odd enough.

After a while, Kruso stood up and walked out.

'Losh ...'

In his military way, Kruso turned at the door and took a step into the twilit room. For a moment, he simply stood there, a few tightly folded sheets of paper in his hand. Ed recognised the quad-ruled paper.

Three stanzas, then Ed realised: it wasn't Trakl, it was Kruso. Kruso's tone that turned Trakl's verse into something of his own, *his own words, his own thoughts*, a dreadful transformation.

His friend could not get past 'Sonya's white brow'. The sheet of paper began to tremble even before the 'snow moistens her cheeks', and he burst into tears, without restraint. He wept — he howled like an animal.

'Losh!'

Kruso was still standing upright. He shook his head violently, his hairband worked loose, and his long hair covered his face. Big Kruso, poor Kruso, stood in the middle of Ed's room and gasped for air. With nothing but his voice, Ed's companion had turned the world of memorised verse that filled Ed's head like tinnitus into an abyss of sorrow, had turned Ed's hard-baked hoard into his very own, unfathomable grief.

'Thank you, in any case, thank you for this.' Kruso held the sheet of paper out in front of him.

Ed tried to put his arms around Kruso, but the man was so large and difficult to embrace that he gave up and stood next him like a helpless boy.

'We didn't always live here,' Kruso began. He slowly composed himself but spoke so softly that Ed had to lean forward to be nearer to the voice that could mean everything.

'When we were brought to this place, I was six years old. My sister was ten. One of my mother's sisters had married a German physicist, an important man. They'd met in Moscow during the war, you saw the institute, the Radiation Institute ...'

Kruso's rigidity relaxed, and they sat together on Ed's bed. 'When my father left us there, we didn't know it would be forever, I mean, that it would turn into a story of step-parents ... Rommstedt, my uncle, X-rayed everyone and everything in his institute, my sister and me as well. We were his favourite subjects, I think. We were nice and small, and fit easily in his equipment. When he could do his research on us, he was very happy, almost affectionate. He constantly stroked our heads, but only to make sure we kept still. I always had the feeling that he was wiping away my thoughts with his hand.

'The time before Hiddensee is very distant, like a forgotten continent in another, an earlier century, in which I happened to be in the world, in a completely different world. We often sat in front of the fireplace. The first thing I see is always this fireplace in my father's office. The hide of a camel was spread out on the floor. That was my favourite place. "I rode on that camel, back then by the Aral Sea," my father always told his guests, who then looked at me and nodded. And so it was if I had ridden as well. I was a great Tartar general, as big as my father, riding a camel on the steppe. There were always people who came to his office and spoke German, some of them threw me a suspicious glance mid-sentence, as if I might betray their crude, incomprehensible secrets. I rode and stared into the fire, because that's where our country and foreign lands were; I was five years old, and the entire steppe lay before me, do you see, Ed?' He held the page with the Trakl poem in front of him as if his own story were written on it.

'The fireplace was painted light blue — that was the steppe. Inside it was black, that was the night we had to fight our way through, my troops and I. Constant darkness and enemy fire. One thing I remember clearly: on the mantel, a section of the light blue had been chipped off, and the broken spot glittered like ice, ice and snow — it was always cold on the steppe. My sister sat behind me on the camel, her name ... right, well, you already know, her name is Sonya.' The poem in his hand began trembling again, but he opened the sheet of paper and smoothed it out.

'As we were riding over the steppe, my father, the general — I don't know if he held that rank at the time, or ever, for that matter, but for all of us he was *the general*, he was wearing those wide epaulettes, you know, Russian epaulettes are almost as broad as your shoulder — so one time, right in the middle of a conversation, my father rushed to the window and shouted something down to the parade ground, to the soldiers. On that day, they were doing drills, the longest drills were on Sunday, and something usually displeased my father. I believe the drills were very difficult. They had to march in formation, following lines drawn on the asphalt, circles and rectangles, it looked like a dance. You couldn't actually see much because the chimney of the boiler house right across from us had been built directly in front of his office window, maybe on purpose. But he could feel it. Two hundred boots, in time. The entire house shook, the floor where I was sitting shook. When something wasn't quite right, I first saw it in his face, the way it tensed up. He could stand it for a moment but then enough was enough. Actually, I never saw him that way any other time, he was not an angry man, maybe for him it was like a violin playing the wrong note in a symphony.

'In any case, the sound of the boots — it was always there, like the sound of the ocean. And the singing. The soldiers of the guard detail had their quarters on the other side of the grounds, almost directly behind our house. The entire area was surrounded by little wooden guard towers and a wall topped with tangles of barbed wire; it was called Russian Military City Number Seven. I often thought about that number as a child and tried to imagine the other six Russian military cities. They were just like ours, with large villas, parade ground, shooting range, apartment houses, potato warehouse, coal depot, prison, and playground, and with a boy like me sitting on a camel in front of the fireplace, seven brave fireplace Budyonnys in seven German Russian camps, almost an army, and of course I was their leader ...' Kruso looked at the poem as if studying a drawing. After a while, he set it aside.

'It was said that a Prussian prince had once lived in our house. That's the only reason my father had wanted that house for his headquarters. He wasn't the commanding officer, but the deputy. He was called the *Zampolit*, and to this day I don't know what that means. Occasionally, he spoke of Prince Oskar, even the name seemed made up, but he, the great Zampolit, could claim in all seriousness that he would have liked to meet this Oskar, "the last Mohican of the Hohenzollern", as he liked to proclaim, which seemed odd to me even as a child, but maybe that's because I didn't understand the words. In any case, he was reasonably knowledgeable about history, and mentioned other names of people who had lived in our city Number Seven — Hindenburg, Oppen, and Oskar were always among them. I believe he'd have liked to show Oskar that his vegetable garden had been turned into a great big parade ground, or how everything had been painted nice shades of light blue and Russian green, or that on his personal orders a sauna had been built in Oskar's cellar, or also our pig sty — back then we owned our own pig, it lived in a shed on the balcony ... I believe it all had to do with the fact that my father didn't really hate the Germans; he understood them, I mean really *understood*.

'Because both of my parents were German-speaking, the only ones in the entire Red Army, I believe, they often took care of negotiations with the German authorities. That may well have been the general's only duty. I believe there actually were secret-police officers in his office who couldn't put together a proper sentence after six or eight years of studying Russian. That would make my father furious, though he liked to show off with his German. His mother was a Volga German, like my mother, and his father was Russian. When there were problems, if things became difficult, they went to him. He had to mediate, explain, even apologise. In the name of the commanding officer, or in the name of the military, or in the name of all the Soviet republics, depending on the gravity of the case. Something was always coming up, a dead body in the woods, someone deserting or getting shot by accident, murdered, raped, robbed, or run over by a tank, things like that were always happening. Of course, I could hardly grasp that as a child, but still, I packed everything that was discussed in the general's office into my fireplace, into the expanse of the steppe, and I retrieved some of it later and made sense of it. It's all still in the fireplace, Ed, the whole story, in the Fireplace of Truth, as you'd probably call it.

'Some tried to avoid the socialist fraternal kiss, but my father wouldn't allow it. I saw how he pressed his lips to their cheeks, and with that, somehow, they lost everything. All the courage they'd been able to muster just to enter Russian City Number Seven was sucked out of them immediately. And finally, there was prosecution by the military police. As soon as the visitor was gone, everything would happen very quickly. If the guilty party lived in our city, my father had him brought in right away. A sea of marching boots outside and inside, my father who would say, "Three years Sakhalin," or "Ten years Omsk." I never witnessed it. The sentences were always handed down in Oskar's garden hall. That was the room next-door. But that's how it would have happened.'

Kruso emptied his glass in a single gulp.

'A ride through the steppe, with all the problems, only a real general could survive that. A general like the one who called himself my father and probably still does to this day, although ...' Kruso fell silent. 'He could stay very calm, but occasionally ... Occasionally, I was afraid, not actually of him, but of the black maw that led up into the chimney. If I leaned forward a bit, I could see him. The general shouted, and I leaned a bit into the fireplace, and then a bit more, until I could feel the draft on my face, and the enormous black mouth gaped wide with its sour smell. Sometimes, I dreamed of a future in which I would reign from my seat in front of the fireplace with a book I'd written; four hundred pages of commands, which I would read out loud, softly and serenely, like a novel, in a room full of Budyonnys, full of good, determined horsemen.'

Kruso stood up and poured the last of the wine into Ed's glass. Ed felt a pure, warm gratitude.

'I believe my father's Volga German made him somewhat indispensable, and so we were never sent back as officers usually were after three or four years. They all went, we stayed. A German anomaly in the vast body of the Red Army, somehow outside the *nomenklatura*. My mother would gladly have returned. She missed her family and her circus. She never felt at home in Russian Military City Number Seven.' Kruso sobbed, composed himself, and folded up the Trakl poem, as if that part of his story had been told.

'My parents always spoke both with us, German and Russian, sometimes even Kazakh. Somehow, it was connected to rooms. For example, in the kitchen we spoke German, which is why even today I think Chef Mike must be Russian, but there he is with Viola and her endless Radio Germany ...'

He fell silent and seemed to be thinking.

'It would be good if we could turn off Viola's juice at some point. She brings too much uneasiness, too much nonsense into the building. All her mainland chatter, that has nothing, absolutely nothing to do with us, with us and life here ...'

'It would be a shame,' Ed objected cautiously. 'After all, Violetta, I mean Viola, is the Klausner's oldest inhabitant, and she has the name of a woman who ... I mean, you know, like in *Crime and Punishment*.'

Kruso stared at Ed for several seconds as if he did not exist. Then he continued his story.

'When my father met my mother, she was a circus artist in Karaganda, where there were a lot of ethnic Germans, former Volga Germans. It was a permanent circus, in the city centre, with a large building. She showed us pictures. One was of her in a glittering white costume, she looked so young, like a child, a circus child. My mother was very popular in the army. She performed for all the regiments, Masha, Manyushka, the little mascot, the tightrope walker, an act that every soldier in the victorious Soviet army must have seen at least once in his life, and so on. You know how the Russians love the circus. She taught me a few things, little magic tricks, although

I was too young and too clumsy. Sonya, on the other hand, mastered everything very quickly.

'After I was born, my mother was very ill and didn't perform for a while. She didn't want to go on tour, she didn't want to perform at all, Sonya told me later. Then she took it up again. I'm sure the general, I mean, the man who acted as if he were our father, convinced her to. It was good for him, for his image among the troops. Because not all regiments had halls with high-enough ceilings, she often had to perform outside, on parade grounds that were covered with sand or with the soldiers' narrow mattresses. For a safety net, they would string up camouflage netting between the lampposts around the parade ground — those lamps were always lit, always and everywhere. As they did for ceremonies or parade reviews, the officers sat on the tribune. The soldiers were allowed to gather, company by company ...' Kruso's voice had changed; he was talking about his *Mama*.

'They used Mama's performances as occasions to award distinctions to the officers and soldiers, and sometimes also to deliver punishments. The officer slapped the soldier's face with an open hand, left, right, not more than that. Once, I don't remember where, Mama was suddenly called up front. She seemed completely surprised and also afraid, naturally, and tiptoed in her white ballet shoes across the soldiers' mattresses, which smelled quite foul. She looked like she had come from another planet. She was given the Soviet army's highest honour, a medal of distinction. Our father-general pinned the medal on her himself, I still remember what a hard time he had getting the needle through the silver-spangled costume and that I was afraid for her. In any case, he managed somehow and gave his military salute, he saluted his own petite wife in her silvery leotard, then he kissed her as well, after which his uniform cap sat crookedly on his head for the rest of the presentation. His lopsided cap, his embarrassed smile, and the thousand soldiers around him, the childlike joy in their faces, I believe that she did it all for this ...

'I always sat up front, in the first row. The commander gave me candy, Mischka chocolate, in the blue and white wrapper. On the wrapper was a small picture of three cubs and the mother bear. Sometimes there was ice-cream, too. Often, the smell of garlic from the soldiers' uniforms made me nauseous. Maybe it was fear, too. It wasn't so easy for me to understand why she always had to climb up so high, onto the wire, why she kept putting herself in danger, right in front of me. I couldn't allow myself to think that my mama could fall, or she would fall — that was certain.

'The best option was to think that she would *never* fall, and to think it constantly and to think of nothing else, but that was exhausting and I never managed to keep it up long enough. Evil always seeped in from somewhere, the evil, forbidden thought that had to be destroyed with heavy defences and a league of monsters, for which I invented an entire army, and weapons that couldn't possibly exist, they were so enormous, but somehow the evil always found its way into my head.

'The second best option was to distract myself. To smooth out the candy wrapper, endlessly, with my fingernail. I tried to stop paying so much attention to my mama, but it didn't work. It only worked when I effectively broke off almost all contact with her, all my feelings, and retreated into myself completely, so that the only things left in the world were my fingernail and the Mischka wrapper and nothing else.

'When I was six, she fell, the day after my birthday. I heard a hollow sound. That was the impact. A dull thud, like a sack falling. Suddenly she lay before me on the ground. One of her legs was bent sideways, as if it were no longer hers or as if someone had stuck it onto her body. One of her magic tricks. Her head was stuck between two mattresses, as if she were trying to crawl away, to disappear ...

'Of course, I didn't understand a thing. It was a circus. And I had no choice but to laugh; I laughed. I was caught in the second-best option, without any real contact to Mama, you understand, Ed?'

Like a candy wrapper that had been meticulously smoothed out, Kruso carefully stowed the paper with the Trakl poem in his pants pocket, and, as if he were still caught in the second-best option, he did nothing but look out of the window for a long time.

'A few officers rushed to her side and bent over her. At some point, I was told to stand up. *Wstan, moj maltschik*, they said very softly. My hand was wet, and there was a sticky puddle of melted ice-cream in my lap. It was the third of July 1967. I was six years old. Six years and a day.

'Starting in the early 1970s, the Soviet army flew home its dead. My mother was one of the last ones who remained here. I'm sure she wouldn't have wanted that, after all, she had always wanted to return home. She was carried through the military city in an open coffin, up the Ulica Centralnaja and down to the metal gates, past our house twice, and then to the memorial for officers of the secret police who had fallen in the war. A sergeant marched in front, carrying Mama's medal on a small cushion. He marched in goose-step, so hard that his heels banged on the street, otherwise there was not a sound. I stood on the steps in front of the door, I wasn't allowed any further. Still, I caught a glimpse of her and saw she was wearing a red costume. Adults were buried in red, children in white. That's what my sister told me. She stood next to me the entire time.

'They kissed Mama at the cemetery gate and then again at her grave, that's how they did it. At the graveside, she was saluted, like a high-ranking officer, which was definitely against regulations. A small orchestra played "Loyal Comrades". They didn't sing any songs. My father had them shoot salvos, one salvo after another. Everyone loved her and I loved her, too, I just couldn't kiss her. I don't think anyone judged me for it, except for me. I was ashamed. Instead of laughing, I tried to cry, but it didn't work. I just couldn't escape from the second option. My sister performed little magic tricks at the grave, everything Mama had taught her, without trembling. From that point on, I knew that she was the one I had to hold on to for the rest of my life — not that I thought of it as the rest of my life, but I felt it, felt it very clearly. We had no idea how we could go on without Mama.

'Then the consequences came. The general had probably made too many enemies. It came to light that there had never been any official permission for the tight-rope walker's performances, as they put it. Furthermore, the circus had had a deleterious effect on the soldiers' morals and battle-readiness. That was that. My father was transferred to Russia, but because they needed him or for some other reason, soon he was back again and rather strange. What exactly he does, or where he is, no one knows. We haven't heard from him in a long time. But it doesn't matter, Ed, it doesn't matter at all. When I think of Mama now, I always see the wrapper with the three bears. They're playing on a tree trunk. One is up high, the brave one, the one I always wanted to be. Below is the timid one, who won't climb any higher, and on the ground is the third, standing off to the side and not doing anything, just looking dreamily into the forest. And in the forefront is the mother bear, her mouth wide open, roaring like a wolf. Why she's roaring like that is something I've always asked myself.'

LIPS

Ed turned his face to the side because it was even better that way. The girl hadn't noticed him. He lay in the water as if dead. He could feel stones on his body, the sand, bits of ground-up bricks. The sea enveloped him, flat and sluggish. The sea cradled him. It was the moment to give it all up.

The girl was playing in the waves. She threw herself into the water, not boisterously, but deliberately, she rose languidly and staggered backwards, but only to get a running start. When she'd had enough, she squatted at the edge of the waves, just a few metres away from Ed. Maybe she hadn't noticed him, an animal lurking, a piece of driftwood in the tepid surf. Ed noticed that she enjoyed the way the water played around her ankles. The foam slipped between her legs and wet her swimsuit. She stuck her hand into the sand in front of her and turned it slowly this way and that. Then she held still. She stared at the horizon as if there were something to watch, but neither Møn nor any ships were visible. Ed realised she was passing water at that moment. He briefly caught sight of the narrow, steaming channel in the sand, and saw the passing waves douse and erase it all. Once again, he submerged his face in the water. He waited, but the girl didn't leave.

At a certain point, Ed had no alternative. He turned onto his side so the girl wouldn't see his erection. As if he had to remember laboriously what walking is, he strode stiffly up the beach. He had grown thinner during his stay. His work on the island seemed have made his body more taut, more slender and sinewy, and like all esskays his skin was evenly tanned and shone like bronze when he stepped from the oily steam of the dishwashing station into the open air. He no longer wore a headband. Like Kruso, he wore his longish hair pulled back in a short ponytail. He had never worn it that way before because he hadn't wanted to look like a girl. He used the hairband his friend had left behind in his room.

The midday break wasn't finished yet, but Kruso was already standing at his sink. He lifted his hands from the water and grabbed one of his towels.

'I'm sorry, Ed, it should never have happened. The esskays in charge of distribution ... They're often just too drunk.'

It took Ed a moment to realise Kruso was talking about C.

'Sometimes, it's just too much. I can't oversee everything, and again and again there are problems that come from the interaction between open and centralised allocations ...'

'Is she still on the island?'

'Who?'

'C., the castaway.'

Kruso kept his eyes on Ed.

'I knew it, Ed, I ...'

He took a step — maybe he wanted to hug his disciple — but Ed had quickly turned to face the sink for coarse cleaning, and reached for a pan.

'That's not what it's about, I mean ...'

'What is it about, then, Ed?'

'Nothing.'

'It is only ever about *that*. About what we're all' — he made a broad, sweeping gesture — 'championing.'

Ed nodded. For a moment was amazed at Kruso's acceptance. And along with it, the sudden return of the terminology of centralised allocation in a place so far removed from housing authorities ... But first, he had to breathe, to get some air. He sucked in the dishwashing station's vapours, the iridescent broth in which his hands were circling, a decoction full of strands and clots, a mash of organic scraps. There was no doubt he was about to lose consciousness: C. was still there.

She entered his room quietly, and immediately crawled into his bed. She smelled freshly washed. Her hair was still wet.

'I don't want to bother you.'

'You aren't bothering me.' He would have liked to lie down next to her right away.

'Where did you shower?'

'Don't you know?'

Ed forced himself to stay at the table a bit longer. He read a few more lines, stretched his arm out to the window, took a deep breath, and tried to determine if the light on the horizon was moving. A clean, salt air had blown in to the room with C.

He stood up, paced across the room, turned around, and straightened one of the bricks supporting his table. A delicious sense of anticipation washed over him. He sat at his table and wrote a sentence in his notebook. It was a dirty sentence — he had never written one like it, not even in puberty, when words like 'fucking' and 'shagging' were hardly comprehensible and remained inaccessible as expressions of a darker, coarser world. If it did come up, they would talk of 'boinking', using a warmer, gentler expression, like one that probably came from the Thuringian dialect. 'So did he boink her?' — the question was more tender, more childlike, whereas 'fucking' was a harder, more direct, and cutting matter. Ed remembered discussions in which they'd argued about the difference between 'tart' and 'whore' when they were just fourteen. A strong faction claimed that tarts were only in it for the money. But what they didn't clarify was whether it was possible, for example, to call a tart a whore. Not possible, according to his friend Hagen. According to Hagen's theory, one could assume that whores always did it for free. Ed had his doubts. At any rate, there must be whores somewhere in the world, although it didn't seem all that believable — women who just did it, with anyone and for free. It was almost a miracle. Back then, Ed had eyed every woman in his vicinity. His friends' mothers, neighbours, teachers, the saleswomen in the supermarket. What were the signs, and, above all, what signals were needed to get them to do it with you? That, after all, had been the greatest mystery, and fundamentally still was.

'What are you writing?' C. whispered.

'Nothing. I just have to finish something quickly.' He realised he was playing the intellectual for her benefit, and he was suddenly embarrassed.

'Where are your things?'

'In the forest, under a tarp.'

'There's enough room here.'

'We all have our things there. They'll stay there as long as we can manage to stay here on the island.'

All of a sudden, it became clear to Ed how little he understood about Kruso's larger plan.

'Are you doing well, I mean, how do you like it — here?'

'Very well,' she said softly. She smiled tiredly and turned towards the wall. The shadowy lines of her shoulder blades, upper arms, and hips all seemed to Ed indescribably precious. He took off his things without a sound and nestled against her.

'And can you feel it, the freedom?'

Over the following days, Kruso expanded the scope of his confidence. When they were alone in the dishwashing station, his murmuring sometimes swelled, which caused Ed to move more carefully in an attempt to make less noise, which was almost impossible in the chaos. Kruso's deep, monotone voice seemed to be caught up in the words alone, as if he were speaking only to and for himself, speaking into the sink, into the greasy broth, and not to Ed. The plates, the scrubber, the pots, the Romans, the entire surroundings changed — the dishwashing station turned into an *expression*, an expression of something else that had to be handled with care. For a long time, Ed was unsure if Kruso expected any reaction whatsoever, if his presence made any difference at all, or if the silverware in the sink or the dishwater were more important.

Ed only ever got an indirect answer. The fact that Kruso was reciting his poems to Ed in the dishwashing station was taken by the crew as a sign. Edgar, the new *plongeur* (Rimbaud), was finally accepted. Rimbaud immediately considered Ed part of his audience when he stormed into the dishwashing station with new books and ideas. He often began with as simple and catchy a quote as possible, which he would then write down as 'wisdom of the day' on the slate board with the daily specials. Time and again, there were guests, mostly day tourists, who, in their thoughtless hurry or in complete obliviousness, ordered the daily wisdom. 'Two orders of *Panta rhei*, please,' or 'We'd like *God is dead* ...' Before they had a chance to explain that their order was the result of a mental short circuit — brought on, no doubt, by being in holiday mode — for which they could excuse themselves with a chuckle (although such orders' kinship with a dish called 'Dead Granny' in Saxony was not to be denied), Rimbaud was called over, and he would begin, with complete gravity and without the slightest condescension, to deliver a short speech on 'Panta rhei' or 'God is dead', apologising at the same time for the fact that neither 'Panta rhei' nor 'God is dead' was available as an entrée, 'no, not yet, maybe later, of course under Communism, as we all know, utopias seldom become realities' — thus Rimbaud would wrap up his brief excursus and recommend the stuffed cabbage.

It was not unusual for him to flourish a sales check over the heads of the bewildered guests as if it held his most important notes, but he never looked at the slip. He just used it to direct one long sentence after another in the air over the tables. Most likely, he simply needed a bit of paper between his fingers when he talked, an old habit from his days as a university lecturer in philosophy in Leipzig on the Pleiße.

'Fame, when will you come?'

Without actually waiting for an answer, Rimbaud speared the sales slip on the needle near the cash register, and puffed the question once more from under his moustache, no longer as a question but instead as a little melody:

'Fame, when will you come, will you come, will you come ...'

Since the book dealer's last visit to the bee house, Rimbaud had been leaving books by Antonin Artaud in the nest. 'This season's favourite,' Kruso murmured in the steam of the clean, almost boiling hot water pouring into the sink in a thick stream. The books had titles like *To Have Done with the Judgement of God* or *Van Gogh, the Man Suicided by Society*. Ed had to admit that Rimbaud's readings of Artaud left him at a loss, and he realised how little he knew about matters of poetry, despite his verse hoard. 'There where it smells of shit / it smells of being.' That made sense. However, Ed would never before have imagined that anything like the 'Pursuit of Faecality' was possible — as a poem. 'There is in being / something particularly tempting for man / and this thing is, justly, / CACA.' Surely it sounded different in French. Whatever you thought of this, you could always learn something from Rimbaud.

Even more than Artaud's writing, the pictures of the author in the appendix (taken by a photographer named Georges Pastier) made a deep impression on Ed. He had never seen a man without lips before. Artaud was a man without lips. His chin jutted out, his nose protruded, and instead of a mouth there was only a hollow that drew

a long line that reached almost from ear to ear, actually more of a slit
that sketched the possibility of a mouth. If the writer Antonin Artaud
did, in fact, have lips, then they had to be internal lips; that is, he had
spoken with internal lips. Ed could only remember seeing a similar
physiognomy, although not in this extreme form, on the famous
author Heiner Müller, held in high esteem by those esskays who read
books, who was meant to have said — constantly quoted by Rimbaud
— 'Artaud, the language of torment!' This, again, immediately made
sense to Ed. At this point, it would have been Rimbaud's privilege to
establish the connection and point out the correlation between lips
and literature, but instead he quoted Müller again: 'Read on the ruins
of Europe, Artaud's texts will be classics.'

Would, for example, a literature of the thin-lipped and the lipless
make any sense then? Ed's question annoyed Rimbaud. And Ed
conceded the point. His objection was primitive and an expression
of his high spirits. Yes, Ed was feeling high-spirited. He was, in fact,
filled with primitive elation, because he was the man who had had C.
And C. had lips, endless lips.

THE TRANSFORMATION

20 July. '... suddenly starts whispering, gets out of bed, sings, and does a few awkward dance steps, with a gleam in her eyes. Or when she goes to the toilet in the middle of the night, feeling her way out into the hallway and raises her arm in the air, softly snapping her long fingers, snip, snap, snip, like steps in the air ... That is, she doesn't do it for my benefit, not for me to see. Sometimes, we just lay very still and ... How can I put it? I don't believe it has anything to do with me, and probably not with us, only with her.'

'Very possible, Ed.'

'I've never been cheerful that way.'

'You're cheerful in a different way.'

'Not since G., old rascal.'

'You found Kruso. You found me. You're not completely alone in the world.'

'There's something I haven't told you.'

'Please, Ed. You know I'm just lying here, in this pleasant cave by the sea, gradually becoming one with the tides. And you come visit and talk to me, I mean, that's the best that could happen to me, Good

Lord, I mean, a fox *in my situation* ...'

'It was our first morning together. C. like a vision in my bed. As
if I'd imagined her. When she pulls her hair back behind her ear and
looks out at the sea ... With complete aplomb, you know? She says
she doesn't do anything to her hair, no particular cut, just her hair, like
her bangs, which she trims herself, maybe with her pocket knife. So
she looks out the window, and her face has this pre-Christmas glow,
and everything glows with it, the horizon, the pine trees, everything.
Then she suddenly asks me, if I like it better *this* way.' Ed blushed.

'You were asleep when she came into your room, right? It was all
a dream and everything you did was ...'

'A dream. But still, I thought she wouldn't have come back *because
of that.*'

'I understand.'

'Yes, you understand.'

'In a certain way, she was the first.'

'Yes, damn it.'

'So you'll think of her now whatever happens next, my friend. She
is your debut, your confirmation, and the album that goes with it, in
which you will gather all your pictures to come.'

'All this has nothing to do with G.'

'No, Ed, nothing at all.'

'Everything with her remains ...'

'Untouched.'

'Yesterday, we were on the beach. C. was drawing. She always
carries a little sketchbook with her, and her tiny pocketknife to
sharpen her pencil — it always has to be very sharp, so she's always
sharpening ...'

'Tell me, Ed.'

'At some point, C. wanted to go to the island cinema. That
afternoon, *Little Matten and the White Shell* was playing. In the
evening, it was *Bear Ye Another's Burden*, and the late show was *Until
Death Do Us Part.*'

'We live in biblical times.'

'And the first plague is already here. An entire company of exterminators are fumigating the Klausner. That's the only reason I'm able to be here with you now.'

'Thanks to the roaches.'

'When C. and I came back from the cinema, the premises had already been cleared. A few slept on the consecrated spots, and a few throughout Kruso's distribution network. The news didn't reach us. Nothing was cordoned off, everything looked the same. Maybe the heat had also made us blind.'

'You're telling me, Ed.'

Only then did Ed notice the agitation with which the fox was looking at him. Inside its little bony eye-sockets was a kind of semolina porridge that seemed to be stirring itself.

'Oh, you old rascal, oh dear, I'm sorry ...' Ed hurried to the water and grabbed a handful of sand from between the stones.

'Sandman, dear Sandman ...'

'I beg your pardon, Mr Fox!' Ed tried to joke as he carefully let the sand fill the fox's eye-sockets, first left, then right. His friend sighed with relief.

'Forty degrees in the sun, and I had my window closed because of the storm Viola was always warning us about. Once an hour, there was something about storms from the north-west, and refugees in the embassies, but no one was really listening. As if we were somewhere *beyond the news*, and I believe that's how it is, old rascal, we are not of this world. In my room, it must have been at least fifty or sixty degrees. Even from the stairs, I heard a kind of rustling, like silk, or as if someone were secretly unwrapping a present. I said something about airing out the room, opening the window, fresh air, looking forward to it with all my heart. I turned the light on and ...'

'What?'

'Something you don't understand just seeing it. First an explosion, silent, with no centre. You only see the thick brown wave spreading in all directions, everything is flowing, the wall like a wave is how I'd put it, and you see it reach the corner and pile up, a gleaming, seething foam, crackling somehow ... You know, I'm not afraid of cockroaches. And I don't think C. was either. But we still screamed, both of us, as if we were being skewered. I went at them with my arm over my face, like in war. I was filled with rage, real rage, and all of a sudden I was holding my big notebook. I just started hitting, non-stop, with sweat running off me, and when I looked around ...'

'What, Ed?'

'Not sure if I can ...'

'You can do it, Ed, you can.'

'I'd rather not.'

'Do it the way people talk about things they want to keep at a certain distance. They use a different person — he, you, she, it.'

'You mean because they feel it all too deeply?'

'Not necessarily.'

'Keep a certain distance.'

'So what does he see then, our friend?'

'He turns around and sees that C. is also thrashing about like crazy. She's using her sandals. With each awkward blow, she gives a compact little war cry, with the same stress in her voice as women tennis players have when they serve. It always sounds a little desperate, but on the other hand it's a pure expression of will, you see?'

'And?'

'And then we started our, ummh, they started their joint hunt. They hammered all over the place, they shot their way free, so to speak. Her sharp bang-bang, his loud smack-smack, small calibre and large, almost like music, as if they were Bonnie and Clyde. And suddenly she broke out laughing. She lay on the bed, staring at me, and laughed ... Sorry, I'm saying "I" again. I can't get the story together any other way. I'll say "I", and maybe you could think "he"?'

'I is another.'

'Rimbaud says that that's only true in French. And only in an earlier time, when people still knew what another is.'

'In French?'

'Yes, you little rotting psychic, that's the point.'

'I thought so.'

'The laughter just burst out of her. She lay there, on the bed, flailing with her arms and kicking her heels against her rear-end. Her entire body rose and fell, and her shoulders twitched, that is, she laughed and screamed at the same time, she screamed, "Yes, Yeeesss!" and "Crazy!" and "Aaaah!", and then she started hiccupping. A deadly fit of hiccupping. Hiccupping like I've never seen before.'

Ed's shoulders were also twitching.

'Maybe it was the shock. After a while, she could only pant. Her eyes were getting bigger and bigger. She looked like a clown, her eyebrows raised high, and I started to get worried.'

'Not surprising, Ed.'

'You know, I've had experience with cockroaches. From my time in the army. Eighteen months with the little beasts in my room. They came in through the heating pipes, right from the Leunawerke chemical factory into the barracks. The old ones were really fat, probably mutants, chemically resistant over generations. But after a few weeks, I knew how they behaved. I knew them, you could almost say, I knew how they *thought*. For example, I knew that their complicated little bodies reacted to air pressure, I mean, to the most minute changes. They know even when I'm just starting to lift my notebook. When I turn a page, they can feel it in their hiding places, and I'm sure they register every word I write, word for word, translated into the tiniest frequencies. In a certain sense, they were like readers. They not only knew my chocolate or the dirty laundry in my closet in the most minute particulars, they also knew what was in my letters home and my euphoric attempts to write poems, word for word ...'

'You squashed your readers.'

'The secret is: never aim to hit where they are. No, you always pound right in their escape path. And C. caught on when she saw me on my rampage. And when I realised she'd understood my experience, my assurance, I no longer felt any disgust, on the contrary, it was intoxicating. Through C., we'd somehow become allied, the vermin and I, hunter and hunted, the old communal fate.'

Ed took a breath. Something moved in his fox's eyes — something like interest, Ed thought.

'Naturally, you can't compare it to the three or four cockroaches in my army locker. They were always there even long after I stopped keeping anything edible in the food compartment. Sometimes, I thought it was always the same ones, and waxed a little sentimental, probably from being confined. Even though I'd already killed hundreds. It was almost part of our morning exercises. Before we went on leave, we had to assemble for roll call. Two steps forward, open bags, and dump out clothes. "Shake, shake your bags!" — that was the sergeant major, Unterfeldwebel Zwaika, a bloated lump. He could barely speak and could hardly see, he forced everything through his nose. I think it was his only idea. There were no regulations or anything about this. "Doan' wanna give your woman a heart attack" — that sentence was muttered before every leave. He probably meant well.'

'Now you're avoiding the subject.'

'In a hiccupping fit, you hold your breath, raise your arms, and so on. But C. was only twitching and not making any sound. So it was an emergency, I'd say.'

'An emergency?'

'Yes, as if she were grabbing the first available lifeline.'

His fox groaned softly.

'I said, someone thinks *a lot* of you.' I mean, I was completely helpless.

'Yeah-ack,' she said, and pulled me to the bed. Around my feet, there was a sound like a thousand munching caterpillars, but the flood gradually drained away, and the noise slowly faded away. Then there was just C. and her soft smacking noise, very soft, just that, nothing else. Everything around me was soft, like velvet, and suddenly, no idea how — suddenly I could do it. I could look in her eyes while I was doing it.'

Ed fell silent.

The sea had begun breathing again with its dark foundation and light overtones. It was almost cool. Ed pictured C. His hand on her head. Her eyes, her high, sweaty, somehow egg-shaped forehead and her hair that she didn't do anything to. Just stroking his thighs, just hooking him into her circuit of energy. A few hairs were stuck on his cock, and took on the current. A faint dizziness, as if she had lifted him, very gently, over the border.

'These bugs, Ed ...'

'I believe it was the only way, I mean, at that moment ...'

'... they transformed you, right?'

THE KRUSO ENERGY

In their intimacy founded on poems, Kruso and Ed had found each other, and each passing day strengthened their companionship. Kruso now joined in the closing-shift cleaning of the dishwashing station, and often even took over rolling the bin with the food scraps outside — all tasks that had obviously fallen to Ed as the Klausner's most recent hire. When Kruso sprayed down the station, Ed leapt about like a dervish, the short scrubbers in hand. In a manner only Ed was capable of, he seemed to stop mid-stride with the rinsing spray from the tap on his heels — it was a kind of dance, a prelude to the evening. In the end, Ed dried the floor with a rag; Losh rolled up the hose. Following a sudden inspiration, he put his foot on Ed's head, but without any pressure. Ed grabbed the foot and leant it weight.

On the whole, it was more than closeness and more than confidence. Essentially, it was a common alienation that underlay their friendship. That both were unable to speak about what weighed most heavily on their souls seemed to bind them closer than any confession. They simply didn't have the words, and understanding meant not deceiving themselves about it. In any case, nothing could be rectified. The source of their unhappiness (which also determined their actions) was better off elevated in a poem. They had recited Trakl's 'Sonya' to each other, and Losh had given Ed the photograph, the beautiful smile in the worn plastic envelope, in which Ed also recognised G.

Often, too often, Ed had held the photograph and touched himself. When he looked deeply into the young woman's eyes, his story and Kruso's became entwined. 'That you're not completely alone in this world,' Ed whispered, and kissed the photograph's pale cover. He was immediately ashamed and felt his feelings drain away. He couldn't have loved G. all that much if he was already no longer able to recall her features exactly. On the other hand, he was now able to think of her without the tram. He could see her sitting in her chair. She was speaking to him. Her mouth moved, but he couldn't hear her. She was serious, and what she was trying to tell him seemed important. In the middle of a sentence and without taking her eyes from his, she reached behind herself and rubbed a leaf of her lemon geranium. The room filled with the lemon scent, and Ed felt his heart constrict. He stood in the cool pit of a well, surrounded by walls made of dead verse, huge gravestones thickly covered with writing that had consumed his pain and transformed it: into distance.

Through the smudged window, Ed watched Kruso as he inspected the food-scrap bin and stuck his hand in it now and again. Although (or because) he had hardly slept since C. had been staying in his room and although (or because) his eyes were now filled with tears and his grief could return, he felt safe in the dishwashing station. He contemplated what had stuck on the sides of the sink from the ablutions: a few hair elastics, pine-needle bath oil, the wrapper from a bar of Palace Hotel soap. The washcloths on the line strung between the shelves were still damp. Only with great effort did Ed resist the temptation to bury his face in them.

When Ed came up to his room from the shower, a sheet of the old Klausner stationery lay on his bed. Bit by bit, he had got to know the poems that Kruso, as he was fond of repeating, wanted to collect into a volume. 'There is nothing better than putting together a volume!' At first, Ed regularly found a poem on the foot of his bed; then on his pillow, in the middle of the hollow left by his head — in place of my head, he thought.

He would picture it when he was still in the shower: the yellowed paper with the lines unevenly lined up to the right or left and the letters with the bloody caps. He pictured Kruso entering his room. Ed imagined it as a kind of mark of respect; as if his friend gave a bow when he set the poem down — Ed could let himself go that far as the water rushed over his ears, and he abandoned his body completely to the joy of being where he was.

Møn was visible. Ed tried Speiche's glasses, which still lay on the sink. He couldn't have explained why. He rinsed the lenses and rubbed them clean with the hand towel. For the first time, he saw the fine white line of surf in front of the chalk cliffs. And the forest along the coast, a dark stripe, fifty kilometres away.

'Ah, Speiche,' Kruso called. He was suddenly standing in the room. He had brought his white wine. He offered some to Ed, took a swig, and sucked in his cheeks — his eyelid was stuck at half-mast. He rubbed a hand over his face as if he were already tired, but it just signalled the beginning of his speech.

'You work in the dishwashing station. You repeat everything into the sink a hundred times, as many times as it takes to get it right. Actually, what you'd most like is to sink completely, to be submerged, but in the meantime the little circles your hands make in the water are enough. Add to that the muffled, barely audible sounds from underwater. The swaying to the right and left when a plate sinks to the bottom, sinks like a ship. From this the position of your verse.

Or the muffled sound when something hits bottom, stacks of it. You can save it all, clean it, pile it up, dry it — every noise is a cavern, a language, Ed. You understand this, you live amidst noise. And that's the only reason you ask what it means: you have to say it all one hundred times, to yourself. You can forget what the words mean. Let's call it shattering the semiotic triangle. At first, you can hardly stand it: the clinking of glasses, of cups, the clattering of plates, the rattling of silverware, then the intolerable heat, the sultriness, the filth, the grease, the dizziness and nausea ... An enormous loss, that's what it feels like. But nothing is really lost, no one is, Ed, *no one*. You just keep on talking softly to yourself, with your own voice, you knock at the words' door with your voice. Hundreds of times, to yourself. And at some point, you'll hear it ...'

Losh's innocent tone. It would hardly have sounded different in front of the map of truth — biblical, chant-like. Ed began to understand, in the core of his memory hoard, what it might be about. Poetry was resistance. And a path to salvation. A terrible possibility. Kruso showed Ed the books, the collection of at most twenty books he called his 'library'. Among them were writers like Lev Shestov and Gennady Vorsterberg, whom Ed had never heard of, and others like Babeuf, Bloch, Castaneda.

'Thinking makes things ridiculous, Ed. Everything becomes an anecdote. We never reach poetry's innermost core. The surrealists are ridiculous, too, because they tried to solve the problem through technique, not to mention the Dadaists, who destroy everything and then lie in wait for someone to come and claim that it has meaning. But what we need is our voice — it's music, it listens for the words of the world. What we need is our voice and a space filled with absence — a place in which to reclaim time.' Kruso's large, open hand gestured towards the room's floor: the ground opened up, a few walls turned like pages, and Ed saw the dishwashing station. He saw two poets, next to each other, standing at their sinks. One great poet, who in the future would walk in and out of the world's best publishing houses, and a second poet, wrapped in a sheet like a toga with a handful of aluminium cutlery in his hand, with which he actually knew how to write and steadfastly took notes at the great poet's side.

Ed treasured Kruso's confidence, and, although Kruso might forget him now and then during his speeches, Ed didn't care. He could have listened to Kruso for hours. His voice bathed the world in a new light. Essentially, it was all attitude, no more and no less, a complicated form of existence that was, at the same time, the only possible one. Kruso's being was attitude, and it was all Kruso — a strange mixture of severity, almost chasteness, and self-control on the one hand, and on the other, resolve, almost fanaticism, and a penchant for the fantastic and the illicit. A chaste fanaticism, if such a thing was possible, a striking blend of innocence and absoluteness, which no doubt also won over the esskays. On top of that was his saintly earnestness, a silently vibrating aura, or, how to put it, the Kruso energy.

Everything could be valuable, everything meaningful. As if it were just a matter of hearing, of seeing, of living, from this very moment on. The possibility of finding a line, a word that rang true was hidden everywhere around him. Even work in the wasteland of the dishwashing station obtained a new gravity. The driftwood, the oven, the pig-slop bin, the most trivial details of catering, it could all become part of a poem. An individual voice, an individual tone — it was a light, a lighthouse, from which Ed now always took his bearings. The word 'conquer' flitted through Ed's mind.

For a moment, Ed wondered if Kruso was present at the ablutions. He wondered if Kruso had seen them all, touched them all, if he washed them with his expert hands and if he used washcloths to do so. Ed pictured C. crouched in his sink, the sink for coarse cleaning. He pictured her long, flawless back, the endless row of her vertebrae. He pictured the white tips of her knees in front of her breasts, her hands pressed against the bottom of the sink. And he pictured Kruso walking from sink to sink, handing out fresh little bars of Palace Hotel soap.

THE CONCERT

There was no one in the bunker. Ed had wanted to go alone, to clear his head, but after just a few steps he was declaiming to the waves at his feet. 'This is the autumn that will break your heart' or 'Don't cry for me Argentina', lyrics from hit songs on his parents' magnetic tapes.

At first, his father had tried to cut out the chatter of Jauch or Gottschalk, the unspeakable propensity of radio announcers to talk over a song's opening — it made his father suffer, and nothing could ease that pain. He knelt in front of the tape recorder, one finger on 'Play' and a second, already cramping finger on the fire-engine-red 'Record' button. His torso was leaning into the wall unit, the universe above him curved by the strain in his two index fingers. Both buttons on his infinitely precious Tesla B56 (later B100) pressed down at the exact same moment, but then Jauch had to say one more thing. 'Loud mouth!' his father roared. He believed the chatter was pure chicanery. Then, at last, the soft clicking, the tape started to move with its own particular delay, which often caused yet another second to be lost: '... cry for me Argentina'.

The door was gone, only a gap was left, through which Ed reached

a small space filled with excrement and scraps of newspaper. Before
he ducked out again, he heard the voice. It was Cavallo, standing on
the bluff above him. Could Cavallo have followed him, Ed wondered,
but rejected the idea. Cavallo was leading someone over the grassland
to the dump, which was so thickly beset with seagulls you could only
guess at its contours. When they followed the access road into the
hollow, the birds rose reluctantly, and with them a heart-stopping
stench, thick and stifling with rot.

Then Ed heard a rumbling, and with it a kind of song without
voices, more of a croaking, like the seagulls and their pitiful cries.

'They even got a licence to perform from the local council,' Cavallo
was explaining as Ed caught up. Ahead of them, the sea gleamed
through a swath between the moraines that reminded Ed of Celtic
royal tombs. The sun had turned and begun its daily drama of descent.

They were greeted exuberantly, cheek against cheek, by people Ed
hardly knew. Then Kruso's cheek, too.

'Where were you?'

'Why?'

'Why are you so late?'

Ed wanted to make a joke about his complete lack of a sense of
direction, but Kruso immediately interrupted him.

'Please, not again, Ed.'

The evening was a chaotic jumble of various performances, drinks,
and nervous jumping around. In the centre was a four-man band,
their guitars and electric organs hooked up to an old car battery. The
electric organ was set up on a hard suitcase, in front of which a pale,
thin boy was kneeling and staring apathetically through his overly
large glasses. Bottles gleamed in the dune grass: Stralsunder, Stierblut,
Strangler, and Kirsch-Whisky, too, as far as Ed could make out. The
drum kit was half buried in sand, and a metal cart had been made into
a kick drum. Ed recognised Chef Mike's Stern tape recorder, which
they were using as an amplifier for the guitar. A campfire burned not
far from the band, and a few esskays fed it with wood as eagerly and

conscientiously as if this were the most important job they could ever have in life.

Ed felt disgust and a touch of contempt. He wished he were back in his room. All he wanted to do was wait there, just wait, wait for C. Maybe they would sleep outside this time, between the moraines, for one or two nights, until the poison of the exterminators ... Cavallo pressed a bottle of Stierblut into Ed's hand.

The singer of the band had started to give a wild, rambling speech. He pushed the Hiddensee cart around in a circle, calling it the 'machine' and repeatedly ramming it into the small group of esskays, who leapt aside, shouting and laughing. Now and again, one would fall into the cart (when the singer's aim was right) and quickly jump out again. 'The machine, the machine, is in league with the god of the sea ...' the singer crowed. He seemed deadly serious. He wore brown, worn lederhosen, and his upper body was bare but for a bandanna around his neck and a leather wristband on his left arm. Ed could barely understand him. The song mainly seemed to be about a drink someone was supposed to mix for him. 'Mix me a drink, that will take me somewhere else': it was more croaking and squawking, with no rhythm or melody. Ed stood in the half-darkness just outside the periphery of the yellow-reddish light that flickered over the dance floor as if it were part of the campfire. The dune smelled of sweat. Ed thought of cockroaches. The mugginess had returned, and the dancers took off their clothes.

When the band stopped and the punks and bluesers among the esskays had finished their tired applause, a man with Asian features stepped shyly into their midst. He elaborately placed a cassette in Chef Mike's tape recorder and started to dance. Cavallo, who had returned to Ed's side, whispered 'Dance of the Khmer' into his ear. 'Scenes from the Apsara Dance,' added an esskay, standing behind Ed and breathing down the back of his neck, 'from Cam-bod-ja, *capito*?'

Like everyone else, the Cambodian was barefoot, and like the bluesers he swung his long black hair, only he looked less desperate while doing so. His dance was a dance of pride and sensuality. In the middle of the song, Kruso stepped out on the dance floor and went to hug the dancer but made him lose his balance. The dancer stumbled right into the reeking crowd of esskays, who lifted his small, slender body right into the air, like a victor. Enthusiastic cheers, from Ed, too. The little Cambodian's large white teeth flashed above their heads.

Then Kruso gave a sign, and his reading began in slow, dragging rhythms and with all the unbelievable tension inherent in his broad-shouldered body. The book's title was *The Night of Lead*; it was the same leaden darkness that sank over the gathering at that moment.

Kruso's voice. Kruso's tone.

The hypnosis lasted long after Kruso had shut the book. The sea rustled softly and cautiously: 'You can adopt my tone.' A line that seemed to come from beyond. A core formed within the rustling, and suddenly there was order and discipline. Ed's heart pumped, his eyes shone, he entered into a state of promise.

Kruso pulled a small bundle of notes from his pocket and put it in Ed's hand. 'The program for Island Day.' He hardly needed to raise his voice, it was so quiet. And, as if it always were his task, Ed distributed the small handwritten pages to the esskays.

'What is to come, what has been prophesied?' the singer croaked, and the band started up again. The song seemed to be well known. Shouts of 'Bap-tism, bap-tism, ba-aa-ap-tism!' rose, individually at first, and then in chorus, whereupon the singer pushed the metal cart (the machine) into the middle of the space:

'Go forward, youth, youth take hold
break your own path.
No compulsion, no drill, only your free will,
to determine your future hencefo-o-o-orth ...'

Ed shuddered. It took a while before someone was ready. Ed noticed that a girl tried to hold that person back, but the lederhosen-clad croaker immediately put his hand on the sacrificial victim's (Ed thought of sacrifice) shoulder and it was sealed.

'Go forward youth, go forward youth,
look freely into the light
that will never lack ...'

The band started playing a furious, hammering rhythm. The victim, who wore nothing more than bathing trunks, willingly let helpers tie him to the machine with his arms bent backwards. His legs were bound crisscross to the shaft. Finally, the esskay who had acted as a kind of assistant the entire time and who was wearing only an apron (and who, like an Aztec or a labourer in antiquity, had pulled the cloth tight between his legs, pulling his genitals upwards and pressing them into a shapeless something) put a tube with a small red funnel on the other end into the victim's mouth. He slowly turned in a circle.

'Charitable donation, charitable donation,' he murmured, and everyone around him tilted the necks of their bottles towards him. He himself offered a swallow of champagne. 'Slowly, slowly, friends,' the one wearing the apron said, and after each donation he lifted the funnel into the air in a kind of victory sign.

During the entire process, the cart was raised and lowered in a quick, almost measured rhythm. Despite the sandy surface, the vehicle, with its large wheels and thin tyres bounced high into the air with each bump. The victim's girlfriend alternately whimpered and giggled. She seemed to be drunk. In the meantime, Ed had recognised the victim. He was a dishwasher in Norderende, the very esskay who had whispered the word *Crusoe* like a secret message at Ed when he first arrived on the island.

The machine was not used for long. In an extended procession, the dishwasher was wheeled down to the shore. Ed felt his stomach tighten.

The cart was pushed into the sea, as far out as the ceremony seemed to require — there was hollering, and among the white caps the dishwasher's body was soon drenched, gleaming darkly as the cart hit a rock and tipped over.

With each new wave, the man's head was underwater; the esskays at the drawbar could hardly control their laughter. The dishwasher also seemed to be laughing, at the top of his voice, or shouting for help — it was hard to tell with the noise of the surf. In his euphoria, the man in the apron started pouring the rest of the champagne into the waves. 'Go forward youth, youth go forward ...'

In two, three bounds — faster, in any case, than Ed or anyone else could grasp what was happening — Kruso had crossed the beach. With the flat of his hand, he slapped the man in the apron so hard that he fell right down and lay sprawled. Then Kruso grabbed the cart, but its frame was already sunk in the sand. A few of the esskays, who seconds before had been laughing, leapt to help him. They grabbed the fetters and straps that hung down the side. 'No-one, no-one ...' Kruso yelled, setting the rhythm.

'This is surely not how you imagined life on the island?'

'A lot has changed,' Ed countered.

Kruso had no doubt recognised him by his step. Or he was simply sure that it must be Ed who had hurried after him. For a while, they walked together without speaking. Ed's courageous friend seemed completely calm. He was carrying the book, and Ed wondered where it could have been the whole time.

A salty spray hit them in the face. Moonlight gleamed in the stones on the shore. A few sentences whirled in Ed's head; suddenly he had a *good feeling*. But before he could speak about C. (and maybe even G.), Kruso offered his explanation.

'They call it slamming. When the machine crashes on the ground, the mixture explodes — schnapps and champagne — right into the brain. It's like being shot into another world. You don't need much alcohol for it, the effect has to do with physics, not chemistry, you see, Ed?'

'I never was any good at physics,' Ed answered, embarrassed by the intensity of his desire to speak with Kruso.

'Before they called it Mass. They did it once a week. Somehow, it always ends in the water. For them, it's about the sea, which they revere, pray to, and so on. Primitive, but understandable. For their old singer, slamming was about gear changes, circuits in the brain, consciousness-expanding brain programming, and such things. But he left the country last year. Since then, it's gone downhill. Even the Buddhist tree ...'

'The Buddhist tree?'

'Yes. A tree with a hundred arms, branches, to be exact. One of a kind, a marvellous tree. Some say it's an enchanted tree. It's on the Capri-path, right on the coast. They use it for their acceptance ritual. They sit up there. They drink and wait to see who falls first. Almost everyone is caught, and nothing happens. They claim the tree brings luck to everyone who needs it. But I really advise you against it, Ed. You don't need to do it. By now, they know you and accept you.'

Kruso's concern. Ed was touched.

'A lot has changed,' he began again.

'You're right. We get to our poems less and less often, isn't that right?'

'Our holiness!'

Ed's answer was too quick. A crazy mixture of rejection and inclination.

'I know why you're here, Ed.'

Ed was silent. Then his gaze clouded over. He was simply exhausted. The sleepless nights had made him thin-skinned. But the wind dried his eyes, and he began to speak almost despite himself.

'The photograph of your sister, Losh. It reminds me of G., my girlfriend, who was run over by a tram a year ago. I know it's crazy, but sometimes I have the feeling we lost the same person.'

Kruso stiffened, in so far as that was possible when walking over a rocky beach.

'You're not a castaway, Ed.'

'I'm not?'

'No. Two nights before you arrived, I dreamt you were coming. I saw you coming. As was written: "now was the time to get me a servant, and, perhaps, a companion or assistant". Kruso turned his face to the wind and laid a hand on Ed's shoulder. He gave a soft chuckle, but maybe Ed had misheard and it was a sigh or even nothing at all.

'That's just Defoe, Ed, don't worry. For Robinson, Friday is the guide, at least he dreams that Friday's one. A guide who helps him get off his island, get away from his bad luck. In his dream, it's Friday who shows him which places to avoid so as not to be eaten, where he can venture or where he can't, and how to get food ...'

'But that's not how the story goes. In the book, Crusoe rescues Friday, the story is exactly the opposite.'

'Are you sure?'

'Maybe you saw me in the port the day I arrived?'

'No, Ed, just in a dream. At first, I naturally had doubts. But the poems confirmed everything.'

Ed was careful to walk so that his friend's hand wouldn't slip from his shoulder. He considered the fact that it was impossible to see down to the beach from any of the Klausner's windows. He had noticed this a few days earlier. Until then, he must have been blind. And he must have been imagining things on the day of the allocation when he saw the beach and the barracks through Kruso's binoculars, under Kruso's hand.

His friend was walking on the coast side and so seemed even taller. By simply turning his head, Ed could have lain it on Kruso's chest. He noticed that Kruso was also trying to walk at an even pace, which was difficult on the steep beach. Ed's shoes (Speiche's, to be exact; he'd been wearing them for several days) were completely soaked because he had walked through the gently rolling fringes of the waves instead of swerving around them.

Kruso looked at him.

Or he looked right past him at the lights of a patrol boat that passed them at the time.

Or he looked at the tiny lights further out, in the channels of the deep-sea vessels and ferries to Sweden that passed as slowly as years. Ed felt the hand on his shoulder clench. He turned his head and felt, at that very moment, Kruso's lips on his face.

THE SPRITE MARÉN

... still, so still as if only the house were listening to the rushing sound of the pines that was taken up by the surf, softly, muted, then thematically elaborated and varied by the stone sinks and amplified by the metal sinks, which sounded like drums under the falling water with their dark rumbling, a domestic sound that cocooned Ed in a sense of well-being and contentment because it was *like back at home*; the hollow sound of water flowing into the bathtub, and the humming of the flash heater heard from the living room or his bedroom, Fridays at six p.m., immersed in the rushing sound.

But this was not his childhood bath day, the best evening of the week; it was simply: this night. Nights were announced by the drumming of the washing, which was followed by the sound of steps on the stairs. There was rarely any whispering, just the soft closing of doors, everyone knew their way, and that was one of the mysteries for Ed. Only then, gradually, did Viola re-emerge, the 'Evening Concert'; later, the newscaster's voice, differently constituted than during the day since he had to speak against darkness and sleep — the man in the studio, therefore, stressed certain words and let others fade almost completely, with long pauses between them and with the sound of papers being shuffled this way and that as if the speaker were desperately searching for the next sentence or choosing it only then. Yes, he's alone in the night, alone with his voice, Ed thought. Ed thought of C. and thought *I want*, and he knew what exactly he wanted to do, and also what next and next and next.

He went to the door once again and listened.

The news followed the 'Night Radio'. A new report on refugees in Hungary, more crossing the border daily, certain words repeated over and over again, or were they just particularly audible amid Viola's fluctuations: embassy, special envoy, sanitary conditions. Ed lit a candle, blew out the match, and swore. His lips had brushed against its tip. 'A north-west stream of cool sea air is flowing towards Germany. The eastern edge of an almost stationary high over the eastern Atlantic and associated disturbances will bring changeable weather over the coming days.' Ed felt ill. Viola loved the weather forecast, the only report she fished from the ether.

The door opened, soft and strange. In the flickering candlelight, the gable in his room receded, but the stained wall slid upwards again and again, slowly at first, then faster. Ed hastily put his hand on the light switch.

'Who are you?'

'I'm Marén.'

She was small. She had short, curly hair and the face of a sprite.

'Marén. You got the wrong door.'

'I don't think so.' She looked at the floor, then back up at Ed or past him, at the window, as if she already knew that this would be the most difficult moment.

'Where's C.?' Ed asked.

He was only imagining this sprite, and he hoped C. would still appear or would suddenly emerge from its tiny body.

The young woman's face cleared. 'Yes, in the afternoon she was still there, in the forest, but not for the soup in the evening. She had

accommodation with us for a long time, longer than any of us, I
believe. Her time must be up.'

Gliding as in a dream, the sprite Marén moved to his bed. As if she
were following some higher law that Ed was bound to recall sooner
or later. She began to take her dress off smoothly and carefully, all the
while avoiding looking at Ed.

'And you're Edgar, right?'

Ed marched. He could feel it on his arms, his chest, all over his
skin — something was going to explode. His lust was now external,
and he marched straight through a space in which his wounds were
glowing. They were so raw and sensitive that everything hurt, both
what he touched and what he did not touch. The underbrush hit
him in the face, branches that broke underfoot — the forest smelled
of rot.

Too dark, but he could feel the sleep that filled the base of the
valley. He drew closer and recognised the outlines of sleepers, the
shimmer of a plastic tarp, sleeping bags, the sound of breathing,
twitching in dreams. *Buried alive*, Ed thought, and the image of a
mass grave overwhelmed him. As if compelled, Ed took another
step, then someone grabbed him from behind and pulled him to
the ground. Ed tasted Kruso. Kruso's lotion, Kruso's hand over his
face. In the hollow, the bulb of a tiny light flashed and went out. Ed
groaned softly, and Kruso uncovered his mouth.

'Where is C.?'

'Did you think she could stay here forever?'

'I just want to know where she is.'

'Don't be childish, Ed.'

'And the sprite's got to disappear from my room.'

'Your room? Who do you think you are? It's one of the Klausner's
rooms, one of its choicest cabins. Don't ever forget it. C. had five days,
more than anyone else here, you don't seem to have noticed. Who do
you think made that happen?'

'I want ...'

'Yes, Ed, you want. And yes, I have to say, we were surprised after what we understood from you. No allocations to Ed, those were the instructions.'

'You choose your own castaway, you said.'

'Sure, Ed. *The first time.*'

Kruso gestured toward the sleepers' grave. 'The allocation has to have criteria, it has to be just and disciplined, or else there's no sense, you understand? Freedom and order are always colliding on our path. Don't ever forget how you yourself were accepted. You found yourself a cave here. You've thought only of yourself for long enough.'

Ed's throat tightened. He wanted to lunge at Kruso, and immediately felt ashamed. He could hardly breathe. He had lost his best friend — in one second. Now he was simply tolerated. Not even.

'Of course, you're free to go at any time. I can't stop you.'

In his friend's eyes, Ed had failed; even though he had always done everything. He had been a good companion, the best. It was as if Kruso had stripped everything away with a single sentence.

'You dreamt me up.'

'And now you're a part of the Klausner, is that not a dream?'

In the courtyard, all was still. There were no lights on in the dishwashing station, just the small violet fluorescent light on the bar shelves. They sat at the waiters' table under the window. Kruso tipped Kirsch-Whisky into a coffee cup. He had put an arm around Ed's shoulders and led him slowly, like an injured man, back to the Klausner. Ed shivered, and his teeth clicked against the porcelain. As if his body were registering the withdrawal right then. Insanity still flickered in his eyes, but his anger had evaporated. He blew puffs of breath into his cup. As if it had only been about finding Losh. Only about that. Not C. And not G. either.

'You should have stayed in your room.'

Losh sounded worried.

'You like being there. Of all of us, you're the one who spends the most time in his room, and it can stay that way.'

Inside the Kirsch-Whisky it was warm and good. As if the Kirsch-Whisky had drunk him. When he raised his head, he noticed a pair of slender, bare feet under the next table. Someone is lying there asleep, Ed thought. Everyone just needs a place to sleep, shelter, accommodation where ...

'Is C. safe?'

'She's fine, Ed. She had her time.'

'Is she coming back?' The refrigeration unit started up with a jerk and set the glasses in the bar rattling. The steel jugs gleamed in the half-light as if freshly polished. Ed knew they were brown and crusted over inside, some almost black.

'She's not really gone. Now she's one of us. Those who have been enlightened all stay in contact, every man, every woman.'

Ed exhaled and pushed his cup into the middle of the table. He hadn't exactly understood. He was starting to forget what sentences meant. He was now living in a cave, surrounded by noise. There, one spoke softly to oneself, in one's own voice. There, it felt wonderful to hear the sound of these words, to feel Kruso's strength and energy.

'They're practising freedom, Ed. There's nothing anyone has to do, nothing *you* have to do.'

'Don't they think, I mean ...'

'They're learning, Ed. For some, it's not easy. Some are surprised and confused. It's normal. They suddenly discover so much with freedom, all their buried needs, often all at once.'

The rushing still continued through the night. Ed was caught in it. The rushing reduced him to the size of an ice cube, while the outside grew ever larger.

On the base of one of the steel jugs one day, Ed had discovered one of the most forbidden signs in the world. Eagerly and without thinking, he scraped his brush several times over the inside of the jug, and the sign shimmered through the crust. Suddenly, Ed realised the responsibility they, the dishwashers, carried. It was almost more than he could bear.

The new girl moved her arm and Ed woke. 'Two-oh-four a.m. There is no traffic announcement.'

The rushing still continued through the night. Ed was caught in it. The rushing reduced him to the size of an ice cube, while the outside ...

THE CASTAWAYS II

There was no sign, no password. Just before midnight, they simply walked into his room. They stood in the dark. No one turned on the light. Viola played the national anthem.

Not one of them turned on the light, as if that were a proviso. A certain protection, perhaps, one of Kruso's rules. Their contours blurred and blended with the things, and so they were still there in daytime, on the table, on the bed, on the floor; his room gradually took on the aspect of a shipwreck. A strange and a familiar shipwreck, the shipwreck of an entire country.

No one who had to feel around for the light switch, no one who had to debase himself. Many wanted to give back, Kruso had said, but there wasn't anything that anyone had to do, and there wasn't anything that he had to do.

And that's the way it was.

Everything happened on its own, without a face.

Monika, the little invisible one, soon brought Ed a second blanket, which he rolled himself up in when he eventually switched to the floor to get some distance.

But there were also some among the clandestine sleepers who did not want to get too close and so didn't dare use the empty bed. Without a word or sound of any kind, like ghosts, in fact, they closed the door and stretched out on the floor.

And so it was that on some nights, no one slept in the bed. Instead, it got crowded on the dirty floor, on which little piles of dried up, dead cockroaches lay, as neatly and systematically as if a burying beetle had carefully collected them. Half-conscious, Ed wondered what animal could possibly eat cockroaches. Their crackly little bodies probably contained all imaginable vitamins, trace elements, and precious ingredients that, in the right dosage, would make you almost immortal or at least sensitive in some way that would make it possible, with their help, to read not only with just your eyes, but also with your skin, in complete darkness, for example.

When Edgar awoke (usually he woke with a start, drenched in sweat, with an erection so hard it was painful; sometimes he tried to stroke himself the way you calm a child, but he encountered only an alien, uncomprehending limb that stuck straight up and seemed to have begun leading its own life, independent of Ed and far beyond his efforts to maintain — how to put it — his dignity) and heard the breathing, the breathing of others as well as his own, lurking and circling, a conversation of air. It went on until he recognised the rhythm and adapted to it and could sink back into sleep, descending into crazy dreams.

Not all qualities were swallowed by the darkness. Some of the castaways radiated a strong sense of self-assuredness and self-confidence. They were proud, not at all bitter, yet full of dreams and plans (one of the island's main effects). Some of them spoke with Ed, quietly; they whispered in the darkness of his room, told him their names, gave information freely, and were grateful. He never met any who just wanted to pump him for information, which was no doubt due to Kruso's selection, his carefulness, and his *criteria*, of which Ed had still not managed to form any clear idea. A few of them seemed to be embarked on a listless shipwreck that did not interrupt their life of boredom. It was as if they were simply following some duty (to be happy, perhaps), an idea of longing, that had reached their ears along with the reputation of the island, but nothing meant anything to them. With them, it was as if a lull in the wind had entered the room. They were mockers, nothing more. Others seemed to Ed like fallen existences, their movements slowed and inhibited by the anticipation of the next defeat. Some just stood there for a long time in darkness on the doorstep and did not move. Like timid, frightened animals who had reached their refuge but still couldn't trust it. As if they had to preserve a difficult fear, Ed thought.

When he pretended to be asleep, he was sometimes overcome with a profound sense of pity. He saw his own flight, the search for a place to sleep. He could read his own desperate thoughts in the clandestine sleepers' breathing. Some of them talked in their sleep, with their faces to the wall: they were suddenly loud, voiced complaints of two or three words, and quieted down again. Some wept, held their breath for a long time, and gulped so as not to sob. Ed never knew if their eyes were open, if they were looking at him in the dark ... No, he'd managed it better, and now he almost felt ashamed of that, and these were the moments when it didn't seem wrong to him to take these night beings into his warm arms.

He had not needed an alarm clock for a long time. He had internalised the time to light the oven, even when its measure slipped away overnight. He reached for the doorknob and felt his way downstairs, down the servants' staircase, across the courtyard, down the crumbling stairs — and only then, in front of the oven, in the Black Hole, did he take a breath, a deep breath, and pull on his clothes.

In the evenings, Ed stayed on the beach for a long time to discuss a few things that had happened to him in his fox's cave — to pour out his heart, as they say. Before sunset, he took rushed, nervous walks across the hills and the highland forests. For hours, he strayed here and there under the lighthouse's circling limb of light and hoped he wouldn't meet any one.

It wasn't the castaways, no; he was the one who abased himself. He felt disgusted, and tears filled his eyes. He picked up the photograph of Sonya to remember G. (as he had begun to do more and more frequently), but what he felt was pure longing. Suddenly, G. seemed to escape him again completely. He compared it to the smell of a food that was long withheld, and he was hungry, completely starved, or even more: he was addicted. His abstinence reversed; even his pain was pervaded with lust. It was a kind of suffering, on the flip-side of which an incomprehensible glee intoned obscene, avid songs.

At ten o'clock, the bicycle patrol. The incessant rattling (like mocking, artificial applause), with the two soldiers on bikes rolling down the concrete paved path towards the village. The sound of their voices on the wind, the gentle shimmer of their machine guns in the fading daylight. On this path, the pair of sentries would cross the entire island, all the way to Hassenort, a spit of sand jutting into the sea on which a watchtower had been built and supplied with the latest technology, according to Kruso, binoculars with which you could see every single pubic hair on the beach — and every refugee for three nautical miles. There was also a light machine gun and 'enough ammunition for us all', as Kruso put it.

Ed leaned his shoulder blades against the base of the lighthouse. The lights of Rügen, so close, as if you could wade across to them with a few steps, knock on the window, and say: I'm here. He felt the old longing for a dwelling, a cave for his almost incomprehensible desolation. From island to island, and on and on ... Ed listened to the voice that had said this, and wanted to ask if it was referring to his entire life.

The sun-warmed stone against his back. First, it was a shudder; he could feel the roots of his hair. Then it was nothing more than a gentle, utterly pleasant pressure; it began beneath his eyelids and moved from there to his very core.

It was in him; it was there.

GRIT

They're all just pretending, Ed thought. He spread his legs to stand a bit lower. He had to bend far forward, brace himself, and push his member downwards to get an angle at which he wouldn't aim over the toilet bowl, over the Klausner, into outer space.

It was a reflex, primitive and powerful. A kind of cannibalism, Ed thought. Since C. disappeared (C., easy-going, happy, dancing, the number one on his list), he was wallowing in a maelstrom of desire. There was an expression for it. 'Screwing your brains out', for example, one of the few captions under a drawing scratched into the grey-green paint on the toilet tank. A wild doodle, mostly a heartily laughing penis, covered with flakes of paint. Who knows which season it dates from, Ed thought, and remembered the photograph. He was thinking of the crew of 68 at the moment they were being photographed, all the women and men with bottles to their lips; they were all just pretending.

It was painful.

He looked impaired.

He raised his head (as much as he could) and looked at the

drawing. Maybe Rimbaud had done it — 'your brains out' — maybe it was a quote from Artaud. The grinning member, now right in front of his eyes, looked livelier than the limb between his legs; its features were mocking, and Ed felt the old sense of inferiority. As if C. were merely a ghost and the laughter was never on his side. And he was still sitting up in the tree of truth in the middle of a burned-down forest, in a charred clearing, a fourteen-year-old boy speaking openly but shyly to his friend Hagen of 'boinking' (Claudia Cardinale's lips and Hagen, who says, 'I'm getting a hard-on,' and Ed, who softly answers, 'Yeah, she makes you want to boink her'; it was probably the first time he'd said it, the first time he'd seriously talked about *that*), instead of using harsher words, which seemed inconceivable, far removed from him along with expressions of an unvarnished, ruthless world, a world that got down to the nitty-gritty, as they say, and one he would probably never be able to cope with.

The cascading noise of flushing behind him (shameless, endless) on the way back down the corridor. Kruso's door, Chef Mike's door, the door of his neighbour, Cavallo, who rarely, almost never, made any noise.

Ed cautiously opened his door. A draft of air and a movement in the room.

'My name is Grit.'

The scent of the Palace Hotel. He could smell the dampness of her hair. With wet hair, she felt her way towards him and offered her hand as she had once and forever been taught to do. Ed had to feel around for her hand, and when he found it he found it was small, smaller than Grit's smell.

'Hello.'

Grit explained very softly that she wanted to lie down on the floor, which Ed wouldn't allow. She was agitated. She seemed nervous, and started speaking right away.

'Thanks for taking me in, I mean, Kruso, I mean Kruso says that all of us here are ... companions in misfortune, but this is my first time on the island and ...'

'Hello. My name's Edgar.'

'I know. Kruso told me your name, and he described everything very well, told me how to get to the dishwashing station, which sink, which room ...'

They talked.

Her whispering was like a rustling from some unknown corner of his room. The nights also served as a way for them to assure themselves — Ed had in the meantime come to understand this from what the castaways had intimated, in a whisper, quietly, often in half sentences and barely comprehensible. They needed to assure themselves after the experiences during the day, their education on the beach, and the incomparable, drastic effect of the island — exactly as Kruso had predicted.

Yes, Kruso was his friend.

Yes, a real friend and a close one. His friend and master.

They laughed a little. Ed talked this way for the first time. He was able to express his admiration undiminished, without embarrassment. He admitted his reverence. He found an echo in Grit. Or maybe he was the echo. Grit took him much more seriously than he had ever taken himself — as a dishwasher in the Klausner. Through Grit, Ed understood his role; he was a crew member on Kruso's legendary ark, which had taken Grit in. For Grit, Ed was proof. He was an example of what freedom *looked like* for anyone who cared to learn.

Grit recounted what the master had explained to them on the beach. Ed felt like he hadn't seen his friend for a long time and as if Kruso had returned to his room with Grit and sat in his traditional place at the head of bed ...

'He says that we, I mean us here,' she touched Ed's chest and perhaps touched herself somewhere as well, 'build the smallest cell. That's the first and sometimes also the only possibility of immediate community that replaces deformed relations. He says that freedom is actually already present, within us, like a profound inheritance. He says that, these days, it's particularly difficult to assume this inheritance. And it's essentially demanding almost too much. But here on the island, it's possible, here by the sea, and whoever isn't afraid will feel its innermost heartbeat.'

She kept talking.

He had asked her to.

No one turned on the lamp.

The illuminated don't need light. Only shady characters do.

Would she repeat what she just said? She did without hesitation, as if it were nothing more than another precious opportunity to accept the teachings.

And suddenly everything fit together. Ed began to understand Losh. First shoulders, then hips. He shifted her slightly to the side, gently, then with more force and determination. She lay on her stomach. He held her by the waist, like a vase. He waited and listened. He closed his eyes and covered her body with his. She kept talking when he was inside her. It was as if he were repeating after her, in that tone, with those words.

'Please one more time, one-more-time ...'

'Yes,' Grit whispered, 'yes.'

When Grit, unknown but strangely familiar, made no other sound than the deep breathing of sleep (her arms crossed in front of her chest), Ed felt his way down to the cellar and took his usual place in front of the furnace. He slowly unscrewed the furnace hatch and looked at the remains. Cinders, dirt, and ash encrusted in complicated geometric shapes. In the centre, a blue-grey pile full of rusty, mostly hand-wrought nails or studs burned out of the driftwood, remains of ships that had been bound somewhere and maybe were stranded by a war or a storm ... His face grew warm. His eyelids drooped — the open oven warmed him to the base of his eye sockets. For one crystal-

clear moment that would never return, he felt as if he knew all the
fates of this country. Their number was limited, five or six kinds of
fate, his own among them.

DOSTOEVSKY

When Ed returned from the sea to the dishwashing station, there was ringing in his ears. It was like having a small siren right in his head, but he remained calm and set to work again; he countered the ringing by making noise with the plates and cutlery, and after a while it stopped.

Even more than the pans, Ed hated the big ladles. He could not have explained why, but his dislike had grown into a full-blown antagonism. He tossed them contemptuously into the sink and rammed his fist into their empty bowls, hectically, much too roughly, and without looking at what he was doing. As a rule, it was simply a question of time until the ladle managed, using the full extent of its malice (and the law of the lever), to hit Ed in the face with the ugly little hook at the end of its metre-long handle. Like a prehistoric reptile that had been declared extinct centuries earlier, the ladle shot out of the dishwater with its thin coating of greasy suds, splashing the caustic swill in Ed's eyes. Blinded and swearing, he waved his hands in the air — and was hit full force by the hook at the ladle's other end.

'The stupid pig!' Ed roared. It was an insult beyond compare.

The outsides of the ladles' bowls were often blackened, as if they'd been held in the fire to brew some concoction, perhaps one of Kruso's magic poisons for the holy soup — 'goddamn shaman,' Ed muttered, scrubbing at the aluminium.

The temperature had risen in the meantime, and the air in the dishwashing station had become heavier and stickier. A sharp vapour rose from the sinks in which he swirled his hands: the detergent was making his mucous membranes smoulder. 'Goddamn shaman, goddamn creatures of the night here ...' Ed was afraid he would faint in the fog of vapours. Since his room had been put on Kruso's distribution list, he was numb with exhaustion. 'Sidle, ladle, collapse,' hummed in Ed's head. Ed swore under his breath. He was festering and burning inside. He felt imperious and angry, eager for a long-overdue confrontation: 'What kind of goddamn herbs, Losh, and anyway, what's the point of this stinking soup, why the toga-clad spectres in the dishwashing station ...' Inspired by the detergent, his temple branded with the impression of the ugly little hook (the ladle, that pig, had put its stamp on Ed), he announced that he had reached his limit, and *absolutely*. Ed stared, unthinking, into his sink. A plate spiralled down to settle on the bottom of the sink, and he briefly pictured C. as silverware — round, gleaming, he saw her forehead covered with foam, a light, damp something that trickled through her hair and into her eyes and had to be wiped away.

After the shift, it could take hours for his vertigo to pass.

Ed wondered how the others did it. Chris or Cavallo, how they managed to sit unaffected at the breakfast table while he stared dully at his toast with marmalade or tried to catch Kruso's eye. Ed found it hard to resist the temptation to rest his head on the personnel table. There could only be one explanation: the others slept. They had all adapted long ago to Kruso's *system*. Aside from Rolf, Ed was the youngest in the Klausner, not a greenhorn anymore, but a beginner in every respect. His sexual experience was limited and, yes, rather superficial, as he himself had to admit. C. was the exception, a beginning, a fall.

Ed was not alone in his exhaustion. The high season demanded its tribute. In the midday chase through the small approach lane between the bar room and the dishwashing station, there were more and more collisions. Dishes splintering; sauces, schnitzels, and roulades spraying onto the floor. On top of that, cursing, jostling, even wrestling, and finally one giant commotion. Then the counter-couple had to make the circuit and, like mother and father, calm the situation. At once comforting and strict, they talked to Chris or Cavallo and brandished small glasses of bright-coloured, high-proof liquid, as if they were using hypnosis. In the rush-hour surge, the counter-couple's parental function became indispensable and more important every day.

According to tradition, each waiter had his own glass. These drinking vessels, given the alluring name of 'end-of-shift glasses', were kept in a special compartment in the bar, which Rick had labelled 'Private' in blue pen on white tape, the so-called goosebump-tape. For Rimbaud, it was a tumbler that had a heavy base with bubbles in it; for Cavallo, a small goblet of pressed glass, but neatly cut; and for Chris, a replica of the half-litre boot with the inscription, 'Glückauf Sulzbach-Rosenberg', a gift from a Bavarian tourist in gratitude for the zeal with which an East German had served him, as the man had ceremoniously declared. The exoticism of the story was still tangible. Indeed, very few guests from the West strayed onto the island. From their perspective, the eastern island seemed just as distant as the West did to the esskays; in other words, infinitely far away. That may have been the reason no one really reacted to Viola's news broadcasts, which for days had been playing reports of refugees heading west. These broadcasts seemed of no real importance (and were scarcely believable) compared to the story of the boot from Glückauf Sulzbach-Rosenberg.

As the season progressed, it was more and more often necessary to have a drink before the end of the shift, and by July schnapps at breakfast was no longer an exception. Ed had seen how Rimbaud let Rick prepare his morning drink in a coffee cup, a dose of Korn and peppermint schnapps that Rimbaud called 'meadow pipit'. Rick considered it his duty to *have on hand* plenty of the crew's favourite drinks, as he put it, which is why Lindenblatt ('Debroer Lindenblatt') and apple brandy (Mona's favourite drink) were only served to the crew — 'goods received in kind,' Rick explained. Consumption was recorded and deducted monthly from their salary. Often earnings and expenditures were evenly matched. Chef Mike drank a mixture of kiwi (short for the Kirsch-Whisky, the cherry brandy) and Korn; once in a while, he also drank Soviet champagne with canned pineapple juice. René and Cavallo drank kiwi with kali (coffee brandy); the ice-cream man now and then drank Rosenthaler Kadarka, a wine imported from Bulgaria that was popular everywhere for being extremely sweet. Ed drank kali straight or the Wurzelpeter, herbal bitters he knew from his time in the army. It wasn't easy to get hold of, but Rick had registered Ed's preference indulgently. Karola drank Gotano (a vermouth) or beer punch, her own specialty: a mixture of fruit juice, brandy, wine, and beer that she mixed herself in ten-litre buckets and left to steep in the cellar. The beer punch was in great demand; along with the shandy Rick called 'Potsdamer', it was one of the Klausner's legendary specialties, and a new batch was mixed every three days. Krombach drank Goldkrone, a brandy Rick considered *white lightning*. Chris was often seen with egg liqueur in his cocoa mug. Rolf drank vodka and coke, a mixture that had just come into fashion in the dance halls. They all drank Stralsunder.

Despite all the difficulties, the kitchen rose like a cliff above the surf. Chef Mike was king, and when the king bellowed, covered in sweat, it was no time to delay. The primacy of the kitchen and gentle authority of the bar was beyond question. Nevertheless, there were increasingly frequent instances of not just René but also Cavallo or Rimbaud behaving with condescension or presumption. Only Chris never did. A hierarchy that had survived from olden times re-emerged, according to which dishwashers were on the lowest rung, fathoms below the rest, certainly beneath the kitchen and bar staff, especially beneath the wait staff, even if none of them really were waiters or dishwashers, but a lecturer in philosophy, a doctor of sociology, a poet who wrote good poems, a life artist on the edge of a steep cliff, or, as in Ed's case, a student of German literature.

But was he still one, actually? No.

And did he actually still want to be one? No.

And did he find the idea of returning to this old way of life even conceivable?

No answer.

And the others, what were they?

Had they dropped out or been thrown out? Legal and illegal at the same time, outside the so-called system of production (the mechanical nerve centre of society), they were no Heroes of Labour and yet were awash in labour (didn't gastronome sound like cosmodrome, evoking outer space, earth, mankind?), not useless, therefore, in any case not parasitical, just completely outside and far from the system, like cosmonauts from the cosmodrome, all of them dedicated to the nebulous star of a liberated life that was mirrored in their shining eyes like the reflection of the earth on helmets when the heroes of space travel left the mother ship for a 'stroll in outer space', as the euphoric news reports put it ... Yes, they were all heroes, Heroes of the Season, Heroes of This Life, all together and each alone, end-of-shift glasses in hand: 'To proscription!', 'To the proscribed!', 'To the island!', 'To Kruso!', 'To the sea, the endless sea!' Rick filled the glasses again, the glasses of promise, glasses of defiance, and glasses of self-will.

Ed had, in fact, heard of esskays who, it was said, published in magazines and anthologies (what a magic sound these words had), self-declared poets, self-published authors to a certain extent, who could be certain of general admiration when they arrived at the beach in the evening and talked about the possibility of new works, so large and full of life, that it seemed they could only have come from the sea itself, only from the sea and only in this place.

Ed's pace became slower, and he made mistakes. A stack of plates fell from his hands, whereupon René started drumming on one of his vats in imitation of a fanfare. Kruso came right over to help him pick up the pieces. 'It's important we get them all.' Ed pictured the bare feet on the tiles. *The arriving feet*, he thought.

Ed's friend slaved away without respite and offered Ed words and glances. He managed, apparently effortlessly, to link their time with the poems, forays, and walks at night along the beach. Words and glances, as if Kruso knew about Ed through Grit just as Ed knew about Kruso through Grit; he therefore knew everything about Ed. Kruso's eyes were so markedly kind and patient — no, Ed was not at his limit, not completely.

The Klausner careened but held its course.

Everything that occurred didn't just happen; each catastrophe was a necessary part of the whole process. As if the tension required to keep the chaotic machinery of the company vacation home high aloft over the sea could only be achieved with the help of collisions, curses, and quotations ('Why do the moon and the man slide together so submissively to sea?'). The only important thing was not to change course — a point made by Rick, whose bar-room wisdom was crucially important at the time.

Once, it was Rimbaud's turn. Although he tried desperately, he wasn't able to escape from his recitation. His unfocused gaze and the feral tensing of his lips, a pitiful expression.

'Fame, when will you come?'

The attempt to submerge the head of the Klausner's most intelligent waiter into the cool water of the cutlery sink came too late. Declaiming fiercely and imperiously, Rimbaud freed himself from Kruso's grasp and stormed out onto the terrace, his arm loaded with plates he had grabbed while rushing past, which he then threw onto the tables of the unsuspecting and completely startled day tourists. As he did so, he bared his broad white teeth beneath his moustache, leaned on the back of a chair in the beer garden as if it were a podium

in a large auditorium. However, Rimbaud did not then address the
crowd of holiday-makers who were gathered, as always, in great
number. Instead, he roared into the ear of the guest who had sat down
on precisely that chair:

'I don't know why ...' (pause, teeth, trembling moustache)

'but it always seemed to me' (a multitude of teeth, teeth all the
way to his throat)

'as if he no longer lived in prison with me.' (bite)

Or rather, a failed bite, since Chris and Cavallo grabbed him
at that very moment and pulled him away. Rimbaud dragged his
bottom teeth over his moustache as if he wanted to pull it down.
'Dostoyevsky,' Cavallo groaned, 'now he's onto Dostoevsky ...'

By the afternoon, Ed had almost forgotten his hatred for the ladle.
With the coffee sets, it was simpler and easier, and at the end of the
shift he was drinking kali with Cavallo. His work was done. They sat
in the courtyard and shared the balm of contentment in silence. Chef
Mike joined them at some point, heaving his walrus body onto the
bench. Cavallo poured; no one spoke. They were not sitting facing
each other, but in a row like prematurely aged schoolboys on their
school bench. They stared at the pines along the forest's edge, which
had begun to glow in the evening light. There was nothing better
than this.

After a while, the yellow of the pines darkened and seeped into
the bark until it was completely absorbed and the trees finally began
to glow from within. Cavallo was filling their glasses when the
question came.

Why is the light of the pines trees so kind to our eyes?

The unexpectedly aged schoolboys thought this over, sitting on
their bench. Cavallo gave the answer.

It's the pine trees' soul shining.

It's related to our own souls, Ed added, you can also see it in
paintings by Bonnard, for example.

In that case, the soul's colour would be a shade between yellow and brown, Chef Mike thought, and said, 'I still have to prepare potatoes for tomorrow.'

The chef stood up with a sigh. Cavallo patted his shoulder.

EARS

Kruso's criteria? Rimbaud says: It's all poetry, and, in that, Losh is never wrong, 'despite morally dubious sources'. Chris claims I'm the only one who gets allocated almost only women. With men, it's different. With Tille, I was even still in the sea, because of the waves, it was heavenly. All my tiredness was washed away. Tille wants to study photography or cinematography, but can't get a place at university, not a chance. He's teaching himself how to do it, he does drawings, reads, he's full of energy. He's saving up for a good camera from the West. I would have liked to show him the cellar.

The fir tree behind the shed raked the six a.m. dawn light into broad stripes. Everything was silent. Since Ed had charge of the furnace, his day began near the woodpile, at the chopping block. He piled a few pieces of wood onto his arm and disappeared into the cellar with them. Sometimes, he saw the manager coming along the bluff, approaching the Klausner with short steps, as if under hypnosis. A white, neatly folded hand towel was draped over his shoulder.

In the Black Hole, Ed could hear Krombach setting up his cubbyhole, pushing his chair, straightening his bed. At some point, the clattering of a typewriter as he typed up the daily menu. Ragout fin, solyanka, fricassee of chicken, steak with peppers, hunter's schnitzel. Ed sat in front of the furnace and stared into the fire. His desire was still there, but seemed detached, foreign, and only there to make him crazy. Sooner or later, it broke over him and whispered something like 'ears, oh those ears!' and suddenly nothing excited him more than small, nicely formed ears. It was absurd. Some ears smiled incessantly and some remained serious and resolute. An ear's expression could be the exact opposite of the expression on the person's face, the expression of the eyes, for example. Usually, the ear was much more honest, more straightforward. And as a rule, ears appeared more innocent than faces. C.'s ear with the small mole on the auricle surpassed all others in this respect. At first, before he'd got used to the sight, he had sometimes thought 'a crumb', his hand prepared to brush it away discreetly. In the end, this crumb had contained everything, expressed everything. 'My dearest ear, my most beloved,' his desire whispered, painting a few images as well. Beautiful ears were like one's sex, or more than that: an always visible orifice. There seemed to be more than a few ears with wicked expressions in the world.

The day before, on his way back from the beach, Ed had seen a man with violent ears; he bit a child in the neck. Only a moment later was the movement recognisable: the slight raising and lowering of his head, the surprisingly long tongue under the collar. The man was licking the boy. Then he gave the child back his ice-cream, the dripping cone he had been holding at arm's length the entire time. The man's kneeling posture and extended arm suddenly took on a chivalric aspect; the criminal aspect had vanished. My father would never have licked my neck, Ed thought. He looked at the thermometer

on the hot-water tank. The roaring noise of the fire after it was lit, like
a current that engulfed him, washed over him, calmed him. This was
his place, in the cellar, by the furnace. Here, he could be alone; he
could sit quietly with the objects.

He liked to walk around and inspect the closets. The supply stores,
the safe, the Ur-hermit's zinc tub, with the inscription 'Hermitage
at Tannhausen'. From above came the first noises from the kitchen.
Chef Mike's shift had begun.

The passage to the drinks cellar ended with a steel door, always
unlocked. Behind it, six degrees and the refrigeration unit's hum. At
the beginning of each season, a truck filled with liquor drove to the
Dornbusch highland. Everything that could be stored ended up in
the drinks cellar. There was a trapdoor in the floor behind the bar
that led to the drinks cellar below. One problem for the bar was that
the labels peeled off the bottles in the cellar's mouldy dampness.
They rotted away, became covered with mildew, and turned brown
with time. Because the cardboard boxes in which the bottles were
delivered also rotted, each bottle had to be taken out separately and
carefully — Rick had taught him that. He often assisted the barman
now. 'Führer-concrete, indestructible!' Rick called when going
down the grimy concrete stairs; it was one of his favourite stories.
The Klausner had the soldiers from the navy to thank for the 'blue
stairs', as he called them (because of the adamantine concrete's blue
sheen). They had been stationed in this forest inn at the beginning of
the war so they could set up their anti-aircraft batteries and bunkers
in the north along with their underground conduits that apparently
crisscrossed the entire highlands.

'Beyond a doubt, the same material — good old German bunker
concrete!'

Since the beginning of the month, the Klausner was going
through ten barrels of beer a day, a thousand litres. Ed washed the
barrels, which stank terribly. Rick set the tap, a device that dated from
before the war, with a CO_2 connection and a manometer. When he

hammered the stem into the bunghole, Ed had to tighten the bolt with the gasket. Now and again, it went awry and they ended up wading in beer or red shandy. Rick always remained completely calm; he swore, but very quietly. For Ed, Rick was the most even-keeled person on the island. Rick said the island had enlarged his soul. He believed drinking was good. After all, they weren't tapping the alcohol of unhappiness here, but the alcohol of bliss. 'The soul rumbles and wants even more happiness,' Rick would say.

Rick's dreamy gaze and his thin, gently arching eyebrows that curved up slightly at the ends instilled a sense of trust in everyone who entered the aura of his bar. Rick emanated goodness. And yet, he was a giant; at first sight, too big, too massive for the bar. But as soon as he came into contact with glasses and drinks, his movements became lithe, catlike. It was a pleasure to watch him work; every move of his hand flattered his surroundings. Indeed, he almost entirely filled the space behind the bar, so his wife, Karola, often took up position in front of the bar and did her work from there. It didn't seem to be a problem at all for her. With her slender arms, she could also reach the tap and work the two enormous coffee machines, the coffee bombs as Rick called them. Each bomb filled forty pots of coffee. In all, around three hundred pots were served (or 'drawn', according to Rick), that is, seven to eight bombs a day.

Rick had wisdom and Karola could do math. She kept every price in her head. For beer (.56 marks), Korn (1.56 marks) or shandy (21 pfennigs a glass), it was easy, but the barwoman also knew the prices of the countless wines, all the Murfatlars, Cotnaris, and Tokajis, not to mention the Czech, Polish, and Russian schnapps, or sparkling wines that were just becoming the fashion and were extremely popular among the Klausner's guests. 'She's got a head on her, that one,' Rick would say.

Karola was one of those whom Ed pictured as *homegrown Berliners* — proud, daring, quick-witted. She had a snow-white denim suit she sometimes wore to work. Her movements were energetic, and everything about her inspired respect, even her red hair, which she wore piled up in a small tower that swayed dangerously with every step but never collapsed. Karola added up the daily receipts for Krombach, and it was she who oversaw the crew's bar tabs — no one else could have managed.

From the beginning, the counter-couple had treated Ed very well, almost lovingly, like parents — or, at least, in a way he missed being treated. Rick had chosen him for the drinks cellar. He had become Rick's assistant, instead of Rolf or René. And every day, Karola brought him fresh tea in the dishwashing station, now and then giving him and Kruso her ice-cube massage as they worked. She placed the ice on them like a tool and made long, flowing movements with it as if slicing. 'Just keep working, kid, act as if I'm not here. Trust me, it's the only way you'll really relax.'

Like Krombach, the counter-couple lived in one of the tiny log cabins that surrounded the Klausner. Rick called them chalets. They had no running water, no toilets, and very little space. 'How much does one really need?' Rick would ask, and launch into one of his bar room lectures. The conditions on the island made people more peaceable. 'As if someone had stretched out time, Ed, into infinity.'

THE ROOT

Ed's experiences had taught him that the desire C. had kindled in him would not release its hold just like that, but then suddenly it was gone. The castaways whispered their names in the darkness, and only a few seconds later he had already forgotten. He couldn't even remember if they'd spoken. He often fell into a coma-like sleep, and no longer wondered how he would be able to stand being close to this or that body in the darkness. The secret was simply to fall asleep.

From these days of sleep, Ed surfaced as someone else. He now trusted Kruso's system of allocation without reservation, and hardly even saw his companions' faces anymore. Yet more: the vague idea that first occurred to him with the castaway named Grit, that all these clandestine sleepers had been chosen as Kruso's emissaries, became more definite. He could hear Kruso's thoughts, even the melody of his words. Pronouncements that slipped into his room just before midnight in the shape of castaways or as utopias-become-castaways, Ed fantasised. One could smell them, one could listen to their voices, one could (now that his brazen lust had finally quieted) learn from them when they lay stretched out beside him or on the floor or paused in the doorway barely visible in the darkness — the range of different temperaments, Ed thought. He knew already, knew perfectly well. Nonetheless, his guests now seemed different to him, changed, mostly without the signs of failure or world-weariness.

When they fell silent, he softly encouraged them to keep talking, to tell him *everything*, the entire story of Kruso's great freedom. Most understood Ed's wish. He was like one of those children who want to hear their favourite fairytale (the story of their favourite hero) again and again. Some thought it was an examination, a final test, a kind of admission charge for the night, for the precious lodging on the bluff, one last thing before sleep, which could hardly surprise them after the seminars on the beach, the soup, the ablution, and the hours making jewellery.

Once they began talking, their lives (with all the hardship and conflicts) seemed elevated by the indescribable effect of the island, as many described it, lifted up by the sound of the sea and its ceaseless motion, from the coolness of the water in the morning and the wind that always blew straight through one's eyes and into one's head, freeing all thoughts. The stories always returned from the view up on the highlands and over the island back to what was called the *greater island view*, which had opened their eyes with its unfathomable beauty and recalled the beginning of a memory into their consciousness, a memory of themselves. Indeed, they often mentioned a completely childish desire to take the island's entire silhouette, as it lay stretched out so vulnerably before them — the sea to the left and right, and, in between, the tender, fragile stretch of land — and press it to their hearts ...

There were rarely any clandestine sleepers who did not speak about how they realised, after gazing for a long time into the fog in which the furthest, southernmost tip of the island became blurred — the tip was actually rarely visible, in fact, it almost never was — that their former lives seemed foreign and burdened to them now that they'd been completely *changed*. One of them whispered to Ed in the

darkness, perhaps not very aptly, that his former life was left behind,
cowering, forsaken, forlorn, shamefaced, surrounded by things, like a
melancholy, alcoholic dog in its doghouse. Still, Ed wanted to hear it,
to hear it all. He could feel the incomparable warmth of hearing stories
in the darkness. He felt the warmth become a common heat as he
listened without moving. He sensed how they all belonged together.
How they effortlessly were confidantes of this country, longstanding
confidantes of a calamity that had lasted for an eternity and would
continue to last forever and yet seemed to contain a promise — if
enough passion could be mustered. The promise lay deep within the
calamity, Ed thought, a paradox he had otherwise only encountered
when reading certain poems that meant more to him than anything
in the world. He could think of this now: his verse hoard was silent,
the tram was gone, there was no more ritch-ratch he had to yank on.
Instead, there were hints of shame, shame and disgust across a broad
range. But in the end, he was simply too tired for this, too.

There seemed to be no fitting comparison to describe the island's
effect, and many claimed that there were no words for it in any case.
All there was to say was that on this spot, called the *greater island
view*, they had begun to feel again, to feel buried roots, as Kruso
called them, the image to which all images wanted to return. They'd
begun to feel 'simply at home', in the words of the castaway who had
spoken of the drunken dog in its doghouse. With his bitter account,
he lingered in the doorway for a long time before he stretched out
next to Ed and immediately fell asleep whereas Ed kept listening. Surf
and rustling pine trees.

As different and occasionally bizarre as the stories of night figures
were, and as varied their presentation, delivered standing or lying
down, hasty or half-asleep, Ed was still able, through the darkness,
to hear Kruso's voice in each of them, an afterglow of Kruso's words
in the words of the castaways and homeless, who struck Ed as almost
chaste, as untouchable. And sometimes it was as if Kruso were
whispering directly into his ear, as if he were caressing Ed with the

particular tone, the slurred consonants, the elisions ...

'The island is the first step, understand, Ed? The island is the place. Here most of them can feel the inner root after just a few hours. It grew into us from pre-history, not from birth, say, or more recently as some want to believe, no, I'm telling you: since the birth of thought. If we can touch the root, we feel it: freedom is there, deep within. It lives inside us, deep in our innermost self. That's the freedom I mean. It's our deepest self's thought, our self's thought in history. We don't need to do anything other than wake this thought. Often, it's imprisoned in unconsciousness. There are all kinds of imprisonment, Ed. Fear, nightmares, cramping, apathy. That is the dross, the endless dross, that covers us as long as we live. A heavy sediment of pride, power, greed, possession: rusty, poisonous, ashen dross. Of course, sometimes, the root has already rotted away or dried up. Those are the lost ones, the shady characters, abandoned beings. But not the castaways, Ed. Otherwise they wouldn't come to the island — they have *sensed* the root.'

Kruso's tone.

Ed remembered. He pictured Losh, how he would walk up and down the beach and talk. Ed had stretched out above, on the edge of the bluff, and looked down at the group that suddenly appeared sitting on the beach in a half-circle. He had gone on a foray alone. He had looked at the waves and tried to understand the rhythm of a diving cormorant. Twenty seconds, twelve seconds, twenty seconds. He had fallen asleep, and when he woke, they were there. They were making jewellery, threading bird bands and bending dental wire, drop earrings, twenty marks a pair. In Utopia, one works for three hours in the morning, then there is a two-hour break for 'literary studies', according to Thomas More; Kruso had read it aloud to him.

The wind picked up; the surf drowned out their words. One of the castaways raised a hand, probably Grit, who always wanted to know everything. Ed couldn't tell from behind. Kruso answered and pointed out over the sea. The sea. Its sheer size, its supremacy. And the ridiculous borders. That's why people come here, Ed thought. They want to see the ends of the world, to have it always before their eyes.

The cormorant had disappeared. In the light of the setting sun, Møn jutted from the sea, higher and more real than Ed had ever seen it. A fine, trembling line of surf separated the water from land, and from the chalk cliffs that slowly turned from white to light grey and in that form seemed to be related to the bluff on which Ed lay. Møn is like a mirror, Ed thought. A mirror in which you can see yourself reflected in the other world, the archetype of longing. The sun slowly lowered a golden bridge over the water, which rolled into shore in massive slate-grey waves that bit deeper and deeper into the western coast of the highlands every year. In the middle of the bridge, the blood-red outlines of hearths flashed, the plan of a settlement on the ground. An undersea glow and glistening reflection, as if the mythical city Vineta might burst through the surface of the Baltic Sea at that very moment, might emerge in space like a third power, a third place that would put an end to all reflections, once and for all.

'Sometimes it's laborious work,' Kruso lectured, but he was not referring to the bird bands or dental wire. 'First, you have to ... the root ... Each and every one of you ... that is ...' The wind had turned again.

Oceanographers had discovered the sunken settlement not long before, exactly halfway between the two coasts. 'Imagine, they live down there. They sit at their tables, go for walks. They're free. They're all free ...' It was a pleasure just to say the word — Losh, who knew that this sea was a grave.

The wind was blowing to the west. It carried his words out over the water, over the golden bridge. Ed saw two wide, strong currents flowing into each other, and suddenly they looked like rivers of light.

'No one should ever flee, never ...'

'Many know ...'

'Half the lan ...'

'Freedom draws us ...'

'... called to ser ...'

'A pilgrimage like no other ...'

'... go on,' Ed whispered. He never wanted to fall asleep before the castaways had finished talking, but sometimes it happened. He simply couldn't keep his eyes open. Once again, he experienced the heavy, unadulterated exhaustion of his childhood that allowed him to slip from a fairytale into a dream, from this world into the beyond, from one story into another, without barriers, without borders.

In a dream, Ed saw that the island was too full. The ports, the moors, the highlands, and the beaches, thick and dark with people. They were even on the breakwater and on the stones from the ice age that towered out of the water along the shore. They looked like giant, sluggish seabirds, but without feathers. Their skin was burned by the sun. He could hear their murmuring even at night. It blended with the sound of the sea and floated up to his window. The beach was filled with filth and rotting seaweed, out of which dead fish peered along with other detritus.

ISLAND DAY

'It's your sign, Ed.'

Kruso had taken a square piece of packing paper from his neck pouch. He pushed it across the table.

The black spot, Ed thought.

It was the sixth of August, the rest day of all rest days, the day on which the different rhythms of the entire island lined up so that not a single establishment was open — a yearly constellation, as reliable and rare as a solar eclipse, in the middle of the season. It was the esskays' day.

'Our signs correspond to the ancient house markings of Hiddensee,' Kruso continued softly. 'It's a particular form of writing, like the runes that used to be branded onto things and animals, even into the land, the earth, whatever one owned.'

He smiled and looked Ed in the eye.

'So it was since Hithin and Högin and King Hedin of Hidensey ...'

As Kruso expanded on their island's fateful role in the sagas of the north, he pulled piece after piece of the creased packing paper from his neck pouch. 'The eddas, then, but also in Gudrun, in which the king ...'

He apparently carried an entire alphabet of runes around his neck, not just the proceeds from the jewellery business. In the end, there were probably even more signs than marks making the greasy leather pouch bulge so uncomfortably. Ed found this supposition somehow reassuring.

'It will be a long night,' Kruso continued. 'Because of the celebration, we'll start the allocation in the afternoon.' He sounded grave and worried, as he always did when speaking of the castaways. Krombach stood up, nodded at everyone, and retreated to his office.

'Acceptance at three o'clock. The soup should also be ready by the afternoon, please, and the ablution as well. Washcloths and soap at every sink. The signs are on the sand, next to their heads or feet, just keep your eyes peeled.'

It was all meaningful and absurd at the same time. And not a single person seemed to harbour serious doubts. Only in René's expression was there icy scorn. Since he and the little invisible one were a couple, they were exempt from the billeting, as were the counter-couple and doubtless Krombach, too.

'Good,' Kruso said, and conjured up a fresh apple cake from behind the bar.

'From Mother Mete!'

'Mother Mete, a good soul!'

Rick served schnapps. Karola sliced and served the cake, while Kruso poured freshly brewed coffee, which required him to make a full circuit around the table with the heavy, steaming steel pitcher. He served each person at the table with equal attentiveness and laid a hand on Ed's shoulder.

'Let's start the deployment, friends.'

Everyone began talking. Chris gesticulated. Rimbaud bared his teeth. Chef Mike jumped up and demonstrated a few shots that would have gone right in, one hundred per cent, if ... He was almost shouting, and he twirled his towel in the air like a lasso, 'right in, one hundred per cent!'

'I say Ed goes on the left side, in Speiche's position,' Kruso called. 'You take left midfield, Ed, secure the back, move forward when they attack, and put yourself forward.' Kruso's tactics were completely drowned out by the general commotion.

Ed nodded automatically. He had always played leftfield. Kruso must have known that. After all, he had seen Ed coming. He had dreamt him. And he had binoculars in his room with which he could see into things, see far into their past ... Whether he was playing backfield, midfield, or offense: always left. Although he wasn't a left-footer. On the left without actually being able to play left, Ed thought, not even 'for domestic use', as his father had once put it. Over the years, Ed had always carried within himself the same vague feeling of disappointment (despite what could be considered a solid balance sheet). His sense of phoniness, yes, of imposture, was revived. A kind of unease that overcame and weighed on him here on the island as well, especially now and then when he was with Kruso.

'You don't need to be a left-footer to play left!' Ed burst out much too forcefully in the hum of voices. They had moved on from deciding the team's positions long before.

'I'm in the backfield, but I'll put myself forward. I'll put myself forward!'

For a moment, the table was quiet. Ed had jumped up and knocked over his coffee cup.

'Good, Ed, very good,' Kruso said. René's shoulders shook.

Ed felt uncomfortable stomping around amid all the runes. The soft sand made each step awkward and difficult. After a while, he inevitably had the feeling that his legs were growing shorter and that he had to raise his head now and again so as not to sink down completely. A few of the signs were made with surprising carelessness, using tiny, almost invisible shells, black pebbles, or thin twigs, some with just grass or seaweed. But it was important that they be made neatly because they were so similar, Ed thought. The girl with his sign sat far to the front, near the water. She was staring out to sea, as if help were coming from there, a ship with seven sails ...

Ed recognised her shame. Her breasts were small and still white. She twirled a lock of her blonde, shoulder-length hair around two fingers. A ship will come, Ed thought.

Her name was Heike, and it was the first time Ed was taking a castaway to the Klausner himself. Maybe because until then he had been the only one without his own sign. He was still mulling over what he should do next and what words he could use to explain it, as Heike got undressed.

'Is that your sink?'

'Yes.'

It was his sink.

'The sink for coarse cleaning,' he added, and blushed.

Heike climbed right into the stone trough. First, she set one foot on the slightly lower metal stand for the dishes. She crouched on it for moment as if she were imitating a larger, rare bird, then stepped into the sink. She already knows all about it, Ed thought.

'Is the water OK?' Ed asked like a hairdresser. Or a minister — *at his first baptism*, the thought flitted pointlessly through Ed's mind.

'It's fine,' the girl said, 'just right.'

She had turned, and held her head bent forward slightly, no doubt as a request for her back to be soaped up.

Ed calmed down.

He saw the flawless row of vertebrae, strange and unreal, and the soft skin stretched over them. He took the washcloth from the side of the sink and ran it down her back, slowly and carefully, back and forth, from her neck down and then further still, between the two sides, gleaming with suds and taut from bending forward, down to the invisible source of this vertebrate animal, the point of greatest temptation, which he reached almost distractedly and where his hand hesitated for a tiny, not even measurable instant.

'Your hair,' Ed murmured, 'now your hair.'

If he knew anything, it was this. He'd seen the hair when they were burying the amphibian ...

In the meantime, Chris had arrived in the dishwashing station with his castaway. They used the sink on Kruso's side. Their presence instantly simplified the procedure — this was the ablution, an important stage in the process, nothing more and nothing less. And suddenly Ed knew what to do. He was a dishwasher at his sink. He washed, scrubbed, rinsed. Heike obediently stretched her head forwards. She was so small that she had plenty of room in the sink. Ed raised the hose, but it was too short. The girl had to turn again and hold her head directly under the tap with her forehead on the bottom of the sink, as if in prayer.

Chris treated his castaway like a patient. He said, 'That's right, that's the way' and 'just this spot here' and 'we're almost done'. The straightforward completion of the ritual eliminated all shame. And doubling the procedure made it seem almost normal. Chris circled the sink with his short, energetic steps, no differently than when waiting on tables on the terrace. The water channelled Heike's hair into the drain and down the pipe to the mouldering grate, where the hungry amphibian snapped at her split ends with its slimy grey jaws ... From every hair, a mushroom; from every ablution, a soup. Baptism and rebirth. Ed fantasised as he — with almost dreamlike certainty — raised the short hose again to rinse the soap from Heike's back.

The drying towel was laid out ready.

Like Aphrodite, Heike rose from the sink. Ed held the Roman out for her. The stiff cloth made a dark sound, a sound of reliability. And as the castaway wrapped herself in the large, perhaps century-old sheet and stood in the dishwashing station like the outcome of a long, tenacious dream, Ed finally understood: all these castaways were pilgrims, pilgrims on a pilgrimage to the place of their dreams, to the last place of freedom inside the border — just as Kruso had said. And he was no more than a helper, a kind of assistant on the way.

Auxiliary staff in the Klausner, part of its sworn fellowship, which
had its own laws, a special trust, and perhaps only this duty.

Seven against seven. Cheering came from all sides, successful plays
were celebrated with applause, while Khmer drumming thundered
hollowly and incessantly. It was the island Cambodian with his flying
hands. He could drum and dance at the same time. By the end, Ed
had played in four games of the tournament. Their team was chosen
from the crews of the Klausner and the Island Bar (their 'family', as
Kruso put it); each half was ten minutes long. Many of the games
were an endless series of fouls and apologies, fouls and professions of
friendship, fouls and hugs, cheek against cheek: there were players who
stood like that for a long time after sliding tackles right in the middle
of the field, immersed in the usual signs of affection. The families
from the Hitthim and the Dornbusch were considered strong, but
could be defeated. Indian from the Island Bar played sweeper; Kruso
played midfield; Antilopé, a waitress from the Island Bar, played
forward. Ed was surprised at how confidently and powerfully Chef
Mike leapt and flew between the goalposts despite his heft. 'He's a
passionate goalie, an unconditional goaltender,' Rimbaud remarked.
'That's what makes him so frightening and unpredictable.'
    Everything was different than at night. Ed's castaway was not
swallowed up by the darkness; she remained completely visible. Her
fair skin, her face, on the sidelines for the entire tournament. Now
and then, she shouted something at the players. Ed forgot that just a
few days before, he had been at the end of his tether. Rimbaud fought
like an animal and debated every play, which made for constant
interruptions, but no one really seemed to mind. Indian, his hair tied
back in a ponytail, crossed the field in enormous strides: he appeared
to move slowly, almost sluggishly, because of his large, angular body
that upset all ratios, as he was, in fact, fast, unstoppable. He executed
a diagonal march, opening the game, then passed to the forwards,

to Santiago, who lurked, or Chris, who jumped about like a dervish, agile, shrewd ... Ed saw Kruso running in front to his left, and received a pass. He was not as fast, but it was hard to steal the ball from him. Ed moved up quickly and put himself forward.

'Losh!'

The drums thundered, and Ed felt an old, almost forgotten sense of pride. He pictured his favourite players from childhood and imitated them. Kotte, the fighter, the striker that no shove or tripping could bring down. Hafner, the technician. Dörner, the sweeper. One day, Kotte had suddenly disappeared, at the height of his career. His only trace was in the small print of the games' stenographic records in the *Sportecho*. No picture, no report, just his name listed as top scorer, repeatedly, constantly, Kotte, the future defector, exiled to a third-tier league. Ed had often daydreamed about him and wondered how Kotte could have kept on playing, how he was able to keep on shooting goals.

Not only the esskays, but also the inhabitants of the island, day tourists, and holiday-makers had gathered around the soccer field. A few were reported to be *famous*, among them a tall, thin man with glasses whom people called Lippi and recognised from television. Next to him was another man, who, despite the heat, wore a leather jacket with braided epaulettes and to whom fans enthusiastically called, 'Hey, Quaster!' Mostly, the conversations were about individual esskays, about their legendary work in the legendary establishments of Vitte, Kloster, or Neuendorf. The suntanned heroes of the season were held in unadulterated admiration for their island lives, outside the law and apparently completely free of commitment. Their solidarity, therefore, was all the more astonishing. In short, the tournament became a celebration of the esskays, a festival in recognition of their caste. Rather than misfits from the dregs of socialism, they were seen as the progeny of King Hedin of Hidensey's brave hordes, just as Kruso must have planned.

Uniformed men appeared during the final match. Some of them

gathered behind Chef Mike's goal, as if they wanted to use the old fishnet hung between the goal posts as camouflage. Something happened, but during the game it wasn't possible to follow very closely.

'Losh! Losh!'

Ed had moved up and put himself forward.

I'm putting myself forward, Ed thought.

His friend looked up, and Ed saw rage in his eyes.

Glasses were handed round as soon as the final whistle blew. On the way to the beach, Ed heard the name 'Willi Schmietendorf' mentioned several times with great respect: Willi Schmietendorf, manager of the Dornbusch Apartments, who had donated a barrel of beer. 'Beer from Willi Schmietendorf's!' was the fanfare that drew them to the sea, and it sounded like 'Victory on all sides!' Without a doubt, they had earned the admiration, without exception, and Ed was happy to belong to them, perhaps for the first time. Together, they raised the mugs that looked like they were made of small bullseye panes that had been pressed together and in which the sun was refracted. For a moment, a golden light hovered like a halo over their sweat-soaked heads. Anyone hit on the temple with one of these mugs would die immediately — Ed didn't know where that thought came from, *die immediately*.

The castaway did not leave his side. Together, they scaled the dam with the narrow tarred promenade, half-covered in drifted sand. At first, Ed felt a warmth, as if he were being caressed, tenderly, unexpectedly, a warmth flooding over his face.

'What's that?'

Her thin voice vibrated in the wind, and Ed looked out to sea for the first time. A long row of grey patrol and torpedo boats were blocking the horizon. In the twilight, they looked like a floating wall, a steel boundary just a few hundred metres off shore. Either the gunboats had been decorated or the flags planted on them were part of their equipment, a kind of war finery perhaps, Ed thought. It was a grandiose, essentially irresistible view.

Like ants, the soldiers lugged in firewood. An enormous bonfire ate into the evening sky and divided the beach. The smell of burning blended with the iodine smell of the sea. On the left, various cautious groups of esskays lingered, huddling amid the remains of their adder stones, driftwood, and rubbish-strewn sandcastles. Some drank beer, other sipped schnapps from bottles. Trench warfare. It pained Ed to see the esskays' heads sticking up helplessly from the hollows — bewildered, intimidated, like children forgotten on a beach, surrounded by a world that had suddenly become hostile and strange. They looked around searchingly, as if they were waiting for someone who could explain everything to them. Explain what they were to think of the things that happened here, on the day of their own celebration, on their own beach. 'Shit on the soldiers!' or 'Brain them with your beer mug!' — unrealistic, of course, but some sort of guidelines would have been vital, and if Kruso had offered one with his usual earnestness, who knows?

To the right of the fire, three officers from the observation company stood near a personnel carrier, its broad tyres half-buried in the sand. They were smoking cigarettes, and looked like they had little to do with the entire scene. Ed recognised Vosskamp, the commander of the island, and his staff sergeant. Evening was setting in.

Out in the grey wall, the motors sprang to life. The three mid-size ships spun their anti-aircraft cannons anticlockwise three times in sync. There were a few gutsy whistles and some booing from the dunes. Also one single, solitary cheer, the kind you hear in recordings of big rock concerts — a lone, lunatic hoot transformed in the recording into a second of enigmatic eternity. Whomever it escaped regretted it immediately: two of the three cannons spun again, but this time only ninety degrees. Their dark mouths, with their small, circular silence, were now aimed directly at the shore. Silence fell on the beach again.

Where was Kruso?

A sailor appeared on the deck of the middle gunboat and showed various flags. His movements were choppy, a kind of breakdance. He was lit up by the spotlights on deck. The man was very short, and only visible because of his vigorous movements. Although none of them understood his dance, the esskays did not take their eyes off the flag-waving dwarf.

There were different shapes and colours, a chaotic game of colourful crosses and squares. These signs could be read as either auspicious or ominous. The ship's name, *Vitte*, was written on the prow. 'They call it the sponsor ship,' someone whispered close to Ed. It was Indian from the Island Bar. He should know after all these years.

'Sponsor ship,' Ed repeated softly. He, too, had found his sponsor. And today, he himself had become a kind of temporary sponsor. First baptism, then sponsorship. Fundamentally, everything here was based on sponsorship, Ed thought. It replaced friendship and was almost stronger than love. He was pierced by the offence the action on the beach must represent to Kruso.

A soldier whose torso protruded from the hatch of the personnel carrier answered the sailor's flags with his own, which were handed to him swiftly, as if by magic. Someone who knew the answer in advance must have been sitting in the driver's cab; someone who knew what should happen next. A salty spray mist wafted over the beach, and Ed rubbed his eyes.

When the centaur spoke, the dwarf on the ship kept his arms down, his hands crossed and against his upper thighs: this made him almost invisible. Without a doubt, the theatre with the flags signified danger. It was threatening, but to Ed it also seemed convoluted, fussy, toothless, and, yes, peculiarly *intimate*. An odd melancholy suffused the scene, as if one were accidentally witnessing the final conversation between the last practitioners of a dying art about the end of the world. However, it could only be about whether or not they should lay waste to the waiters' beach, with its hills, cigarette butts, and condoms, its sandcastles and remains of camp fires, its bars made of fish crates and stashes of schnapps, and with it, of course, all the esskays, the whole pack of useless, superfluous drop-outs — *reduced to dust*, shot through Ed's head.

The esskays gradually remembered that they were, at bottom, fearless companions, at least in relation to their countrymen. Bit by bit, they approached the fire, since it had got cold on the beach. The grey of the boats became blurred, and they seemed to have completely forgotten the cannons or simply didn't care about them anymore. In the same way that they didn't think much of anything that threatened them. It was a primitive but striking bit of wisdom, in which Ed suddenly recognised the secret precondition of their free existence.

Indeed, more and more of them arrived and settled down around the fire. Some hauled fresh wood. Openly and frankly, they drew the soldiers into conversation and embarrassed them with their boundless offers of alcohol. It seemed as if, in doing so, they were explaining why the origin of their freedom was sacrosanct, and in the reflection of the flames this message began to glow.

Ed and his castaway sat on the periphery in the dunes' half-darkness. A couple of the soldiers couldn't keep from staring at Heike's legs, so he briefly pulled her close — after all, he was still responsible for her. He was immediately overcome with the longing to be her washer again. Even the driver of the personnel carrier was looking at her, but it was hard to confirm that exactly since the fire was reflected in the windshield. His face is burning, Ed thought.

A blond guitar player with combed-back hair, the ice-cream man at the Heiderose, sat down next to Heike and started playing 'Blowin' in the Wind'. Ed contemplated whether or not all ice-cream men were loathsome. Rimbaud came by and brought them schnapps. Ed wanted to ask him where Losh could have got to and what was going on here, *what kind of rotten betrayal*, but first he had to drink. Rimbaud spun stories of long-ago regattas and fleet reviews ('when I was a child'), wonderful celebrations with speeches, parades, the Marine Corps ball, and the garrison band — he had trouble pronouncing the words 'garrison band'. He pronounced them like two burps strung together, 'garrri-son-barrrnd ...'

'Alright, I'm hungry!' The castaway had jumped up. She cut Rimbaud off mid-sentence with her offer to get some soup. *Soup against soup*, Ed thought, and, although Kruso's soup inspired only disgust, he felt the prick of betrayal again. 'I'm putting myself forward ...' As if he had just now put the key to the black box named Edgar or Ed on the personnel table: 'I'm putting myself forward ...'

But Losh had disappeared.

On both sides of the field kitchen, soldiers watched over the serving. At the sight of the castaways, they stiffened like tin figures. Her heels shone as bright as taillights — she had a peculiar way of twisting her feet in the sand which made her hips move in a continuous, circular motion while she held her arms out stiffly, almost ceremoniously.

She's marching, Ed thought, she's marching.

'Naturally not here,' Rimbaud continued undeterred, 'but in all the larger ports, Rostock, Greifswald, Stralsund.' Several times, he mentioned the phrase 'Baltic Sea Week', 'including a tour of the torpedo boat, including the flags of all the Baltic Sea States, the beautiful blue and yellow of Sweden everywhere, and Denmark's red and white, and, interspersed among them, banners like "The Baltic — a sea of peace" or "The Mackerel — a fish of silent rapprochement", and so on.'

Rimbaud was hitting his stride. Adrift, Ed careened through his wild ramblings. 'Blow-wo-wo-wo-woing in the wind.' A cloud-fish in the sky darkened. For a moment, Ed had to lie back: he was gasping for air. When he closed his eyes, he saw the photograph of Sonya, which in his imagination had become a picture of G. — he no longer fought against it. He felt longing. Longing for the dead, that's how he referred to them now. Grief constricted his throat. He was drunk.

'The freedom I mean,' bubbled up from the noise of cutlery at his side and:

'All streets lead into dark decay' and 'Warning, strong current, hold onto balls!'

The small circle slowly dissipated in silence. Ed imagined the gun barrels sinking thoughtfully in the dark, rising, and sinking again.

The surf's applause.

AMBER LEGEND

He danced like a locomotive frozen onto its rails. Only his upper body moved. His legs were stiff, set slightly apart and his arms bent, left, right, back and forth, as when walking. No movement in his hips, no swaying, no turning, just now and again a sudden, completely unexpected bending forward, more precisely a catapulting of his body forward into the void combined with a violent, sustained circling, tossing, and shaking of his head, which was the real point, because dancing meant mixing air and hair ...

It was Valhalla-style, invented and based in the Valhalla, the most important dance hall in his home town, where the blues bands played — Gypsy, Sit, Fusion, Passat, and the band with the drummer who jumped up in the middle of a song to bang his shaved head against the gold gong that hung above the stage like a giant halo.

At some point, during one of the band's breaks, the first DJs had trickled into the room with their ridiculous hits. At first, they were still timid and holed up in some niche at the foot of the stage, but soon there were only discotheques left in the city, even the dance floor of the sacred Valhalla was overflowing with dancing kids, fourteen, fifteen years old, who followed stupid choreographies instead of jumping up and down like animals in a cage or at least swinging their heads around — which would have been pointless in any case because their hair was much too *short*. And on their faces there was no trace of that revolt, that longing, drunk with life, that drove the bluesers like a horde of dervishes over the dance floor, not in pairs, no, all of them, all together, their entire tribe filled the hall with their hair ... And no, in those faces filling the discos there was nothing, or nothing other than makeup, no sign of the feeling, the rhythm that made circumstances dance, no battle and no utopia. They did not belong to the tribe *before time*, before society and its order, which was completely contaminated with banalities, constraints, rules, contaminated by their agony and which lacked the most important things: honesty, solidarity, perhaps love ... No, nothing. Nothing but glitter-covered void, that's what the faces in the discos were.

And suddenly they were old, the bluesers, who called themselves *punters*; only a few were in their early twenties, like Ed. In their early twenties and old. The disco had conquered their tribe and banished them to the villages where wooden steps led down to tiny rooms over smoke-filled bars where there were still bands, where glasses were still crushed with bare hands, and one punter would remove the shards of glass from another's palm with the incomparable tenderness required for that operation. Driven out in the countryside in the evening on a decrepit Ikarus bus, they had to walk home, long tramps over the fields that were their steppe, their prairie, even in the coldest winter, from Trebnitz, Köstritz, Korbußen, or Weida, stumbling for hours with glassy eyes through the pitch-black darkness of the Osterland, with snow in their hair and ice in their beards. Those who were too weak fell and wanted only to lie there, but that wasn't allowed, no punter ever abandoned another, never!

Ed lifted his head. In a moment of suddenly clarity, he recognised the small bits of mirror, and between the shards the outline of Africa. Faces sank into the crowd and emerged again, a painting of a battle.

A few esskays, fleetingly, and in front of him the snow-white face of his castaway, with her round cheeks and half-closed eyelids. She had made the oddly reasonable suggestion of looking for Alexander Krusowitsch in Hitthim, where a disco for the esskays had been planned to the end the day. The night wind from the sea had cooled their temples. Walking in the sand had been tiring. They had ended up in the middle of a herd of sleeping canopied beach chairs. For a long time now, Ed's head had been too heavy to bend and peer into each one of these enclosed beings with their freshly cooled odour of artificial leather and sun lotion.

'Losh, goddamn it, Losh!'

They danced in small, dreamy arcs, with hands outstretched, insofar as possible, and upper bodies swaying. Little seagulls, Ed thought, because now they were in the forest. His arms were stiff with cold, and his neck was stiffening, too. I am the forest, Ed thought, the last harbour, first wash, then feed, the sleep, sleep, last harbour — but then the sea flooded the shore, the jealous sea ... Ed slowly froze in his movement; either he was going crazy or he was already a part of the legend. He gasped for air. Tears shone on his cheeks like amber in the shabby light of the homemade disco ball that revolved like the globe it once was in an earlier, better life, without bits of glass but instead covered with Africa, Asia, and the Urals and with 'name-the-industrial-conurbations-of-the-Soviet-Union!' Situations, without splinters, but instead covered with Ed-the-schoolboy, almost blinded by the desert yellow of the drab economic map, while it showed Samara and Volgograd, full of the East, full of the West, oh planet earth full of sorrow (shards), oh you poor despoiled, mistreated world, oh world that spins, spins, and torments with its false reflections, but now Ed was simply standing there.

Weeping forest.

Amber legend.

With great effort, he raised his arm, touched the seagull, and pointed to the front of the room.

Best friends cause each other pain, Ed thought, it's a sign. He fell to his knees and hugged the vomit-spattered toilet bowl.

'I'm very sorry,' the castaway said softly to his back. Her voice contained everything; above all, understanding. Things that Ed had never said, never even thought before marched like finished, typewritten sentences through his brain, with bloody caps, entire legions of *his own words*, like verse set to the right and left, in the shade of windswept trees, that's how they passed; somewhere it was written: We kissed, understand?

'Are you OK? I'd rather not stay too long, I mean, it's the men's toilet,' Heike whispered.

Without looking around, Ed raised his arm and let it drop: Go ahead.

The bowl stank. From its depths rose the picture of a punter from back then, *complete punter*, about whom all the bluesers agreed, Steffen Eismann, his best, his only friend. What if he came in now, into this horrible room, and stretched out his bloody hand, what if ... Ed broke into a cold sweat. He tried to stop the image, and hugged the bowl even tighter. Behind him, a man pissed his endless stream into the newly tarred latrine, which probably drained directly into the port. His pissing thundered in Ed's ears and disco music thundered from the toilet bowl. It smelled of urine and shit, and he tried to chase Steffen Eismann away. But all the tables were watching as Ed gently pulled out one shard after another. The back of Steffen's large hand on the cool, beer-soaked tablecloth. After each shard, a look in each other's eyes. It was about honour and some girl, probably (Kerstin or Andrea), it was about music and the feeling of being in rhythm, in the rhythm of this separate, other existence on this separate, other earth. 'Freedom ...' Ed whispered into the toilet bowl, 'freedom is always also ...' No, that was wrong, 'freedom is different ...' No. 'The freedom of others is — freedom?'

It was pathetic. Ed couldn't finish *the sentence*, the sentence that probably everyone here knew, had to know, Luxembourg, London, deportation, emigration, that endless series of offenses and outcasts, the caretaker in Halle with his bottles, the man without hair in his armoire on the street in the centre of Berlin, and all the castaways here, and all the esskays, my esskays, Ed sighed, I've taken them into my heart, Rolf, Rimbaud, Cavallo, large-hearted Rick, generous Karola, and Chris, her severe Harlequin — but what about Ed? The thought was painful. What or who could *he* be in it all?

'I'm putting myself forward. I'm coming up from behind and putting myself forward,' Ed whispered in the toilet bowl's suffocating stench, and it finally burst out of him: a sustained howl, ignited again and again in the depths of his intestines, 'Kru-sooooo, Kruuu-soooo,' as full of despair and longing as any final cry, alone on the high seas.

'The stupid pig!'

Strange — they were suddenly in the narrow doorway to the bar room, and yet they managed to push past each other, Ed and the ice-cream man, the ice-cream man and Ed. But then Ed let out the yell, loud and resounding over the harbour, the boats, the bodden: 'The stupid pig!'

René was immediately at Ed's side. He tried straightaway to pull him to the ground. In his surprise, Ed was almost overcome with fear, a fear that coursed through him like elation: yes, he wanted to fight, no matter what the cost, he wanted to beat the stupid pig!

The first blows — an enormous relief. Then the pain, searing, first under his eye. After each hit, Ed had the face of a child, undisguised, helpless, but mostly astonished. Something was being pounded to pieces and from the midst of it all, the child Edgar B. looked out at the world: Why am I here? And why alone?

What happened next was no longer comprehensible. René grabbed him by the hair. Pulled far forward, almost to the ground, Ed tried to stay on his feet. He tried to get away. René's fist in his hair negated everything Ed had believed about the world and his place in it. A blow landed every second, unchecked, unpredictable. Pain from his right eye socket stabbed him to the centre of his head. With a powerful jerk, the ice-cream man forced him to his knees, but Ed reared up ...

A moment of astonishment.

Ed put his hands to his head, as if he had to examine himself first: here's my head, there's my hair. My hair, Ed thought. His hair in René's fist.

Maybe the lapdog wanted to — wash himself a little? Lapdogs know all about that, from dishwashing and the entire hocus-pocus. Wouldn't that be best for little lapdog? Ed heard the questions. They came from far away even though René was standing right next to him and trying to wipe away the blood-smeared tuft.

Here's my hair, there's my head ...

Faster than Ed could comprehend, the ice-cream man had grabbed him and shoved him down the incline to the dock. High season, Ed thought nonsensically, but the water was ice-cold and his cuts burned. He felt his contours; he was trapped in his body. He managed to push away from the dock. He made it to the first cutter, and felt his way along the planks. The wood, the algae, the moss — he felt gratitude and, at the same time, something hard, a force that wanted to push him down, under the water. He sank into the mire, surfaced again. His legs felt like lead, and he gasped for air.

René was now above him, far above with a rescue pole in his hands. His aim improved with each blow. He pushed Ed through the harbour basin like a billiard ball. Ed swallowed water. A rusted ladder floated past. He tried to yell, but it was no more than a thin, feeble howl.

'Hey, little lapdog.'

Someone on the dock laughed. The crazy boy.

Before Ed lost consciousness, he saw his father. When he resurfaced and took a breath, he felt a cool breeze on his face, the chill night air over the bodden. He saw the outlines of the buildings along the harbour, the bulwark, the Hitthim, streaked, blurred; a few of the windows in the hotel were illuminated. He saw a man walk up to the window. The man was his father, there wasn't any doubt. His father, who very soon would open the window and stop everything with a single command. But then the man just drew the curtains, and his shadow faded.

HIS FIRST ROOM

His first room. It has no windows and no door, just an opening. It's a passageway, and some light shines into this passageway. All this dates from a time before language, and so Ed can't answer the calls from outside. It's strange enough, being there with someone calling him. No one could have said what purpose the windowless chamber behind the bedroom had been meant to serve. Storeroom, broom closet, later a space to store a knitting machine neatly wrapped in brown oilpaper. It's on the damp, mildewed back of the house, facing the creek, the saltpetre side. He hears the flowing water. He hears the stamping of the animals who come to the edge of the creek to graze. He hears it all without knowing that the creek, its borders, and the animals exist. Sometimes, one of them will rub its flank against the timbers and lean with his breath against the wall. His first space. His first room.

Those who are outside the room, calling to him, are basically happy for his earth-deep sleep and the silence he emits. He is the only possible child, who unfortunately still gives trouble. Everything the old woman does far above him is accompanied by a soft, sweet, strange sound. It is a sigh, his first noise. Everything must be accompanied by a sigh. Boiling the diapers, getting the wet nurse's milk from the community nurse, the long walk to the neighbouring village, there and back with a little aluminium pitcher, step by step. The dark plop or boop when she removes the black rubber lid with the initials 'E.B.' written in chalk, and then the sigh — from deep within her soul. Things are counted with sighs and put in the proper order, one after the other. Hours are sighed into days, and days to weeks and years. A deep and ancient lament has become her own. She shines over little Edgar's crib. Her face is a bright spot in the electric light, and smells as old and mouldy as the house.

'Edgar!'

Edgar — yes. There in the chamber, that's what he must become, he has to get used to being that, little by little: Edgar, Ede, Ed. Until the words 'knitting machine' arrive and step into his consciousness, the silent brown mass next to the wall across the room is a small horse wrapped in cloth. His horse, it talks to him when darkness falls. They resemble each other in their cocooning: Ed in his capsule under the covers and the horse in its cloth. Winter sleep. It is his best, his only friend, with those agreements, unspoken, that are only possible between best friends. If, for example, by chance he didn't wake up one morning, his horse would chew through the tether with its strong white teeth. As soon as its strong, dark horse head had shaken off its bridle, it would go to Ed in his bed. It would only have to turn, carefully: then it would wake Ed with just its horse's breath, it would breathe new life into him.

'Edgar, Ed! He moved, didn't he?'

Everything can evolve from sighs and a horse's breath: a name, a language, a song, an individual existence perhaps. But at some point, his mother returns from the hospital and the sighing woman disappears forever. He continues to listen for her for a very long time — Nothing. Instead: soft, cheerful talk, a new odour, a new face, and boundless love. He still doesn't know her. He tries to sense her. A sigh is his first word. His mother cannot understand him.

'Edgar, can you hear me?'

Yes, but his eyelids are very heavy. It's better to keep them closed. The capsule that contains him ends with the cover that is pleasantly soft and protects him up to his chin. But from there downwards, its space seems to extend far, through his bed and the floor, into the cellar, and on into the depths, to the ore, his native ore, which radiates and draws him gently and benevolently in.

'Hello, Edgar, can you hear me?'

'Uranium, pitchblende, isotope 235U! Neurosis that penetrates to the core!'

'What was that? Did anyone catch that?'

His verse hoard had spoken.

Someone shakes him.

Someone pinches his arm.

Underwater, I'm still underwater, Ed thinks, and wants to say it.

Three saints emerge from the mist.

Krombach, a stranger, and the island police officer.

COLD HANDS

He could not find his face. When he raised his hand to feel it, he touched something unfamiliar. A mask, perhaps, Ed thought. He tried again but fell asleep during the attempt.

Kruso bent over him. His large, dark horse head. His large white teeth. Ed could not feel the kiss.

I'm sorry.

When he woke again, he tried to smile, but it didn't work. His eyebrows jutted out like a small balcony. His nose, too, protruded into the room like a shadow. He looked into the room through a kind of tunnel. At the end of the tunnel: sink and armoire. He thought of Speiche: some day, he'll come to collect everything, his toothbrush, his shoes, his sweater, and glasses. Maybe I won't be here anymore when he does, Ed thought.

From this point on, there was always someone in his room, a gallery of guests, endless, dreamlike: the island police officer, the island doctor, Krombach, Cavallo, Rimbaud, the entire crew, and a strange man with photosensitive glasses, who said he was an inspector from the sanitation department. And above all, Monika, Mona, the laundry fairy, every day. She was suddenly no longer invisible, and Ed's room was filled with the scent of this change.

'It's good that you're awake again, Ed. You should drink, drink lots of water.'

She lifted a cup to the level of the tunnel and touched it to his lips. He took a deep breath and the underwater noise returned, the ugly snorkelling in his head.

'Where is Kruso?'

'You have to drink, Ed.'

'What happened?'

'He disappeared. They grilled each of us, for hours. They turned his room upside down, but my father ...' She looked him in the eye and nodded.

'Where could he possibly be?'

'The island people say that a few men in civilian clothes tried to encircle him after your last match, and since then no one has lain eyes on him. How stupid of you, Ed, the whole thing. Completely senseless. By the way, René is missing, too.'

When Ed woke at midnight, his door was ajar. A cool draft on his forehead. His head was heavy, and it took him a lot of effort to lift it. What Viola had been talking about in her newscaster voice gradually dawned on him. Once again, there had been refugees; in fact, there had been talk of a veritable flood of refugees, slipping through the fence, over the border in double-time.

Ed tried, repeatedly, to imagine the fence.

He saw people running. He saw rusted old wire mesh and a landscape that looked like the steppes. The fence remained a mystery. The Hungarian border mystery. Suddenly dated, suddenly open. And no one fired a shot. How was that possible?

'It is now eleven fifty-seven p.m. To close the day, we'll hear the national anthem.'

Ed's heart began to race. He cowered in the middle of a grandiose desolation. Strangely, he thought of the movie *Spare Parts*, a West German film, if he remembered rightly, that nonetheless made it into the cinemas. No other portrayal of an escape had imprinted itself on him so clearly. A man jumps out of a motel building and flees into the desert, chased by an all-terrain vehicle. Those chasing him are hunters of men. They want to butcher him and sell his organs. Ed had seen the movie as a fifteen-year-old in his local cinema, still called the 'Moving Picture House'. The words were engraved on a wooden sign, the way you'd have seen 'Saloon' on a sign over the door to a Western bar. The sign hung over the concrete slab path that led from the main street into the back courtyard, where the small room was. No thought was given to how the room could have ended up there, and with it the movie *Spare Parts*. Ed listened to Haydn and watched people running, running for their lives.

With her arm outstretched, the island doctor held the photograph against the window pane. Holding a pen in her other hand, she circled his right eye socket. His skull peered into the room.

'A small fracture, probably sustained earlier. No idea how often this happens to you.'

'What?'

'Fighting, drowning, getting beaten up?'

She was slim. Her dark hair was pulled back severely into a ponytail. She waved the X-ray in the air as if she wanted to brush Ed away with a large gesture. She looked paled and haggard; it was difficult to pinpoint her age.

'Your nose is broken. At first, it was hard to catch because of all the swelling.'

Never happened before, Ed wanted to answer, but the doctor spoke quickly as if she had no time to lose.

'A transport would have been too dangerous because I couldn't judge your head injuries.' She was sitting on his bed, and fell silent, as if she had momentarily lost the thread. 'Besides, we had level-eight winds during the night.'

'It was calm in the port,' Ed murmured to show he was paying attention. His voice sounded strange, and it took effort to speak. His upper jaw hurt. Once again, the doctor circled his fractured eye socket with her pen. The X-rays gave off a grey light.

'In your case, we were able to use the X-ray machine. Strictly speaking, it's not a medical instrument, but the images are better than anything we ...' She became lost in studying the photograph. The ballpoint pen traced a fine line, barely perceptible under the eye socket. A small, almost invisible fissure in the large, smooth Gulf of Mexico. She looked at him thoughtfully for a moment, as if she wanted to hear his opinion. Then she let the image flutter onto his bedspread.

'Please keep this very carefully. I will come and collect you in a few days. I believe we need a second X-ray, Mr Bendler.'

'Thank you, thank you very much.' Ed managed to feign the trust that could be expected of a good patient.

'You should thank your friends here.' She waved her hand to include all of the Klausner, and vanished.

Ed pulled his knees into his chest, slipped his hands between his thighs. Realisation slowly seeped into him. Tears stung his cheeks. He felt his golem head; at night, his head became so large that he was afraid to move it on his pillows.

'Losh?'

It was dark. Ed had heard footsteps. The soft crunch of tar paper, steps along the roof over the dining room and up to his window.

Losh.

He climbed over Ed's typewriter and the oversize notebook. He stepped on Speiche's eyeglasses and knocked the small kidney dish with the cotton wool that Monika used to dab Ed's face off the table.

For a brief moment, silence.

Only the heavy breathing of Ed's friend on the tiny table, his sweat, his stink. For an instant, he was the nightmare that perched at night on every writing table around the globe, whistling softly, an infernally good song, its own sound, whistling until the words under its claws decided they would rather die than mean anything.

'Losh!'

'Quiet, Ed, quiet.'

'What happened,' Ed whispered, 'where were you?'

'You're my only friend, Ed.'

'I looked for you everywhere, but in Hitthim ...'

'I know, Ed, I know. Where's the photograph?'

'There.'

The nightmare slowly floated down from the table onto the bed. He took Ed's notebook and leafed through it until his sister's picture fell into his hands.

'Did you see her?' He studied the photograph.

Ed sat up. It was too dark. Losh's face was a pale spot, nothing but a faint outline of what had been lost. In the last weeks, Ed had begun to understand. He had begun to remember. He felt the despair and the loss. It was the same each time, as if he were hearing it for the first time: a tram, the final stretch, just before the last stop ...

'Of course, Losh. I look at her photograph every day. You know how much they look alike, Sonya and G.'

'No, I mean, did you see her *out there*, in the parade, on one of the boats?'

Kruso's words were rushed, and Ed did not understand the question. He probably misheard it.

'Why did you come in through the window, Losh?'

'I just need to rest for a while, that's all, a week or two. I have to

think, Ed. I want to try to move the allocations north. Somewhere
on the beach that can't be seen from the observation tower. A lot of
things need to be improved. The herb beds, the mushroom cultivation,
the whole process, especially the distribution, and new, more secure
quarters, really good hiding places.'

'Losh ...'

'In the winter, we're going to work on the bunker, you know, the
underground connection between the Klausner and the old anti-
aircraft battery. Shaft, tunnel, all buried. We'll dig it out, we have
time. We have provisions. Seclusion, everything. November to April,
six months. Then we can put up half the country down there, can you
picture it, Ed? We'll hide them all. Until there's no one left over there.
Hundreds will sit here, at long tables, on fixed benches, underground,
hidden. Hiddensee! Here on the island, there will be more free people
than ...'

'Losh!'

The two remained silent for a while. Just the sound of breathing,
the smell of sweat.

'I'm sorry I wasn't there.'

'What do they all want from you?'

'Me, you, everything.'

He was silent.

'Where's Heike? And what about René? Is he here in the
Klausner?'

'He's no longer one of us.'

'What does that mean, Losh?'

'Don't worry about it.' And then: 'You can stand in this part of
the harbour. No one drowns there, Ed.'

Kruso's hand on his face, as if he wanted to close Ed's eyes. It hurt,
but it also felt good. Maybe I only imagined him, Ed thought. Maybe
it was all just a dream. Speaking tired him out.

'Did you see her, out there on the ships?'

Kruso carefully felt the part in Ed's hair. He carefully bent Ed's ear.

His hands were cold. He had seen Ed coming. He knew everything. He knew there was nothing better than cold hands on your skin.

'Why do the moon and the man ...'

'... slide together so submissively to sea?'

TCHAIKOVSKY

All afternoon, the sun shone on the gable. Its light lay on his bed, and he could feel its warmth. As soon as it became light, the swallows began their flights. They lived in a row of shrivelled little igloos they had painstakingly built over the course of weeks on the beam above his window. Not very professionally, in Ed's opinion, rather as if they had not got used to the drooping building. Occasionally, some mud would crumble onto the window sill, the table, the notebook.

Around eleven, the noise of the holiday-makers started up. Single voices, crystal clear, and short, sharp cries of madness, like those that children give when playing. Karola's laugh like a caesura, a break in the drama of sound. Chris's 'solyanka!' and 'schnitzel!', the Klausner at lunch hour. Only a few metres away, there were hundreds of people who moved over the island as through a good life. People who hadn't done anything wrong, for the most part, anyway. They arrived on boats in the morning and they disappeared again in the evening. Lunch at the Klausner, coffee at the Enddorn, or vice versa, seven hours on the island.

For the time being, he could not go anywhere, that much was

certain. He was an elephant man, hidden away, frightening to look at. He had looked in the mirror once and decided not to do so again. He had to keep calm.

He waited for his meals. He waited for the next questioning. It was either the island police officer or the man from the sanitation department. And maybe René would even come by again, a tuft of hair in hand. I'm very sorry, but you know ... Ed got up and paced around the room. He pictured it to himself. He could only picture things. He looked out of the window now and then, but was careful to make sure no one could see him. Speiche's glasses were broken. Not the frame, just one of the lenses.

At night, the Klausner lay as still as a ship on the bottom of the sea. There were no more castaways; no feet on the stairs, no sound of rushing water from the dishwashing station. Viola was the only sound. Ed opened his door a crack to hear her better. Then he sat on his bed and dreamt. He no longer knew if he had wanted to sleep or had just slept.

The puzzle of the Hungarian border recurred every day now. Every day around one hundred, it was said, the numbers remained constant. Ed listened and shook his head involuntarily. It made him dizzy.

This time it was rolling hills — Hungary, as pictured on the Lindenblatt label, Kruso's favourite drink. The label showed hills and a copse. A copse in Hungary, behind which the refugees crouched before leaping up and running, running for their lives.

Kruso had disappeared and the ice-cream man was missing as well. 'I think you know what that means,' the island police officer had said. Ed closed his eyes and fell asleep immediately. He had learned to use his swollen face as a mask: *I'm still too weak, too tired, in no condition.* The island police officer touched his shoulder hesitantly: 'Mr Bendler.' The questioning, the third session in two days, was not finished yet. 'Mr Bendler, finally, I must ask once again what injuries you inflicted on the ice-cream man René Salzlach or might have inflicted on him in the harbour on the evening in question during your *confrontation.*' Ed was not incensed by the question. The evening in question lay years in the past, in some darkness or other, in the harbour water, which tasted of oil and algae. At a loss and apparently exhausted, he moved his head back and forth on the pillow; he let his face speak for him.

On the following day, he felt better, and on the subsequent evening his appetite returned, for the first time since the fight. He had specifically thought of it as a fight, as if the whole event could still be removed from the contours of its senselessness, as resistance or loyalty or courage. 'I also did it for you,' Ed murmured, and pulled himself together.

Kruso had invented the Island Day, but at the critical moment he had disappeared. It was childish to think this way, unfair, maybe stupid, but the disappointment stung deep. The esskays had also let him down. And evidently, there were things that Losh had kept from him; maybe Losh didn't trust him. For a moment, Ed longed to have their evenings together back, their promise. It was more than mere disappointment. There had been a — how should he put it — revelation. As if he had grown very close to Losh on those evenings. And as if Losh had not noticed at all.

The dishwashing station was neat and cleaned. He left the light off. In the kitchen, Viola's magic eye was enough of a guide for him. He moved quietly. He took two slices of bread and an onion, and sat on the chair under the radio. His life was no longer in the present. He remembered the portable radios from his childhood, which he held on his lap during family outings as he sat in the handcart. He began trembling, inexplicably, from grief and joy at the same time, if that was possible. *Probably just an effect of my injuries*, Ed thought, *a small fissure in the Gulf of Mexico.* He chewed his bread gingerly and gnawed at his onion. The pain was gone, actually, only a light stabbing in his upper jaw remained.

'To mark the end of the day, the national anthem.'

Ed thought of the man from the sanitation committee. Initially, he had commented on the working conditions, disappointed and full of empathy, but then he had only asked questions about Kruso and his role in the 'company vacation home collective'. Although it was hot in the room — so hot that Ed had begun, as if under some compulsion, to spy for cockroaches — the sanitation inspector wore a black leather jacket, with a large number of very practical pockets. The jacket made a soft chewing sound when the man straightened up or lifted his arm to brush his straight black hair from his forehead. His photosensitive glasses gradually cleared. Eventually, Ed could see his eyes: a dull, light blue.

No, this man was certainly no outcast. He had his proper place, he was an integral part of the generally accepted circumstances, and yet he also gave off a sense of desolation. It was a coarse, extensive desolation, with none of the fascinating details that Ed admired in the caretaker of the German Studies Institute and had, to a certain extent, also recognised in Krombach or Rimbaud, although they lived in completely different circumstances — indeed, they had settled in an almost completely contrary world. Perhaps there was an invisible, underlying mycelium of futility in which they were all rooted, from which they all originated and grew? A rootedness that extended deep, very far down, yes, even to the other side of history, where the continuum of emptiness reigned, that powerfully alluring void, which Ed had turned away from with such difficulty before the beginning of his journey.

He had not jumped.

When the man mentioned in passing that Ed's papers — he actually used the words 'personal file', although Ed was just a seasonal employee, a casual dishwasher, a scullion, *plongeur*, without a shred of ambition to rise to the position of kitchen hand or even counterman, in any case Ed had never considered anything from the *perspective of a gastronome* (cosmodrome), he had ultimately been busy with other matters and circumstances — in short: when the heliomatic man mentioned that although there was no registration form for the island or a certificate of health in Ed's personal file (at first, Ed thought he had said 'parasitical'), the situation could *surely be resolved along with the problem* — then Ed no longer had any doubt about who was sitting on his bed.

'So, Mr Bendler, tell me a bit about yourself, for example, about your wonderful friendship with Mr Krusowitsch, about whom, believe me, we've already heard quite a bit on the island.' He pursed his broad, ugly mouth as if for a kiss, and Ed blushed.

Ed recovered slowly. The swelling subsided, the wounds healed, but he still felt weak and rarely left his room. He often slept during the day and spent his evenings with Viola, sitting under the radio's shelf. He liked the emergency broadcasts for motorists best. One night, Cavallo came into the kitchen, turned on the light, and waved at Ed as if he hadn't expected to find him anywhere else.

'Enemy station?'

'As always.'

While Viola played Tchaikovsky, Cavallo buttered bread, cooked eggs, and washed apples. Ed marvelled again at this slender, reserved figure. He admired the way Cavallo moved his hands, his confident, smooth handling of the knife, as if Tchaikovsky had composed his movements. In the end, he packed everything into a small box.

'Right then!'

'Very hungry.'

'Endlessly. And you, Edgardo? You're holed up here with Viola, but you don't catch much, do you?'

'Exactly.'

Ed knew that Cavallo was wrong, wrong in every case. Cavallo went over to Ed and hugged him, but the dishwasher remained seated, since he hadn't understood until just then that this was a final goodbye.

Ed listened to the concerto until the end. Vladimir Horowitz on the piano. Then the program preview, then the anthem, then the midnight news and an emergency bulletin: 'Mr Dorgelow, presumed travelling in the vicinity of Hamburg in a green VW Beetle, licence number HH PN 365, is urgently requested to call home.' As Ed fell asleep, he heard Monika's voice in the corridor.

TRAVELLING THROUGH THE
REGION OF LONGING

They were going to try through Hungary, Karola told him, her voice filled with respect. She'd brought two bottles of Lindenblatt on a tray, already uncorked, along with several glasses. Ed learned that Mona had *never really* been married to René, and therefore could not officially be prevented from leaving. Ed had his doubts. Everyone was gathered around him except for Krombach and Chef Mike, who had gone to the harbour for a late delivery. As if his room were the appropriate place to toast the departure, which had come about so abruptly and without any ceremony at all.

Some sat on Ed's bed, some squatted on the floor. Rolf sat on the stool near the table and looked out the window without speaking. Him, too, Ed thought, they're all waiting. Alexander Krusowitsch, travelling through the region of longing with a great, glowing annunciation, licence number unknown, is requested to contact his family immediately. I repeat ...

After two weeks of the indefinable vacuum that had followed

the Island Day, the day of the esskays, the ultimate day off, things
happened very quickly. Cavallo and Monika left the island early in
the morning on the first ferry. Monika of all people ... How could
she leave as long as René was still missing? A small, senseless ember of
jealousy pulsed in Ed's chest. Not Tchaikovsky, but Mona, the little
invisible one, had determined the number of sandwiches.

Following a kind of last will and testament Cavallo had written
in ballpoint pen on a receipt, Rimbaud distributed his friend's books.
Ed was given a brochure about the history of the Naples Stazione
Zoologica. On the cover was a picture of a villa on the Gulf of Naples
with canals that flowed directly from the sea into the building's
underground vault — as if invented by Jules Verne. He also received
an essay on *Faust in Italy* by Paola Del Zoppo, and Goethe's *Italian
Journey*. Ed opened the latter to an underlined passage: 'Old horses.
Here, these valuable animals stand around like sheep that have lost
their shepherd.'

Around nine, Chef Mike entered the room and immediately
filled it. It was a strange, disconcerting moment that stayed in
Ed's memory for the rest of his life. They learned that Kruso had
been arrested. Arrested and taken to Rostock for questioning, it
was said. Illegal border crossing, resistance against military bodies,
suspicion of subversive organisations — suddenly everything
seemed possible. They had apprehended him in a cave in the
boscage on the Bessiner Haken in the bird sanctuary. The crazy
boy in port had spoken of handcuffs. Kruso had been led through
town in handcuffs. There had almost been a riot in front of the
Island Bar, not just esskays, but the regulars, too, had all stormed
outside, and Mother Mete had lain down in the road like a corpse,
and that sight was the final straw *for everyone*. 'In any case, they
ended up taking Kruso down to the harbour without handcuffs,
and he boarded the ship without handcuffs!' Chef Mike roared as
if he were announcing a victory.

Ed stared at the Lindenblatt label. It was misted over. He saw

Kruso's finger, the way Kruso gently rubbed it over the label, pointing at something, giving some kind of sign, for him, for his life.

On the following afternoon, Krombach entered his room. He still smelled of Exlepäng. His face was pale but shining, freshly lotioned. Ed expected a short talk. His dismissal, perhaps. The manager pressed his hands flat on Ed's table and looked out at the sea for a while.

'The swallows, eh?'

'Yes, since the baby birds hatched ...'

'They can't withstand much, these bird nests.'

Krombach took a deep breath, wiped a few flakes of mud from the table, and closed the window. Only then did Ed understand that Krombach had just lost his daughter, or at least he wouldn't see her again for a long time, if ever.

'You know Alyosha. You two were close.'

Ed was silent.

'He was a poor lad when he started here. He developed really well, astonishingly well. Those who came later hardly know anything about him, about his story and what happened back then. But he showed you everything, the hiding places, the Map of Truth, even his poems, from what I know.' He turned to face the bed and looked Ed in the eye.

'I mean his own poems, which he typed on our old Klausner typewriter.'

ROMMSTEDT

Ed almost fell on the stairs down the bluff. Holding a piece of ember with coal tongs, he had burned off a section of the shower curtain and wrapped the map in it. He turned on his flashlight and listened. He had decided that from now on he would do everything very calmly, *one step at a time*. He had never understood the expression as advice, simply as a saying: one step at a time — he had more than enough time before the midnight patrol.

There was still light over the water. A bright, almost white band, surrounded by darkness.

'It's already late.'

'I'm sorry, it's probably the very last time.'

'Maybe, maybe not. If you run into difficulties, you'll let me know, right?'

'I had bad luck, old gaffer, just bad luck,' Ed murmured, and felt around the cave. All that was left of his fox was a hard, bristly piece of leather. He carefully pushed the carcass aside and started to dig a deep enough hollow.

A week before the Island Day, Losh had hidden the map and his poems in the cellar, as a precaution, he'd said. There were forty, maybe fifty poems — Kruso's *volume*.

Ed carefully levelled the dirt and pulled the carcass back in its spot. Again, the flashlight. His fox was nothing more than the sole of a boot.

'And the map, you hero?'

Ed stared into the cave.

'What are a handful of poems compared to the map, the Map of Truth?'

It took Ed almost an hour to reach the Radiation Institute. He was not strong enough yet for the walk, but it did him good to be outside, to move, to walk in the open air with the cool night air on his face. He had to return along the top of the bluff and between the hills down to the bodden. The wound under his eye began to throb, but he was no longer afraid of being discovered. He now followed older rules: the first, fundamentally childish conviction of friendship and what that entailed when the friendship was real and singular.

The door to the old transformer house that Kruso had called the tower was unlocked. Ed tried to keep the draped wool blankets off his face, and finally found the way up. A few drawers hung open. The map had disappeared.

'Too late, too late!'

Ed almost sank to his knees.

'Don't be afraid, young man. I'm just sitting here.'

The figure in the easy chair warded off the beam of Ed's light.

'Please ...'

A cat was perched on the stranger's lap. Its head was as large and heavy as a child's. Kruso's cat. Its flat, broad paws clasped the man's knee.

'You did a lot of sighing when I saw you last. How is your face?'

'Fine,' Ed answered automatically. He could not manage more.

His eyes gradually got used to the darkness. He understood that it was Professor Rommstedt sitting across from him, Kruso's uncle, director of the Radiation Institute.

'I took a few X-rays of you, as you probably know.'

Ed tried to collect himself. The professor offered Ed his hand. Ed went over to him quickly. The man was tall, even seated. The cat opened its jaws.

'The picture, I mean the shot, was meant to have been very good, the island doctor told me.' The professor in his chair fell silent, and the half-stuttered sentence echoed until its triviality was evident.

'The picture, yes — a picture is certainly the least of it all here. But never mind. I'm happy you're here. I'm glad that Alosha had a real friend on the island.'

Ed wanted to answer, but Rommstedt parried. He asked Ed to light the candle on Kruso's desk.

'Yes, they were here, even before I got here. But what does that mean? Presumably, they are always around, they know everything, see everything, who knows. They came for the first time after Sonya's death, or rather, let's say after her disappearance. Alosha was nine years old. At the time, they interrogated each of us, even Alosha, who was completely devastated. For a long time, he didn't say a single word.'

The professor fell silent. Maybe he was in a state of shock. He seemed to have been waiting for Ed or for someone else. He wore a heavy black jacket and baggy brown corduroy trousers. He looked as if he had just finished working in the garden. Ed couldn't see his face clearly, just short silver-grey hair.

'That summer, the two of them had their own sandcastle, down on what today is the waiters' beach. They'd written on the castle with stones, white stones, black stones, gravel and basalt, a kind of mosaic they had worked on all day long, a real work of art. It had their birthdates and their names, Sonya and Alosha — Alosha from Alexander, his mother had called him that.'

'The artist.'

'They were on the beach. Alosha had seen his sister go up to the water, but certainly not more than that. "Wait here long enough and don't go anywhere" — that's what she said to him. That he should wait there *long enough* for her, in their sandcastle. Nothing more. Later, he told us the story in tears. He waited, but she didn't return. And fundamentally, he's still waiting, even now. He won't go anywhere, he's waiting for her. Perhaps you know what I mean?' Rommstedt bent forwards, and Ed saw small tufts of grey hair that grew from the professor's ears, as if his hearing were sending feelers into the darkness.

'Losh never talked about that.'

'I know. Losh from Alosha, right? Losh and Ed, these two.'

Ed wondered if Kruso had talked about him, had mentioned him now and then when he talked — 'Ed' like 'um', nothing more than filler.

'When their mother died, my brother-in-law sent the children to live with us. They were inseparable. But actually, it went deeper. They were made for each other, their entire difficult history, their tragedy had destined them for each other. One couldn't live without the other.'

Ed leaned against Kruso's desk, on which a few books were piled. More than half of the titles were missing from the worn dust jackets. From the remains, Ed recognised Benno Pludra's *Little Matten and the White Shell*, and Camus, the brown Reclam edition of *The Plague*. Nothing forbidden; no books from the West.

'What was strange,' the professor continued, 'was that on the day she disappeared, two or three greys were out patrolling on the water, not far from shore, closer than usual, in any case, surprisingly close as the islanders recounted later. Actually, no one was worried about the ships. They're a daily sight, you don't even notice them. With time, one hardly notices the border either.'

It was silent in the tower. The candle flickered, and the professor's easy chair seemed to move away slowly, drifting off into nothingness.

'Only with difficulty did we get Alosha out of his sandcastle. He stood there as if rooted to the spot, staring at the sea, trembling like an aspen leaf. At night, he would run back to the beach, to the same spot. The greys were still out there, at anchor, with their lights. He screamed, and we had to pick him up and carry him. He lashed out, and we finally had no choice but to bind his hands and feet. We put him in our handcart and pushed him home, across half the island. He screamed the entire way, I don't believe there's a single person on the island who didn't see us then.'

'Who are the greys?' Ed asked.

'The patrol boats. Border troops. I thought you'd been initiated. From then on, Alosha kept a kind of logbook. Until they came and confiscated everything, we didn't understand what he was up to. I would never have dreamed of reading his diary. He rarely spoke to us, and even less to his father, the general, when he came to visit. I believe Alosha hated him, but he hated us, too, ever since we carried him off the beach like a piece of luggage. But I beg your pardon, I have no way of knowing what Alosha, I mean Losh, has already told you about — these things. I mean, about his sister.'

'I have a photograph, it's ...'

'A photograph of Sonya!' the professor interrupted him. 'That's good, yes, that's very good. Excellent.' He was surprised and tried to hide it.

'At any rate, for seven years he noted down every one of their movements, coast guard, gunboats, minesweepers, every manoeuvre. Kind, time, the boat's course, and always whether or not there were lights, what kind, what colour. They asked him repeatedly why he had drawn an extra circle around each green light. Until the end, they couldn't explain it. Today, I'm sure that he saw them as a kind of sign — a sign from Sonya. He believed in the green light.'

Ed thought of Losh's question. If he had seen Sonya 'out there'.

'Naturally, they convicted him. Suspicion of border violation, desertion of the republic, treason, whatever term they were using at the time; he had just turned seventeen that year. One said that we'd raised a clan of border violators. From their point of view, we're the ones who cause injury: to the homeland's skin, to its sensitive body. Like bad blood, a pus-filled boil that suddenly bursts, that wants out.'

Ed wondered if he should tell the professor about the inspector from the sanitation department, but the feline shook its head slowly. It was a continuous and comforting denial, which completely captivated Ed. He thought of Matthew. His wounds were buzzing, and he would have liked to lie down and sleep on the spot.

'I made a few discoveries in the field of radiophysics, as you no doubt are aware or perhaps even can sense, if I may put it that way. After our foster-son's arrest, that was finished. All my experiments were suspended and my colleagues transferred to Berlin. The equipment is still here, well taken care of. Once in a blue moon, there's a case like yours, then I turn on my power station, and, yes, you were an unusual patient, Mr Bendler, a great sigher before the Lord, if you'll permit me.'

Rommstedt laughed softly.

A pitch-black tone was audible in the professor's bitterness, and Ed resolved to heed it.

'What happened to the diaries?'

The question seemed stupid and superfluous.

'Alosha was sent to a youth residential home, to Torgelow. Actually a prison. The Nazis interned deserters there. They released him after half a year, relatively early. Not everyone has a general for a father. We took action, too, but that's beside the point. He was expected to prove himself in the socialist-mode production and so on. Strangely, he himself suggested the Klausner. He had often been there even as a child, the seasonal workers liked him. Now and then, he helped collect glasses and wipe down tables, and they would give him ice-cream or lemonade. He spent a lot of time there. He was their little mascot, and most of them knew his story. Of course, there's no one left there from those days. Good people, scattered to the four winds. No matter. He was offered training as a skilled worker in gastronomy.

But Alosha turned them down. He just wanted to be a dishwasher, an unskilled labourer. In the end, they agreed. I believe they saw it as a kind of penance, the Klausner as work camp, washing dishes as special treatment, penal labour, temporarily. Something that would knock the nonsense out of him, a good precondition for him to make something of himself later, a recognised member of society, 'my hand for my product', along those lines. An absurd idea from today's perspective. But, back then, things were different here, the country was different, the island was different. There was no society outside of society. There were seasonal workers, fine, but not this caste and all their fuss, some of it is simply tasteless, don't you think?'

'I've hardly been a part of it, until now.'

'Didn't you ever spend a night in the Buddhist tree?'

'Losh said it wasn't really necessary.'

'Not really necessary, very good! That clever young man spent ten years washing dishes, his brain all foggy, his hands sodden, and without producing anything — not really necessary, right?'

The cat rubbed its large, round head between the professor's thighs. This time, it was nodding, nodding hypnotically.

'In the winter, I keep him officially as the caretaker of the radiation ward. It's absurd when you consider that he has refused to enter the main building since his return from Torgelow. That's when he moved into this brick building, the old transformer house, used even before our time as temporary storage for lab waste. He calls it the tower. In the winter, it gets icy in here, but that never bothered Alosha. It's his fortress. He sits at the telescope, writes, and forges some plan or other.'

'There are people who claim they saw Sonya that day, on the street, in the village.'

'There's a lot of talk on this island, my young friend. There are twenty current rumours about Sonya's disappearance, and every long winter a new one is added. Don't forget that Alosha is now very well-known here, maybe the best-known person on the island. After

Torgelow, he started speaking with absolutely everyone. He must have brought something back with him, something that has been driving him since then. He only talks to us about places to sleep in the main building, clandestine quarters for the poor devils who come to the island with nothing at all, just themselves and their longing for the wide world in their bags, every year there are more of them ... No matter. And, yes, I'm sure he only wants to do good. But they all take advantage of him, every one! Nonetheless, he tries to win over every single drunken esskay for ...'

'... the organisation, for rescuing the castaways, for their enlightenment and ...'

'Lord, yes, those are his concepts — homeless, castaways, the sacred places, all that. Alosha played pirates and castaways as a child, constantly. Maybe, please forgive me, maybe it would be better if you paid a bit more attention, observed things more closely, and drew your conclusions a bit more carefully.'

'I have always stood by Losh, at his side, that is ...'

'Yes, of course, you misunderstand me. There's no doubt it was good for Alosha that you ... stood by him. I'm convinced that he sees you as a companion, above all in his — how should I put it — in his despair. As obsessively as he kept his diary back then, so conscientious and deluded was he in creating what he later came to call the *Band of the Initiated*, I was told. A kind of underground to accumulate inner freedom, a spiritual community, something of that sort; without the injury of borders, without fleeing, without drowning. No small illusion, rather an elaborate delusion, which makes me very sad, as you probably understand.'

'You're mistaken.'

'Alosha is a young man full of longing. Are you one too, Edgar?'

'Losh helps others!' Ed's sense of justice, white-hot.

'His despair, his bitterness, it was all longing once. His longing is simply too vast.'

'Losh takes care of everyone! That's what he does. He is brave and full of ... He took me in and not just me. He taught me a lot. It's certainly not possible to understand everything right away, and sometimes I was too weak or simply too scared and ...'

'And now you're his friend. Now you want to help him. That's understandable and quite wonderful, and that's the only reason I'm talking to you. That's the only reason I'm telling you this story instead of throwing you out of this house, reporting you, or ...' he gently stroked the cat's large head, 'setting this baby on your throat.'

The professor smiled and for an instant Ed saw a row of black-lined teeth. Irradiated, Ed thought.

'We must have faith and hope for the best. I simply wanted to teach you a few things, to warn you, perhaps. The map is gone, as you can see. And Alosha won't return for a very long time, if ever. What would you think of a walk through the radiation ward?'

THE OLD LIFE

18 August. He stood for a while and stared at Speiche's bag. (Arrested.) Then he closed the armoire, sat on his bed, and pulled his own bag from under it. (For a very long time, if ever.) The zippered side compartment, where he kept his diary: he hadn't made any entries for weeks. His diary had fallen asleep. (Torgelow.)

He leafed through it. Blue lines, empty days. The rough paper that gave him a furry feeling in his mouth. SR for sunrise. SS for sunset. And the old appointments. '23 April: consultation with Professor W. about the Romantic exam; introductory topic Novalis, 1.) The "Encyclopedia", Attempt to redefine the world and its knowledge, 2.) "The Meaning of Illusion for the History of our Will", 3.) "Europe and Christendom". '8 January: A film about Max Ernst in the Film Club 66.' What had made the deepest impression on him were the pictures of the house being built in the desert, sun and wood, the painter's own house, as he had planned and built it, creating a cave for his work, far from everything, undisturbed. Every six weeks, a gallery owner from New York came to check if anything had been accomplished in the interval. '3 May: Dissertation defence of Knut

Mewes, an old friend of G.'s.' A few times, he had visited him on
Wolfstrasse, a heavy man with big eyes and heavy beard, informal,
a Wieland specialist. '2 February: coal.' '14 March: Veterinarian.'
'25 August: Yatra.' A film? Indian music? In any case, something he
had written down and planned months before. Like the trip to his
parents' bungalow (to work, if possible). Entry from 30 June, long
past. He had noted the train times from Halle to Zeitz, from Zeitz to
Meuselwitz, the bus from Meuselwitz to Kayna, by foot if necessary,
it wasn't far.

And so on.

He felt as if he were leafing through a dead man's appointment
book. And again, he felt as if his old life were still there — a strange
feeling. He had snuck away from the life that had been planned
for him. Now it seemed unfamiliar, but still destined for him. He
wondered if that life were waiting for him there, in the room with
the two shabby armchairs and the Vertiko dresser, and the lemon
geranium.

Lonely and left behind, Ed thought. My old life, leaning against
the oven. It was left standing there, by itself, alone. What an affront.

He paged through the book some more and began to count: sixty-
eight days since he arrived on the island. Sixty-eight days. Not even a
year, although years had passed, without a doubt.

He wasn't thinking *this way* explicitly, but at some point he began
counting off the days until the end of re-registration period for the new
semester. He added them up again. He had only missed three weeks
of the most recent one, not more. He could have been ill. Of course,
he didn't have a medical certificate. But the special circumstances, his
unstable condition, some kind of diagnosis, psychological problems.

He had begun thinking of G.

He could think of her again without hearing Trakl and all the rest.
He pictured her hand balled into a fist to write, and the little smiling
animal (like a mouse) that she drew in her signature with flourishes
and dots when she left him a note. 'Come to the Corso after the

demonstration. Can't wait to see you!' And under that, the mouse. It was 1 May, the holiday celebrating workers and their struggle, a lovely afternoon off after the parade, and their tradition: first the Café Corso and then to the bar called the Gosenschänke.

'I had psychological problems,' Ed practised saying. It sounded convincing.

Ed thought of Krombach.

'So, you're healthy, really healthy?'

Then his lies.

He just pretended. He had wanted to disappear, disappear completely. This was impossible in a country in which every position was somehow connected to another — university, registration office, sanitation department? *But not the Klausner*, Ed thought, *not the ark!* He shook his head, but his head was still heavy and it made him dizzy.

HIS OWN SOUND

SR. Four forty-nine a.m. It was still dark when he left. He crossed the woods and took the concrete path. Through the soft soles of his suede shoes, he could feel the signs. It was as if he were standing on his father's feet again and his father were walking forwards, the old game, Sunday afternoon after he had finished his *exercises*. They started after breakfast, around nine. Around ten came the first tears. Ed lost the ability to add two plus two. Then the worst: his father's resolution to explain mathematics to him again *from the top,* from the very beginning. 'What can you possibly hope to do without the foundation on which everything is built?' What followed was impatience, fits of anger, a rushing sound in his head. Sidelong glances at the clock. It had to end at some point. And then it was over. Ed's father lifted him up and held him close. Then he set Ed down, feet on top of his own in slippers. They strode in big steps across the orange rug (Ed with his arms wrapped around his father's hips) to the balcony and back to the bedroom door, back and forth, with big steps counter to their own internal walking. With each step, Ed had to surrender his own sense of direction, grounded deep within his body: resistance, abandonment, relief, in each and every step, and rejoicing — after all, it was a game ... *Letting yourself go*, Ed thought.

No one seemed to have seriously considered the possibility that he might leave the island.

In fact, neither the island police officer nor the inspector had said anything that would have required him to stay, anything that would have implied he was under arrest. They found him suspicious. And he was ill. And he belonged to the Klausner, practically forever. Something made them feel certain. Maybe his face. But his wounds were healing even though he still looked like a marked man. *As if I had no life of my own*, Ed thought.

When he put his foot down flatter and harder, he could feel the imprints in the concrete slabs. A few, as far as Ed understood, indicated the quality grade of the concrete. Others resembled hieroglyphs, writing from the pyramids, Ancient Egyptian, Aztec, Sumerian perhaps. 'They free us from all gravity. If you hit them just right, they will relieve you, heart and soul, from the burden of existence,' Kruso had told him, and sped up. His stiff-hipped gait over the signs. The fixed square, in the middle of which were Kruso's privates — Ed thought of the word, and it flashed in front of his eyes, in the centre of the movement. The path headed downhill, past the greater island view. His pace was now a run, without effort, a light bounce, each step covering two or three slabs, from one sign to the next. With every impact of his foot on the ground, something burst inside Ed. After fifty metres, he was freed of any sense of embarrassment: two grown men running down the slope like children. 'Come on, come on!' Kruso yelled, running even faster. Ed felt the springiness. Their loping stride. The island lay spread out before him, and he was set to fly over it. A rising and falling of the world, up and down; his spinal cord melted and began to flow, a feeling of omnipotence. It streamed into him from behind and filled him up. He rejoiced. He leapt and rejoiced, he could not resist. '*Davai, davai*,' Kruso shouted. Land and

sea had become one. Ed breathed in the sea air, the smell of the island.
He ran through the air, as in dreams.

Fifteen minutes to the harbour. In any event, it was to be expected
that the boats were under surveillance. First, he hid behind the
remains of the harbour latrine, a boarded-up shack from a bygone
era. He shoved his bag into the bushes and sat on it. He was now in
the depths of defeat, just him on his own.

It soon became light, and the first ferry passengers arrived. Only
the locals used the early ferry, people who worked on the mainland
or went there to shop. They greeted each other and knew the captain.
Ed envied the islanders their laconic way of being with each other,
interactions that involved few, if any, words, but consisted of gestures.
A curt nod, an incomprehensible phrase, expressions of their
resistance to the countless strangers and their chattering invasion,
the cacophony fundamentally alien to the north that flooded the
island every summer. There was also a border against the esskays and
their unrestrained gossip about the island, the sea, and life. Even
on crowded ships, the natives were immediately recognisable. They
seemed completely impervious to the surrounding din, as if they
had permanently walled off their existence, yes, as if they had been
inoculated and were forever immune to the repulsive species called
holiday-makers. The worlds did not mix. Only someone like Kruso
moved in both spheres ... Arrested, Ed thought. Not for a long time,
if ever. Torgelow.

The short gangway, made of boards with a metal pipe for a handrail,
was dragged to the boat. Ed stood up. The straps of his travel bag cut
into his shoulder. That's when he saw them, the counter-couple. With
a handcart full of luggage. Ed was still uncertain, something in their
bearing seemed odd, as if they trying to not be that — and maybe
they weren't? Ed hesitated. Once again, he shoved his bag into the
shrubbery, and walked in an arc — back towards the harbour.

The counter-couple. Two seconds full of joy. The way you meet an acquaintance unexpectedly and greet him more enthusiastically than usual. In the next moment, Karola's expression had already become guarded; Rick was looking intensely at the ferry.

In a rush, Ed had explained that he had only wanted to collect one of the Klausner's carts from the harbour to transport the bread. As he did so, his glance fell on the cart with the luggage and the name 'Zum Klausner' in red paint, and his lie hung there as if also painted in red.

'Fine, hang on,' Karola said abruptly, and started to unload their bags in her energetic way.

'No, don't, there are plenty of others, other carts, back there with the other carts,' Ed quickly assured her. Blood surged in his head, but what else could he do — he helped unload. And finally, as if it were the only reason he was there, he also helped stow their things in the bow of the ferry. The gap between the pier and the side of the boat, his fear of drawbridges. The moment to confide in each other had passed. No chance to ask where they were headed. One of the messages or the mystery of the Hungarian border? No questions.

The luggage: it was *everything*. Glasses clinked in one bag; a night-table lamp encrusted with shells and pieces of amber stuck out of another. Something large, something immeasurable had shifted. And things were still shifting, inexorably, incessantly, as if they were part of the movement of geological plates (a deep, childish feeling), and, when the counter-couple had crossed the drawbridge and the motors started up and the metal hull began to shudder, they were already as far from each other as if on different continents.

The ferry's horn began to blow, and the crazy boy appeared. He was guiding the ferry on its departure. The rear of the boat slowly moved away from the side of the harbour and moved into the harbour basin. The boy's right arm circled in the air like a windmill, and the hull turned onto its course. With a muffled hum, the steamboat began its trip. Ed breathed in the diesel fumes, the blue-black poison that burned his mucous membranes.

Karola's lips were tight, as if she had decided not to say another word, neither about the Klausner nor about its sworn community, for whom the counter-couple had served as parents. Maybe they didn't trust him — in fact, they surely didn't. What else could they think about his sudden appearance in the harbour? Coming for the bread, even though at this time every morning he sat in the cellar tending the boiler. Coming for the bread, even though Baker Kasten never had the bread before eight anyway ... Only then did Ed notice the tears, and Karola did open her mouth in the end. The diesel motor revved, so the only thing that reached him was the movement of her lips.

Ed stared at her. He raised an arm, doubtfully, hesitantly. Inadvertently, he had landed on the wrong side of the parting.

'When else, Ed.'

Did she say that?

Yes, without a doubt, she had.

Or was it something else?

'It was nice, Ed' or 'Take care, Ed' or 'Whatever you want, Ed.'

Take care. And she'd made some kind of sign at Ed, as if she wanted to caress him and then as if she wanted to caress the Dornbusch as well, the highland and the entire island. Caress it very tenderly, as was possible from such a distance. She and Rick had stood at the railing for a while and then they'd disappeared.

Ed still couldn't believe they'd gone. It was even harder for him to accept what they'd taken him for. Betrayal from all sides. The idea of the counter without the counter-couple.

Herds of day tourists passed him. Departure of the next ferry and the one after, without Ed. The coachman Mäcki and his bear-horse, which gave him a questioning look. The crazy boy with his mouth open: he sat on a plastic chair at the edge of the harbour with his legs crossed and his upper body turned to the side, as if he'd been

overcome with a sudden wave of disgust. But it was only in reaction
to the wind: the boy bent his head so that the wind would blow into
his mouth more easily. He grunted and roared into the wind and gave
long, drawn out cries like a seagull or a baby. Ed realised as he passed
him that this was no boy, no child, and hadn't been for a long time.
His face was old.

Since Ed's embarrassment did not lessen, he continued to pretend
he'd come for the bread. He dragged his bag from the bushes and
threw it into the handcart. Too late, he remembered the bottle — the
Blue Strangler, unbroken. He unscrewed the top, listening to the soft
crackling. He drank, and heard the whistling — against the western
moon.

The door to the Hitthim was boarded up. Ed wondered if it had
been damaged *in the fight*. How he and René had covered the long
way to the harbour basin, he couldn't remember. He looked around
as if there might still be some traces. As if the ice-cream man might
come out from behind the chestnut tree that stood halfway between
the Hitthim and the harbour basin, the only tree far and wide. I'm
sorry, but you know ... A tuft of hair in his hand.

Ed recognised Santiago's silhouette behind the counter in the
Island Bar, He looked at the ground, skirted a hole in the sand,
and passed by. A light still burned in the display case outside the
Gerhart Hauptmann House even though the sun was high. Instead
of Hauptmann's poem, an announcement for a reading by the writer
Rainer Kirsch hung behind the glass, the launch of his new volume of
poems. The blue in Ivo Hauptmann's watercolour was faded, and rust
had spread from the thumbtacks. For some reason, Ed felt close to
the painter Ivo Hauptman, perhaps simply because he had managed
to be a son.

Ed left the handcart on the path and trudged northwards on the
waiters' beach. It was completely empty at this hour. He climbed over

the wire that separated the beach from the stabilising coastal dunes. After a few metres, he dropped to the ground and fell asleep. Once again, he saw the hand that had blessed him at the first breakfast; then Losh's hand on his shoulder.

When Ed woke, the sun was shining in his face. He could feel it healing his wounds. He pulled the bottle from his bag, drank, and fell back asleep. He dreamed his camel dream, the dream with which he had first made his break. When he woke the second time, he saw the Klausner, the ark. Those missing: René, Cavallo, Monika, Karola, Rick, Kruso, and himself, more than half the crew. He drank, ate the onion he had packed for the crossing, and the two slices of bread. Pushed by the wind, the tips of the sea grass traced geometrically neat circles in the sand. And with it, the surf, the soft, constant rushing sound that had enveloped Ed's thoughts like a warm, protective cocoon.

Then he heard it. The first time. The sound dwelt within him. His own sound, as good as a fate of his own. He just had to follow it. Two weeks until the end of summer, four weeks until the end of high season, Ed thought, and closed his eyes again, but only for a few seconds.

THE BLOOD WILL COME LATER

The island's Capri-path ran close to the edge of the escarpment. It was so thickly lined with trees and shrubbery, that there was seldom an open view of the sea. Ed breathed in the smell of the forest, which, together with the noise of the surf, inspired some vaguely Asian associations. Before the flights of tree-root steps, long carpets of pine needles had piled up. They returned each of his steps, soft and springy, as if walking were pure grace and as if the way home had long been ready: yes, I'm coming, I'll be there at the sinks and the furnace, dishwasher and boilerman, and if I can move fast enough, I could also help at the bar, with the lemonade, for example, the seltzer. Rimbaud and Chris will have to take over another part. Maybe Rolf could do the coffee. The ice-cream hatch will stay closed — no loss.

Ed hardly felt the weight of his bag. The horizon was white, as if smudged. In the foreground, he could see the outline of a patrol boat; the more clearly it emerged from the fog, the more unreal seemed to him the plans he had had just that morning. The unspoken requirements — he was now fulfilling them. He felt at home in the Klausner as nowhere else.

He remembered how, on afternoons after school when he was a child, he had headed off on his own through the forest, all the way to the forest's edge. He had never thought about it before: he had always gone all the way to a small moss-covered embankment with a view of the fields in which the end of the world swayed or stood still. Then, sooner or later, it was time for him to head home.

He picked up a few large leaves, rolled his pant legs up to his knees, and squatted in one of the ditches. They reminded him of bomb craters. The undersides of the leaves were covered with small white hairs that felt surprisingly raw against his anus. He had to be careful because the leaves tore easily. He kept squatting for a while, as if turned to stone. A warm wind that blew in from the sea played between his legs and gave him goosebumps.

'I've almost got it!'

Ed froze, then he recognised the voice. It was the good soldier. He was crouching just thirty or forty metres from Ed, trying to light a fire. As he broke small branches and blew on a flame Ed couldn't see, the soldier talked to himself out loud. As if in the next scene of a shadow play, a second person, who had remained hidden behind the trunk of a tall, dark beechwood tree until then, was pushed onto the stage. His outline immediately came into focus. There wasn't the slightest doubt: it was Kruso.

Or not. *Too much Blue Strangler*, Ed thought, and remained in a squat. The light of the setting sun projected shapes into the forest, desired images and voices. Ed tried to concentrate on his pants: pants, belt, shirt. A flood of joy had begun to throb inside him, and his hands shook. He couldn't help it.

In the next scene, Kruso's silhouette melted with the good soldier's. Ed was almost blinded by the sun's rays that penetrated the underbrush from the sea. He heard laughter, almost a snigger, and then he heard the Kruso-figure explaining something in its earnest tone. It pointed at the trunk of a tree, and all of a sudden Ed recognised the tree. It was the Buddha tree, the tree with many arms and bottles — the tree of inexhaustible drink, as the esskays called it — their enchanted tree.

Their embrace was long, tight, and full of meaning. The good soldier pulled a few bottles out from among the roots. They clinked bottles, drank, clinked bottles again. They laughed like thieves who had pulled off an utterly unbelievable heist.

Ed's joy was completely pure and immediately outshone all his defeats — the loss of his room to the allocations, the loss of C. to the rules, all the sleepless night, the wounds on his face. He felt as relieved as a child who suddenly realises all his fears and worries were ungrounded. He had lost a friend, he had lost the island, and now he had got everything back — in a single blow.

'How are you doing, Losh?'

'I'm doing well, Ed, really well.'

'Didn't they ...'

With one wave of his hand, Kruso swept the question aside. They drank and laughed. They were laughing! Ed thought of handcuffs, interrogations, a cell in Rostock or Torgelow, maybe even torture ...

They embraced again. They would talk later, for sure.

Ed could read a few things from Kruso's big, warm cheeks and from his chest, his heartbeat, in which their friendship and an iron will throbbed. Ed thought of Rommstedt, the radiation ward, but this moment overpowered every doubt. Cheek against cheek.

'Ho-ho,' the good soldier said. With a secretive expression, he pulled a razor from his pack — that is, later, Ed wasn't sure where it had suddenly come from, that cheap, dull blade encrusted with dried soap.

They followed Kruso a few steps towards the shore. The fireball sank, the red sun; in a few minutes, the sea would swallow it.

First, the question of where they should cut themselves. It had to be a *good spot*, Kruso declared. With the word 'cut', Ed's first thought was of the pulse, then the soft white inner arm with the blue-green delta under his skin. He felt hardly any fear. He was probably drunk. Like a craftsman testing a tool, Kruso felt his own tanned, hairy arm. He found a suitable spot above his wrist, 'always visible, a scar for life, more precious than gold' — Alexander Krusowitsch could say such things without seeming ridiculous.

Of course, he went first, vigorously and without hesitation. To Ed's surprise, the good soldier grabbed the blade next. Kruso encouraged him, which did not annoy or hurt Ed, which it might have done since the soldier was suddenly on the same level with them, the two companions, on the same level with their reunion (his friend's return home, which merged with his own return — good thing he had left his bag behind in the ditch), a reunion filled with a joy on which everything to come could be built ... Yes, it was a victory. And the more Ed thought about it, the less clear it was to Ed why the good soldier should be allowed, just like that, to be the third in their bond.

'Brothers, to the sun, to freedom,' Kruso enjoined, then lapsed into an incomprehensible murmur. Brothers get up to the light. Ed's heart caught the hint. You have to open yourself up, stand together, *let go*. And the soldier was certainly not one of the shady characters. Kruso knew what he was doing.

The blade was greasy with the good soldier's blood. Ed was surprised at how easily it bent and how hard it was to hold between his thumb and index finger. Ed's father had shaved dry and, when Ed was fifteen, had given him his old Bebo Sher electric shaver.

One jerk — no blood.

So Ed tried again, and his hand cramped as if he were a child determined to write even though he is not used to the writing implement. His hand slipped, and he missed the previous cut. The thought of how good he had been in drawing a straight line freehand was completely useless at this moment. 'Exactly as if you'd used a ruler, Edgar!' his mother had often exclaimed, full of praise. But on his own skin, it was different. Skin doesn't give way, skin slips away.

What he later recalled: that he would have liked to say his useless thoughts out loud. Maybe he had, in his fear, too much force and would, for example, damage a valuable vessel. For a moment, the absurd thought flitted through Ed's mind that he might be *dry* inside or that there simply wasn't enough of the sap of brotherhood flowing through him, which now needed to be brought out in the open and displayed. It surely had something to do with his low blood pressure. Since his earliest childhood, he had got used to drinking coffee, not just at family celebrations, but also on weekdays, coffee and cake, every afternoon with his parents after work, 'real coffee beans!', the proud exclamation about the costliness of the bitter drink they had to dilute for him with milk or water, 'the blood will come later …'

'The blood will come later,' Kruso whispered soothingly and with a note of concern in his voice when he saw Ed fumbling with the blade on his skin, his movements hectic and nervous as he attempted to deepen the cut he had made.

Kruso and the good soldier held their bent arms together as if they were comparing watches. The good soldier's wound seeped a bit along the edges. Kruso's blood dripped right onto the sand. He put his foot on it and then twisted it as if he were crushing a cigarette.

Suddenly blood.

It poured from all his scratches and cuts, in every direction: it overflowed. In a complete rage, Ed dragged the sticky blade once again through his flesh, pointlessly — the blood quite simply did him good.

The sun disappeared. The sea became dark and massive. The trees' outlines were now tangible. The night sound of the surf was powerful and even stronger up where they were. The island was like a stranded animal, breathing in sleep or on the brink of death, in, out, in, out … Ed saw a large, shining chrome stethoscope, saw it push into the wrinkled, grey skin and disappear; then the muffled heartbeat: Dr-Dr-Dr-Dolittle. It was all ludicrous compared with the three of them up there with the cleanly bleeding arms. The entire history of their childhood was ludicrous, as ludicrous as the term 'border violator', as ludicrous as the world in comparison. They listened to the long, continuous rolling of the surf, and they pressed their arms together, hands balled into fists. Ed felt a warm thread of blood trickle down his elbow, and it was the right moment: he slowly slid out of his cocoon, through a tunnel of sighs; he stretched forward, let himself go — and won two brothers.

PAN

It was all over with the clandestine quarters. The castaways trotted along the beach like sheep without a shepherd. Their pilgrimage gradually ebbed, but new faces still cropped up daily to follow the predetermined paths of freedom. There were always a few who had heard something about donkey stalls, waiter's rooms, or gravedigger huts, and a terrace with wonderful views high above the sea where you could get something to drink and warm soup every day. A few stayed on the beach for a few nights. At one point or another, they were tracked down, charged with suspicion of desertion of the republic, and summarily escorted to the next ferry, not without a threat that 'officials would be calling on them' and that they would 'hear from us again soon, very soon'.

The mood among the esskays was subdued. They were withdrawn, suspicious, sparing with gestures of fellowship. Part of the caste had already left Hiddensee and headed south, it was said. Not much more was said about them, as if the subject were somehow taboo, like a serious illness, or silenced by the reticence lovers experience when their relationship suddenly ends. That almost nothing was said about the *new developments* that played a role hourly for Viola and were already the second or third item in the news reports — this initially seemed to Ed to be a measure of general caution. Only gradually did he begin to understand that it was primarily due to a desire to hold on to an advantage based entirely on the island and the islanders, an almost ancestral sense of self-confidence and self-assurance that was secretly connected to the island: they were island people and would always remain island people. They wanted to protect this rare, yes, unique enclave from the challenges in the rest of the world, with its trials and tribulations, its threats and temptations, all its demands and intrusiveness, its boundless appetite for islands ...

Kruso took over the bar duties without any fuss. Chris and Rimbaud gave their all to waiting tables. Ed practically washed the dishes by himself. He was strong enough, and he had the confidence. Since his return to work, he worked almost without stopping. After work, he sat in his place under the radio to rest awhile and gnaw on his onion. Notably, the reports about a so-called picnic, a pan-European picnic, they called it, at which more than six hundred refugees crossed the border into Austria, fit seamlessly into the world of images with which Ed imagined this southern region, with its bushes, vineyards, and a wire fence that was presumably gaping with holes. A deadly escape had turned into a picnic; people arrived carrying blankets, baskets, maybe Hungarian salami, too. Pan emerged and made music in European fashion ... Exhausted from his day, Ed slipped into this bizarre dream in which a metal wall turned first into a ramshackle fence and then into sweetly whispering reeds.

During the day, these events were not a topic of conversation. Only Rimbaud, on whom Cavallo's disappearance weighed (although he would never have admitted it), made a comment now and then, caustic quips, pronouncements about the situation, like blows, but the ends of his sentences trembled. He hadn't left any books

PAN

in the nest for quite some time, and at some point he had stopped writing philosophical mottos on the menu board. Instead, he started delivering monologues about politics, and preferred to hold forth on politicians in the West. It sounded like he was reciting a cynical poem, yes, as if Antonin Artaud had risen from the dead to spew his faecal scorn over everyone and everything.

Rimbaud liked to insult the guests. He commented on their appearance, their orders, their, in his view, more than deficient intellectual and verbal abilities. 'Each according to his ability!' he would shout over the tables when he stepped out on the terrace with a tray full of beer glasses. With the exclamation, his imperious expression. Like a general the night before the last battle.

Rimbaud's hair turned grey during those days. His moustache was stuck together, his eyes were round and shining when he speared the charge slips next to the cash register, but he hardly ever raised his head anymore. 'Fame, when will you come ...' He slowly turned into a spectre. When he stormed down the racetrack to the dishwashing station and banged the dishes down on the rack, he looked like he was about to vomit.

As so often in recent days, the counter-couple's absence was keenly felt: Karola's magic tea, the ice, her cold fingertips on Ed's back. And Rick, who never considered himself too good to apologise to the guests for his waiters, always without reproaching his colleagues. Only good words and paternal reminders passed from his lips as their old bartender lined up the staff's personal glasses on the counter's SprelaCart-laminated surface and filled them to the rim with the sticky, sweet balm of consolation.

27 August. Krombach lugged piles of bed linens across the courtyard, his face buried in the laundry. The last of the good smell, Ed thought. The manager had taken over his daughter's tasks, and completed them like memorial service. Krombach also set the tables in the

dining room: breadbasket, tableware, the condiment set with the orange mustard jar in the middle. Like a busboy on his first day, he traipsed back and forth in front of the bar. He filled the salt and pepper shakers, and stirred the mustard in those pots in which little pools of water had formed in the middle of the surface and the edges had turned dark brown and hard.

'Good morning, Mr Bendler!'

Ed whirled around; a soup bowl banged against the side of the stone sink. The sanitation inspector raised his hands and smiled his photosensitive grin. He must have snuck up the ramp to the dishwashing station. Ed tried to concentrate on his work. The inspector dropped into a crouch with a flourish and poked around the drains for a while. Maybe the dishwashing fumes had wiped his memory. He suddenly sprang up, grabbed Ed's arm, and told him to report to the registration office 'at the end of the shift'.

Kruso had taken up his forays again. Ed didn't understand how he could risk making his rounds again. The circuit on the first day off after his return was like a victory parade. He was greeted almost everywhere they went, often with a loud hello, drinks, food, small gifts. At the Dornbusch Apartments, he was given an entire bottle of peppermint schnapps. At the Island Bar, Santiago prepared him a meal. Still, no one was prepared to return to the old arrangements. People changed the subject, poured another drink, recounted island anecdotes. No matter how often their old impresario tried (in the most indirect, delicate, and respectful way), he met with evasions, excuses, and occasionally simple silence. In his disappointment, Kruso began using phrases like 'by any means' and 'the situation requires'. The longer he spoke, the emptier the esskays' faces became.

In those days, Kruso took very long walks. After work, he hiked to the relatively isolated southern end of the island, where he was less known, but he didn't find any new confederates there either. The old readiness for enthusiasm that was naturally connected to the idea of freedom and the purest form of island patriotism, was suddenly gone. From Kruso's point of view, it was a regression into seasonal stupor, a kind of sickness, an infection — it all resembled the course of a plague.

The suspicion occasioned by Kruso's quick return was serious. His reputation as a hero (led away in handcuffs) had become doubtful, and there were rumours.

'Kruso, a Russian?'

'But he speaks German.'

'And his accent? Those funny words?'

'Maybe some kind of Thuringian dialect.'

'He's not from there.'

'But he's not from here either, is he?'

On days that would have been allocation days, Kruso sat on the terrace of the Klausner and drank. A few esskays came and brought excuses from others. At work, Kruso now mostly spoke with Rimbaud. Occasionally, he would go see Krombach in his office. At night, he sat with Ed, whose blood-brotherhood scratches (seven cuts) had got infected in the dishwater. But it wasn't worth mentioning, not in front of Losh when he came to visit Ed in his room, almost as before.

Ed had plenty of questions, but Kruso looked at him questioningly. As if it were up to Ed to address something, to name it, a disaster, an invisible wound. Generally, he asked Ed to recite some Trakl, ideally the verses in which his sister appeared. There were many of these, twenty or thirty poems, or perhaps more. Kruso himself never recited anything anymore. He explained that he was *no longer pure enough* to do so, whatever that was supposed to mean. He said other strange things as well. The only thing he wouldn't talk about was his arrest. Ed decided not to pressure him. Kruso only asked his friend to recite Trakl, and insisted until Ed actually tried.

Ed got through four lines, then stopped. For a while, he tried to continue soundlessly, only moving his lips, then gave up. His face became blank, completely expressionless. At the moment, his cheeks were too big and had the same firmness as a nursing infant's cheeks. The place of deepest tenderness. For a few seconds, Ed looked at his friend with new eyes, but he could not bear it any longer than that. He softly read the poem out loud. He did his best, made an effort, and after a few verses he noticed that he was able to hit the right tone. His heart beat harder. In his voice vibrated the power, the rhythm, enough to doctor the invisible wounds with poetry, poetry of a melancholy and grief that outdid everything.

They drank Lindenblatt. They were talking about migratory birds and bird bands, when Kruso suddenly reassured him that he had not been with René. Been what, Ed asked, and Kruso explained that he and a few others had simply helped him, although essentially it was too late and he was still sorry for that. But now Ed was well again, after the radiation treatment. What treatment, Ed wanted to ask, but it wasn't important. An X-ray, maybe several, whatever. He felt secure in his friend's presence. Now, in fact, his brother.

THE MACHINE

'How are you doing?' Ed asked.

The boot sole had a bony face, patches of fur. The new, mocking grin couldn't be attributed to any species, but it was still his fox, its empty eye sockets completely attentive.

'When will you bury me, Ed?'

'I'd like to read something to you, please.'

Ed ceremoniously pulled a piece of paper from his pocket and began reading:

You can ask me and I will tell you openly what I think and know, and I would like to maintain that same degree of openness with others, but I can't when I am working with you ...

'What do you think?'

'Dreadful.'

I cannot lead a double life. I have to be able to talk about everything I see and think with those involved. The mere idea makes me anxious.

'And how's that?'

'Terrible, Ed. What's with the anxiety? Do you think anyone is interested in your anxiety? Show it as a real weakness instead. You're a talkative person. A bad character. You can't keep anything to yourself, you always blurt out everything. You're constitutionally completely unsuitable and so on. You have to admit. On top of that, you're a moraliser about truth. You're incapable of lying, even if you wanted to, you know? You assume responsibility, you prove your vigilance and class consciousness by warning others about yourself.'

After Vitte, Ed continued along the beach. He could feel inclusions of the old fear, mummified, half-petrified, imperishable fears, ready to rise again. Once again, they had begun transmitting their positions, their status, their childish labels and names like 'Helmut's dog' or 'Going blind in your sleep' or 'Ravenous, evil sandman', and so on, along with the more superficial ones called 'Exam in ten days' or 'Obstacle course' or 'Code red'. Languages also hibernate somewhere deep in the body if not spoken for a long time (like Russian, for example), like words unused for ages and feelings you don't ever want to feel again, all endure this way, deep inside oneself, Ed thought.

A side door of the Free German Trade Union Federation hotel, Zur Ostsee, stood open. A dark-panelled room, dimly lit, the white tablecloths like small sails, lost in the room's expanse. A waiter, bending over a chest of similarly dark wood, sorted cutlery into compartments for knives, forks, and fire. Ed looked at the ground and slipped by. He continued on in this posture. Black and white stone tiles in the entrance to the lobby, an intimation of coolness and a better life.

The door to the registration office. Ed hesitated briefly then entered. The woman behind the typewriter looked up and gave a wide smile.

'Please go right in to the back!'

She must have been familiar with the entire procedure and so Ed interpreted her peculiar cheerfulness as a dubious, perhaps desperate, attempt to escape her role.

The door to the back room was ajar. The sanitation inspector came to greet him. Halfway to Ed, he thrust his arm in the air like a traffic cop on duty, and, for the first time, offered his name: 'Rebhuhn, at your service!' With his right hand, he gestured towards a chair that was obviously meant for Ed. His left hand pointed to his own seat. They sat across from each other on opposite sides of an elongated table, around which stood ten or twelve more chairs.

'How are you, Mr Bendler?'

It briefly occurred to Ed that the staff breakfasts had recently been especially subdued and silent. The ends of the table were unchanged: Chef Mike and Krombach, like bridgeheads. The one drenched in sweat, the other in a cloud of Exlepäng and face cream. On Ed's side, only he and Rolf were left, separated by a few chairs, since the seating order remained unchanged. To his left, the counter-couple was missing; to his right, René. They had *distanced themselves* from him, and it was his own fault ... Sometimes this thought overpowered him.

'Mr Bendler?'

The inspector was wearing the black leather jacket with the many practical pockets. His photosensitive glasses shimmered a soft light brown. On the chair at the head of the table was a flat briefcase, as if it were presiding over their meeting.

Ed brushed the hair from his face. His wounds had healed. He didn't know what to say.

'Excellent treatment from Professor Rommstedt, right? Did you speak to him at length? How do you judge him? We had some problems with him earlier, which is always a shame — with such an excellent scientist, if you know what I mean. We need science! More than ever. We need hand, heart, *and* mind! Surely you've heard about our 32-bit microprocessor! Neither ox nor ass!'

'I was still unconscious during the — treatment. And what I wanted to say was ...'

'Of course. You were not conscious, Mr Bendler. But it's now time that you came to. How is your friend doing now, after his happy return home?'

Ed looked out the window. A muddy courtyard with deep, broad tyre tracks, as if a tractor had driven in circles. In the middle of the mud circle was a discarded vehicle, and next to it the island police officer's green moped with a helmet hung on the handlebars. The sea was only one hundred metres away, but Ed couldn't hear it.

'How are you managing now, up there in the Klausner? And was else do you get up to, in the evenings, say? Back to poetry? Or drawing maps? Visuals for the castaways and the homeless, as your friend calls them, so thoughtful and caring with his Slavic soul, isn't that right, Mr Bendler? Speak frankly and unburden your own heart!'

Rebhuhn. *'Partridge' is an odd choice if it's a made-up name*, Ed thought. He wondered if there were a tape recorder in the briefcase to capture the self-criticism he had prepared with his fox's help. Again, he pictured the B56, his father's Czech tape recorder in the wall cabinet, the little gears to spool the tape and the fire-engine-red record button — 'Don't cry for me Argentina'. Ed had often rewound to that song and ...

'I'll just say it between us, more or less. If your friend weren't so thoroughly Slavic — or how should I put it, Mr Bendler? — then he wouldn't be walking around free anymore, wouldn't have been for a long time, now. You do understand that, don't you? Or let's just say: Soviet jurisdiction. A father in Potsdam's Russian Military City, Lordy! A general! But you've known that for a while. However, we're the ones who get stuck with the aggravation, the work, the consequences, as if this here were Sakhalin or Saint Helena! But not just us: you, too, and the professor, the Klausner, everyone he draws into his circle. That's exactly what you don't seem to realise, Mr Bendler, how much danger ...

First the DJ's voice, his fake enthusiasm, which even the soft, swaying beat of the song's opening couldn't stop, and so it forever spoiled the first measures. But Ed was already stretched out on the carpet, his arms outspread, in anticipation of the unearthly voice of a singer named Julie Covington. He was fourteen years old and actually hated everything that could be considered pop music. But he just lay there on the carpet, and soon his tears began to flow.

'Alexander Krusowitsch is my brother.'

That isn't exactly what he had wanted to say.

Not exactly what he had prepared.

But it was his sentence. A pretty good one.

He was still looking out the window.

His second good sentence was already circling over the tyre tracks in the courtyard.

'Aren't we all Slavs, up to the Elbe, Mr Rebhuhn?'

A second later, he was no longer sure if he had said 'Slavs' or 'slaves'.

The sanitation inspector stared at him, then at his notebook, as if he had to force himself to turn away from Ed's appearance in all its repulsiveness. A dirty, little seasonal worker, fickle, unstable, difficult to assess. Dropped his studies despite good prospects and hasn't learned anything in life yet aside from a few poems full of dull, incestuous lines.

They left the registration office, but they weren't finished. Rebhuhn led the way. The idea of being seen with him was unbearable. Two cyclists, some people out walking, tourists on their evening stroll to dinner, often served as early as six o'clock in the vacation homes. They entered a building diagonally opposite the registration office. A small, shadowy hallway with a flight of stairs to the basement at the end. First, a low-ceilinged, neon-lit room that looked like a classroom with its benches and chairs. It smelled of disinfectant or maybe it was rat poison. Ed felt a slight vibration and then he heard the humming noise. The inspector went to the front of the classroom and pulled a rod from under the teacher's desk. He stared at the rod's red lacquered tip, spun it gently, and brought it to his lips as if he wanted to kiss it. Finally, he pursed his lips and blew an imaginary bit of dust or chalk from the lacquer, which then seemed to shine or glow, but it was just a reflection of the neon light. Each movement of his hand seemed casual and confident, unlike his movements in the registration office. Only then did Rebhuhn seem to come into his own. He perched on the table, his posture nonchalant and superior. The handle of the rod beat lightly and almost impatiently against metal. Ed had stopped in the doorway to the classroom, a student waiting for his punishment. The chalkboard was pristine, as if nothing had ever been written on it.

Ed regretted having come. He could have refused. (Couldn't he?) He could have forgotten, unintentionally, but he had been afraid and had the feeling he just had to get through it. He simply needed to take this step to prove that he didn't feel contempt for the inspector (which he, in fact, did) and by showing him this bare minimum of respect (consoled him, Ed thought, consoled him for all the deceitfulness and ugliness in his appearance). He would open a way for his retreat and reveal his complete ineptitude for conspiracy. A refusal at the outset, however, would have been impossible, unacceptable. First, you have to respect the deadline, then you have to pull your head (carefully, slowly) out of the noose. But Ed's fear had returned. Abject fear, beyond thought.

The inspector approached Ed with little rhythmic double beats, first against the benches, then against the wall. A previously invisible door opened, Sesame opened. All routine, Ed thought, the usual routine. The only thing odd, was that *he* was experiencing it, now, at this moment.

The humming noise swelled, grew loud, a breath-taking stench hit him. They entered the machine room. Rebhuhn stood to Ed's right and greeted the machinist. The machine consisted of a steel frame in the centre of the room with a bulky cover that gave off a milky glow. It had a head, but no face. In any case, no lips and no ears, just teeth. It had hair, clotted with sand and algae, parts of limbs on every side, translucent and grey or green like a film drawn over moss, a swollen foot. Something like a foot. It wasn't the machine that was humming, it wasn't humming ...

Ed stepped back, looking for the door out, but the machinist blocked his way and pushed a white enamel pail against his chest. At first, Ed thought the man wanted to put the pail on his head, but he was just trying to pull the handle over the crown of Ed's head. The handle seemed to be an extra-large one. There was no doubt: the pail was designed for this purpose. Still, a few of Ed's hairs were pulled out. The sanitation inspector began talking before Ed was done vomiting.

'This body was in the water for three, or at the very least two, weeks ... Mr Bendler, are you listening to what I'm saying?'

Ed spat.

'Good, that's better. Mr Bendler, can you confirm that this dead man is René Salzlach, ice-cream seller at the company vacation home Zum Klausner in Kloster, Hiddensee?'

The machine. A clump of putrid jelly.

The inspector tried to maintain his didactic demeanour, explaining the condition of the corpse and repeatedly looking at Ed as if he had to monitor his attentiveness.

'René Salzlach is a typical case, a typical border violator, I'd say. Key characteristic: these people overestimate themselves, it's part of their personality, isn't that right, Mr Bendler? That's why they underestimate the distance, the cold, and the sea. And then it's up to *us* to rescue them, but of course we can't be everywhere at once. We can't always be in the right place at the right time.'

The unit's hum thundered in Ed's ears — it turned out to be a cooling unit. He wrapped his arms around the bucket and held it tight against his chest. He was now the camel, the camel in his dream with a feeding bowl around his neck. The red tip of the billiard cue circled, swung in a few arcs, as if it were writing in the air. The milky remains of René now formed a surface of glass or ice, on which the balls rolled back and forth, disappearing one after the other into the dark, decaying opening of the machine without a sound.

'Yet where, we must ask, did these injuries come from, Mr Bendler?' The writing stopped abruptly, and the red tip sank towards the milky grey being. Ed's eyes were filled with tears from gagging. He felt dizzy. He was freezing.

'This haematoma, for example. There isn't the slightest doubt that the victim suffered it before he entered the water. For lay persons, it may be difficult to recognise, even for me, but we have experts, Mr Bendler. We have laboratories, boats, divers, we have a 32-bit, if you understand my meaning!'

First the touch, then the thin streak that bound the pointer to the machine. He thought he was going to faint. His knees started to buckle. He wanted to drop into a crouch, but the machinist grabbed him from behind and held him upright. The handle on his pail made a long squeaking noise.

'So, Mr Bendler, what do you think? Maybe you don't remember, at least not clearly? Don't worry — that happens to everyone. At first. But once you start talking to them, you find they usually have a lot to say.'

There were papers for Ed to sign on a small metal table with wheels that was rolled up like a serving cart. There were four or five pages. As he bent forward, the pail handle squeaked.

EXODUS

On the fifth of September, Chef Mike was missing at breakfast. Krombach appeared, cleared his throat, and read a goodbye letter scrawled in grease pencil on a piece of wrapping paper in capital letters. The letter mentioned a wife and child who lived in the hills on Rügen, Chef Mike's wife, Chef Mike's child. It mentioned a family trip, the opportunity for a new beginning after so many years and so on. It closed with a sentence that used the phrase 'in these difficult times', along with a request to be forgiven 'for everything'. Until that point, Ed had never heard a single word about a family. He pictured Chef Mike with sweat running from every pore as he wrote his goodbye letter 'To the crew', as laboriously as one of his supply orders.

'As you all know, Chef Mike was reliability personified and ...' Krombach had started in on a kind of eulogy but broke off and limited himself to the observation that 'under the present circumstances' it would be nearly impossible to find a new cook.

'And what for, really?' Kruso whispered. He was sitting ramrod straight, as usual. His hands lay to the left and right of his plate as if he wanted to soothe the table.

'Rolf, what do *you* think?' Kruso waited until the assistant chef looked at him.

'First: the menu,' Kruso continued. 'From today on, short and simple. Only what you can manage, straightforward, easy dishes. Second: during peak hours, you, Werner, can give a hand in the kitchen now and then.'

Krombach remained silent. From Viola came the news report, incomprehensible, then a traffic report, incomprehensible, then 'the morning prayer will be given by Pastor Thomä from Darmstadt.' It was the first time that Kruso had openly taken command.

After the end of the holidays, the stream of holiday-makers dropped noticeably, especially the number of day tourists. The ferry schedule was changed. The crew worked hard, and with great effort they were able to keep the Klausner above water. Ed enjoyed feeling exhausted at night. The sweet rest and lack of any consideration greater than a last drink so he could sit unthinking for a while longer outside on the terrace. It soon turned chilly, and at midnight the moon poured its light onto the tips of the pine trees.

Ed forgot his dream about the rotting camel the way you block out nightmares that are too bloody. Actually, it was more abrupt than what is usually called forgetting, as if something had been hacked off and had fallen into the cell's darkness — still there, but invisible. What remained was a sensation of an even closer bond with Losh and a vague but rampant sense of guilt in connection with René. Even without Ed saying anything, word had got out that René had been found and pulled from the water in several pieces with a fishing net. If Ed were near, conversation seemed muted, conjectures were offered in a lower, more questioning tone. People were willing to make allowances for his somehow direct involvement with this fatality, the most decisive departure of those days.

The small, simple dishes were popular, and Rolf fought his solitary battle in the kitchen. People accepted the reduction of the menu as they accepted everything on the island. In fact, they didn't just accept it, they embraced it as a sign of good fortune. The red shandy was flat, but it was served on the island. The thin coffee tasted exceptionally good because it was proof that one had made it *all the way here*, to this terrace high above the sea with the most enchanting view in the country, a day they would never forget.

On the other hand, it seemed as if the guests in the late season were draining the contents of the glasses and cups more and more quickly, as if they wanted to drink this strange summer rapidly to an end. Orders piled up at the bar. Kruso swore, so Ed stopped washing dishes and hurried to help his friend. It was their daily battle, and Ed sensed the depths of their bond in the struggle, the few words, the accidental contact (like the most tender caresses), an almost blind understanding when they proved, together, that the Klausner was unsinkable.

19 September. Two weeks had passed since Chef Mike's departure when Rimbaud did not appear at breakfast. Rolf poured the coffee and offered to check the bee house and wake his colleague who had probably 'tipped back a few' until his eyes closed the night before. Kruso gestured towards the door with his head, looking at Ed all the while as if he were Kruso's man for such things.

A despairing sound filled the entire clearing; it seemed to come from the ground and not from the hives. A dead queen, Ed thought without knowing why. Ed called Rimbaud's name. He slowly opened the door, and a sweetish haze hit him. The bed was unmade. The room smelled of sleep and food scraps. Ed went to the bookshelves as if that were the reason he had come, and only then did he notice it. Bits of honeycomb lay on every shelf, dripping honey onto the books. Rimbaud's little library (no more than two hundred volumes) looked like a soft, flowing golden block and in it a living being, tough, organic, the outer shell of a fantastical embryo. The nectar dripped constantly, unimpeded, as if the honeycomb held a boundless supply or as if it were flowing from the books themselves. The books looked very content under the sweet, murky, meandering flow, as if pensive or meditative. 'In consolation,' Ed murmured because the honey seemed to be consoling the books. Yes, honey and books belonged together, books and honey, a peculiar ambrosia. But it was deceptive, of course. In truth, the books were as sad as spilled honey. From now on, the books were thinking, there will be no more waiter to carry us into the dishwashing station and read aloud to the dishwashers, and there will be no more dishwashers who know how to respond with poems, that is, the dishwashers' poems will no longer be found anywhere in this world, and hence there will be no hope for their books, thus is the circle broken. 'No, not yet, there is still time,' Ed whispered, 'I promise you.'

The honey library. Ed could not have said how long he remained sunk in this slow trickling, this most gentle demise. Because he didn't want to return yet, he sat at the small table under the window on which a pencil and a few runes lay, perhaps left over from the Island Day or from allocations in earlier times. His foot knocked against a coal bucket for which there was no actual use in the bee house given that it had no oven. Ed pulled a few crumpled sheets of paper from the bucket and smoothed them out. Most of them only held a single line, a kind of heading, and nothing more. 'For here we have no lasting city, but we seek the city that is to come', Hebrews 13:14. Ed recognised the quote. It was the motto on the mortuary in the island cemetery. On another page, there was a short treatise on bees. Under it, the signature of a bee-like man whose chest was covered with fine hairs; his bee face wore an expression of bitterness or at least aggravation. His two limbs ended in feet he held pressed together in front of his genitals (or the place where his genitals presumably were). He looked like he was rubbing the soles of his feet together.

He could have been taken for a Buddha, if anything, an allusion to the bacchanalian cult of the esskays around the Buddha tree, but thin, twisting claws grew from his toes and his beard ended in a trident — without a doubt this was the strangest being Ed ever laid eyes on.

Without a word, Ed laid the sheet of paper with the bee treatise and the drawing next to Krombach's plate (laid it there unintentionally — out of residual respect for the director), but Krombach handed the sheet without a glance to Chris, who pushed it towards Kruso's end of the table. Kruso thanked him with a strange formality, like someone who had to remind himself of his own dignity. He tentatively raised the paper to the light, threw it a glance, and set it back down. He chewed with his head lowered, swallowed, picked the paper up again and began to read out loud.

'The reproductive caste of honeybees ...' Kruso swallowed and began again. 'The reproductive caste of honeybees — queens and drones — will travel great distances to mate. A queen will let several drones mate with her in flight. In order to facilitate mating of creatures with superior characteristics, areas must be found which impede the arrival of undesired drones, such as islands. The goal of breeding is a subspecies that is industrious with a gentle nature and limited propensity to swarm — characteristics of the *Apis mellifera carnica*, the Hiddensee subspecies.'

The refrigerator at the bar shuddered on and drowned out the sound of the wind in the pines. The first autumn storms would soon come.

'This message is proof,' Kruso explained, 'that Rimbaud will return sooner or later.'

It was too late to point out that the message came from the coal bucket. At the same time, Ed had to wonder why he had smoothed the paper out so carefully and brought it back like a petition from the bee house.

'Some are leaving us now,' Kruso began softly. He stood up, and his face disappeared in the darkness above the lamp. 'More than a few

of whom we could use, yes, we urgently need them here.' He leaned
his hands on the table and his large, vulnerable cheeks returned to
the lamplight.

'Some will return, in fact, many will. They abandoned the island,
but soon they'll realise that even with valuta ...'

Even in Kruso's speech, the word shimmered like a piece of gold in
the dark. It gleamed and jingled stealthily and it *smelled good*, valuta,
western currency, what a lush, dignified sound. Eastern currency on
the other hand was recycled food scraps and aluminium cutlery ...

As if he had divined these thoughts, Kruso paused and looked
down at Ed. 'Only the illusions of freedom have a price. Freedom
itself is priceless. And it consists first and foremost of duties, dammit,
not privileges.' He had dropped his 'it-can-hardly-be-expressed-with-
words' tone.

'A better way to put it might be: those who leave us now are
denying the responsibility they have to this place. They are thinking
only of themselves. And now you're the ones who are left carrying the
burden, you, with your work, each in his place ...'

'All right, it's fine,' Chris murmured, and poured schnapps in their
coffee cups. Rolf gazed at the floor and looked pale. He had pushed
his chair back from the table.

'... not least for the castaways and the homeless, who will be
around for a long, long time, washed up on these shores from a sea of
hardship, a sea in which you can suffocate without dying.'

For a moment, Ed had the feeling he should offer Kruso his
condolences. He felt pity for some reason and was immediately
ashamed. After all, it was his brother who was speaking, full of
passion, and wasn't he right in the deepest sense? Nonetheless, he felt
as if he were standing on a large ice floe that was floating further and
further away as Kruso listed *the instruments of liberty* (the Klausner,
the island, the sea) and *the instruments of slavery* (valuta).

'I would just like to say this: our herbs are thriving. The mushrooms
are growing, the soup is simmering, the rooms are ready — we now

have a very nice number of sleeping quarters, more than ever before. Isn't that right, Werner? And soon the whole dormitory will be free. That's how we should see it. Everything will cool down. Autumn is here, winter is coming, and you are ready. I thank you for that!'

Something was underway. Continents were shifting. It would be almost impossible to run the Klausner with just the five of them. The mention of winter depressed Ed. Christmas, presents, cold, some great regret, a deep sadness — as if he were supposed to make provisions and now it was too late. Kruso's ice floe, in the meantime, had moved far off, so they could no longer understand him. All that was left was his silhouette on the horizon, his cheeks' pale glow, his mouth opening and closing.

Once again, Chris poured Korn whisky into their cups, Korn and Kirsch-Whisky, half and half, the way Chef Mike preferred.

'Why do the moon and the man ...'

'... slide together so submissively to sea?'

A few voices were missing. They stood and drank. Ed knew Losh's cheek (large, soft, unshaven), but now his hugs felt different than before when it was still about a photograph and a poem and someone who was missed more than anything in the world.

The days of the skeleton crew began. In the morning, Kruso removed the unoccupied chairs from the personnel table and spread them around the bar room. In Ed's eyes they remained there, the departed, at various tables, like outcasts even though they were the ones who had decided to jump ship (as Krombach put it).

They held down the fort. Chris waiting tables, Rolf in the kitchen, Kruso at the bar, and Krombach, who appeased the company vacation guests. On Wednesdays, Krombach still led the social evenings, telling stories about the island and letting his grey hearts have their say. Without looking, and with arms raised over his head, he tied heart after heart and tossed them into the women holiday-makers' laps. Krombach blossomed on these evenings. Ed saw him later, still on the terrace with a few guests. He heard their voices and laughter as from a great distance, laughter from a distant past. In the end, only a short, portly woman with a glowing white cardigan was left at his table. Krombach held her in his arms as if she were his very last handhold. His half-bald crown phosphoresced in the terrace lanterns' glow, maybe because of the Exlepäng, Ed thought. He had to think of the swimmer who had swum more than twenty kilometres towards the north-west while escaping and at midnight had clung onto a navigation buoy with a gas-powered light that gave off enough heat to protect him from hypothermia. Cavallo had told him the story along with the man's name, Mittelbauer or Mitbauer. In the morning, when Mitbauer wanted to continue swimming and cover the remaining kilometres, a large ferry from Lübeck called *Nordland* came by. From the railing, which towered as high as a house over the swimmer's head, the captain asked the refugee if he should take him onboard for a stretch.

'What do you think the swimmer answered, Ed?'

'What?'

'Why not. He said, *why not.*'

The swimmer's answer pleased Ed beyond measure. 'Why not' was an elegant way of saying *yes* in which possible reasons for a *no* had been considered. Why not. Cavallo's refugee stories had a different tone than Kruso's. His were good, satisfying stories.

Ed looked out at the terrace one more time and realised that no more ships would pass by for Krombach. The white cardigan was the end of the line. His last buoy.

On the evening before the day off, Ed was completely exhausted. Once again, he had had to pitch in at the bar and so still had some dishes to wash after the end of his shift — 'bulldozing the dirt' was what Rick called it. The bits of food on the plates were hard as rock, and the coffee stains seemed scorched onto the cups. Immediately after work, he lay down in his bed. His wet, dirt-encrusted cotton shirt gave off a nauseating smell. After Mona left, no laundry had been done. There was a humming in his head and a thundering in his ears. He left his room again, went down the Klausner's stairs on the bluff. He had not been down to the sea in days.

On his way back, he felt faint. 'October, and the last honeyed pear / has enough weight to fall.' With his fatigue, the verse hoard had returned, noticeably quiet and, how could he put it, *sympathetic*. They no longer dominated him. Climbing the stairs, he thought he would fall backwards into the sea. He felt a pleasurable heaviness in his head and a suddenly alluring faintness, flashing with the remains of his old, long-overcome temptation to let himself fall. He looked around. A silver goblet lay on the water, its base reaching all the way to shore. A black column supported the moon.

Ed walked around the Klausner in a wide arc, and entered the dishwashing station from the courtyard. He left the kitchen light off. Viola, who was playing a Handel concerto, was enough for him to orient himself. He took an onion from the refrigerator and scraped the remains in the potato pan into a small, greasy pile. Then he sat on the chair under the radio. And there, leaning against the refrigerator with the frying pan on his lap, he finally fell asleep.

WEST GERMAN RADIO

26 September. *It is now seven minutes to midnight.* Viola brought the coming day's program like a fairytale. The narrator's soft bass only squeaked a little at first, but then it scraped noticeably on the bottom of things. Every word seemed to have the same value for him. Every sentence was spoken as if with numb and at the same time paternally soft lips. Ed listened and let the voice soak into him. He dreamed of the time when he was a child and had tried to make contact with extraterrestrials. He had set the portable radio on the desk in his bedroom. He had turned on the short-wave receiver and searched the ether, millimetre by millimetre, with the white tuning button between his fingers until the signal sounded. *That is our program preview. West German Radio. To close the day, the national anthem. At twelve a.m., we will return to the air with — the news.* Now and then, the extraterrestrials' broadcast fell silent, which Ed took as a request: 'Hello, hello, I am here, please come. I live on planet earth in Gera-Langenberg. Charlottenburgweg 24. German Democratic Republic. Can you hear me? Please come. Over.'

The national anthem was unspeakably beautiful, and called up the forbidden as if in celebration, the old lyrics, sick with longing, about *Deutschland über alles*. The music and lyrics seemed indissociable. He thought the word: indissociable. Dr Z. had spoken about the anthem in his seminar. The way the poet August Heinrich Hoffmann von Fallersleben had sat on an island, then in English possession, and from that island in the north (sick with longing) had looked on his sundered land. *Twelve a.m., midnight. West German radio — the news. According to the Head of State and General Secretary of the Communist Party Gorbachev, perestroika in the USSR can no longer be called a revolution from above. Offering simple solutions for enormous problems would be to deceive the people. Discipline is now more important than ever.* It wasn't easy to undo the snaps, but eventually Ed managed to free the transistor's small wooden case from the stiff leather sheath. He could whisper into the receiver more easily: 'Hello, hello, where are you? When are you coming? Over.' His lips brushed against the metal loudspeaker cover and left behind a moist imprint. It made his lips tingle. The extraterrestrials had begun their broadcast again ...

Ed slept through the news, the weather forecast, the traffic report, and most of *Rock Time*, during which they played music by Jimi Hendrix. Dozing, he heard 'Hey Joe' recorded live — the guitars accompanied a kind of squawking, as if from crows, seagulls, or chainsaws. 'Hello, hello, what is your planet called? In case you need a human being, I'm always alone in my room at night. Over.' He had opened his window for the extraterrestrials even before making contact although it was already November, and the cold air blew over his neck as he alternately pressed his ear and his lips on the cool metal of the loudspeaker cover. The strangest part of broadcasting: his own voice. Its whispering between his lips, the hissing, the humming in his head, the grousing between his eyes, and above all the strangeness of its sound. As if it were stirring deep below, at the bottom of his own voice, an unknown, all-powerful being, something that could only be stopped by another constant whisper. It was the sound of death — that's what he would call it later.

He slept through the one o'clock news, the weather forecast, an announcement by the Hamburg marine weather service, and an emergency call from the General German Automobile Club. He slept through the second hour of the *Rock Time* show, in which they played folk music, including the song 'Some People Say Go Away, Some People Say Stay' by Melanie. Then a kind of interval signal, seven clear notes as soft as a music box melody used to lull children to sleep. He slept through the ARD night concert and the sentence spoken in a kind of night-blind voice: *We greet all listeners of our regional channels.*

The extraterrestrials had fallen silent, and so Ed had begun fiddling with the telescoping chrome antenna. Since that didn't do any good, he stood up and paced back and forth around his room holding the radio on his shoulder: 'Hello, hello. I can't hear you anymore. Please answer! Over.' He had climbed onto his desk and was waving the radio in the air with outstretched arms. It couldn't be a problem with the batteries. 'Where are you? What happened? Hello, please answer! Over!'

Ed woke and took a gulp of the coffee liqueur he had brought to his seat under the radio. Then he slept through the opera concert, which began with the overture 'Dawn over the Moscow River' by Modest Mussorgsky, then a Monteverdi madrigal for eight voices. Shortly before five o'clock, the marvellous music box's seven notes sounded again. It was the call sign. Or the extraterrestrials, three times in a row. He dozed through the press review. Now and then, Irish music. The snow line had fallen by 1,500 metres. *Those who want to get out no longer believe the leaders.*

THE SEVEN SAMURAI

On the seventh of October, Krombach announced his resignation. His speech was short, more of an organisational talk, a kind of final report. The manager had been making his preparations all afternoon. He had taken over the kitchen and hurried back and forth across the courtyard. Despite the national holiday, the coachman Mäcki had brought eels from the harbour, a few special wines, and two cases of Staropramen beer that had come to the island on the tugboat.

Mäcki's cart stood in the courtyard until evening. Ed went down to greet his bear-horse. It seemed to him to have come from some distant past. He brushed his fingertips over the horse's smooth coat between its eyes, and it jerked its head in the air. Ed remained standing for a while, waiting for his thoughts to come. Instead, it began to rain, and he went back in the house. The weather was gradually turning cold. The heating in his room did not work.

At the agreed-upon time, they sat only as a threesome at the table. At some point, Krombach raised his hands, and they started eating. Rolf and Chris had hinted they'd rather go to the Hitthim, to the yearly 'Republic Dance', which Ed did not pass on to Krombach. The eel was good as far as he could tell. There were also potatoes, Russian caviar, and later some kinds of cheese that he didn't recognise. Kruso poured the wine; they drank quickly and in long drafts.

Krombach told them that he had abruptly cancelled the last round of holiday-makers, 'rescinded, you might say, because of severe staff shortages'. The parent company of the VEB Smelters and Semi-fabricators in Niederschöneweide had immediately relieved him of his position and initiated an investigation. The Director of Hospitality had outdone herself on the telephone. 'Criminal' was the mildest of her accusations. She went above and beyond in expressing her conviction (in fact, she downright screamed her conviction, Krombach told them, caressing his bald head with his fingertips) that he had always been swindler, a double-entry bookkeeper who bartered goods and illegal accommodation, in short, a saboteur of socialism, and therefore the whole affair hardly surprised her, didn't surprise her at all, in fact, no one was at all surprised, and so on. In the end, the Director of Hospitality asked him how he was planning on answering to the seven workers and their families, all in all twenty-four citizens of this country, who had been waiting for their holiday spots for years and had worked hard for them for years, if not decades, and had distinguished themselves — or, and this was her last question, did he happen to have a few other islands in his vest pocket?

The vest pocket fits, Ed thought. He was sure that Krombach had worn vests during his time in the palace ...

'Other islands!' Kruso's voice was almost shrill. 'What did you answer, Werner?'

'Nothing. I've now been summoned to Berlin. On top of that, the Director of Hospitality called for an audit commission, accompanied by the forces of law, who are probably already on their way.' He poured another glass and raised it. His hand was trembling, but it didn't seem to bother him. It didn't embarrass him.

'So then. I'd just like to say that I don't have the slightest intention of' — he took a deep breath — 'answering to these seven, to these seven *workers*, to these' — he searched for a word that would be big enough, at least for a moment, to encompass his bitterness — 'these seven samurais from Schweineöde.' Schweineöde was what Kruso called Schöneweide when he had been drinking and started in on the parent company in Berlin. He himself had only been a leaseholder, leaseholder of the dream of one day owning the Klausner, the ark, in another era, in a late life. 'And I don't see any reason not to share this with you, one on one, in this group — more or less.' He made an expansive gesture, as if they were all still at the table, his entire crew, the sworn community. 'Unlike some others who, how to put it, jumped ship without a word, right?'

He threw back the contents of his glass. A short silence fell. Krombach was breathing heavily, then he had to burp, and immediately began singing. Very soft at first; it was more of a hum.

'Out on the breakwater, where the old lighthouse stands ...'

They joined in.

The tablecloth blinded Ed. The sight of the leftover food was making him nauseous. He squinted and saw tears running down the face of the manager of the company vacation home.

'Out on the breakwater, they looked over the wide, wide sea, out on the breakwater, their hearts heavy with longing, out on the breakwater ...'

By the end of the evening, Krombach was completely drunk. As was Kruso, who sat as if he'd been turned to stone on Chef Mike's chair, on the other end of the table, at least twenty nautical miles away. And Ed, too, who bobbed up and down in the stream of events and had to listen onerously for the meaning of things but was no longer able to grasp their meaning.

AUTUMN, AUTUMN

Day was dawning when Ed climbed down into the Black Hole to light the furnace, and it had hardly got any lighter when he climbed out again. A raft of small fires floated towards him from the bar room. He rubbed his eyes to chase away the camel that should appear any moment, but it wasn't his dream. In the middle of the personnel table, there was a cake with plain white candles. The cake looked like it had been blown up. The candles were much too large. In the crumbled cake, they looked like sticks of fresh dynamite, ready to explode any minute.

'Thirty-five, my friend, you don't need to count. No one here needs to!' Ed noticed the table had been set for everyone. Plates, cups, glasses, and cutlery for twelve people. He saw Sonya's photograph, like a silent offering, a small grave at the head of the table. It was a place lovingly set by parents at a breakfast table in anticipation of the child who would come out of his room at any moment and pad into the room, still drowsy and in the blessed certainty that he stood in the middle of a warm, fundamentally good world. To the left and right of the photograph was a thirteenth place setting — knife and fork,

surrounded by candles. Ed saw the light on Sonya's forehead: it was
his photograph. Kruso stretched his arm out to Ed, but didn't reach
him. Instead, he waved it impatiently about. The dynamite started to
flicker.

'You have to blow them out, Ed!'

'The birthday child blows out the candles.' He said it quickly,
without thinking. Maybe simply because it was his picture, his own
little dead person.

'Blow them out, dammit!'

'I mean, they're not mine to blow out, Losh.'

'So then. So then, Sir Edgar ... The birthday child isn't here just
now, she is — still on her way, out there somewhere!' He waved his
arm at the sea. 'That's why she can't come today, get it? Is that enough
for you?' Kruso's cheeks were grey, leaden. 'Strictly speaking, it's the
nineteenth time she has missed her birthday. And strictly speaking,
today she became older than her mother ever did, rather strange, isn't
it?'

'I'm sorry, Losh.'

Ed had an idea, but he was also worried.

'Let's do it together, Losh, I mean the two of us, like — her
brothers.'

Kruso stared at him and muttered something angrily in Russian
without bothering to articulate it — rather, he spat it out. Ed
wondered how he had managed to bring the plates and glasses to the
table in one piece and set up the candles. Losh's face was blank, but
then, as if he finally got it, the corners of his mouth tightened.

'The-two-of-us!'

Ed lowered his head.

'Besides, there's no one else here,' Kruso prattled, 'all gone, Ed,
gone, gone, gone! — even though there's champagne for breakfast,
Soviet champagne with Kirsch-Whisky.' He poured schnapps into his
half-full champagne glass. Ed was still expecting Krombach to come
out of his cubbyhole or Chef Mike to show up at the table, a sweat-

soaked supply list in hand — he wished they would.

'To Sonya, Solnyschka, Sofiya, to Sonya Valentina Krusowitsch, thirty-five years old! Long may she live, long ... Dammit, Ed, can you imagine, I sang *that*, me, Ed, her tiny little brother?'

'To Sonya,' Ed replied, and raised his glass. He thought of G. Of the day they found Matthew, still blind, his fur still sticky.

The movement of their heads towards the table, suddenly energetic, hungry, lips pursed — as if they were both trying to kiss the photograph at the same time. Ed almost forgot himself in the process; he blew, sputtered, breathed in smoke.

'You'll stay, little brother, right? You'll-be-good-and-wait-for-me-right-here!'

Kruso's head swung drunkenly in explanation of why it would be absolutely necessary.

Ed wore Speiche's sweater for the first time. He shook it out, felt it, and pressed his face into the wool. It smelled of tobacco, and for a moment Ed felt something like gratitude.

'Closed for inventory' — when he came back from the sea (a roaring, raging sea, at the sight of which you wanted to faint or at least to fall on your knees), he found the sign on the door. The bar room smelled of smoke.

'Happy birthday, little one.'

His face sprinkled with drops of wax.

Ed paused indecisively. Then he picked up the photograph and took it back to his room. He slowly went down the hallway, opening all the doors. There was no one left.

Kruso was sprawled on the bar asleep. His right hand hung in the sink, holding a glass. Ed pried it from Kruso's fingers and placed his sodden hand on a dry surface.

His friend had knocked over a few clean glasses with his elbow, and one had broken. Ed covered him with tablecloths and slipped a dry cloth under his head. Kruso's cheek rested briefly in his hand.

Ed started with the shards. Then he cleaned up the personnel table and, to be on the safe side, the bar as well. One thing led to another. Without hesitation, he threw the remains of the cake in the garbage. Chaos reigned in the kitchen. He went to the basement to check on the furnace. He spoke a few words into the embers, then put the cinders in the ashbin. He had spread a cloth over the ashbin to keep the wind from blowing the ash around. The work reminded him of his father, but this time it was his responsibility. He piled up the dirty pans in the sink and left them to soak. He waited until he could be certain there would be no tourists on the terrace (now and then, he heard voices, calls, the rattle of the doorknob), then went out and wiped the menu board clean. All of a sudden, he could no longer bear the thought of *today's special*. There were too many false hopes in the world already. 'Yet even the false ones are warranted, more than warranted, and therefore not at all false, neither true nor false, apparently, you have to admit it, just admit it for once,' Ed whispered, and relaxed. He had begun talking to himself. He checked the supplies in the refrigerator. Working calmed him down. *Haven't seen my bear-horse for a long time*, Ed thought and pictured the horse's head. His thoughts slowly began to circle around the head's contours, vague and still hesitant, but he could clearly feel that he himself was doing the thinking. They were his thoughts.

'We have two hatches, Ed. One for drinks and one for ice-cream — the ice-cream hatch, we call it. That is, we're going to close everything up, the terrace, the door, the bar, and the hatches out front. It's war, Ed, the Klausner in a storm, on a difficult course, with a *reduced crew*.' He pointed at Ed and at himself, nodded as if he were in agreement with himself and the plan, and finally made a random detour as if to

imply that help was not precluded, but was not absolutely necessary
either. He had come to only in the late afternoon. He had washed,
shaved, and put on fresh work clothes. The trousers were too short
and barely reached his ankles. Ed sat under the radio in the kitchen
and listened to him with an onion and two slices of bread on his plate.
He had thought Kruso would request his help in some way, maybe
even beg him. Now he understood that it was completely self-evident
to Kruso that Ed would stay, that they would keep going.

'You know, Rick always called the hatches *valves*, and from now
on I will, too, which has nothing to do with him. I'd like to propose
we now call the hatches *valves*. Want to?'

'Want to what?'

'You're not listening to me.'

'Yes, I am, you're talking about the hatches.'

'Calling the hatches *valves*, I mean, starting immediately.'

'Fine, Losh.'

'OK then: two men — two valves, that is, when everything is
going well. But more often it will be: *one* man — *two* valves, here
and there, back and forth, you see, Ed? And the other will work on
the ammunition, sausages, meatballs, and so on, small calibre. Always
with lots of bread, lots of mustard — that calms tempers. Delivery
straight to the ice-cream valve or, as always, to the serving counter.
Either way, we'll have to do some running, Ed, you or me, but that
doesn't matter, right? Right behind the drinks valve is the bar and
the coffee machine. There's not much distance to cover, no problem.
There, things will go right out, all the liquids.'

Almost every day and often before noon, Vosskamp now showed up
on the terrace with a few of his soldiers. It wasn't a real inspection.
He ordered coffee, added a lot of sugar, and stirred for a long time.
He leaned an elbow on the shelf in front of the drinks hatch, made
a few comments about the weather, and asked after Krombach. The

commander acted like an old neighbour, the officer of a friendly ship that lay just a few hundred metres to the north, just off the shore. For the manager, Kruso invented a business trip to the parent company in Berlin. Once again, Ed admired his companion, the way he was able to control himself and offer news with apparent willingness, despite Vosskamp's arrival on Island Day. Maybe it had something to do with Kruso's arrest (about which he never spoke) or with the presence of the good soldier, who sat on the terrace with a few others on Vosskamp's sorties, looking nervously at Ed and Kruso the entire time. Their *third brother*.

They had turned the Klausner into a fortress, that was obvious. The doors and windows were all locked, the curtains drawn. Everything was shut tight except for the two hatches — 'two valves from which to shoot,' Ed whispered.

After a few days, the commander asked for a tour. He went through the empty rooms with apparent regret, ignored the dirt that had spread over the floor and the tables, and strode through the kitchen in his shiny boots, offering Ed his hand. Ed had no choice but to shake it. He spoke with Kruso in a muted, bland tone, as if he were talking about a bereavement they had both suffered, if not on the same level.

The following evening, Kruso explained to his friend Ed why they had to remain on guard and why it all came down to holding on, especially now with the borders in a state of alert, when overreactions couldn't be ruled out. For the first time, he mentioned Viola and her news from the mainland, from cities like Leipzig, Plauen, and Dresden. 'We'll give a sign through the valves.'

They sat at the counter until late into the night and then, wrapped in quilts, they went out onto the terrace again. The weather had turned. The foghorn blew all night. The navigational beacon seemed to spin faster, and the Christmas pine moved its stiff limbs as if to express its fettered despair. At every noise, Losh raised his hand and stared into the darkness. He began to talk: about his sister and their time together in the Radiation Institute, their games, their hiding places, and how enormous the building had seemed then, how endlessly long and labyrinthine the corridors that had no windows, just frosted glass panes behind which lights burned day and night, and about the mysterious machines that could send rays through their heads and which made him think his uncle could read their thoughts. 'I was sure that was the only reason he wanted us to come see him in his lab once a week. I was afraid of those appointments because of my bad thoughts, and tried to hide. That's when I discovered the tower. It was full of rubbish, thousands of X-ray images in wooden crates, an army of skulls — at some point, they burned it all. Our own images hung in the laboratory hallways. I think he liked them especially. All I saw were skulls over which a ruler floated like a halo; the millimetre markings glowed white. When I stood in front of these pictures, I was afraid of myself. I mean, afraid of what was invisible inside me.'

Kruso quietly lectured Ed about the asylum that the Klausner's terrace could still represent. He talked about the *returnees* and claimed there would be more than a few of them as soon as they saw through the deceptions of the consumer world. '*They* can't recognise it, Ed. But many who were born there and have never known anything else, who don't sense their unhappiness anymore. The entertainment industry, the cars, single-family homes, fitted kitchens, why not? But for them it's part of their bodies, a natural extension, the source of their thoughts and feelings. Their souls are trapped in a dashboard, deafened by hi-fi or vaporised by a Bosch stove-top. They can't feel their unhappiness anymore. They don't hear the cynicism in the word *consumer* — in the word alone! Its animalistic sound, full of cowbells and herds driven over the hills of affluence, grazing, chewing, consumption, digestion, and more consumption — eating and shitting, that's the life of a consumer. And everything is set up just for that, from the consumer's birth to his death. Consumer protection functions like a fence, it's the paddock on the pasture. The consumer-advice centre registers every movement within the herd and calculates average usage, not by kilometres as with motors, but by years, decades. How high is the use considered, for example, over a lifetime? And how long does it take before a consumer is consumed? The word alone, Ed, this cow-eyed word, would be proof enough — if people only had ears.'

For a while, they remained silent and listened to the foghorn that blew every twenty seconds, 'buh-buh-buh', then a pause. 'We've got an important after-season ahead of us. I think we start with the quarters again soon.' Ed was sad that he couldn't agree, and he avoided contradicting him. Ed's duty was to stay at his companion's side, to watch out for him, to protect him, if necessary, even from himself. At the same time, he enjoyed the idea that it was just *the two of them* who were holding down the fort: two best friends, running the Klausner on their own and therefore achieving something essentially impossible with their work, like heroes.

Kruso had great hopes for the next scheduled allocation even though at the moment there was nothing to allocate. It would be more about maintaining contacts and the 'Organisation', the 'Family', or what used to go by those names. He drank even more than he had in the summer, and his talk grew vague. He repeatedly called the Klausner's two valves 'the heart valves of freedom'.

Ed peeled onions as he had in his first days, onions and potatoes. He had inspected the stores in the cellar and the cold store and drawn up a list. Following Chef Mike's example, he put together a shopping list and drafted an emergency menu: scrambled eggs, meatballs, bockwurst, with a side of bread or roasted potatoes. He was now the Klausner's commissary of stores. He was chef, sous chef, and dishwasher at the same time, the epicentre of a relatively enormous kitchen, which filled him with a certain pride despite the setbacks.

Nothing demonstrated more clearly how far he had come since his decampment. Before the words 'doubt' and 'grief' could enter these reflections, he bit heartily into his onion: Robinson dreams up Friday and Friday appears. Kruso had not been wrong to bet on Ed, to trust him, had not been wrong when he had seen in Ed something that had never been before. Kruso had dreamt correctly.

During these days, Ed paid a great deal into the account of unspoken requirements — he must have more than broken even. The feeling of falsehood or whatever was the source of Ed's constant feeling of depression (or whatever had weighed on him) when he was at Losh's side or among the esskays, all those, that is, who had distinguished themselves through *insubordination*, had been wiped out. Furthermore: he didn't leave; he didn't do what all the others had done.

Among the stores in the cellar, there were a few hundred rusty tins of pears that must have been left over from an earlier year. The labels had rotted off. Ed cleaned the tins and carried them up to the kitchen. He suggested to Kruso that they sell the pears as compote. And the cakes from the cold store that had been ordered for the last round of guests on company holiday (the seven samurai and their families) could be offered as 'dessert'. With a knife, Ed indicated the size of the slices he intended to cut from the cake, which was made from some rubbery fruit jelly — little morsels 'for thirty or forty pfennigs a piece'. Kruso, who was constantly rushing back and forth between the valves to serve drinks and food at the same time, stared at the knife then threw his arms around Ed.

'*U menja brat I sestra!*'

He ran back to the hatches. Yes, they were now truly like brothers.

On the day of the traditional allocation, only five esskays showed up, whom Ed hardly knew. No castaways, no homeless. No one had brought any contributions, and it soon became clear that the esskays just wanted to drink and watch the sunset. Although Ed served them well, they complained that the drinks usually served on the bluffs in late summer weren't offered. Kruso returned to the bar and mixed the drinks. Ed was outraged, but his friend gave him a sign. With glasses in hand, the small group went to the edge of the bluffs, to the highest point, in view of the barracks, which none of them seemed to care about.

They drank and looked out over the sea. The wind was so strong on the escarpment, that it tore the laughter from their mouths and left them standing there stupidly with their mute grimaces of lips and teeth as the glasses in their hands turned to ice. The low light of the sun lifted the chalk cliffs of Møn from the sea like a miracle. Indeed, the island of longing seemed to have grown larger in the past weeks or to have moved closer. Perhaps it had something to do with the fact that the sun now set much further to the left, much further south than it did in the summer, and in autumn its light was completely different. *Mostly, it's the chill in the air*, Ed thought, *the air is clearer and the wind sweeps the view clean.*

Streaks of storm clouds flew in from west over the sea, at a slant across the mountainous waves constantly rolling onto the shore. These waves, if one believed the marine experts, would slowly but surely swallow up the Dornbusch, along with the lighthouse, the barracks, and the Klausner, one by one. Minutes after the sun set, the sea was nothing but a dark, eternal mass. The storm whistled its singsong on the lighthouse column at their backs. The clouds drifted in large, light-grey masses, billowing like the smoke of a giant chemical plant — 'bunabuna,' Ed muttered, and thought of the Bunesians and the suffocating emissions of their enormous steel battleship at the gates of the city he had fled.

He took a step back from the cliff edge and suddenly all was still, as if there were no more wind, or anything else in the world. Once again, he pictured G., the way she had crouched next to the light well in the courtyard and tried to lure out the tiny cat who had fallen in with a bowl of milk: 'Matthew!' Maybe it was Sonya he meant in his thoughts. He suddenly felt too warm. ''Tis Autumn — Autumn yet shall break thy heart ...' Though Ed's memory hoard of verse had resurfaced, he couldn't remember the author's name. The rest of the poem was also shrouded in fog.

'Tis Autumn — Autumn ... The forgetting had begun.

GOODNIGHT

At night, the silence froze in the empty rooms. Outside, the trees or the sea or time roared, but they were inside, sheltered, not transient. Kruso drank. He stared into the dark dining room and rubbed his hands as if he were trying to wipe something away, but it didn't work. Then he held still and spread his fingers. It looked like he had a cramp. Now and again, he would wander into the kitchen to straighten a few things. Or he ran to the dishwashing station to get the bottle of the fabled skin cream. Since their hands no longer soaked in dishwater for hours every day, they'd become like old, sun-cracked leather, like brittle, mildewed gloves, gloves you couldn't get rid of, no matter how hard you tried.

Sometimes, the two men acted like strangers.

Ed's attempts to start conversations sounded hollow and petered out. It wasn't easy to withdraw now that there were just the two of them in the Klausner. Suddenly, every retreat meant something. On evenings when they sat together for a long time, Ed felt a certain embarrassment. But they drank their way through it, and, in the end, when Kruso went behind the bar to wash their glasses, the cutting board, and the knife (nothing was left lying around anymore), they were drunk enough to no longer feel their separation at night was artificial or forced. Still, it felt strange when Kruso wished him properly 'Goodnight' and added 'Sleep well', the way parents do, and Ed immediately answered with something similar, which turned them both into children again, children in striped pyjamas. In fact, their work clothes, which were too thin for the autumn weather and, now stiff with dirt, flapped around their joints, reminded Ed of such pyjamas — prison stripes or pyjamas.

They paused a moment, cheek against cheek, unshaven, dirty, somewhat run to seed. Ed felt faint remains of pain behind his eyes — the tiny fissure in the Gulf of Mexico. Kruso bent down to him since he was the taller child, the older brother. It could not be denied: they treated each very cautiously and carefully, not only at that moment. Perhaps also because they knew they had the whole autumn and the entire winter ahead of them. One evening, Ed had asked his friend when they were saying goodnight (they were already standing in the hallway, outside their rooms) if he should get the manuscript of poems from the hiding place. Kruso just shook his head and closed his door without a sound, so that Ed wasn't sure if his friend had even understood the question — something always remained unresolved between the two of them.

At night, Ed felt a tremor. In his dream, the Klausner slipped into the sea, slowly, deliberately, with all its hatches bolted, like a battleship leaving the shipyard. The bar stuck out of the roof, the bridge. Ed saw Kruso leaping about on it, swinging his binoculars, and shouting commands. The ship set its course. All doubts dropped away — pure joy, indescribable.

NO VIOLENCE

14 October. The autumn holidays had begun. Once again, boats full of day tourists arrived, even if fewer of them made the effort of climbing up to the Dornbusch. Most of the late season tourists settled for a walk on flat land, from the bodden to the sea and back, and because there was nothing better to do on that route they would take a spin through the island museum and one through the Gerhart Hauptmann House, with hazy memories of a play called *The Weavers* or with nothing at all in their heads aside from the sound of the sea. Ed remembered Kruso's stories of illicit meetings that the esskays had held in Hauptmann's study in earlier years — at midnight in almost complete darkness because it was easy to see into the house from the road. Rimbaud had apparently given a talk about his namesake entitled 'Ophelia, or the Poetry of Drowned Corpses'. He talked for an entire hour without notes or an outline.

'You should have seen the esskays, how they hung on his every word. All those dead bodies, Ed, it was as if they were floating past in the darkness, fantastic, as if they were alive or at any rate holy — Hauptmann's study was an aquarium filled with corpses, and there he was at Hauptmann's desk, like a reef sticking out of the water. It was the first time I wished I could have been a student, a student of Dr Rimbaud's in Leipzig on the Pleiße.'

Despite the general indolence, there were always enough tourists out walking to form a reasonable queue at the Klausner's hatches, at least at lunchtime. Kruso leapt back and forth between the two valves, the heart valves of freedom that were always a bit too far apart to keep an organism as large as the Klausner going without faltering. When orders were called to him, Ed brought out his dishes. To speed up the process, he would place them on a side table in area behind the ice-cream hatch — it had been his idea. He was also responsible for the coffee machine, and sometimes he was even able to help at the bar as well, which his comrade (*comrade in arms*, Ed thought) didn't always seem to appreciate.

The company vacation home was running, even if they were like prisoners behind the valves, at which they had to bend down to catch a glimpse of the outside world — and there was rarely time for that. As a rule, they only had their voices, and the clientele remained at chest-height. Once in a while, the sun came out, which livened up the tourists. 'If it works, I'm telling you, they'll stop in their tracks.' There was no doubt: the man was talking about those fleeing the country and something that could prevent them or even make them turn back, as Kruso had predicted. The word 'dialogue' was making the rounds; people kept talking about a 'readiness for dialogue', which Ed understood as challenge. He bent towards the hatch, pushed the beer through it, and looked the man in the face. The man nodded at him but then turned and went to sit on one of the terrace chairs. No one wiped off the tables, Ed thought, and decided he would clean them that evening — 'If it works,' Ed whispered.

He noticed that Kruso was serving particular voices for free or for only a symbolic charge, doubtless people he took for castaways, but who, in fact, were spongers taking advantage of his friend's generosity. Occasionally, they formed a small following who sat lazily around the terrace and expressed their dissatisfaction 'with the service'. A few days later, they had disappeared again.

The holiday week consumed their strength. The tourists' endless thirst and bottomless hunger and their talk, a general sense of dissatisfaction, a commotion that spread and spilled through the hatches into the Klausner. On the last day of the week, in the middle of the rush, Kruso suddenly lost his cool. He left his post, shouted, and stormed outside. The guests poured in through the open door.

Only when a stranger appeared next to Ed in the kitchen and grabbed one of his meatballs, did Ed notice the change. In reflex, he'd whirled around and almost stabbed the man with his knife. The man hysterically shouted, 'No violence!' Ed then had great trouble herding back outside all the people who were standing in the dining room, staring incredulously at the floor strewn with food scraps and other garbage. The guests seemed much more confident than in the summer, positively unruly, and not easily intimidated. Although the tables in the area behind the hatches were piled high with glasses and stacks of plates, a few sat down immediately and raised their hands to place an order or to get his attention. Indeed, it all resembled a spontaneous gathering at which demands were to be voiced along with criticism that had remained unspoken for too long, but the place was *here* and the time was *now*. Confused talk about embassies and trains carrying refugees filled the room; a few had begun serving themselves from the bar. Ed's voice soon cracked: he issued commands, made threats, and gestured wildly with arms outstretched, still holding the knife, which he occasionally swung back and forth like a machete through the underbrush. He could feel himself growing, surpassing himself. Still on the doorstep — Ed was already grasping the door handle — an older man turned to Ed and confronted him. He got so close, Ed couldn't avoid his protestations of equal parts speech and spit: 'Go right back in, boy, you can *all* go back into your shithole of a prison ...'

Ed was completely exhausted, but the sense of injury weighed more heavily. He washed his face at the bar. At some point in the evening, Kruso showed up again, without an explanation or word of appreciation. He held a large beer glass (the bullseye kind), which he threw straight at Viola, who immediately fell silent. The glass didn't fall to the ground, because the radio's brown, grease-encrusted cover ripped and Viola engulfed it completely. A disquieting silence fell.

Even though the terrace was only sparsely filled for days and a measure of calm had returned to their business, Kruso rushed back and forth between the two hatches. He walked with that stiff, pounding gait that Cavallo had sometimes used to intimidate his guests. Indeed, it was a kind of marching. Kruso scrubbed the serving shelf in front of the drinks valve as if it were the most important plank on their ship. Then he polished a few glasses at the bar, washed them once more, and polished them anew. Afterwards, he was back at the ice-cream valve, wearing the stained white apron that René had worn last. He banged the ice-cream scoop against the side of the aluminium vat below the hatch, a short, squat vat that had not held ice-cream for a long time. It emitted a mouldy smell that amplified the banging.

Ed was busy in the kitchen. It would take days of work to clean up the chaos of pots, cutlery, and food scraps, everything that he had had no choice but to leave lying around. The work did him good, as did the noises in some way. At least the vague busyness out at the valves was better than Viola's silence. Lately, he often thought: I have followed the wrong course. My life got on the wrong track when I left construction and my crew and submitted an application to study. Only the Klausner, only my work here, has set me straight again ... With all his strength, he lifted a steel cauldron in the air and banged it on the ground, again and again, until a semi-circular piece of coal was knocked loose and fell into the empty sink. A black, silver-gleaming moon that had been burned onto the bottom of the cauldron. With his index finger, Ed pressed the planet into little crumbs of coal, which he then pushed together to form the letters Y and E and S: YES.

THE BLACK BAND

René had returned. Ed woke and heard the voice very clearly, his nasal, arrogant way of talking, 'what'll it be then, young lady', and even before Ed understood, he saw the ice-cream man, the way he cracked jokes (political jokes) and sniggered at them himself, and Ed saw the white billiard balls come pouring out of the dark, putrid hole, one after the other, into the vat or right onto the scoop, 'fifteen pfennigs, please'.

Ed crept quietly downstairs. All the lights were on. He made his way through the dishwashing station and the kitchen. He stopped before the swinging doors to the dining room and peered through the gap between the two wings. He saw Kruso sniggering as he hectically tore off the ice-cream man's apron. His expression changed; he turned serious. He rushed to the cash register and raised his head. 'Fame, when will you come?' Then he put his index finger on his upper lip as if he were thinking, and yelled something to the chess board: 'd5 to d6!' The game had been set up. Kruso sniggered again (René's effeminate snigger appealed to him even though it was clear he was embodying Rimbaud at that moment) and hammered some imaginary sum into the register with his index fingers, fifteen or twenty characters, as if he were typewriting, one of his own magical poems, perhaps, and then, in fact, he froze for a moment into a wax figure of himself — apparently, it wasn't easy being Kruso. He took a rapid half-step back to the cash register and gave a small whinny. He galloped to the bar, mixed a glass of kirsch-kali, and sat down at the chess table, on Cavallo's side. *'Perché questo silenzio?'* Cavallo's impersonator asked softly, then made his move and drank. A second later, Kruso rose ceremoniously, and with his hands he made a protective gesture over the chess table that could have been a blessing or could have meant something like 'Good luck' or 'Stay friends forever!' None of them had ever done anything remotely similar, and so it must have been a gesture from the narrator of Kruso's play about the old Klausner. The narrator moved much more slowly than the other characters. He needed much more time. As if in slow motion, he backed up to the bar, turned, and caressed the tap — some kind of bridging, perhaps an awkward interpolation. 'The barrel is already all, tss-tss-tss.' Kruso had tried to say the universally despised sentence with Rick's calm, gentle tone, yet he himself was no longer calm, but dissatisfied — something was wrong. The caresses turned into something more forceful, a kind of milking, but the tap stayed dry. Rick-Kruso banged the flat of his hand on the bar: the glasses clinked. He reluctantly bent down, jerked open the door to the cellar, and disappeared down the stairs ('Führer-concrete!'). Soon, sounds of an argument drifted up, and soft cursing: the beastly cellar, the damp, the mud you're always in danger of slipping on and breaking your head open. Then: 'Mis-er-able, mis-er-able filth!' Presumably he was trying to tap the barrel and having the usual trouble. Only Rick had been able to do it, but he had needed an assistant, someone to tighten the screw for the gasket around the bung hole while he inserted the tap. So Rick-Kruso called for Ed. Ed-Kruso answered, 'I'm coming. I'll be right there!' Ed-Ed stood there, barely breathing. For a few seconds, he waited for his self to appear, then he crept silently back to his room.

Throughout the day, a clear, almost wintery peace reigned. In the evening, the cocoon of the Dornbusch engulfed the Klausner with its numbing roar. A beam of light from the navigational beacon swept across the floor of the dining room, a room that seemed to have been shifted out of their radius and was no longer accessible. They also no longer sat at the personnel table (not even for breakfast), but at the chess table near the bar with a view of the terrace. They drank a lot, Lindenblatt in the afternoon and kiwi, kali, or peppermint schnapps in the evening, sometimes mixed with corn whisky or Blue Strangler. With it, they ate smoked ham cut into cubes; they had enough in the cellar. Earlier, Ed had thought nothing of ham. Now he chewed it slowly and deliberately, like a farmer at the end of the day. They were flexible with regard to meals. There were no rules except for Ed's onions. Kruso made a new dish rack from old wire — for the coming season, he emphasised, and at such moments the bitterness drained out of his voice. He sanded down the wire and painted it with leftover paint from the cellar. Some paint dripped onto the table, but he didn't seem to care. Blue paint that had also been used for the seesaw on the playground and the metal frames of the covered tables on the terrace. Ed went into the kitchen and made coffee; they talked about God and the world.

Ed told his friend about his first and only family holiday on the Baltic Sea, in Göhren, on Rügen, in the summer of 1973. The three of them, father, mother, child, had stayed in a small Free German Trade Union Federation hotel in the middle of the village. He had slept on a cot next the wall under the window. Ed collected shells and hid them under his bed in a plastic cup, where they began to stink.

One morning when they'd come to the dining room for breakfast, he noticed black cloth on the frame of the portrait that hung over the breakfast buffet. He didn't know what the black band on the picture of *the goatee*, as his parents called the Chairman of the State Council, was supposed to signify, but something told him (he was eight years old) that it would be better not to talk about it out loud. He waited until they had all sat down with their breakfast rolls and cheese, then he stood up again, ran around the table to his father, and whispered in his ear: the black band. His father's reaction to this small discovery was so disproportionate that the scene was burned into his memory. Instead of going to the beach with his family, Ed's father sat in his room the entire day, listening to the radio. He also listened to the radio turned low throughout the following night; he had shoved the little transistor halfway under his pillow and so only very muffled sounds reached Ed. An endless murmuring about the goatee's rise to power and how it ended. Above all, the murmuring was about *the inner German line*, of which Ed formed an impression for the very first time in his life: a bloody line through the middle of Germany, as if drawn with a scalpel, one commentator claimed, right through towns, houses, and families, a deadly obstacle, insurmountable.

Ed looked at Kruso and attempted a brotherly glance. There was a border between them, too. It was better when they were telling each other stories. The stories helped Ed overcome his inhibitions, his fears. 'We always have a few tanks ready for emergencies.' The goatee had said this in a peculiarly high, thin voice that was on the verge of cracking, and it was played again and again. It appeared to have been his most important sentence — in any case, it was the one that stayed in Ed's memory from that night on the cot, and so he told Kruso about it. In addition, it occurred to Ed that he hadn't yet learned how to swim at the time and he had felt a deep fear at the sight of the sea (he saw it for the first time on that trip). Kruso nodded and looked into his eyes. Robinson and Friday. They had returned.

Their table stood so close to the bar that Kruso only had to turn around and reach for the bottle in order to refill their glasses. They spent a great deal of their time on 'cleaning and mending hours', as his companion put it. They cleared the drains, although these were hardly dirty; they chopped firewood, repaired the palisade around the Klausner, and tried to wash their laundry in the stone sink in the dishwashing station. Monika's washing machine would not start.

First Kruso had tried, then Ed. It was a WM 66, a model Ed knew
from home and the usual one around the country. As a child, Ed had
thought the WM stood for Weltmeisterschaft, the World Cup. He
was convinced the machine had been named after the 1966 football
World Cup. As with so much else, Ed had never asked any questions
about it, and to some extent he was still that distracted, easily
influenced child who believed the world resembled his own dreams.

Of all the deserted rooms in the Klausner, only Mona's two rooms
seemed homey. Sometimes, Ed lay in her bed and pressed his face
into the pillows. As he breathed in the smell of the sheets, he thought
of C. Then he stopped thinking of C. and thought of G. Ed tried to
remember sex with G. He was ashamed of how little he could recall.
Two, three scenes, no more than that. Maybe it wasn't important. It
was just a matter of how grief filled space within him. And finally, it
was a matter of not mixing anything up. His desire was just one part
of it. A few images from the nights flitted past. Marén, Grit, Tille,
the castaways' stories in the dark. Sometimes, they were still there
when he woke suddenly from sleep, and he had to pleasure himself
two or three times in a row before he could fall back asleep. In the
final moment, it was always C. Her laugh, her hiccupping, her raised
eyebrows. C., the way she had looked at him.

The days trickled into the sea. The delegation from the parent company
whose visit Krombach had announced had still not arrived. Neither
of the two friends answered the phone. After it had rung constantly
one day, Kruso rushed into Krombach's cubbyhole and ripped the
cord from the wall. Ed no longer believed the Director of Hospitality
would come. Everyone could guess that this was not the time for
delegations and oversight committees. Even Vosskamp hadn't shown
up for days. It all fit Viola's news reports and her commentaries about
closure of all borders, before the beer glass hit her. Not long after,
Kruso found confirmation for his thesis: how important it would be

to hang on, to persevere, to build a base camp (he used that term), a base camp for everything that was now inevitable. Ed thought of his parents in Gera; he had begun to worry. They would believe he was still in Poland, at the International Student Summer, separated from them by one of the borders that had suddenly been closed.

Ed now used the bicycle to buy supplies. He no longer needed the cart. Just a backpack for bread, milk, and a few additional things. They had everything else in their stores. He enjoyed riding through the forest and the descent on the road paved with concrete slabs, which could shake a person's bones from his body and descale the brain (Rick's theory). A few days earlier, Ed had seen his companion in the village and immediately made a detour. It was as if he couldn't meet Kruso outside of the Klausner. As if something might unavoidably be said that would call everything into question. Also, the truth was, he was embarrassed to have seen Kruso standing there between the metal carts in the harbour, prattling absently, his head bowed, like a shepherd surrounded by his herd. Kruso was gaunt, but his face was completely smooth, almost childlike. The grey hairs in the curl over his forehead seemed to multiply by the day.

Back from his errands, Ed went to the kitchen and unpacked his backpack. A voice that seemed familiar (his own) came from the dishwashing station. He put things away in the refrigerator, and minutes later he was no longer sure if he'd really heard it or had just imagined it. He went quickly to the bar room to gather a few old schnapps glasses. Actually, everything was already done and there was no real work left to do, but Ed stayed at the bar and started rinsing out and putting away again the glasses on the top shelf that had not been used for a long time.

The two of us, Ed hummed — he wanted to think over his next steps, about his responsibility for Kruso and the restaurant, but his head was empty. First the farewells, then the skeleton crew, then 'two

KRUSO

men, two valves'. He looked out at the empty terrace and saw himself framed, with a reverse look into the window at the bar. *Wait here long enough and don't go anywhere.* Sonya's words before she swam out to sea and turned into a green light.

After a while, Ed heard pots clanging in the kitchen and something that sounded like Chef Mike's wheezing, and, as if in answer, Ed clinked the glasses lightly: Chef-Mike-Kruso and Ed-Ed. Together, they mimicked the Klausner, the last hope of all the freedom-seekers in this land; yes, in the meantime they had come to represent everything about the old life up here on the bluff, where no one came anymore that autumn. Ed rinsed one glass after another as Kruso stood right behind him, bending his head towards him as if he could smell Ed's thoughts.

'Are you ready, Ed?'

Ed jumped. He'd almost dropped the glass. 'Ready?'

'For the allocation this evening?'

FINAL ALLOCATION

It was already getting dark in the afternoons. Ed looked outside but couldn't see anything, and he turned on the terrace lights. Kruso raised his hand as if blinded or maybe he had waved at Ed. At first glance, it looked like his head was wired. The rain had thickened his long hair into strange struts that seemed to be supporting his raised head. The upper half of his head gave off a golden glow in the light of the metal lanterns that stood watch over the beer garden.

'Looks like no one's coming today.'

Ed felt his obligation, but also that it was important to be considerate. His friend was untouchable. Near and yet untouchable. For a very brief moment (too brief for him to grasp things fully), Ed recognised that it must have always been this way. Kruso was like him. Otherwise, they couldn't be together like this, near, but each keeping to himself, trapped in the capsule of their lonely, chaotic existences, to which a rare constellation of fate or an all-controlling cosmodrome had granted parallel orbits.

There were three glasses on the table, already half-full of rainwater. Kruso sat very straight, a saint contemplating his place in eternity, Ed

thought. With his right hand, Kruso gripped the wine bottle. His left
hand rested on his lap. And over everything, a rain so fine that you
couldn't feel it fall, but the air was saturated with it, a cold rain that
congealed into a thick mist in the light of the lanterns.

'Maybe it'd be better to come inside now, right?'

'Yes, please wait for me inside, Ed.'

'We could keep an eye on the terrace from the chess table.'

'If no one's here now, then no one's coming.'

'It's the beginning of November, Losh.'

'You don't know what autumn is like. You were never here in
the autumn. The allocations are different in the autumn. Autumn is
different.'

'We could leave the light on. We'll put Chef Mike's Stern-Recorder
in the ice-cream hatch. You can hear it across the whole island.'

Ed gradually talked himself into his new role. Now he was the one
who had to take charge. For a moment, he felt a need to press Kruso's
large, wet head to his chest and to rock him like a child who has hurt
himself, to rock him until he was comforted, until his eyes fell shut
— *everything is OK.*

'Yes, Ed, yes. But give me a moment. You go ahead and I'll follow,
just in case.'

Ed understood he couldn't accomplish more than that. He
thought of one of the umbrellas left behind by the guests, but it
seemed inconceivable. An umbrella was absurd. After a while, he went
out into the rain again and draped his parka over Kruso's shoulders,
gently and without a word. It was as if he were completing a valuable
painting, yes, perhaps that was his real task at Kruso's side.

The coat turned the rain-soaked man on the terrace momentarily
into a kind of abandoned military commander, a general without
troops. A hero who was beginning to freeze. Although Ed was deeply
worried (a worry that had been constantly deepening since the day
Mona and Cavallo left them and started the exodus), he felt a kind
of satisfaction or gratification at that moment. Everything he did

happened for the sake of this story, as if he alone were responsible for its being told someday.

When Rebhuhn raised his head, the light of the desert sun began to flow along the metal frame of his glasses, a shimmering in all the colours of the rainbow. The Bedouins were pulling their camel over a rough metal frame; Rebhuhn was the team captain. The team captain's job consisted primarily of cutting open the camel's neck, which two or three players held as low as possible and stretched tight between the posts of the metal frame. The cutting was an art and was considered a privilege. Rebhuhn was explaining everything: the knife this way, the skin that way, then the cut, like lightning. Essentially, it was a matter of triggering a cramp-like tension in the camel's body, a contraction, Rebhuhn elucidated, hard and persistent, enough for a firm, even playing field. Rebhuhn bent down under the frame; the Bedouins fell to their knees. They each carried a billiard cue.

FAIRYTALE OF LIFE

In the morning, Kruso was gone. Driven by guilt, Ed roamed through the Dornbusch, but kept returning to the Klausner in the hope of finding his companion there. Because he was rushing, a branch whipped across his face. He was filled with a nameless rage that immediately turned into a sense of helplessness.

The consecrated sleeping spot was covered with leaves, and the outlines of the hollow were hardly visible. Under the leaves lay the mummies in their sleeping bags, castaways, forgotten searchers for freedom, clandestine sleepers who had turned black in their sleep, buried by leaves — these thoughts made Ed nauseous, and he marched quickly on.

The honey library was almost completely destroyed. The books had turned into a shimmering brown swarm of ants, woodlice, and cockroaches. Only a few linen-bound volumes still stood upright, though buckled and decayed. The shelves were a wall of blackened honeycomb. An enormous charred dollhouse. Ed watched the new recipients rushing rapidly back and forth apparently without any plan. They had eaten themselves into a frenzy of sugar and cellulose.

Ed stepped closer and recognised the remains of a few volumes by Anton Kuh and Peter Altenberg, *Harvest*, *Gleanings*, and *Fairytales of Life*. A few isolated pages hung out as if they were reaching a hand out to him. Artaud was gnawed clean.

Ed had to calm himself; he wasn't completely alone in the world. He took the bicycle and rode down to the village. He left the Klausner unlocked, which didn't bother him. Everything felt different now. Over the door to the parsonage hung a sign with the words 'The Reformation continues'. Ed stopped and read the notice posted in the parish display case. In an 'open letter', the islanders called for a 'process of renewal'. The undersigned protested against the dilapidation, littering, and overdevelopment of the island.

Santiago hugged Ed. Cheek against cheek. An old black-and-white television had been set up in a corner of the Island Bar. 'They want to drink, but now they want to see the demonstrations, too.' Another new addition was a washing machine in the basement that heated water for the dishes. Santiago no longer had to heat water in the cauldron; he was distinctly happy about this. Ed's question about Kruso surprised the esskay. He brought both hands to his cheeks as if something very bad had happened. It was the gesture the golden-haired girls in the Soviet fairytale movies made when they learned their beloved had been killed by a dragon or turned into an animal.

Ed went through the clandestine quarters. The path to the summer cabin was nowhere to be found, overgrown, covered with sea buckthorn. A few of the hiding places looked ruined. There were food scraps, empty jars, and newspapers left in the entrance to the stone caves between Kloster and Vitte. The smell of excrement reached the path. The small brick house behind the Hauptmann House (room for two people) had been broken into. Two bicycles were leaning against the front of the so-called headquarters in the woods above the harbour. Ed felt a flash of hope, but the shack was empty. All he could see through the smeared window were a few worn chairs and a rough map of the island, drawn in black paint or tar on the wall, its outline strewn with crosses as if it were an island of the dead. Ed realised the crosses marked the clandestine sleeping quarters. Their number was far greater than Ed had suspected or than Kruso had confided in him. The woods were filled with cold, unhealthy damp. In the woods, the wreck of an indefinable machine squatted between the trees like the skeleton of a dinosaur, visible from a distance. The garbage had disappeared under the leaves. It smelled of winter.

Finally Ed ran along the beach one more time, heading south. At some point, he just stood still, staring out to sea, the cold roar of the surf filling his ears. The sea — the promise. Every other area seemed to Ed to be exaggerated, maimed, turned grey under domination. He'd always had the feeling that the sea was trying to tell him something, that it held something decisive for him, a solution to his life. There was the abundance of roaring that was its breath, surging, endless, all-encompassing. There was no body, no vessel big enough for this being made of breath, this pneumatic giant. Instead, it contained everything; it gave breath to his thoughts or brought them to a standstill. It rocked him in his sleep and washed around his dreams and shaped them into something that was unfathomable.

Wait here long enough and don't go anywhere.

Long enough.

This was the place where Sonya left her little brother. Ed realised this and could no longer move, not one centimetre. The place of farewell took possession of him.

Dear Sonya.

Dearest G.

Ed lost her at that moment. The pain, the despair, the self-pity. Immeasurable, irrepressible grief. Edgar, Ede, Ed, to whom all this had happened, now he could be that person. The news had reached him.

Dear Losh.

The observation tower behind Vitte hovered in the fog; the border patrol probably had him in their sights. It was simply inconceivable, the idea of swimming away from here, of going into the water. The place could hardly have changed since then. A run-of-the-mill beach, visible from all sides, a few breakwaters, dunes, a view of the Dornbusch hills to the north. 'She was a very good swimmer, Ed,' Kruso had told him.

Ed thought of Island Day. The place where he now stood, as if frozen to the spot, was only a few hundred metres away from the parade ground. It was the place of the little brother looking after his big sister — for a few seconds — then going back to his game.

Wait here long enough and don't go anywhere.

What should he wait for, long enough? First for his sister, who had swum out to sea while he pushed the warm sand here and there with his plastic shovel. He could only see her head, if it was even she, very small, like a net buoy, a swimmer between the waves. He stood up and walked to the water. He stood without moving, holding his plastic shovel tight against his chest. Should he shout, yell, as loud as he could? Or was he not supposed to right now, long enough?

Ed imagined Sonya swimming out, then the wall of patrol boats, then a ship's propeller or a shot. Or Sonya, who swam out, pulled by an aqua-scooter — in broad daylight, that was absurd. Rather, Sonya, who walked up the beach to the Dornbusch and stayed hidden until nightfall, next to the inflatable dinghy, between the buckthorn bushes. Everyone knew that this launching place on the tip of the coast lay in the blind spot of the radar that Vosskamp's people used for surveillance of the sea — an MR-10, Kruso had told him and drawn the measuring system's radius in the sand.

Eventually, Ed managed to move again. If you went closer to the water, you could hear a great agitation inside the breathing — thundering, aggressive — but underneath was a much higher tone, a gasping, a panting, as if the sea itself were struggling for breath, as if it were on the verge of suffocating ... It was the childlike sighs of the dead. Ed couldn't help such thoughts. He saw René on the pool table, the apparatus René, the stinking machine with missing parts, feet, legs, which were drifting about, rolling, turning, being prepared right here on the bottom of the sea. And he saw Sonya, saw her walking over the waves, completely intact with an emerald on her forehead, the amphibian princess. And he saw Kruso, his brother, untangling the nets of the Vitte fishermen underwater and declaring the fish caught in the net free. Bubbles came from his mouth, and his long black hair seemed to be floating in jelly, and no one could help the fact that Ed broke into tears.

Wait here.

Long enough.

The metal gate at the entrance stood open. In front of the sandstone building below the radiation ward, there was a vice. It had been welded onto a metal rail and held a metal box in its jaws. The metallic green paint on the steel sides was chipped, and the lid was sticking up. At first glance, it looked like the vice was waiting for its master to come and praise it and release the prey from its jaws. Coins gleamed on the cinder-covered ground, and papers were strewn over the path — charts, records, maybe experiment protocols. Ed picked up one of the bundles, heavy with rain. It was all in Russian.

He found identity papers with the emblem of two letters, J and P, combined to form a torch — *Young Pioneers*. He opened the pass and saw Kruso as a child. A dark hooded anorak with light dots, a bandana, early traces of dark rings under his eyes over his large cheeks, and a furtive, almost fearful look. Next to him, the stamp of the island school and the Young Pioneers' ten commandments. His picture was the portrait of a child who knew that he would never be good enough for these commandments. It had never occurred to Ed that Kruso must have been a schoolboy on Hiddensee after the move from Russian Military City Number Seven, a Russian boy in a German school. Without a mother, and suddenly without a sister either. Having lost everything he had, and like a remnant in a place that was not a home.

A light drum roll sounded. It came from the metal lid of one of the lanterns; the rain had set in again. Ed was worried about Kruso. He wiped the pass on his chest (Speiche's sweater) to dry it provisionally. The door to the old transformer house was open, but the tower was empty. The labyrinth of wool blankets had vanished, and the lower floor was completely visible. Around the room, rusted bins were attached to the walls with metal bands like medieval prisoners. Ed called for Kruso. Nothing moved. For a crazed moment, he thought his companion might be locked in one of the barrels — Jonah on his way into the sea. He inspected the barrels. Their markings had rusted away for the most part, only pine trees or skulls and crossbones, with traces of writing in black and red. 'Pick me up and hurl me into the sea.'

After some time, Rommstedt opened the door, but did not cross the threshold. He didn't seem to recognise Ed at first, but smiled and did not stop smiling the rest of the time. There was very little light in the hallway, and Ed briefly thought he heard noises — there was someone there, without a doubt. Ed tried to convey in hasty sentences what there was to say about his friend's disappearance, beginning with the others' disappearance, or rather, *all the others*, except for him. He half-turned towards the vice as if it were important for him to include that step in his search. Rommstedt also looked at the vice, but seemed to be looking at the vast, stormy sea beyond as well. Then he asked Ed to give him a moment, and closed the door. A short time later, he opened the door again and invited Ed into the ward.

He looked at Ed with interest, so Ed repeated his question about Kruso. The air in the hallway was stale and smelled of food and old sweat — it stank of Rommstedt's loneliness. Ed briefly wondered if Rommstedt weren't also an outcast, like the caretaker in Halle, educated, academic, but out of commission and therefore in despair, deeper than despair.

As on his last visit on the Schwedenhagen, Ed sensed his predisposition for this place. He was tired and his knees were buckling.

'Do you know, by any chance, where Kruso ... ?' The professor stroked Ed's head. 'How are you feeling, Mr Bendler? You've healed wonderfully well, haven't you?' Ed needed to sit down. He had to rest, for just a moment. Rommstedt dragged a chair forward in a sweeping motion that seemed to extend infinitely into the depths of the ward: a thin, singing scrape along the linoleum that rushed towards Ed through the empty hallway. At the same time, the building's floor plan turned, and all the rooms within the ward shifted to the sound of an electrical hum ... *Of course, that's what it's built for*, Ed reasoned, sluggish and drowsy, and he therefore wasn't surprised that the chair coming up behind him and gently pressing against the backs of his knees was in the middle of the laboratory, right in front of the large, blue-grey photographic plates. He could also hear that the hum was coming from the plates. *It's no more than that*, Ed thought as if he'd understood what was most important. Once again, he formulated his question about Kruso, his brother, but only in his thoughts because Rommstedt had started speaking.

He listed the previous names of his institute as if they were honorary titles. 'Institute for Radiation Research, Institute for Radiation Sources, Heinrich Hertz Institute, Central Institute of Electron Physics.' Clearly the great fire of 1970 was a definite break, combined with the loss of the institute's own observation tower. In common parlance, however, the building had always been called the Radiation Institute. 'Beginning with our success in fighting paediatric osseous TB, luminescence research, our invention of energy-saving lighting ...' It was a lecture on the history of his institute, solemn, proud, a lecture about experiments begun (under his direction) decades earlier, 'you must imagine, everything done with our own materials, certainly no different in the end than with all great research families, just think of Becquerel, Curie, or Röntgen.' Experiments, Rommstedt emphasised, that could soon be pursued with every resource, at least that's the way he saw the situation, 'because we are the people, young man, and we will stay here on this island, won't we, because we, here, are the people!'

He stroked Ed's head again, but this time more as if he were testing the rounding of his skull.

'And so he took you on? With all the rights and obligations?' The professor touched the blood brother scratches. He spoke softly and calmly.

'And now you yourself are almost like Alosha, just as bold, as intent, and, yes, driven by longing, isn't that right? What would you call this last ... whatever is at the root of your separation? What you don't yet possess?' The professor had placed a hand under Ed's chin and turned his head into position.

'How lost, how abandoned one feels, yes?' The humming changed.

'Your particular susceptibility, call it *receptivity*, did not escape me, young man. Along with your perceptivity, your excitable temperament, let's say, your fundamentally spiritual disposition. It's the radiation that relaxes you, isn't it? That returns you to the old days — sleepy villages, doors that open with a sigh ...'

The humming swelled.

Ed saw himself on a mountain of sand, the world was made of sand, murmured languages that rolled out in search, also, of houses, bridges, and streets, murmured languages ...

He saw himself as a child, saw how he would go out in the morning to the mound of sand in front of the barn in the back courtyard and sit on it. He would sit there all day and build houses, bridges, and streets, until the grownups came in the evening and marvelled at his sandcastle, which was enormous and contained everything that held the world together at its very core: a colourful glass marble shimmering softly and the spiral of a long, flawless track.

Twilight had half set in. The grownups' praise, like balm, and their heads, large and dark under the swallows' flight paths.

THE LAST ESSKAY

Ed had not bolted the front door or the servant's entrance, so that Kruso wouldn't be locked out. The terrace lights were lit. Some light fell on the playground, too. In the early dawn, the seesaw's steel tubing towered into the sky like artillery before the battle.

Something moved in the house.

Ed stood at the window for a while, listening. The attack would come from the west, from the sea and up over the bluffs, always from a direction no one expects. As he decided to get dressed and light the stove, Ed barely understood how he could have slept that night.

First, the chopping block. Second, the stove. Third, coffee.

He took charge.

The wood quickly caught fire and burned well. He used the slender pieces of kindling that Kruso had made. Ed stared into the flames and warmed his face. He thought of his military service in the winter camp, sleeping in a squad tent with a pot-bellied stove in the centre. Twelve iron-frame beds and eleven soldiers asleep. He tried to see it that way. He was on duty, and the rest of the crew was asleep. The sea was frozen solid. The earth was frozen. They had had to dig the latrine with a pickaxe; the blows still reverberated in his arms. You were not allowed to sleep on stove duty. He wore his winter uniform. He heard the wild boar outside the tent. He stared at the glow of the embers on the sand in front of the oven. Then he fell asleep. No. He was on duty, dammit, he had to pull himself together. The embers' glow on the sand must still be there.

Ed got some bread, butter, marmalade, and an onion from the kitchen. Some sort of noise.

He stood at the stove and listened.

The sea.

Just another kind of silence.

He generously spooned coffee into a cup and poured boiling water over it. Even as a child, he had heard other sounds behind the noises he himself made, voices calling softly, short Gregorian chants, which must come from those things that use such opportunities to switch with others. He also heard mockery and something that sounded like abruptly stifled laughter. For a while, it was possible to cover it all up with a louder noise, but sooner or later he had to become quiet again and the listening resumed.

It would have been easier to eat his breakfast right in the kitchen, but he carried it all to the bar room and sat down at the personnel table. My place, Ed thought. His first personnel breakfast seemed decades in the past. Next to his plate lay a receipt book. The skin between his fingers was so chapped, he could hardly feel the pencil. He wanted to make a list of things that needed to be done, but he couldn't think of any. A few words flitted through his mind, and because he had wanted to write he started writing, three or four pages' worth.

He chewed slowly and looked at the photographs of earlier crews. The camaraderie shining from their faces was unrecognisable. The oldest was hung high up, in the shadows, a few years were missing. More than a few of them must have died in the meantime, and so these were faces of the dead looking down at him. A dead person's glance is always a little reproving — who had said that? Probably some clever waiter, or, no, a good bartender, someone like Rick.

Ed imagined a photograph of him and Losh, suntanned with gleaming, bare forearms. The two were laughing, and the caption read: Robinson and Friday playing chess, 1990.

'After a bit of time up here, you know how to cross the water, boy.' One of the dead had spoken from the shadows right under the bar-room ceiling, the crew of 1932. The man wore a white shirt and round, black-rimmed glasses; not much more of him was visible. He looked like Fernando Pessoa.

The noise was there again. Something was moving through the house, but not with footsteps, as if the Klausner itself had woken, a rumbling in the walls, a distant, muffled rattling deep in the stone foundation. 'There, they discovered it,' Ed murmured, 'behind the inn, in the forest. The so-called forest inn high up on the bluff hid nothing other than a prehistoric being, in whose body a dishwasher had been trapped for the rest of his life ...'

'Arise, go to Nineveh ...' The Pessoa-man was talking again.

Ed stood up. He crouched down and tilted his head. He knelt in the corners, held his breath, and listened. Essentially, it was everywhere. Experimentally, he pressed his ear against the cast-iron side of the cash register, then against the bar; the beer cooler was still. He rushed through the house, but it was neither upstairs nor downstairs. It moved, it was nowhere.

Time to sit down, concentrate.

His eyes fell on the receipt book. Had he written that?

Yes.

No.

The onion.

He took little pointy and started peeling with stiff wrists. I need a ladder, Ed thought. He wanted to try to fix Viola, but he couldn't even get the word 'ladder' down.

There was a kind of vibration, a muffled clattering, then again a groan, maybe a giggle, but very soft and roaming.

Ed pushed his breakfast things aside and pressed his ear to the table, his arms spread wide. He tried to hold very still. He looked like he'd just been shot. Caption: The Last Esskay. What he heard was a rushing sound, the usual rushing sound. It was always there, in him and in the objects. And he heard the soft rustle of his hair. The wood felt cool against his ear. He heard his blood, his heartbeat, and it calmed him: it's just your clumsy old heart, Ed thought. Maybe the Klausner and I have become one overnight, *topsy-turvy*. He almost laughed.

He had to move around a bit. He carried his breakfast dishes into the kitchen and tried to recall Kruso's lecture about writing. 'Actually, what you want to do is sink completely, submerge yourself, but for now it's enough just to move your hands in small circles underwater ...' Ed turned off the water. It was already pleasantly warm (good stove). He stared at his plate under the stream and felt a faint longing to put his ear against the wet rim of the sink. He asked himself fleetingly what he'd seen — what he might have seen behind him, near the shelves.

Too late.

LOVE

From that point on, just details. The force with which something hit him from behind. The weight and the breathing on the back of his neck. Rolling around on the floor and the animal strength that tried to push his head into the drain.

Ed gasped for air. He sputtered a 'No-no', then 'Ow-owww, owww' and a pathetic 'Please'. In the midst of his pleading, his mouth dipped into the stringy slime in the drain grate. He spat and breathed some of it in — soap and rot.

There was no doubt: the animal from the wall was Kruso. He wheezed and his voice was hoarse. From the sink above him, water poured onto Ed's head and made everything incomprehensible. Again and again, Kruso spat the word 'betrayal' at Ed's neck, along with Rommstedt's name and 'told him everything, everything!' His main word, however, was 'betrayal'. Betrayal of Sonya, betrayal of the Klausner, 'and of my mother, my mother ...' He paused at that point and switched to Russian. A feverish heat streamed from his body, and his breath smelled of illness.

'Losh!' A bubbling splutter.

Only then did Ed notice it: a stabbing pain in his hand. *Little pointy*. Still have to wash, have to finish washing — whether that was his thought or Kruso's poetics of dishwashing was irrelevant. As he fell to the floor in that half-dreaming and then no longer comprehensible moment, his fist had closed around the blade. He had held tight to *little pointy*, pointlessly.

Kruso was kneeling on his back. He stuttered, repeated himself, far above Ed and the waterfall. Far below, Ed's ribs on stone; they were going to crack. The Radiation Institute, the sanitation inspector — betrayal all around. Ed had stopped understanding what Kruso was saying for some time. The grate was pressing into his face and forcing it into a grimace — washed away, the word pulled him into the depths, washed away, into the sewage pit, into the amphibian's realm, washed away like filth, garbage, greasy sauce, and now it was his turn ... Grey slime was his friend. Grey, stringy slime that kept the rusty wires from tearing into his lips. He had other friends, the rest of his verse hoard, for example, brave helpers, ready, as always, to *whisper something* to him. A piece of advice, an idea, in the very last second.

'And softly the dead woman's hand
reaches into his mouth. Sonya's smile is gentle and lovely ...'
A muffled gong, and Kruso seemed to hover.

Ed heaved the heavy body to the side. He doubled up; he couldn't breathe. The water kept pouring; he held his face under the stream and vomited into the sink. He tried to rinse out his mouth; he gagged, and spat.

Kruso lay on the ground as if felled, arms outstretched as if the Klausner's dishwashing station were his final stop. There was blood in his hair, though not much, and it seemed already to be congealing. Little pointy had torn Kruso's shirt near his hip, but there was only a scratch on his skin underneath. His flank had been hit, but not seriously. It had just been the surprise, the sudden pain: Kruso had reared up and banged his head full-force against the steel sink — more precisely, against the rusty steel frame that supported the sink ...

It's where he hit his head, Ed thought, a sensitive spot.

He slumped to the ground. He couldn't stand, he had to wait. His heart was pounding. Only later did Ed ask himself how he could have got a grip on the little knife's handle as his right arm shot backwards randomly.

The man on the ground was completely drenched. He looked very peaceful and relaxed. A light shuddering ran through his body, and Ed carefully felt his forehead. It was hot. Ed found no feeling he could trust, just a fresh wave of fear and panic. And the mechanism of worry that would support him on the basis of some experience he'd never actually had. And in it all was a feeling of disappointment — disappointment was the only feeling he trusted. But there was also a feeling of concern, once again, genuine concern, the concern of friendship, then disappointment anew, bitter and dark, and rage, and, deep within, helplessness. The whole insanity that he could no longer comprehend.

It took an eternity to move Kruso into Krombach's cubbyhole, and used up the last of Ed's remaining strength. He had put together a kind of dragging apparatus from a few Romans. Time and again, the wet body slipped away from him and hit the floor. 'I'm sorry, please forgive me ...' Ed trembled with the effort. He was gagging the entire time, and he urgently needed to throw up.

In the cubbyhole, it looked like Krombach had intended to leave behind an accurate impression. It smelled of Exlepäng. Ed ran back to the dishwashing station and rinsed his mouth out again. His tongue was swollen and stuck to his gums. He picked up the little pointy and washed it. The clean-up-all-traces thought drifted through his mind, wan and unimportant.

Kruso lay in front of Krombach's desk like a hunter's prey. Beneath the worry, a sense of insult spread, cold and silent. The rage of rejection. Ed put the knife on Kruso's chest and breathed deeply.

He thought of stills in a film. He, himself, was now in a film. He was the main character, the last Mohican. As deep as the insult cut into the Mohican's flesh, the voiceover said as the camera showed a lone rider crossing the desert through two towering rock spires, something just as powerful must exist on its flip side. And it must reveal itself now, now or never, open and unguarded, at least for this instant: his love.

Ed stuck the knife into Kruso's shirt.

Or what would you call this last ...

Piece by piece, Ed cut the wet shirt from his body.

Kruso's penis was swollen, but not fully erect. Ed tried to heave the large body onto the high mattress, but that seemed impossible. In a new attempt, Ed wedged himself between the sloping wall and the bed and created a kind of lever. First, he had to prop Kruso's torso against the bed and make sure it didn't slip off to the side or slump forward, which turned out to be a challenge. Eventually, Ed had no alternative but to grab Kruso's hair to hold him upright while he danced around the bed to get leverage. As Ed pulled and tugged, Kruso came to. He immediately put his arms around Ed's neck.

'One man, two valves, Ed, sometimes that's the way it is.'

Ed tried cautiously to take his head from Kruso's embrace, and it worked. He circled the bed and lifted the long, hairy legs as heavy as tree trunks onto the bed.

'Or just one, one valve is enough, Ed.'

Ed picked the blanket up from the floor and covered Kruso up to his chin. He tried to make him as comfortable as possible.

'Edgar?'

'One is enough, Losh, like you said. But now you have to rest.'

'Why do the moon ...'

'And the man slide together ...'

'So submissively to sea?'

They had recited the last line together. As if it were their question.

Once again, Kruso reached his hand out to Ed. Ed looked at the little pointy on the table. Then the hand sank onto the covers, and Ed's companion fell asleep.

'I'm sorry, please forgive me ...'

For a confused, indeterminate amount of time, Ed sat at Krombach's desk and let the waves of shock roll over him. His next action was one of self-defence: he made up a *little plate*. A little plate, as his mother called it, is what she made for him when he was a child, lonely and sad, a single child in his single room, overwhelmed by his schoolwork and by life in general.

'I'll make you a little plate, Losh.'

He washed an apple, took *little pointy*, and cut the apple in slices, which he placed evenly on a saucer in the shape of a sun. As he did, he continuously murmured to himself, 'I'm sorry, please forgive me ...' He tried to eat one of the apple slices himself, but couldn't face putting anything in his mouth. A few tears ran down his cheeks.

He ran to the dishwashing station to rinse his mouth out yet again. He bent over the sink and cooled his face. The traces of the grate hurt. He had to be reasonable now.

He noticed the open doors of the dumb waiter, and the puddle on the floor. The dumb waiter, which was never used, which for years had simply been a recess in the wall, a place for Karola's tea and a few cake tins during the noon rush! How long had Kruso hidden in it? Crouching in this cube. And how did he manage to raise and lower it topsy-turvy?

Kruso was asleep. Ed pulled Krombach's chair cautiously up to the head of the bed and set the little plate on it.

'I made you a little plate, Losh.'

A little plate signified affection and consolation, without intruding on the other's sorrow.

'Should I make you *another* little plate?'

He went to his room and took Sonya's photograph from his notebook. The picture felt hot, as hot as Kruso's forehead, but this came from Ed, caused by the cut on his hand, which now burned slightly. The knife had hardly penetrated the dried, mouldy dishwasher skin, and the cut had hardly bled, only a thin, yellowish fluid had come out. Maybe, being a dishwasher, you no longer had any blood in your hands after a while, but instead just lye, liquid soap.

Ed placed the photograph on the chair so that Kruso would see it when he woke. He felt like a child stroking a half-dead bird he had just shot out of its nest.

Only then did he think of the telephone.

He had behaved as if Kruso were his possession. As if he alone were responsible. Because of some monstrous distortion, the world now consisted only of him and Kruso, only the two of them. Again, he felt nauseous.

Because he couldn't decipher the number immediately, he tore the paper from the plastic envelope. The island doctor was fourth on Krombach's list, a three-digit number. The telephone jack was half-broken, but he was able to plug in the wire. Ed pressed his ear to the receiver. For a time, he listened numbly to the changing tones, a short then a long, very long, drawn-out tone. As if someone would answer even if he hadn't dialled.

WE WHO HAVE STAYED BEHIND

The carpet, the wall unit — as if he had walked into his parent's living room. Mountains of dully gleaming artificial leather — the *sitting-room suite*. Like large animals in a little stall. Ed went to get some air. He could hardly breathe. It seemed even colder in the house than outside.

At first glance, the electrical appliances were missing. Television, stereo, speakers — the dark outlines of their absence on the polished veneer. Behind these, the wounds, the severed cables. A jigsaw, Ed guessed, or a drill. Surprisingly crude for a doctor's house, or at least very different from the meticulous work his father would have spent hours on.

The house stood on exactly the spot where the island had been flooded and separated into two long ago. The private quarters were in the back; the rooms for the doctor's practice faced the street. There were no chairs in the waiting room, just the scrapes from chair backs on the wall, and above them shiny grease spots where the patients' heads had rested tiredly over the years. The long, unnerving wait for solace and death before they could finally return home.

In the consultation room, the cabinets were open, and medications and diet powder were spilled on the floor like snow, scattered around the dented metal bowl of a baby scale. The beige steel cabinet with the patients' files was half-torn from the wall, opening up accounts of all the illness on the island. A battery-powered wall clock lay on the table, as if forgotten, left there unintentionally. Next to it, some empty syringes, a doctor's bag, and rubber gloves. The second hand on the electric clock made a soft clicking noise but didn't move anymore.

It had taken Ed no more than ten minutes to get to the doctor's office by bicycle. He had sped down the Dornbusch, over the concrete path and down the road behind the dunes, against the wind and through the cold of November. The house door was open, the door frame splintered at the height of the lock.

Someone had scribbled 'QUACK!' and 'SHIT COUNTRY!' in ballpoint pen on the eye chart. Next to it was the rail with the centimetre ruler. The slide was pushed all the way up, as if the last person measured were a giant. Ed saw himself against the wall, the wood slide on his head as he straightened his back as much as he could and tensed the balls of his feet. The result always came too quickly, not as if any care had been taken. Measuring and measuring are two different things, his father had always said. Usually, it was 174 centimetres, sometimes only 173, and only once was it 175, and that's what was put on his identification papers. Category: medium-height. When the information was recorded, it was left to each person to provide their height and eye colour — no one looked him in the eye in the police registration office and no one measured him. That surprised Ed, and it was the first time the notion of *possible holes in the system* ever occurred to him.

Ed bridled at the heading, but it was already circling in his mind: silent despair. He saw the words; they were useless. Everything a feeling designated was useless; the generally human was useless — poor material. Medium height and brown eyes, those were the facts. In the light, however, grey-green, like his mother's. In shade, brown,

like his father's. Ed let himself drop. It was the patient's chair. In front
of him, a cream-coloured metal cabinet and his face reflected in the
glass — a look as if he could make himself at home there, just move in
to this cabinet and go to sleep.

— No, I don't know how serious the injuries are.

— He has a high fever, I believe.

— Almost two days, completely drenched.

— I think he hit himself badly.

— Yes, but only a little, really, not much.

— Yes, but not for long, then he came to.

— Yes, I think so. At least, he knew where he was.

— ...

— No, nothing particular. Just that he was in the elevator, our old
freight elevator, maybe all night long.

— ...

— Exactly? A brown ring around a grey-green centre, I'd say —
I'm a mixture of my father and mother, you know?

— Hello, Mr Bendler?!

Someone had called his name. Ed went to the window and saw the
sanitation inspector slowly coming up the street. He wore the jacket
with the many practical pockets. The consultation-room window was
right next to the broken-in door that was just now reflected in his
photosensitive sunglasses. Rebhuhn cleared his throat softly. A living
noise, not intended for anyone in particular, and suddenly Ed felt
very close to him, which sucked the strength from his very bones.

'What was most valuable has already disappeared, Mr Bendler,'
the inspector called in a low voice through the open door. He must
have watched Ed's arrival. Maybe they always see us, day and night,
Ed thought, and all evasions are superfluous, as are all the reports.

'I'm looking for the doctor, Dr ...'

'And I didn't mean anything other than that, Mr Bendler. Or did
you think I held you for one of the looters? Unfortunately, we can't
stop it. There are too many of them, mostly the people next-door.

They're simply faster than we are. When our citizens see their fellow citizens on the street with suitcases and bags, they've already got a crowbar in their hands. But a fugitive's property belongs to the state they're turning their backs on. Ordinance Number Two, you see, Mr Bendler? That is why I must ask you to come out now. I have to seal the door.'

It was odd that the inspector did not enter the house. And strange that he asked Ed, that he had made a request, not a threat, not an ultimatum. For a moment, Ed thought René was standing behind Rebhuhn, without feet, lightly swaying on his rotten stumps.

'Did you understand me, Mr Bendler?'

Ed didn't answer. He was confused. He had left a note for Kruso, next to the little plate, under the photograph, on the stool, next to the bed ... He felt faint. He took a step backwards into the consultation room. He was like the child in his hiding place who doesn't want to be found and feels like he's moving further and further away from the world.

'By the way, I'm pleased to hear that the Klausner is still open for business,' Rebhuhn continued. He was speaking through the open door, his head stuck halfway into the hallway. 'There are people in this country who stand by their work, by their place in society, they don't just throw it all in — that's what I call responsibility, Mr Bendler.' He had called the sentence out as if he were speaking into a tunnel, clearly unsure how much of it would reach the listener.

Ed remained silent.

'This doctor, on the other hand, the so-called island doctor is long gone — so much for the Hippocratic oath! Still, your wounds have healed, healed very well, haven't they, Mr Bendler?'

He remembered one of Viola's reports in the days before she fell silent. A good doctor doesn't desert his patients, an unforgivable violation of basic humanity, and so on — and with it, the voice of the health minister and Viola's commentary, which he had forgotten, as he had the title of the broadcast, maybe *Midnight Update* or *Day by*

Day or *Europe Today*?

'The border with our Czechoslovakian friends has been reopened for the past few days, an important sign of trust. But you know that already, of course. Now everyone can leave, from now on *everyone* — is that not a joke? Are you listening to me, Mr Bendler?'

The inspector's situation was gradually becoming clear to Ed. But what kept Rebhuhn from entering the doctor's office?

'That's why I'm glad, really glad, to see that you're still here,' Rebhuhn called. 'You and our friend Krusowitsch. You're busy with poems, we're aware of that — and maybe that's what this is about, who knows? We can't exclude it, right? More than a few have created their works on this island, big names, God knows. I'll just mention Lummitsch, Cibulka, Pludra, and Gerhart Hauptmann, of course, as well as Joachim Ringelnatz, great minds of bygone eras, representatives of bourgeois humanism. Have you thought of publishing, Mr Bendler? A candidate for the writers' guild — how does that sound to you? We have to stick together now, we men of the typewriter, we typewriters!'

Rebhuhn cautiously squeezed through the doorway and made his way past the consultation room into the living room, which for Ed, at least for the most part of his confused awareness, was still something like home, like his parents' living room: the dark gleam of the veneer, the yellow-brown carpet, the daily vacuuming around the stove, the small galaxy of scorch marks, later hidden under an oven tray — all at once, it all seemed worthless.

'Your other colleague, on the contrary, that ice-cream man, was stupid, very stupid! First the nonsense with the beating, and then he just couldn't wait, and his escape ...'

'What escape?' Ed burst out. He had almost shouted — in any case, he had held his peace too long. His question was aimed from the hallway at the inspector's back, and Rebhuhn flinched as if he'd been hit, and threw his hands into the air. Perhaps it was this gesture, overblown, hysterical — suddenly Ed felt hatred, a hatred that seemed to have been stored up for just this moment.

'What escape?' Ed repeated, slowly approaching the inspector.

'Oh, I beg your pardon, it's nerves, just nerves.'

The inspector took a step towards Ed.

'What I also wanted to tell you ...' He tried to take Ed by the elbow, 'I am authorised to inform you that a rubber dinghy was found, down near Gellen. The usual border violation, I'd say, and a terrible craft ... A plastic milk jug was stuck in the bow with personal effects, some money, letters of reference, no ID, but the photo — his partner for all I know ...' He paused to reflect. 'Everything was secured, Mr Bendler, and the suspicion that had fallen on you for a time ...'

'Listen to me, Rebhuhn. My ... colleague, Alexander Krusowitsch, is ill. He urgently needs care, immediate care, a doctor, a ... He's injured.'

The word 'injured' — it was as if Ed had spat out some of the mixture of soap and rot that coated the inside of his mouth like fur and kept him from speaking freely. He had the feeling he had made some animal noise.

Rebhuhn turned away as if disappointed. With a half-pirouette, he sank onto a faux-leather chair and sighed audibly. A gust of wind whistled against the windowpanes. The storm blew unchecked over the narrow island, as if it had to be swept clean before the final downfall. Heavy as a stage curtain, the drapes behind the sitting-room suite billowed. Ed felt the wind on his face, and noticed that one of the windows was broken.

'Oh-ho! Our friend is sick.' The inspector pressed his fingers tips together to form a small pointed roof.

'Not your friend,' echoed from Ed's felt-covered mouth. His left hand moved instinctively to the scribbled scars on his right forearm. He momentarily sensed his body's smouldering outline.

'It's completely irrelevant, Mr Bendler, whether or not he once was or still is or if he one day will be or will be again, as I believe, our friend — we who have stayed behind have to stick together, understand? All who are still here, *compris*?'

The sanitation inspector crossed his legs, as if to anchor permanently his remaining behind. A gust of wind, the broken window — a large piece of glass crashed to the floor and splintered. Ed leapt at Rebhuhn and forced his putrid breath in the man's face:

'*My* friend, *my* friend, *my brother*!'

Like a young child, the inspector brought his elbow up to shield his face, and waved the other aimlessly at Ed, who was pressing the man's head into the faux leather. The photosensitive glasses slipped. A large insect losing his eyes, Ed thought, just a slight pressure and they'll fall to the ground. For an instant, he saw the inspector's flattened profile; just a hint of mouth and nose, a face like a giant worn-down fingertip, yellow and grey, like the sandy ground in which Kruso and he had buried the bottles against the western moon on the day of desire.

'My friend!' Ed roared again, because shouting felt good. The felt in his mouth had torn and he could finally hear his own voice, and he heard that what he was shouting was true, while the inspector cowered, arms and legs drawn in, contracting to the size of the ridiculous bird he was named after.

The storm had abated and a fine rain was falling. The inspector was in front of him. In single file, they trotted the hundred metres down to the registration office. There was no one else on the street; the village seemed deserted. Even the inspector's gait emitted a sense of loss: short, choppy steps, as if his feet had been shackled for years.

In his office, Rebhuhn gradually regained his composure. A number of files landed on his desk, over which he ran his hands for a time. Something needed to be sorted or enumerated in the air. 'We'll help your friend. We help whenever we possibly can, of course ...' His muttering was like an incantation that allowed him to keep his fear in check, and Ed realised that things were serious for the feeble figure behind the desk, that Rebhuhn was not acting this time.

'I must ask that you not be surprised, Mr Bendler,' Rebhuhn began, 'we will help your friend, we *can* help him.'

Still standing, he dialled the number. Ed stared at the bent index finger that repeatedly missed the dial. 'Please don't be surprised, it's the quickest ...' The connection went through. The inspector snapped to attention, his voice immediately became strong and confident and he continued speaking in Russian. He spoke in short, monotone sentences as if he were giving a report that had probably been expected. He asked only one question, and the answer was just as short and restricted. Each of his words evinced respect and readiness to subordinate himself.

Ed understood no more than two or three phrases. In all the years of instruction, his vocabulary had hardly increased. Rebhuhn dictated latitude and longitude as was no doubt the usual practice of providing location in the military, then he gave the Klausner's postal address — it was the first time Ed had heard it. Rebhuhn pronounced the address with a Russian accent. In the end, he was obliged to repeat his name and rank. He spelled it slowly and clearly, but it sounded expressionless, futile, like a final attempt to be someone.

THE TASK OF THE EAST

Kruso slept. It was a kind of fairytale sleep. Ed touched Kruso's large, unshaven cheek, stroking it with his bent index finger like a father bending over his son's bed one last time at night. He held the back of his hand against Kruso's forehead, then put his lips against it, because the back of the hand's feel is unreliable. A hundred years had passed since the morning.

Ed stood bent over Kruso's face for a time, and for some reason he closed his eyes. He pictured Rimbaud at the cash register and Karola at the bar; even his predecessor, Speiche, sat with all the others again at the table and asked each in turn about his bag, his glasses, his toothbrush. Unreality had reached a pitch in which it was possible for Ed to be wearing Speiche's jumper and at the same time to be taking it from the wardrobe and handing it over, as ceremoniously as if it were his final evaluation report, the admission of a nearly immeasurable guilt he had accumulated as successor. 'Please forgive me, my dear Speiche, I ...'

He couldn't manage to make himself coffee, so he poured boiling water into some coffee liqueur. He drew back the curtains and looked out onto the terrace as if help might arrive there at any moment, a helicopter, perhaps. Or a new Russian MiG, a vertical take-off aircraft that did not require a landing strip, only longitude and latitude coordinates. He tried to drink, but burned his lips.

He went upstairs and started packing a hospital bag. It was cold in Losh's room. He had forgotten to turn on the heat. The shaving kit was tidy. Ed took some clothes from the wardrobe, which was also neat and tidy. Little piles, black cotton pyramids topped with a pair of socks. Ready for action. No pyjamas, no bathrobe — he would need them. (Immediate disapproval from the head nurse: 'No pyjamas? Then this.' A short tunic, open behind, revealing buttocks and back.) Ed stuck most of their revenue in an envelope and placed it in the bottom of the bag. After a while, he fished the envelope back out and wrote his mainland address on it: Wolfstrasse 18, 4020 Halle / Saale. He didn't know why, he just did it.

'My folder is safe, isn't it, Ed?' Only then did Ed remember the poems. Kruso had mentioned them several times in the past few days. He had entrusted them to Ed. 'Let's leave it for now, Ed, until things have calmed down here. Then I'll put the volume together.' Forty minutes to the fox's cave and back — but what if help arrived just then, what if Losh woke up and needed him. There was no room in Ed's head to think any more about it.

He brought the bag to Krombach's office and placed it on the foot of the bed. When the impression that something had been irrevocably sealed began to overwhelm him, Ed removed it again and placed it instead on Kruso's chair at the personnel table. His helplessness was palpable.

Because Kruso was shivering, Ed plugged in the portable heater and slid it under the bed. 'One after another,' Ed whispered, and got a crumpled NIVEA inflatable ball from the shed, washed it, and filled it with hot water. He tried not to watch himself as he did so. He tried to see it all *practically*. For a moment, Ed recognised how unreal it all was. He saw the crew of a phantom ship stranded on the coast of a ghostly island; castaways, islanders, and esskays, they were all phantasmal.

When he went to slip the half-filled ball under Kruso's legs, he saw that his feverish friend was clutching something to his stomach under the covers. It was the photograph. It was Sonya.

'Good, good,' Ed murmured, 'you snapped her up, didn't you?'

He had an idea.

Krombach's Exlepäng. He took a fresh bottle from the wardrobe, and the packing leaflet fell into his hand.

It's never too late, but also never too early ... Care and nutrition, like all ground that will bear fruit ... refreshes and rejuvenates ... The name Exlepäng guarantees quality and effectiveness for far longer than half a century. Ed calculated: 2039. Far longer: 2050? That's what it says, but that's not what it means, no, surely not.

He gently pried the picture from Kruso's fingers, which crumpled it even more. He sprinkled a bit of the elixir into his hand and rubbed it into his friend's hairy chest. 'Just for the moment, Losh, just for the moment, she's coming right back. She'll watch over you. She's coming back, we know she is. She's right here on the chair, waiting for you.' Ed felt the warmth under his hand. Kruso breathed more quickly, his skin became hot, a wave of coughing came, like an avalanche of gravel ...

Alarmed, Ed stepped back. It could all be wrong. It could all have the opposite effect. Ed took the photograph from the chair and slipped it back onto Kruso's stomach.

Only then did he notice: the emptiness on top of the wardrobe. Krombach's grey hearts were missing. They had stopped beating.

Kruso was awake now, but only rarely opened his eyes. Ed mashed white bread, milk, and some buckthorn juice into a pap. Buckthorn was good for everything, the islanders claimed. He added sugar and two painkillers he had found in Krombach's first-aid kit along with a bottle of iodine and a few grey compresses. Following an intuition, Ed also mixed into the mush a few leaves from Kruso's dried herbs, which he had solemnly called 'the season's final harvest'.

The way one feeds an infant, Ed tapped the spoon on Kruso's upper lip, and, as if the reflex lasts throughout one's life, Kruso opened his mouth, but only a little. Ed wiped off a bit of the pap and tried to push the food deeper into Kruso's mouth with the back of the spoon, which he finally succeeded in doing. Kruso swallowed, opened his eyes, and immediately began talking.

'The task of the East, Ed, I mean of the entire East, starting from the Kazakh yurts, from my mother's circus tent in Karaganda, you know, from there to here, to this island, this ark ...' he choked and spat, evidently the mush was doing him good, 'will be to show the West a path. A path to freedom, understand, Ed? That will be *our* task, and the task of the entire East. To show them, who have come so far with technology, economically, with infrastructure ...' he swallowed and continued more emphatically, 'who have come so far with their highways, production lines, and Bundestags, to show them the path to freedom, the lost side of their ... their existence.' He choked again, then had a coughing fit, as if an invisible giant had grabbed his shoulders and were shaking him furiously for a spell.

'Pscht, pschschscht,' Ed said, but immediately fell silent when he noticed Kruso's cutting look.

'It is our task, Ed. To protect the roots from the ashes coming now in unbelievably sweet-smelling avalanches, unbelievably enticing, mild, attractive ashes, you see, Ed?'

In his embarrassment, Ed tried to keep feeding him, but Kruso had stopped swallowing. He just pressed his lips together and squeezed some of the mush out again.

'Freedom attracts us. She recognises her helpers. She recognised you, too. She recognised you, Ed!'

Ed wiped the yellowish ooze from Kruso's stubble as best he could, and wiped his chest. This time, the ablution in the afternoon, flitted pointlessly through Ed's mind. He gently coaxed his friend.

'We must also eat, Losh. To regain strength, I mean, against the ashes, I mean, who else would know how ...'

Because Ed didn't have much to say in this direction (although he did, as so often, feel a profound desire to agree with his companion, to be one with him despite the estrangement), he began reciting Trakl. He had forgotten a few of the verses and even some entire poems. It wasn't bad. He hummed lines and rhymes from other pieces, from the now flimsy compendium of his verse hoard; he hummed it all to himself as if it had never been anything but a single tender melody tuned to a single despairing tone — his own personal tone. Kruso's poems were also a part, even passages he hadn't even known existed before. Something like a poem of his own — as if he himself had begun to write.

His spoon touched Kruso's mouth, and the Sesame opened.

'That's good, Losh, very good,' Ed murmured. 'We'll get there.'

On the way to the dishwashing station, Ed felt stronger and almost content. He rinsed the rest of the mush out of the cup and filled it with water. He dipped his uninjured hand into the cup and felt the stream of water. Little brother, what are you doing, are you asleep or awake? He turned two or three times towards the open doors of the dumb waiter, where there was still a puddle. When he returned to the cubbyhole, Kruso seemed to be himself again. His head lay askew on the pillow. His left eyelid started to tremble. When he opened his eyes again, the eyelid stuck halfway for two seconds.

'Are you hurt, Ed?' He reached for Ed's injured hand.

Fever shone on his face like a mask. There wasn't the slightest trace of the hatred with which he had tried to push Ed's head into the drain.

'This belongs to you, Ed.' He held the photo out to him. It was crumpled and stained with sweat or Exlepäng.

'No, Losh, please, you should keep her *with you* now, I mean ...'

'Take it back. She's watching over you. Until the next allocation, let's say.'

The photo was now just a scrap. A precious scrap as long as the gentle smile was recognisable. *Our very own dead*, Ed thought.

'Let's just put her right here, next to the bed, I mean for both of us.'

Kruso's expression changed. Ed snatched at the photograph, but Kruso would not let go. He held on tight and looked Ed in the eye.

'She's out there somewhere, Ed. You can use my binoculars. Use the lights to orient yourself. Think of the green light. And if ever I'm not here for a while, then — take charge. Promise me that. Promise me, now!'

As if an electrical circuit had been cut at that very moment, Kruso closed his eyes and fell silent.

'I promise,' Ed murmured.

He put the photograph back on the chair. Drops of wax, of sweat, the crumpled face. It pained him.

Anyone, any kind of help. Ed looked at the clock. He swore. What possibilities were there? Finding a doctor among the tourists? Since early November, the island had seemed empty. There was certainly a retired doctor somewhere, slicing his bread and listening contentedly to the sound of the waves. Vosskamp's ridiculous medical centre wouldn't have anything more than Krombach's first-aid kit, and the hospital in Bergen was too far away.

He took the telephone directory out of Krombach's desk.

Ed wasn't used to using the telephone. He had never had one at home. Speaking into a device with no counterpart seemed unnatural; it seemed artificial, almost abnormal. Ed remembered his first telephone call, when he was a child, in the village co-op. The woman had leaned over the counter with the candy jars and held the receiver to his ear. His mother's voice hit him like a blow. He could feel her in his ear, but she wasn't there. He hadn't been able to say a word even though everyone in the store was encouraging him to speak — not a single word.

The directory's dirty yellow title page (an edition from 1986) was covered with dotted lines — an attempt at a geometric representation of long-distance telephone connections, it was easy to see. An imaginary construct with little telephones perched on each junction like spiders in a web. A larger animal resembling a rotary dial had already got itself trapped. A pitch-black, monolithic telephone receiver, tipped upward, loomed over it all like a rare idol or god, half-encircling the telephone network and threatening to drag it all into the abyss.

On the first page, there was a list of 'Acoustic Warning Signals': nuclear alarm, air-raid siren, chemical alarm, and all-clear signal. This was followed by a page of regulations, which Ed skimmed quickly, then the 'Instructions for Use'. 'In the interest of general courtesy and increased accessibility: KEEP IT SHORT!' was printed in bold. Ed dialled the number for medical emergencies. A voice answered with the request 'Information?' This was strange, but maybe all services were directed through the information desk. There was static, and some kind of counter set in. Yet something else irritated Ed. He pressed the receiver to his ear. He was sweating.

'My name is Edgar Bendler. I'm an employee of company vacation home Zum Klausner, ummm ... on Hiddensee, regional district Rostock, municipal district Rügen.' He spoke in a very loud voice and spelled the address.

'Yes?' the man answered, and Ed immediately knew.

'Rebhuhn?

'I'm sorry, I don't understand you. Please state your concern.'

'Rebhuhn, you swine!'

'Hello, who is speaking?'

A click, and the busy signal sounded, droning in Ed's ear. Kruso's arm waved weakly in the air and dropped back down. 'The traitors are everywhere now, even on the telephone. They listen in on everything, the lowlifes. Even the sea is one of the worst traitors, Ed, did you know that? Flow, flow onward, many hours!'

Kruso listed, apparently at random, the places he called the 'root sources': Plauen, Gotha, Pécs, Brno, Kraków, Kursk, Pavlodar, Karaganda ...

Dusk was falling.

Ed turned on the light and unplugged the heater. He got a glass of water from the bar and gave it to Kruso to drink.

'Water is the worst traitor of all, Ed. I mean deep water, did you know?'

He coughed again. His condition was worsening. He had strange spots on his skin, and the dark circles under his eyes spread their shadows into his cheek area.

'It's a shame, a real shame, old onion,' Kruso murmured.

The bar suddenly seemed very far away, and the muffled sound of his footsteps on the floorboards was no longer enough to instil him with any sense of confidence. The rooms slowly began to dissolve; the season was over.

'Ed, Ed? The Dornbusch is burning.'

Ed sat at the desk for a time and then crept into the bed. His companion had turned away and pressed his forehead against the wall. Kruso moaned and groaned until exhaustion pulled him into sleep. Around midnight, he had another shivering fit. Trembling, he babbled barely comprehensible phrases about his mother the tightrope artist and about the three bears on the Mischka chocolate wrapper. Russian Military City Number Seven also came up, as well as someone Kruso called the 'fountain master', the fountain master of Sanssouci.

'The seed of true freedom, Ed, thrives where man is not free.'

His voice grew softer. In the end, it was mere whisper, a stuttering breath.

Ed tried resolutely to transmit some warmth to his friend, but the chills were simply too tenacious. Sometimes, it seemed that Kruso was trying to push him away, to shake him off. Then Ed held him tighter and whispered the poem, 'Evening returns to ancient gardens; Sonya's life, blue stillness. Wild birds' migration ...'

By and by, calm returned. Only the dull vibrato of Kruso's forehead against the wall, as if he could not stop sending his SOS in Morse code, into the Klausner's foundations.

Ed decided to carry Losh down to the harbour in a cart the next morning in time for the first ferry. From there to Stralsund, then to the hospital. Maybe it would even be possible to manoeuvre the cart into the cubbyhole and right up against the bed. *That way I can manage*, Ed thought. He placed his lips on Kruso's sweat-soaked back. Then on his ear. Then his lips again. For a second, the smell of Christmas cookies. Cinnamon. Ed's shoulders twitched, then the feeling flooded over him. Without making the slightest sound, he did not hold back his tears.

TAKEN HOME

The personnel table was loaded with trunks and suitcases engaged in a heated discussion about God and the world and the new travel destination. They were all worked up because none of them could really know what to expect out there on Møn or Hawaii, or in Shanghai. Even Ed's worn faux-leather bag spoke up. Until Godfather Death entered the room and they all fell silent.

'That's not Death,' Krombach's hard-shell suitcase whispered, 'it's just the ferryman.'

Just the ferryman, Ed dreamed.

A star approached him from the darkness.

Until Ed understood what had happened, everything seemed to happen in quick breaths. The large silhouette next to the bed. A coat opening. A belt buckle with the Soviet star. It bumped the glass on the table, and the glass was transformed into a softly ringing grail, full of the music of parting.

'We waited all night, I'm so glad you're ... We waited and ...'

Against the light from the desk lamp, Ed could only make out clearly half of the large figure at first. A grey-haired giant, a knee-length coat draped over his shoulders, as a commander would wear it. Half-dazzled, Ed raised his eyes to the broad, shapeless epaulettes. The empty sleeves and the glowing red strip on the hem of the coat — there was no doubt: a general. Ed still lay under the covers, as if paralysed. Kruso had turned in his sleep and wrapped his right arm around Ed's shoulders — as if he wanted to hold him or protect him.

A second soldier, in a sailor's uniform, entered the room and immediately pulled back the covers. Kruso's grip tightened, but to no end. The sailor pulled Ed from the bed. Then he started examining Kruso, who was breathing heavily but no longer seemed to be shivering.

As if Ed were now part of the troop, he took up position next to the bed and tried to give his report: 'We waited all night, the telephone was dead ...' Just then, shame washed over him. His companion exposed and he — half-naked, a lump of misery, his hands along his trouser seams — had been wearing trousers.

Even the general appeared embarrassed. He picked up the bottle on the table and read the label.

'Ex-le-päng?'

His voice: a dusky rolling sound.

'Sixty per cent alcohol,' Ed blurted out, relieved to have the opportunity. 'I rubbed Losh, I mean ... I rubbed some on Alexander, he had the chills, he's — injured.'

Ed gestured towards Kruso's head and touched the spot on the back of his own. The general dropped the half-full bottle distractedly into his coat pocket. With a slight bow, Ed gestured towards the host of extra bottles in the cabinet, but the large man didn't notice his offer, or overlooked it.

His entrance seemed solemn, not like the response to a distress call. He gave orders only using his eyes. A thin brown strap crossed his chest diagonally from his right shoulder to his left hip, where Ed presumed he had a weapon.

Kruso groaned, and the soldier gave a sign. He had inserted an IV and set up a drip, which he waved around the room as if that were part of the treatment. Ed shrank back in alarm, but the general, who had approached him with rapid steps, only reached for the photograph on the chair. The scrap.

The general's face. Ed recognised Kruso's large, vulnerable cheeks, their endless expanse, grey and sere, Kazakh steppes, with a camel and on the camel, Sonya and Kruso, the siblings, on their way to the Aral Sea. But they never reached it, because with their every step, the sea's shore retreated a bit.

What happened back then? Ed asked.

The question was too vast for Krombach's cubbyhole. Even though he had only asked it in his thoughts, it inundated the room, and the general stepped back abruptly. He had put the photograph back. The medic, who had managed to fasten the drip onto the handle of the office cabinet, followed the general.

In the bar room, there were even more soldiers. Soviet sailors. They sat tiredly at various tables as if they'd already been waiting a long time for their orders. When the general appeared, they sprang to attention and spread a cloud of a sour odour. On command, they broke the legs off the personnel table; the medic gathered up the tablecloths, taking care not to let any ashtrays fall on the ground. The blows to the table were given purposefully, almost solicitously, from which Ed concluded that this was not an act of retribution or a retaliation campaign.

8 November, SR 7:09, SS 4:18. This is how the entry in the diary would have read, but Ed had not used his provisional diary and it never got truly light that day. Like the last forgotten guests of an endless autumn, the frigate captain and two of his soldiers sat on the terrace. When the general appeared, Vosskamp sprang up and saluted. One of the soldiers didn't manage to get his weapon over his shoulder, so he held it upright in front of his chest and froze in that position. The general tapped the visor of his cap and called something in Russian over the beer-garden tables. 'Plechom k plechu,' the frigate captain yelled back, which silenced the few birds that had decided to take on the morning. Vosskamp saluted once more to the general's back, but was already looking at Edgar as he did. Ed sensed his incomprehension but also his benevolence — the look of a shocked parent.

Plechom k plechu.

The medic had bound Kruso to the personnel table top with tablecloths. Their large flower pattern was covered with food and beer stains interspersed with black-rimmed cigarette burns, which Ed briefly took for bullet holes.

Now it was the general who was holding the drip (life) in the air as they made their way down the stairs to the sea. With motions of his free hand, he directed the bearers, who slowed and walked in step as is customary in the burial of the *important dead*. The medic had hurried a few metres ahead to call out the many loose or missing steps. And at the end came Ed, like a useless child skipping behind the procession without understanding what was really happening. Nonetheless: he carried the bag, the hospital bag. Nonetheless: he understood the bag. Containing just the basics, it was not that heavy. No one had asked about it yet.

Kruso hovered, feet first, between the soldiers, like a pharaoh on his final journey. Certain sections of the stairs forced the bearers to tilt the makeshift tabletop stretcher at a steep angle, as if they wanted to show the sea the victim or the victim the sea one last time, from the horizon to Denmark, which floated invisibly in the fog, or to the water of the Baltic Sea, which lay inert and with November's chill behind the head-high sea buckthorn bushes that had overgrown the flight of stairs down the bluff. Yes, for a moment it seemed to Ed as if they were holding out to the Baltic Sea a saint, a martyr, whose body they were about to consign to the tide in order to calm the storm and to end the patrol boats' confusion and, finally, as a sign of freedom and proof that it could be attained right here, in our time, and not just on Møn, Hawaii, or elsewhere — yes, Kruso had to be sacrificed, sacrificed for the future of the island ...

Ed had no idea how such revolting madness could have entered his head. He grabbed his forehead. Maybe he had breathed in too much Exlepäng that night, had smelled Kruso's neck for too long; maybe he had simply gone crazy.

'Losh!'

The soldiers were still holding Kruso out to the sea.

Last of his kind, last living representative, careful, careful! the insanity whispered to the steps on which Ed's feet appeared with fine regularity, feet and steps in endless number, but no, of course not, he had counted them more than once on his lunch breaks before the high season, sweating, breathless, be careful 294 times, the whisper filled Ed's head.

On the last section of the steps, the one that hung over the beach, the wounded very nearly slipped from the soldiers' grasp. Ed saw the Soviet muscles tremble, the tension under the uniforms, the general's hand oddly contorted, his flapping coat — for a moment, he looked like a large, amusing puppetmaster, on whose strings the personnel table danced and with it the whole story of this endless season, accompanied by the dance of four young lackeys in sailor costumes. Kazakhs, perhaps, yes Kazakhs would be fitting, Ed thought.

He noticed that Kruso's eyes were open — his broad face, smooth and white, with incredulous eyes; a youthful and yet leaden face, a child's face with graveyard eyes, it was — Georg Trakl's face. Only Ed and his madness could think such thoughts.

At first, there was no boat in sight, just the armoured cruiser, enormous in the fog, so Ed initially thought the men were simply going to push Kruso out to sea on the table top, all the way to the dark hull on which the number 141 was written. He had never seen such a large ship so close to shore. The bow towered above the water; the stern, however, hardly seemed to rise above water. Between them were two domes like cyclops skulls, from which a pair of gun barrels protruded, long and as thin as spears. Then Ed saw the dinghy. It was beached just a few hundred metres to the north, at Ed's swimming spot, where there was a path to deep water that was somewhat free of stones.

Without thinking, Ed had put one foot on the bow. He belonged with Kruso if anyone did. First, the Kazakhs' alarmed looks (he hated them at that moment), then the general's hand on his shoulder. Not in acknowledgement, not in consolation.

Ed only grasped what happened from that point on in isolated images. The hovering drip. The metal barque. The handing off of the infusion. The dark hollow sound of the personnel table on the thwarts. The medic who took the bag from Ed's hand without a word. The general's shiny shoes half-sunk in the sand. A wave and the dark, wet hems of his trousers. The wet bottoms of his Soviet trousers — the story ended with this image, it contained the entire story.

The general's hand had nailed him to the beach. He could still feel it when the dinghy was hauled onto the mothership and the diesel motor roared and the armoured cruiser or whatever that waterborne fortress was supposed to represent slowly picked up speed. His body became leaden. To lend his stiffness some kind of expression, Ed lowered his eyes. Rocks, algae, rotten hair. Heaviness flowed into him from every direction and the hammering of the diesel didn't subside, it did not stop.

Then the shot.

The crazy boy in the harbour, mouth open wide and arms raised high, then the shot. The coachman Mäcki in the stall with a bottle and his bear-horse, then the shot. The counter-couple with their luggage and bags between bushes, right in the puzzle of the border, then the shot. Chris? Rolf? Speiche? The shot. Chef Mike with his family? And Rimbaud somewhere, neither reading nor writing? Then the shot. Mona and Cavallo on their way south — Rome, Naples, the Stazione Zoologica, then the shot.

Ed dropped to the ground as if he'd been hit, and pressed his face in the sand. For seconds, the surf was still, the landscape touched by thunder. Even the general had gone insane. The line of fire must have passed far over him, over the bluffs, the land — the entire hermetic space filled with echoes. The entire rotten space that was their home.

Another shot and its echo in the cove.

Then one shot after another in respectful succession. As if the guns were imitating a giant's dying heartbeat. Between them, a faint whistling, like the sound of jets flying high above, almost in outer space. But no impacts; no explosions.

With each peal of thunder, the sky was raised slightly. Air streamed in. Ether of intoxicating freshness and purity. Ed tasted sand. A few strands of algae stuck to his face, and he could feel his constricted heart wanting to expand. Twenty-one claps of thunder. Maybe he was losing his mind. He finally surrendered, he tittered at the sand: Salute, salute!

Shipwreck, salute! Two valves, salute! Dishwashing station, salute!

Salute! Salute!

He had understood. It was a signal.

It could all fall apart.

RESURRECTION

9 November. He served in the bar room, but through the valves, which were bolted shut. He had established a provisional neatness, lit the stove, and made coffee. He did it all very slowly, one thing at a time, separating each movement. He made a provisional solyanka with brown bread on the side. Some parts of his body had trouble emerging from the state of shock into the usual flow, so he stalked stiffly back and forth between the bar and the tables. There was something accompanying him *inside*, using his eyes and his ears, with whatever he did, something that had to be treated very gently and very well.

Seven guests came on his first day. Calm, taciturn lovers of the island, loners who warmed their hands on their coffee cups and stared at the terrace through the net curtains while Ed washed cups and glasses or stood motionless at the bar, letting the tap run. The soft stream did him good, as did the gentle snorkelling and warbling of the overflow's waterfall. If anyone spoke to him, Ed answered, 'Exactly!' or 'Why not?', as if he, too, were in the midst of life. There were even moments when he forgot everything and fantasised about

running an inn on his own. Maybe the control commission from
Berlin-Schweineöde would never show ...

His last guest was a young woman who asked for Kruso in the
way that castaways by the dozens had asked for the king of the island.
She was very short and had long brown hair, wet with rain. For two
seconds, Ed pictured her in his room, her hair on his pillows. Then he
gruffly pointed out that the season had ended. November — the end
of *every* season, he emphasised unnecessarily.

It was also unnecessary to shout at the small woman. His name
wasn't Rimbaud. His pain, his grief — the entire loss. He was ashamed.
He thought of the last castaway in his room, a woman named B.,
who had slept in his room the nights before Island Day, the day of
the parade, the day that was the beginning of the end. She had been
at least forty, maybe even older. There was hardly a sentence from
B. that was not accompanied by a puff of smoke. She was a chain-
smoker. She said she didn't want to be a maid-of-all-work anymore —
on the other hand, it's also nice to be a maid-of-all-work. She talked
and quoted Losh: 'Scrapped and valuable people. The enlightened
and shady characters.' There was something dismissive about her;
she was in the process of throwing everything away. Ed slept on the
floor, B. in his bed. She slept, woke up, talked and smoked, then slept
again. At some point in the night, Ed imagined he could taste B.'s
smoky mouth. Even in the darkness, he could recognise her small,
hooked nose and her long, straight neck that became, almost without
transition, the back of her head, as if she had no occipital bone, just
endless neck that constantly whispered to him: lay your hand on it,
go ahead, lay the flat of your hand on it. B. laughed about Kruso. She
called him, 'His Majesty, Lord and Master of the entire island.' She
also called him a rag-picker, and compared the allocation with the last
bus home but without anyone being able to say what or where home
was. Freedom Inn? Boarding House of Lost Souls? She prattled on
about such things without interruption, blowing smoke. It was all a
game to her, an intermezzo. She said she had no intention of making

jewellery for anyone and had turned down the sacred soup. She said, 'I'm not going to eat my soup,' and laughed. She added that she had her own ways of getting intoxicated, without alchemy, and, besides, the sacred soup smelled like shit. Ed was offended, although he had to admit the soup did not smell good. Ed thought B. was in distress. She'd been married twelve years and had got divorced three months earlier. It was her decision, she said. On the day they separated, she hadn't been able to sleep from excitement and joy. They still got along, she said, still saw each other now and then. Ed was completely *stiff* with exhaustion, stiff. Twelve years. Her husband was jealous but had always had a bit on the side. Because she always danced so ecstatically, people often thought she was out of her mind, especially at the office Christmas party. But she wasn't crazy, not in the least. However, she wasn't getting ahead. And now she couldn't imagine anything else. *Here* she had nothing to lose. *Here* there was just this island. The last place.

In the evening, Ed locked all the doors and drew the curtains. He wrote with Chef Mike's grease pencil on a piece of cardboard — CLOSED DUE TO STAFF SHORTAGE — and stuck it behind the glass of the drinks valve. He blocked the entrance to servants' staircase with Monika's ironing board.

There was no one left.

He went to his room, gathered his things, and brought them all downstairs to Krombach's office, where he wanted to sleep from this point on in a cloud of Exlepäng, in the heart of the Klausner. He locked the swinging doors to the kitchen, but left the door to the cubbyhole open so that he had a few metres of open view at night as well.

I saw you coming. Those had been Kruso's words at night on the beach after the baptism of the esskays, shortly before the kiss — he had only been dreamed up, had only been another person's dream. A Friday envisioned by Crusoe in sleep, in his longing.

The bed smelled of sweat. Ed wrapped himself up and stared into the darkness. He had only been dreamed up. But now they'd taken the dreamer away and so Ed couldn't really exist.

Voices woke him the following morning. When he entered the bar room, they fell silent, but at breakfast they were there again. The voices were coming from the photographs of former crews. Nothing that should worry him. No threats, no vulgar remarks, just simple, well-intentioned advice like: 'Don't do anything stupid, kiddo!' (from high up on the right; the year was barely legible, maybe 1930) or 'You should take off, whippersnapper' (1977) or 'Do something about Viola, man' (1984). This last comment sounded like it came from the dead cook whose radio Viola had once been. A giant of a man in crisp whites, on the far left in the picture, still not aware he would soon drown. But since then, he had found out everything, Ed thought; he saw all the crews that followed him, and now he saw Ed, the last 89er, who was not taking care of his radio.

Ed spread jam on a slice of brown bread. They had frozen a lot of it. The time of breakfast rolls was over. He had sawed himself a slice from the five-kilo block of mixed-berry jam, enough to last three or four winters. Finding food would be no problem; he had a sure supply. He could stay here forever, could keep his promise.

He had taken to sitting in his old place again. He had pushed another table to where the personnel table had been, and placed the chairs around it. Twelve chairs — a one-man crew. A room filled with absence.

He brought his dishes to the sink and whispered a few lines into it. 'My good Kruso. My dear Losh.'

He remembered the list of things he had to do. The Kazakhs had stolen the receipt book. No, it was on the windowsill behind him, and next to it was his pen and the ashtray, put aside neatly. The good Kazakhs. He read the list, but it was no list. And not from him. But it was his writing. He read. Three pages of the receipt book, written in Kruso's tone, not by Kruso. He read.

He went back to the dishwashing station and turned on the water. He gathered plates, cutlery, and glasses, and began drawing circles with his hands on the bottom of the sink. 'Good man. Dear man.'

After a while, he dried his hands on the Roman and got the large notebook from his room. He looked at the light-blue grid on the pages. The book lay half on Krombach's side, half on Monika's. He turned it this way then that, first towards Cavallo, then towards Chef Mike, and finally towards himself.

Look, everyone: a present from G.

He leafed backwards and rubbed his hand over the old entries. He caressed them; he caressed G. He could now simply think of her. With his worn fingertip, he could feel the indentation from the ballpoint pen, the way the writing had been impressed into rough, woody paper. She was gone, and he thought the actual word, *gone*.

No one left. Ed stood up and put on his Thälmann jacket. He was wearing it for the first time since he had arrived on the island — the weather was cold enough. He made sure no one was standing outside the door or in the courtyard, some hiker who might not want to respect the closed sign. He resembled a hermit, full of mistrust. A strong wind buffeted his face. He hesitated then took the path to the bluffs.

Walking did him good. The roar of the surf became louder as he descended. The breakers thundered, and a howling had set in, soft at first, then louder, a whistling that rose and fell as if the general's shots had been deflected into an orbit. Kruso's bottles, Ed thought. That toots, it does. That toots them moles in the noggin.

He couldn't think anymore; he could only walk. He grabbed his temples as if he had to remember something or as if he were greeting the sea in that old, almost forgotten customary way. The endless roar — it now penetrated him directly and tried to erase his memory. 'We walk a-long the great wide sea, 'til-the-sun-sets-hap-pi-ly ...' Mother, Father, and Ed-the-child between them, their bright, shining faces, all three walking in step on the sand of Göhren, on the island of Rügen — the only memory that came to his assistance.

All of a sudden, his walk stopped. The beach had disappeared. Instead of the mountain of loam, there was a giant avalanche that extended far into the sea. A section of more than a hundred metres of the coastline had broken off. A few boulders as tall as a man stuck out like the skulls of submerged giants, and between them lay uprooted trees and shrubs. Ed noticed the delta at his feet. There wasn't the slightest trace of where the fox was buried.

Old rascal.

Gaffer.

Ed imagined his fox protecting the folder with his leathery body, and he heard the poems whispering softly deep in the earth. He understood each word and repeated it, and soon his talk expanded beyond the line ends and reached out into the breakers. He declaimed the poems forcefully against the surf; he became cocky and almost fell. Shaken, he fell silent and understood: what the least, the only thing he had left to do was. *For Losh. For Kruso.*

Three days later, on the evening of the twelfth of November, his notebook was filled, single-spaced, a line in every square, covered with writing. He hadn't slept; he had worked day and night. Sometimes, he sat at the personnel table, more often in the dishwashing station at the sink for coarse cleaning or the sink for cutlery, always switching between his side and Kruso's. 'Actually, what you'd most like is to sink completely, to be submerged, but in the meantime the little circles your hands make in the water are enough ... An enormous loss, that's what it feels like. But nothing is really lost, no one is, Ed, *no one.* You just keep on talking softly to yourself, with your own voice, you knock at the words' door with your voice. Hundreds of times, to yourself.

And at some point you'll hear it ...'

In the end, Ed had washed the entire stock of cutlery, pots, glasses, and dishes again. His hands were disintegrating, his fingers like those on a drowned corpse. 'I have to arrange them into one volume. There's nothing better than compiling a volume of poetry, you know, Ed?'

Ed climbed through the trapdoor behind the bar and brought up a pile of Klausner letterhead. He took Krombach's Torpedo from the cabinet and began. He sat at the typewriter the entire night. Certain letters had bloody caps. In the morning, the job was done. Maybe not word for word and not every line, but Ed could hear that it was *right*, he heard the tone. 'The two of us,' Ed murmured.

Writing had emptied him out. A feeling as if there was nothing left to do in life. He crept straight to bed and fell into a deep, dreamless sleep.

Barking woke him in the evening. One of Vosskamp's dogs. It was barking mechanically, without stopping. Maybe a fox near the security gate, Ed thought, or wild boar. Maybe there are only animals left, animals and me. The thought was oddly comforting. He wrapped himself in his blanket and wanted to fall back asleep, but there was knocking at the door.

The control commission.

Ed stayed still for a while and listened to the rain. No one there anymore.

Then someone knocked again.

Ed turned on the outside lights and peered through curtains. The good soldier was at the door. He was in his dress uniform and did not have his gun.

'Be well, Ed, good luck,' the good soldier said.

'What's going on?' Ed asked.

'I'm just wanted to say good luck in case you weren't here tomorrow. So, good luck.'

Ed had no idea what to say, and rested his hand against the door.

'Good luck,' he finally murmured, and 'I'm sorry,' without knowing why. The good soldier turned and disappeared into the night. Ed watched him go. He took the shortcut, the narrow path through the Svantovit Gorge, straight to the barracks.

'Good luck.'

He stood in the doorway a few minutes and listened.

Then he made his way to the dishwashing station to get the bottle of skin cream. The skin was peeling away from his fingertips, and two of his nail beds were inflamed, covered in tiny red bulges. Maybe I was too generous with the cream, Ed thought. He rubbed some of the cloudy slime between his fingers and clapped his hand a few times. Silence fell again immediately, so it started taking effort to clap. Silence demanded silence, that's how it was, 'and that's how it always has been,' Ed murmured. On the other hand, the clapping felt good. It warmed his hands; blood hummed in his fingers, clapping bolstered his spirits. So he kept clapping as he wandered aimlessly through the darkened Klausner — like a damned spirit rattling its chains, Ed thought. He clapped and pictured Ettenburg, the Ur-hermit, whose ashes had been strewn over the sea — Ettenburg, the revenant. He walked along the bluffs in his monk's habit. Now and then, he rammed his foot despairingly into the sand and a large chunk of land would break off and slide into the sea. It was his revenge; bit by bit, the island would vanish into the sea.

Ed climbed the servants' staircase to the top floor. The wind had freshened the room. Kruso's curtains swayed. Ed tried to stick his ruined fingertips into the coarse netting, but the curtain would not be calmed. On the night of the last allocation, Ed had slipped into Kruso's room and looked down at the terrace. The cowl he had draped over Kruso had seemingly melted in the rain into a mirror, shaken now and again by a tremor, a kind of stutter in his back, a cold, wet, lonely stutter. This had pained Ed, but he had still gone to sleep in his own bed. He had only wanted to rest for a moment, just to dry his hair, and rub cream into his hands ...

Hesitantly, he started clapping again. He was careful not to get too close to the window again.

No one left.

No one left.

When Ed went back downstairs, the manuscript caught his eye. Kruso's *Collection*. His book. Ed smiled at it across the bar room. In some way, it had taken over the old crew's place, the place of their collective absence, of their old life in its entirety even though it was nothing more than a small pile of paper, writing with bloody caps, neatly stacked. All of a sudden, Ed had a past.

The gate to the barracks was not locked. The dog run was empty. No guard, no dogs, just the smell of dogs, the smell of a kennel and rotten meat. A light was on in the sentry post, but there was no one there either. Ed entered the compound tentatively. The garages were deathly silent. A Robur truck, a field kitchen, a military motorcycle, and the cycling patrol's bicycles. Next to these were a coal bucket and bags of coal, set out as if in anticipation of discovery by a future civilisation.

Then he heard it.

It came from the ground, from the moraine at the foot of the watchtower. Ed circled the small, roughly cone-shaped hill and found an entrance covered with netting. Two doors covered with steel levers, unlocked, and a third, closed door with a small square window at eye level.

'Out on the breakwater, they looked over the wide, wide sea, out on the breakwater, hearts heavy with longing ...'

The bunker was panelled with wood all the way to the ceiling, like a house bar or a basement workshop — narrow, finely sanded boards with a thick coat of varnish that formed farmhouse-type benches along the side walls and an extra, roofed counter at the gable end of the room. On the bar shelves, Ed saw a television's shimmering green screen. It was turned off. *Cola Bar* was burned in ornate script into the wood above the counter. Next to the television, there were beer mugs covered with disassembled clothes pegs and an array of wooden craft items, arched candle holders, and Erzgebirge Christmas decorations, enveloped in a thick cloud of cigarette smoke.

'Out on the breakwater ...'

Only two seconds, but Ed had recognised Vosskamp immediately, his cap pushed far over his ear, and next to him, the good soldier; the entire observation company was gathered in the hobby bunker, arm in arm, and on the floor a guard dog was stretched out as if exhausted.

'Out on the breakwater, Annegret waits in the evening ...'

Twenty men, Ed guessed, and a hundred bottles. Vosskamp was conducting. A corporal had slumped to the side and fallen asleep on one of the benches, his arms bent over his head. It looked like a victory celebration; as if a war had ended.

One of the dogs started in.

There had been a flash amid the windswept trees, a magical light. 'Ahoy, ahoy, the wide, wide sea,' drifted up from the bunker moraine. Someone had opened the door. The sound of barking was approaching as Ed overcame his fear and reached for the first iron ladder.

The watchtower was manned day and night, Kruso had explained to him. But the searchlight was turned off and no one stood at the telescope. Every step sent a dark roll of thunder through the structure, which seemed to sway slightly.

Ed had seen the glow halfway there. But it wasn't coming from the lights on the frigate or from the patrol boats. Where there was otherwise only blackness, lights flashed in every colour — red, yellow, blue, and, yes: green, green, everywhere green, the green light ...

'The dead!' Ed exclaimed in a whisper. He was probably losing his mind.

The dead had risen — there was no room for any other thought in his head after all that had happened. 'Look at the signals,' Ed murmured. The entire bay was full of them, risen, back from below ground, from their flight, from the place they'd been waiting all this time for this day — the sea had set free its dead.

'Ahoy,' Ed whispered, then again, 'Ahoy there, ahoy!'

Kruso was right. None were lost. None had gone missing forever.

'Ahoy, dear Sonya! Ahoy there, little G.!'

No wonder there was a celebration. No wonder they were singing in the bunker. 'No wonder!' Ed shouted joyfully and felt faint. He grabbed onto the railing; he hugged the searchlight. He wept and finally understood: no wonder.

He couldn't remember what happened next. It was unclear how he regained consciousness, how he made his way down the ladder. He found himself back on the ground, at the gate. One of the dogs leapt at him. He threw up his hands, and the dog fell back into the darkness without a sound; as if it had never really been there at all.

He fell, got up, kept on running. He dragged the first table he could into the kitchen, set a stool on top of it, and pulled the beer mug out of the radio.

A smell of mould streamed from the radio case. All he had to do was bend the silvery tubes back to their original position. Viola came to — she still worked.

'Eight o'clock. West German radio, the news.'

Like a performer in a complicated cabaret, Ed crouched high up near the radio. In the Klausner's kitchen, in the middle of Chef Mike's realm. A lonely, comical figure, but also loyal and perhaps brave.

For a while, Ed wasn't sure he understood. But he knew Viola's voice, and she helped him calm his breathing.

All the borders were open. They had been open for days.

EPILOGUE

MISSING DEPARTMENT
(EDGAR'S REPORT)

I learned of Kruso's death in 1993, on August 23rd. The following morning, I drove towards Potsdam to the Russian cemetery on highway B2 to look for the grave of his mother, who had been a performer in the Red Army. I'd been living not far from there for some time, just a few minutes by car, a half-hour through the woods on foot.

The cemetery lay on a hill among fir trees that stood like columns between the graves, offering shelter and shade. Still, the area had changed greatly in recent years — even 1993 seems long ago now. Back then, when it happened to Kruso, I had no influence on the course things took. It's important to me to state that again, just that. All the circumstances have been explained, as difficult as it is for me to conclude with this. The circumstances don't belong in this report.

I had no point of reference, so I searched the entire area. The officers were buried in the front, near the road, behind them were the soldiers, then the children's plots, and finally, all the way in the back near the fence, the women's graves. Many of the graves' borders were broken, the stones shifted and covered with pine needles. In the middle of the cemetery, there was a grove of honour, guarded by a kind of golem, a cast-iron Red Army soldier, four or five metres tall, with a helmet and a machine gun. This fearless figure was completely focused on the main entrance, to cow with his cast-iron glance anyone who might wish to enter the area without respect.

There were all sorts of toys on the children's graves, plastic cars, rubber dolls, and teddy bears leaning against the gravestones, their legs covered with moss. Soldiers who had died together were also buried together, according to the inscriptions — one company until the end. Often the cause was a downed plane, and the silhouettes of the plane models (bomber, MiG, cargo jet) were engraved in the headstone above the names. Some headstones had portraits, small oval photographs behind glass and bordered in stainless steel. Others had only names, no dates of birth or death — executed deserters, I learned later.

The further away I went from the golem, the softer and thicker the moss on the gravestones became. There were many soldiers who had died very young, especially in the years 1958 and 1959. I could not make sense of that. Even stranger was the large number of children. There was a pinwheel stuck in one of the graves, a little plastic pitchfork in another. I found the tightrope artist's grave near a mound of roots and earth where wreaths and flowers were composted.

I stood there for a while. I have an exact memory of that moment. The day was warm. The fir trees' bark was peeling off in the sun, making a crackling noise as small, light-brown flakes whirled to the ground, as opaque as skin in the light, and I imagined Sonya doing her magic tricks beside the open grave. Then, the salute into the dome of firs, and Kruso-the-child, unable to cry or say goodbye. Without admitting it to myself completely, I had been convinced (or afraid) that I would see Sonya's name under her mother's on the gravestone.

Sonya Valentina Krusowitsch, Kruso's sister.

'And if ever I'm not here for a while, then — take charge. Promise me that,' Kruso had said. It was as if his death had finally put my promise into effect, and maybe that's the reason I happened on the book (everything is by chance). A few days later, on one of my aimless searches through the shelves in the city library, I read the title: *Across the Baltic Sea to Freedom.* The sea-grey jacket bore the subtitle *Dramatic Tales of Escape.* The book was on the 'Recent Acquisitions' shelf, near the entrance, almost impossible to miss. In the appendix, there was an interview: 'Stranded on Klintholm: Harbourmaster Erik Jensen Recounts'. I picked up the book and retreated behind the newspaper stand, where there was a small reading nook with soft brown upholstered chairs in which a few retirees and homeless people spent their days.

The interview with the harbourmaster concerned East German refugees who had landed on Møn. He talked about broken dinghies and crushed folding canoes with no crew. And about the dead who washed up on Klintholm, 'on his doorstep,' he said, or who had been hauled in by bottom-trawling Danish fishermen, or who had been pulled from the water over the years. Nowhere were there so many as between Rügen and Møn, the harbourmaster said.

'We brought them on land here and then to the Forensic Institute in Copenhagen.'

'Could a relative of a missing GDR refugee still find out about their fate today?'

'If he knows the approximate date of their escape and can provide a description or a photograph, then it might be possible. Descriptions of the dead are kept in the Forensic Medicine Institute of Copenhagen University, Rigshospitalet, Blegdamsvej 9, Copenhagen.'

I changed some money and bought a map, on which I drew the way with a ballpoint pen. On the seventh of September, I took the ferry from Rostock to Gedser in Denmark, and from there to Copenhagen, to Rigshospitalet. The cost of the crossing alone blew my budget. The country, the city, they were all new to me, and I occasionally had the feeling of being on an expedition, a voyage of discovery, a test, perhaps, but that does not belong in this report either.

The main building of the National Hospital was a grey building of steel and glass, about twenty stories tall. The woman at the information desk did not understand me at first — because of my bad English. She switched to German and explained the basics, and the forensic department's location and office hours. Her friendliness was reassuring, but the institute had just closed.

I drove along a road that passed directly in front of the forensic medicine building, Frederik V's Vej, a peaceful neighbourhood. There was a park right next door, with a football game in progress. The Rigshospitalet compound seemed enormous, a kind of hospital-Manhattan, surrounded by open areas that symbolised the Hudson. I took a turn through the park and took a picture of a bicycle that had a big black hutch attached to it like a rickshaw. I treated myself to a cup of coffee and started to calm down. I sat on a bench near the football pitch and made some notes — consultation times, the name of the street, the neighbourhood, and so on. My intention was to be meticulous about everything. I didn't want to miss anything. If you've promised something, you have to deliver — the childish maxim. Or perhaps not, it was more of a parental maxim, the goal of a certain kind of upbringing that later could only be quoted ironically for reasons I didn't need to think about because I was certain and my goal was clear. I ate the last of the sandwiches I'd brought with me, and returned to the car to set up for the night.

A good three years earlier, my parents had left me their old car, a 1971 Shiguli, which, as I knew from my childhood, was very well suited to sleeping in because the backrest of the front seat lined up perfectly with the surface of the rear seat when folded back. There were no headrests or bucket seats at the time, at least not in cars from Togliatti. The Russians had named their car manufacturing city after the Italian communist Palmiro Togliatti. Furthermore, the cars were built on Italian licence, 'modelled on the Fiat 124, 1966 car of the year!' — my father had told me these facts an endless number of times when we were driving in the Shiguli, so often, in fact, that they still whirred through my mind now that the valuable car belonged to me and that I was the one behind the wheel, as if these facts were a necessary component of the car, as indispensable as the wheels or the stick shift. What I liked most was the wonderfully soft brown artificial leather, stitched together in stripes, which still smelled of my childhood, of driving and sleeping stretched out on the backseat with my feet against one door, my head against the other.

But my report is not about this either. I was exhausted and could have dropped off to sleep then and there, but I wanted to wait at least until darkness fell. I took one more turn around the grounds of the Rigshospitalet. In front of the wards, there were elongated pools with nervous little fountains. Over the entrance to the forensics department was a sign that read 'Teilum-bygningen'. The woman at the information desk had also said 'Teilum'. For me, it was the *Museum of the Drowned*. The expression had first occurred to me when I was reading the interview with the harbourmaster, and I hadn't been able to get it out of my head since.

The 'Teilum' didn't look like a museum, nor did it look like a morgue. It was a new five-storey building with a façade made of gravel concrete, as were the planters to the left and right of the entrance, in which tiny gingko trees struggled to survive. Through the glass doors of the front and back entrances, you could see the foyer and the adjoining hallways. In the spacious corridors, seating areas furnished with colourful shell chairs in light blue, green, and red had been set up behind folding screens. It was inconceivable that anyone had ever used one of these areas. A lemon-yellow spiral staircase led down to where the dead were probably kept.

When I pulled my forehead away from the glass and took a step back to photograph the 'Teilum' and its desperate colourfulness, which inspired in me a sense of respect that was hard to express (was it perhaps possible to deal with death in a more modern, more optimistic way?), a man came up to me on a bicycle. Without dismounting, he asked me something, probably what I was doing there. He wore a grey security-guard uniform that looked like a locksmith's work clothes. He was grey, too: grey hair, grey complexion. I answered in English. I explained that I was a German writer doing research for a book about the dead, 'about the bodies who came here in former times,' I stammered. At that, the security guard wished me luck and went on his way. He set off at a considerable pace, bent far over the handlebars. There must have been some kind of bike race. Suddenly, I realised he had already passed me several times while I was trying to scout out the Museum of the Drowned more thoroughly.

I climbed into the Shiguli and soon fell asleep. Overhead, the rustling trees of the Fælledparken (the name in my notebook). The next morning, I tidied myself up as best I could. Water from the water bottle, teeth brushed behind the car's open trunk. I changed my shirt and tried to smooth out the wrinkles. Then I went into the park, but the coffee kiosk was closed.

I found a last apple in the car. I contemplated whether it would help my cause to stick to my cover of being a writer, in any case, it seemed to make more of an impression. I had a folder with Sonya's picture, and I'd prepared an explanatory text in English that was meant to explain why I could claim to be a 'relative'. And I had gathered Sonya's personal information (as much as I knew), along with the presumed date of her escape, her presumed escape. I opened the folder again, but couldn't concentrate, and just picked a few drops of wax off Sonya's crumpled face.

'Blow them out, dammit!'

'You have to blow them out, Ed!'

I tried to brace myself. My head was filled with zombies and body parts. I pictured Sonya's dead body in a morgue refrigerator 'on the kingdom's good ice' — utterly absurd, yes, and suddenly it seemed no less absurd of me to have come here, naïve and ignorant as I was.

But, still, not without reason. Yes, I would *take charge*, and naturally I hoped I *wouldn't* find Sonya.

I wandered through the hallways on the ground floor for a while — Auditorium 1, Auditorium 2, the doors were open, a sweetish smell hung in the air. The offices were on the floor above, where there was a kind of waiting area with a cloakroom and a reception desk with two secretaries, one younger and one older.

I started reciting the sentences I'd memorised (my bad English). Even before I could open my folder, the younger secretary reached for the telephone.

'Doctor Sørensen?'

Dr Sørensen spoke German and for that I was instantly grateful to him. In his building, around 3,000 post-mortems were done a year, of course, some might have been drowned refugees found on the coast of Zealand, Lolland, or Falster. He had vague memories of a few cases, but unfortunately only the police had access to the files ... Sørensen wore a white shirt with a large point collar. He tilted his head as he talked, and nodded a few times in a 'things-are-what-they-are' kind of way.

I felt vaguely relieved for a while. I was happy to have been welcomed and treated so pleasantly by the Danes, all of whom seemed to speak German, despite my bleary-eyed, rumpled appearance. I was just a random stranger, but was still the first East German to come to the 'Teilum' and show interest in the corpses of his countrymen, as Sørensen noted, 'Countrymen — can one even use that term now, probably not, right, Mr Bendler?'

I have to admit that Sørensen impressed me. His agile manner, his tanned complexion — today, I would probably feel differently, but back then Sørensen was a man from another world, another (better) life, light-years away from where I came from. I was almost ashamed of the stained photograph, but I still took it out of my folder and pushed it across the desk like a final request. I felt shabby. Sørensen just glanced briefly at the photograph (as at a misunderstanding) and didn't touch it, so I soon took it back, quickly and with embarrassment.

Nonetheless, I must say that the circumstances of my visit were met with great helpfulness, including an offer of a tour through the 'Teilum'. Perhaps because he found it difficult to send me away empty-handed (considering the distance I had travelled to get there), perhaps also because I came from the East and my humble demeanour gave the impression I was interested in *everything*.

Here they spoke of death more openly, Sørensen explained as he lead me through the rooms. I had put on a white coat and was trailing behind him.

One distinct memory has stayed with me. It is of the department's utensils, probably because they looked so familiar to me — knives, spoons, ladles. Organs were removed in groups, first the heart and lungs, then the stomach, intestines, and liver, and last the kidneys, bladder, genitals. They were washed and weighed separately, and most had specimens removed. 'These small plastic containers, for example, are ready for the evidence.' I picked up one of these little cups. It held a white powder. 'Sodium fluoride,' Sørensen explained, 'it stops decomposition.' He took the cup. I dutifully pulled out my notebook, which led the forensic pathologist to comment on my 'unusual interest', as he put it. He went on, 'drowned corpses are putrefied corpses and have a particular odour that is essentially unbearable. You sit in your car on the way home, stuck in traffic, and suddenly: the smell. It sticks to your skin, to your hair, to everything. Fresh corpses are much preferable.' Sørensen laughed and immediately apologised. That was all irrelevant. Most important was curiosity, a certain and perhaps exaggerated curiosity, one must never lose that curiosity.

As I was leaving, Dr Sørensen said a few words to the secretaries. I must have looked distraught. At any rate, the older woman walked me to the exit. In front of the elevator, she stepped closer to me and then she said it: if I wanted to grieve, that is, if I were looking for the

proper place to take leave of my girlfriend (those were her words),
then I should go to the municipal cemetery, to the grave of the
unknown. She pressed a note into my hand: Bispebjerg Kirkegård,
Frederiksborgvej 125, Nørrebro.

I don't remember much about the rest of the day. In a daze, I followed
the usual tourist route and ended up in the port. I came to with a
start — surprised at how small the little mermaid (Den lille Havfrue)
really was. In the guidebook, I read that someone had sawed off her
head in 1964 and her right arm in 1984, but there were no scars, no
traces to be seen. She looked immeasurably sad — pitiful and worthy
of great pity. That was the moment I decided to go to Bispebjerg,
that I do remember. On the way, I tried to imagine the little mermaid
without a head or arm; she did not turn into sea spray, did not
become a spirit of air, no, her decaying body lay between the stones,
recently washed up, but no one did anything. Then police, forensics,
post-mortem, protocol. Still, she had a name; every Dane recognised
her even without her head.

What was unusual about the Bispebjerg cemetery is that you could
drive in it. There was a large, well-paved oval, similar to a racetrack,
and a few smaller side streets. All the roads were lined with poplars or
pine trees. I parked first next to the crematorium and oriented myself
with the map. Various sections were arranged around the racetrack,
signed like highway exits — Swedish, Russian, Muslim, Catholic
exits, and on the other end of the grounds, past the southern curve,
the *tyske grave*: the German plots. I climbed into my Shiguli and
drove there, about three kilometres.

The *tyske grave* was an enclosure with three stone crosses, three
oak trees, and a large bronze memorial plaque. One row further on,
the dead were listed alphabetically, with dates of birth and death,
on smaller plaques. The list concluded with a mention of 'seventeen
unidentified German refugees'.

I don't recall what I felt at that moment. I know I had trouble sleeping in the cemetery even though I felt safe in the Shiguli. And I know that at midnight I crawled out of the car again and went to the stone. In the dark, everything looked different, warmer. I set the crumpled photograph on the grass and kept watch. It was quiet. No wind in the trees, no rustling, nothing happened. No sign. I thought of Kruso, of Sonya, and also of G. I fulfilled a promise as if I'd made it to myself.

'Then you won't leave me, Sonya?'
'No, no, never. I will follow you.'

Barely twenty years later, I saw a man gesture towards a vast emptiness and heard him say: 'There are dead buried everywhere here.' It was a film from the North German Broadcasting System about refugees who had fled over the Baltic Sea. I'd been working until just before midnight and had turned on the television. I'd drunk some wine, half a bottle. It was all chance. I had just wanted to make myself tired enough to sleep — bed-heavy, as my mother called it — and there was no better way.

The camera lens panned slowly (grieving) over the field and finally stopped (prayerfully) in the branches of an old beech tree that was keeping vigil. Field and tree, nothing else. The cemetery was called Bispebjerg Kirkegård, but didn't look anything like the place I'd been two decades earlier, for an evening and a night, to *take my leave*, as the secretary in the forensics department had suggested. The young Dane in front of the camera wore a half-length coat, his hair was blond and hung down to his shoulders. Behind him, there was nothing but grass, and here and there, in the distance, small islands of flowers.

Promises made. It wasn't that I was at the wrong grave and perhaps was taken for a fool. It had nothing to do with being outraged, no: I'd been careless. I had been content too soon and with too little, basically with nothing at all.

In the following weeks, I read everything on the topic I could get my hands on. I didn't find all that much: two books with careful research and analysis, a few articles, a travelling exhibit. One statistic showed over 5,600 refugees, 913 of them successful, 4,522 arrests, and at least 174 fatalities since 1961, washed ashore between Fehmarn, Rügen, and Denmark. The most successful refugee stories had been filmed, not big movies, but good documentaries for regional broadcasting: two surfers who made it from Hiddensee to Møn one November day (on homemade windsurfers); two young doctors in a dinghy, picked up by a Danish cutter; one man who swam forty-eight kilometres in twenty-four hours, from Kühlungsborn to Fehmarn, with five bars of chocolate as provisions. Stories were made of these escapes, and the refugees were made into heroes, people who had risked everything and survived. 'We made it' or 'We reached our goal', repeated over and over, like an incantation.

There was also material on many unsuccessful attempts, but I found nothing about the nameless dead, nothing anywhere. No location, no date, no grave, just a vague reference to a burial in Copenhagen. Strangely, the number fifteen cropped up here and there, fifteen unidentified victims, it was reported, washed up on the coast of Denmark. I asked myself how they could have arrived at that number. Irrespective of the often-cited estimated number of deaths — though one can assume the actual number was many times greater — these particular victims were identified as East Germans. Someone had to have seen the bodies and determined: they came *from there*. 'When our fishermen pull in their dragnets between Møn and Rügen, sometimes they find bodies among the fish. I can remember twelve dead bodies. We brought them to land and handed them over to the Forensics Institute in Copenhagen.'

That was certainly an abridgement of the matter, a restriction to the essential, as is an old harbourmaster's wont, without mention of the police, the forensic pathologists, the district attorney, and the entire thanatocratic apparatus. The bodies had to end up somewhere. There had to be files, post-mortem reports, and a grave that can be located. Maybe not a museum, but something.

First, I wrote to the Institute of Forensic Medicine at the University of Copenhagen, *Retspatologisk Afdeling*, the colourful mortuary. The answer came back right away. The incidents described in my letter were 'interesting and disturbing', but unfortunately they were not in a position to help me. All post-mortems were done by order of the police, and only they had rights to the reports. They had, therefore, to refer me to the police office of South Zealand and Lolland-Falster, Parkvej 50, Næstved. The letter was signed by Professor Hans Petter Hougen, State Pathologist, not by Sørensen, who had probably retired.

A Danish-speaking friend helped me formulate as exact a response as possible, and again an answer came right away. Allan Lappenborg from the administrative office of the South Zealand and Lolland-Falster Police Department explained that there were no cases that fit my descriptions on file in the area of his jurisdiction, an area that covered two-thirds of Denmark's southern coast. With his answer, he included the information provided by the police department's archivist, Kurt Hansen Loï, who wrote: 'I asked older colleagues who were employed here during the relevant time period. The police apparently did not pursue this matter, and probably no deaths were reported. This would confirm the harbourmaster's claim that the death reports were filed with the Forensics Institute. In any case, the police archives in Vordingborg have no death reports from the time of the GDR.'

Although the police archivist's information was more than astonishing, I decided not to write to Professor Hougen again. Instead, I wrote to various administrative offices, basically blindly, with the assumption (the hope) that there would be someone at one or more of these addresses who knew the whereabouts of the unknown dead from a vanished country, at least of the fifteen who were always included on the lists of victims.

I wrote to the German church Sankt Petri in Copenhagen, to the IEDF, the association representing the interests of former refugees from the GDR, to the Stasi Records Agency in Rostock, and to the Berlin Wall Museum at Checkpoint Charlie, as well as to the operators of certain websites that referred to the dead refugees, some of them gave the number fifteen, without date or year, just this final absence. Inevitably, I had begun to think about their *presence*, as if such a thing were possible. I had paintings by Géricault in mind, that is, I thought of the dead as physical beings, as if everything still existed in their remains: desire and need, loneliness and despair.

'The dead are waiting for us, Ed, did you know?'

'But no one ever comes. No one. Not ever.'

All in all, the conclusion was sobering. No one really knew, and the contradictions were piling up. The website operators didn't answer my questions, which I had painstakingly typed into their schoolboyish boxes under 'Contact'. The German Senior Pastor of Copenhagen had just been appointed, and promised to ask his elders in the church council. 'Where the dead are buried is something you should ask the Danish coast guard,' was the IEDF's answer. Dr Volker Höffer of the Stasi Records Agency auxiliary office in Rostock offered his support. About the fifteen unidentified dead, however, he had no information. The number fifteen was probably based on statements of Danish experts in their interior ministry's defence department, but unfortunately he no longer had a contact there. From the Berlin Wall Museum, Alexandra Hildebrandt wrote an email: her institution was also trying to track down the names of the victims buried in Bispebjerg. 'According to my research, we have no records

in our St Petri Church concerning refugees from the GDR,' wrote
Wulf D. Wätjen of the St Petri Church council. Dr Wolfgang Mayer
also wrote on behalf of the IEDF and suggested I enquire with the
German embassy in Copenhagen.

Coast guard, ministry, or embassy?

The answer from the German embassy was sent by Olaf Iversen,
who was on staff in the Ministry of Foreign Affairs: 'I contacted
the cemetery administration in Bispebjerg today. Unfortunately,
they could not give me any information about the anonymous East
German refugees.' Iversen had been in the cemetery office one day
after he received my enquiry. Once again, the St Petri Church council
member Wätjen wrote to me. He, too, had enquired at Bispebjerg
Kirkegård — there was no documentation of the burials, no entries
in the registry. One thing seemed certain: it wasn't just me, but also
the young Dane in the film, who was mistaken — the unknown dead
were not buried in Bispebjerg, neither beneath the bronze plaque in
the military cemetery, nor in the pleasant field next to it.

The embassy secretary offered to get in touch with Jesper
Clemmensen, a Danish television journalist who had written about
escapes across the Baltic Sea and had made a few films on the topic.
Two hours later, he sent notification: 'Jesper C. has written that he
speaks fluent German and would be happy to speak with you directly.'
I had Iversen's completely unrestricted helpfulness to thank for this
important contact.

I wanted Jesper Clemmensen to take me for a serious person, not
some lunatic with an idée fixe. The risk of this would remain as long
as I made calls around the world and sent emails asking *about the
dead* without any institutional support or official assignment. So I
said nothing about Sonya or Kruso, but formulated my quest more
generally — as a matter that almost explained itself and seemed
more than justified. The sentences were ready at hand, as if engraved

in a memorial plaque: to give the victims back their identities, to overcome the anonymity of statistics, to redeem the forgotten from their tragic fate and so on. This was sufficiently weighty and could not be a lie. (All you're doing is looking for Sonya, and fundamentally you're searching for G. because you will never, ever be done with this in your lifetime — because of a *promise*.) (*Longing for the dead*, you even called it that once, didn't you?)

Whether or not Jesper believed my explanation, I can't say. Likely not. Despite this (or perhaps because of it), I had great luck with him, I couldn't have found anyone better. He was on site, he knew 'a few people', he had connections, and he knew whom to call. He knew how to investigate. He spoke of 'sources' ('my source said') and 'useful information', whereas I, with the best of will, couldn't make any progress. I don't like speaking on the telephone, but with Jesper it was easy. Two months passed, during which he ploughed through his country's law enforcement and archival landscapes, including the Forensic Department and the coroner's office as well as the German national archives, before calling me on the afternoon of 23 September to tell me he knew where to find the 'Museum of the Drowned'. The only question was whether I would be admitted without a research contract or proof of kinship.

'The dead are waiting for us, Ed. What do you say to that?' Kruso had asked.

'They don't release the corpses,' Kruso had said.

My flight landed in Copenhagen in the early afternoon. My hotel was just a three-minute walk from the station. Through a large opening in the station forecourt, you could see into an underground tunnel with tracks running north. A few bicycles lay on the macadam. Someone had dropped them into the pit (overboard). The track bed was strewn with garbage and offered a squalid view compared to the square's surroundings, as if trains now rarely ran on those tracks or as

if the tracks led to another, subterranean Denmark to which no one
wanted to travel.

Our meeting was scheduled for that afternoon. Jesper had set it up
with his source. It was cold and there was a light, almost invisible rain
in the air. A few men dressed as American Indians were playing music
on the town-hall square. The chieftain's feather headdress hung down
to his feet. He wore red gloves and a fleece jacket. I tried to let myself
drift with the crowd, but didn't have the patience. I turned into a side
street, where I could walk at my own pace. The road soon opened
onto a square. At random, I chose a restaurant called Café Scandi. The
lunch buffet cost sixty-nine krone. The Café Scandi was tolerable, but
something didn't fit. The ceiling was covered with wavy metal bands
that reflected everything going on below. On the tables, lanterns shone
like navigation lights in heavy, wine-red glasses. I sat at the window so
I could look outside. The sky hung low, and it was too dark for the
time of day. My navigation light started flickering — some draft blew
from somewhere — and when I looked around, I knew: behind me,
the shaft of a dumb waiter had opened. I moved to the opposite side
of the table and looked fixedly at the two hatches. The waiter snapped
them shut with a flourish and sent the dumb waiter back down. Over
the shaft were the words *Persontransport Forbud.*

I thought of my last day on the island. I had drained the black
water from the Klausner's heating system and closed the shutters. I'd
turned off the gas from the beer pump, unhooked the tap from the
CO_2, and cleaned everything again. When I pulled the door to the
terrace closed behind me, I could hear Viola — West German radio.
I didn't feel like I was leaving someone behind. The feeling was more
serious, more final.

The address where we were to meet was Polititorvet 14, 1780
Copenhagen V, headquarters of the Rigspolitiet, the national police
force of the Kingdom of Denmark, also called the Politigården,

located to the south-west of the city centre. Because I entered the square from the opposite side, I had to walk all the way around the building.

The Politigården was a fortress, a four-storey castle built in the shape of a blunt wedge, like an ancient complex, overwhelmingly large and bright. I'd never seen anything like it before, and my first thought was: why here? I was overcome almost simultaneously with a kind of humility and solemnity. My knees went weak.

I crossed to the other side of the street as if in self-defence. A few rusty cone lamps hung over the street. There were no trees and, oddly, no traffic either. I still couldn't grasp the fact that they were lying *there*, there on the ground, in some basement, in the foundations of power on which this building was constructed, this concrete spaceship, that could swallow up all earthly things if it wanted, that was clear, even the dead, even death ... That, or something similar, is what was going through my mind.

'I have his phone number,' Jesper had written in his last email. Jesper's source worked in the Forensic Department of the Danish police force and was 'one of three on these cases' — 'one of three', he stressed, who should know, who should be informed about these things, 'one of three' in the 'Missing Department'. Jesper's translation of the words 'Department of Missing Persons' seemed plausible to me in every respect. That it was necessary to search in the *Missing Department* seemed, after so much back and forth, to be the decisive piece of information.

Jesper had explained the organisation of the archive on the telephone: not only were cases of missing persons registered in the Missing Department, but also all the unidentified dead. Even if you knew or, like the harbourmaster of Møn with his knowledge of tides and conditions, could estimate with great accuracy that the human remains on the beach or in the fishermen's nets had been refugees from East Germany, there would never have been a separate registry for them, no statement of origin, no special category — the GDR never existed in this archive's classifications, in its depositions, exhibits, and death rolls. The date and location of discovery on Danish soil, those were the indications according to which the entire system was organised. In a certain sense, the dead were submerged once again, this time in the ocean of the unidentified, the missing, the unknown — Missing Department.

According to everything I've learned and recorded in my Copenhagen notes (after a brief search, the notebook from my first trip resurfaced, and I continued it rather more conscientiously and, how should I put it, to a certain extent more responsibly than I had back then, twenty years before), the disappearance is threefold.

First: the departure. The refugee is careful not to tell anyone. He also leaves nothing behind, no goodbye letter, no sign. He leaves his identification papers and wallet behind, all to protect those close to him, that is, to absolve them of charges of complicity or aiding border violators. It's a matter of protecting mothers, fathers, sisters, and brothers from the endless interrogations, chicaneries, and prison sentences. For his first disappearance, the refugee removes all the labels from his clothing, *Malimo*, *Modedruck*, etc., evidence that could betray his eastern origins in case the grey wolves (the border patrol boats of the East German Navy) catch him out on the sea. Hours later, the refugee is missed. He becomes a missing person. Many refugees skillfully erase all traces — giving rise to no suspicions even up to the present day. The so-called 'dark figure' — no one will ever know how many of the 'missing' were refugees.

Then, the second disappearance. Diving into the sea, the escape attempt. High seas, the cold, a cramp, only water and waves, with no one informed. Therefore, no consolation and no one with them, just absolute solitude, 'what an insult, what a goddamn insult it is'. Then come the stages of drowning (asphyxiation), five stages are differentiated. Stage 1: the refugee's struggle to keep from sinking, panic reactions, most violent movements, head still above water (inspiration phase). Stage 2: apnea. The refugee is submerged and holds his breath. Stage 3: accumulation of CO_2 in his blood, which triggers inhalation in response to respiratory stimuli. Stage 4: water is drawn into the airways with air, and mixes with bronchial mucous to form a thick, white substance with small bubbles (dyspnea). Closure of the epiglottis, little movement, relative calm. Only then, caused by the lack of oxygen in the brain, do the asphyxiation cramps set in, that is: hypoxic convulsions, laceration of the respiratory musculature, the fight to survive — the refugee loses consciousness. Stage 5: exitus. The dead body on the sea bed. His aerobic metabolism has been derailed, his circulatory system has broken down, his heart has stopped.

The distance travelled underwater also belongs to the second disappearance. The dead refugee is turned onto all fours. His body drifts like a tired, snuffling dog over the seabed, his head bowed down to the ground — scraping his forehead, his knees, his hands, abrasions down to the bone, the bones stripped clean. The extremities hang down and have the effect of a boat's keel. The refugee is under way in the deep with its cold currents for some time. Then putrefaction, decomposition, gas, surfacing, disintegration: the furrows eaten away by eels, gnawing animals, creatures large and small, a constant degradation. More than a few corpses remain below and become one with the tides, part of the Baltic Sea, 'the Sea of Peace', terminus. Some are washed ashore — either on the desired or the hated coast.

Then the third disappearance.

Jesper was waiting for me under the arcades, a porch on the fortress' south side. We had barely greeted each other when his source arrived and led us up a flight of stairs to the concierge. The source was thin, surprisingly young, and had an air of an office boy about him even though he undoubtedly had a high rank. As I entered my name and address into a book and received a plastic card in return, Jesper interviewed his source. They joked, but it was more out of embarrassment as far as I could tell, without understanding a word they said. The concierge in his hutch made of brown-tinted security glass also said something I did not understand, whereupon Jesper came up to me and pinned the card on my shirt pocket. Only then did I really take in his appearance; his head was clean-shaven, and something about it moved me — the unconcealedness of his skull that suited the openness of his character (as if people only wore hair as disguise or deception), at least that's how it struck me at that moment. He wore his army-green parka zipped up to his chin; the hood stood high against his neck like a nobleman's ruff. I pictured myself reaching out and stroking his head: thank you, Jesper.

My card had the number fourteen on it, and Jesper explained that I had to return it before signing out in the concierge's book and leaving. He added that I shouldn't worry, just follow the course things would take. Only then did I realise he wasn't coming along. For a moment, I felt weak. The source touched my arm, and I glanced at the name tag on his chest: a name I can't recall, and under it the designation *consultant*.

To my surprise, the consultant did not take me into the fortress, but to another building, diagonally opposite to it, which was part of the complex of the police-department buildings on this square. It was a five-storey brick building in the Hanseatic style. One of the entrances led, like a tunnel, to the inner courtyard, where we came to a narrow snow-white door. The courtyard made a strangely civilian impression. I saw laundry hung out to dry on the balconies and a string of lights in one of the windows.

The consultant entered a code and said something to me in English. I made an indeterminate but inquisitive noise, and the door opened. In single file, we climbed down a very narrow, twisting staircase to the floor below. Then through a fire door that wasn't locked. There were small steps in the floor that you had to look out for, with steel edges and marked with black and yellow like in a factory. Air-conditioning pipes ran along the ceiling; I heard the deep thrum of a cooling unit and involuntarily thought of Rebhuhn's machine. Fear.

The room was very large, like a factory work floor. Some distance off, a small, brightly lit cubicle rose above the shelves, like the cabin on a cutter. We walked without speaking between the shelves, and I calmed down. Black slipcases, sturdy cardboard, labelled by year. Like drawers, each of these had a metal handle or a grey tab on the front, and each shelf had two or three of these cassettes stacked on top of each other. Again, I felt the urge to reach out my hand. The consultant glanced around and began calling.

When we reached the cutter cabin, he immediately veered off into the half-darkness and disappeared. A man stood in front of me as if he'd been conjured up. He introduced himself right away and asked me to follow him. He wore thin brown coveralls, and in his front pocket he had a glasses case and a voltage tester, an instrument familiar to me from my father's toolkit.

No idea where Henri Madsen (Henri or Hendrik, Madsen or Mattson — the tension was too great for me to understand it all exactly) had appeared from so suddenly, maybe he'd been amongst the shelves the entire time, maybe he'd been standing there in secret, waiting for our arrival.

First, there was a small wooden staircase with a bannister. The cutter cabin was much more spacious than I'd expected. A long desk stood under the bank of windows. It looked like a workbench. Strictly speaking, it was a workbench. Two work lamps and a computer screen. Strangely, there were also tools on it, good, clean tools, a variety of pliers, wrenches, a drill, some wire. There was another, smaller room attached to the back, without lights; his berth, I thought nonsensically.

Henri was tall and had the physique of an aged heavyweight boxer. He must have weighed over a hundred kilos. He offered me a stool next to his workbench and asked me what region I came from. Because my heart was beating in my throat, I didn't notice at first that he spoke German without the trace of an accent. When I told him, he just nodded.

'In 1945, my grandmother fled Germany with my mother, who was still a child. They were on one of the last boats to leave East Prussia and cross the Baltic Sea to Copenhagen. Lots of refugees died here after the end of the war, especially children. Some are buried in military cemeteries with names and dates whenever possible, one year, two years old, even less than a year. You'll find these graves wherever there were German soldiers, virtually all over the world. The German War Graves Commission, Mr Bendler, that means lots of money and good contracts — your dead can only dream of that, isn't that right?'

I had no idea what Madsen thought of me, how he judged me, or what he knew of my motives. He didn't smile, his expression remained closed. Nevertheless, I immediately felt I could trust him, maybe because of the tools, because he was a man of tools. And he had begun speaking without any hesitation. As if the course the next hours should take had long been clear to him.

In his family (in the *German branch*, he continued), there was a distant relationship to Friedrich von Hardenberg. His immediate ancestors had also worked in mining, as had Hardenberg, the poet. 'Our sort have always been drawn to depths,' Henri said. He began to tell me about his family. I could see that he was surprised (and delighted) that I knew who Hardenberg was, and he immediately recited a few lines from 'Hymns to the Night': 'Are you also pleased with us, dark night? What is it you hide under your mantle ...'

Hearing verses of Novalis in this basement hall from the lips of an archivist in the Missing Department was so unearthly that I had to grab onto the wood of the workbench. It was smooth and rounded, or worn away on the edges, but most importantly: it was *there*. I looked out over the rows of shelves that extended into the darkness beyond the range of sight, and answered that my parents still owned a garden plot right where Hardenberg had intended to drill his last geological bore holes, namely between Zeitz and Gera.

'Unfortunately, I hardly know East Germany,' Henri said. He opened a drawer under the workbench and pulled out a sheet of paper. (He only reached for it once, he had everything ready.) The paper was filled with signatures in several columns, written neatly one under the other. He tapped it and looked at me. His thick, blond hair was greying at the temples.

'To be honest, no one here believed that you'd come. I mean that anyone would come. After all this time.'

'It wasn't easy to find you.'

Henri shook his head slowly.

'This is an enormous building, in the centre of Copenhagen. And we were always *here*.' He pressed his hand onto the table to mark the spot again.

I felt a sense of irritation return: Missing Department of the Kingdom of Denmark. But no one in Denmark ever missed *these* dead (Madsen had called them 'your dead'). No one in this country would ever claim their bodies, no missing-person report would be filed here, no trace of anything that could lead to the refugees of those years. For them, there was nothing but this archive, Missing Department. The third disappearance.

Before I could say anything in reply, Henri stood up and turned on a light in the rear section of his cabin. 'I set up a workstation here back then, for research purposes. A reading device and a computer, a Commodore, now out of date, of course.' He touched the small grey screen and we returned to the workbench. 'When the Wall fell, I got additional capacity and drew up a list of regulations for using it. There was discussion of setting up a small reading room.' He looked out into the hall. 'Please excuse any grammatical ... My German has become rusty over the years.' He pushed a sheet of paper across the table, *Rules of Use*.

I seized the opportunity and, almost in a counteroffensive, handed him the file with Sonya's photograph and the information I had collected. He opened the file and looked at the picture for a long time.

'As I said, Mr Bendler, you're not authorised.'

He had not said this before.

'First, I'd need an official notice and a search request registered with the police department in your own country, ideally with government officials who would then get in touch with Danish government officials who, in turn, would contact my colleagues in Forensics in Vanløse. In addition, a request for access requires extensive documentation, more precise information about the presumed date of escape, serviceable photos, descriptive details if possible, and so on.'

He slowly closed my file and rested two fingers on it.

'It's a very long, very complicated way, Mr Bendler. And not everyone is suited to it, you know what I mean?'

He cleared his throat, and we looked out at the shelves for a while, together, side by side, like officers on a lost boat, standing on its useless bridge.

'What I mean is that you're the first one here in twenty-four years, who would have thought? As if no one had missed them, our dead.'

He added that of course that wasn't the case, on the contrary, not at all the case. And, in fact, it was a matter of fifty-two years, since the Wall was built. And in any case, he himself had only been down here for thirty years.

Madsen had got to his feet.

My visit was over.

I wanted to stand up, too, but his hand prevented me. More: it lay heavily on my shoulder, two or three long seconds, as heavy as a rock.

He began a brief speech, which he evidently needed to deliver standing. His head almost touched the cabin ceiling. 'Thirty years and never any cause for complaint, Mr Bendler!'

Point by point, Madsen recounted the variable history of the Department of Missing Persons, which had, as he put it, three full-value co-workers, three good, indeed, excellent policemen with offices in Vanløse. There was no archivist. They never had one, just him in his role of technician. Monitoring all the spaces, especially the ventilation and air conditioning, required a great deal of attention, which is why he set his workroom up down here, with the dead, from the very beginning, at least that was the main reason back then. Over the years, he gradually got used to the circumstances. Through the evacuations, renovations, installation of new storage racks, reordering the files in boxes made of acid-free cardboard, and so on, he had, more or less perforce, acquired proficiency in the organisation and contents of this peculiar collection, and he had been under its spell — there was no other way to put it — ever since, to that very day, in fact.

'The nameless seem suspicious simply because of their anonymity — is that not unjust, Mr Bendler? Earlier, seamen wore complicated tattoos and rings so they could be identified if they washed ashore. Even back then, people knew how bleak it was to be one of the unknown dead in this world. A person without a name is not trusted, worse, he or she is considered repellent and ugly. No name means no origins, no family, neither mother nor father, and so they lie here on the shelves like links severed from a chain. They're still here, but they're lost. This basement is now their only homeland, Mr Bendler, their final home. And in a certain sense, I'm all they've got, the only one who still knows them not by name, but from photographs, reports, a few objects.'

Madsen cleared his throat and paused. His silence wasn't coincidence, but rather a moment of silence. I was neither embarrassed nor nervous, the silence did me good. There was a rumble of thunder from somewhere, perhaps a truck driving by on the street that circled the blunt wedge of the fortress.

In order to better understand what he as caretaker had been entrusted with, Madsen continued, he had secretly and on his own initiative begun to educate himself in all associated areas, criminology, forensics, examination of evidence. He used his time well and — not to make himself seem as important as a caretaker could possibly be in this world — now it was *he* who had the most exact and thorough knowledge of this archive and its contents.

Madsen reached for the voltage tester in his coverall pocket (for his heart, I thought) and glanced at the instrument as if he had to quickly make sure everything he needed was at hand.

'Twenty-four years, fifty-two years, that's simply too long a period of time. No set of usage rules lasts that long, I mean — without users. That's what I mean, Mr Bendler. But I'm just the caretaker here. I, too, am *unauthorised*, you understand?'

I nodded. I understood that he saw me as a kind of envoy, a delegate, a man for all his dead.

'Please wait here and please help yourself.'

He gestured toward a plate of biscuits with a thermos and two plastic cups next to it.

He turned in the doorway.

'With Novalis, the dead are the good ones, Mr Bendler!' Then the sound of his feet on the stairs.

Out in the room, a frenzy of flashing lights set in, a few hundred fluorescent bulbs flickered on. From my place on the bridge, I could see Henri combing the aisles. There was something off with his gait; a slight limp or just the sway of his weight. He pushed a kind of serving trolley in front of him with just the sheet of paper on it at first. The trolley made a deafening rattle on the stone floor, but the more Henri reached into the shelves the quieter it travelled along the aisles.

After a time, he passed the bridge again. He looked up at me and called out: 'Biscuits, Mr Bendler, help yourself to some biscuits!' Then he turned right into the more modern section of the archive.

Four or five enormous grey filing cabinets slid over the floor with a soft murmur. Madsen touched them lightly (evidently there was a keyboard) and they began to move faster like a caravan of steel elephants. The workbench vibrated and the Commodore PC crackled. Madsen moved between these monsters without haste, he was their tamer with brown coveralls and raised arms, and it was a miracle they didn't crush him, or rather it was no miracle when you saw how elegantly the tall, heavy-set man glided through the narrow lanes. Now and again, there was a light, almost childlike lilt to his hips, and each turn was like a caress with a tender decisiveness. With each extension of his hand, another slipcase landed on his trolley

All the convictions I'd carried with me on my trip vanished in that moment. I felt no trace of the loyalty that had perhaps only been a sense of duty, fed by an old guilt now barely measurable, no trace of the thrill of the promise and the will to keep it come what may, proof of *being worth it*, being worth the friendship — none of it played a role any longer. Just this moment of clear beauty, this — what else to call it — dance of death. As if I had come to this underground box only for this, an audience of one man in thirty years.

Not just for Novalis, but also for Trakl, were the dead the good ones — I grasped it that very instant. Trakl was not just trauma, he was also longing. I wondered if it would be possible for me to get to the exit without being seen, if the code was necessary on the inside, too, if I could find the way upstairs without the source.

No idea how what followed could be part of any report. When I picked up my Copenhagen notebook again in those days, I thought it was more likely that *someone else* who was interested in all this had written it, not me. Someone had noted it down hastily over several pages, like this:

- Foot in shoe, rotted stumps. As if bones had been bitten off, M.: tennis shoes act like life jacket. Rest of corpse missing
- Woman: no lips, no nose, face just teeth, arms black, covered with algae, M.: algae groundcover
- Male torso: full of holes, as if shot. Eels, says M., usual animal bite marks
- Woman like a rubber doll, bloated, fringes, shiny. M.: corpse wax, adipocere
- Woman with bare skull, worn away, abraded, skin on all sides, M.: scrape marks, abrasions, face against the ground

- Man in coat, white bubbles on his mouth, M.: foam from lungs
- Man with tree root on chest, black, like a tattoo, M.: subcutaneous hypostasis
- Person, gender unidentifiable, no contour, M.: boat propeller, shredded, disintegrated. 20 pages of text, photos, overview and details
- Male torso, M.: head and arm 4 km away, photographs of places of recovery, dismembered by animal bites, eaten, perhaps scattered by stray dogs.

And so on.

That's how it was written, but I don't remember it. Only what was said. Madsen's talk was like a sound you hear in a dream. Sentence after sentence, without words. We all dreamt this sound: Madsen, the dead, and I. There was no message, no communication in it. It simply sounded in everything. It was in the half-darkness of the hall, in the labyrinth of shelves, in the photographs on the work bench, and only then did something that was said surface clearly.

'Imagine, Ed, they lived down there. They sit at tables, they go on walks, they're free, they're all *free*.'

'All these corpses, Ed, it was if they were gliding by in the darkness, precious, as if they were alive or holy.'

I counted four green lights. Those were the emergency exits, two at each end of the hall. Every dream had to have an emergency exit or it wasn't a dream. On the other hand, there were dreams of great clarity, dreams in which everything fit together, incredibly authentic.

First, I recognised the shirt. He had worn it in the picture taken at the opening of the 1989 season. Then the gap between his front teeth. Then his hair, blond hair, strangely undamaged (angelic — the word was there without my having thought it up, and although I tried to erase it from my mind immediately I couldn't get rid of it). His body, however, was blackened and bloated. Still, you could tell the deceased had been a thin, lanky man. Speiche.

To make sure, I asked Madsen to translate the entire post-mortem and the police report. He understood that I had happened on something, someone I had found but hadn't been looking for, but had found. His trouble had been worth it.

He gave me a shred of Speiche's shirt glued onto cardboard (the clothing card, Madsen said) and a bundle of hair as thick as a pencil in aluminium foil. A number was written on the heading of his file and I asked Madsen about it.

'That's the number of his grave. His number in the row grave.'

'What does that mean, the row grave?'

'That's what we call the graveyards of the unidentified dead.'

'Why row?'

'The deceased are buried in rows. That way they can always be found using the coordinates in this number. It indicates the exact location where the body is buried. As you know, there are no gravestones on graves of the unidentified, no cross, just grass, nothing else.'

'The bodies aren't cremated?'

'No. The deceased are waiting, after a fashion. I mean, on the chance that someone might come to claim their remains. Their graves are kept indefinitely, and these files here, too, are kept forever — not a single case is considered closed as long as we don't have a name. At first, the bodies lie in dormitories in the forensics department, minus twenty degrees Celsius. Some for an entire year or longer. That has happened. At some point, they're taken back to where they were found.'

'Taken back?'

'To where they washed ashore — the community is responsible for them, that's the law. Stege was for *them*, the row graves in Stege, the largest town on Møn.'

Freed from the narrow shelves, the files gave off peculiar fumes that clouded my awareness. It wasn't the musty smell of age, nor the smell of glue or decay, no — the paper smelled ill. I breathed, in and out, that was the essential thing in this world, breathing evenly in and out. The dead were not lying at rest in Copenhagen, not in the

Bispebjerg Kirkegård. In Copenhagen, they were given a post-mortem and all the files and reports stayed there. They themselves, however, travelled back to the sea, they were buried in the sea, provisionally, invisible, in a row.

Copenhagen gave the impression of being an all-around solid city. The houses on the waterfront were built of brick, high-fired, Nordic. Now and then, a herd of broken-down bicycles leaning against the wall of a house, timidly huddled together, like some kind of animal that had found no bolthole. Twilight was falling, lit windows that fill one with longing even though the surroundings are foreign. I recognised the old longing for caves, for solitary happiness, hidden away in these rooms, at this table, in the light of this lamp, under which you can finally feel at peace, far removed from everyone and everything. After recognising Speiche, I concentrated all my willpower on one single point and told Madsen that I would like to come again — tomorrow, the day after, the day after that.

I walked aimlessly for two or three hours, and darkness had fallen when I went in to a café called La Esquina. I ordered something, pulled out my notebook, and started recording everything, all that I'd seen and heard that afternoon. In the end, I even wrote down the name of the café and the address (Ryesgade 76) and that there were deer heads mounted on the walls from which the menus hung, and so on — all mechanically recorded. I looked around the café, at the counters and the people sitting outside, because I knew that I had to write it all down for myself. It was hard to set the pencil down, my wrist was stiff, but I kept writing, my fingers cramped, but I kept writing, I scratched line after line into the paper, all of Copenhagen, without a single thought.

In the back room of La Esquina, there was a hairdressing salon, doubtless the café's key feature. Through a glass door on which the outline of giant scissors had been glued, you could see the hairdresser at work. I had just begun to eat a sandwich (sandwich in one hand, pen in the other) when the hairdresser closed her shop. She had her coat on and was holding a small plastic garbage bag. She knelt down (very elegantly) and tried to fasten the tie, but she couldn't manage it. When she passed my table, I saw that the bag was full of hair — overflowing with hair.

She was still in the doorway when I caught up with her, but I couldn't make it to some corner or even a metre away from her in time. To be precise, I threw up right at her feet. A young hairdresser, she had just finished work, was nicely dressed (and surely had plans to meet someone for dinner, a movie, a concert, or whatever), and I stumbled after her and vomited at her feet, her and me and her bag full of hair, this tangled mess, this tangled, blotchy hairball, this spotted, snarled clump of human detritus. She gave a little cry in Danish, a kind of raspy 'ay' sound, and called something into the café. As I threw up, I roared at her. In my mind, I roared at her and at the street, I roared into the Copenhagen night: Why are you bringing these corpses to my table? What was I supposed to do with these corpses? What?

Months later, before I started writing this report, I saw the dead in a dream. They stood on my path in their fragmentary, almost indescribable condition (post-mortems resemble descriptions of paintings, Madsen had said), asking after their own names. Am I called Boat Propeller? Is my name Rubber Doll? Or is my name Walter? Or Monika? In my dream, it was as if the answer had to be found *now*, as if it were the last opportunity before the dead would retreat from the path, leaving no questions, no traces, as if they had never existed.

But I had left Denmark. I did not return to the archive. From my report, it's clear how unsuited I was for it all, how little I measured up to the task. A report full with negligible details, feelings, and thoughts noted down where facts were essential.

There were other reasons as well. I had entered their space, the territory of the dead. By chance it was I, and writing was my defence, my shield, my cloak of invisibility — without my notebook, I would have seen nothing. *They* had not chosen me for this, nor had anyone else, I was aware of this. I was no researcher, no historian, I was not familiar with the ways of working through the past. I had simply followed a promise, the law of friendship, if you'd like, that's all it was to start with: Kruso's request. And only that. But then I'd crossed a line with the expression 'the third disappearance', when I began to think *just so*.

Nonetheless, my reason returned as I wrote, and the dull burning in my stomach lessened. I went to the shed that lay at some distance from my house. I hadn't entered it for a long time. A rotting carpet of pine needles lay in front of the door. After a while, I found what I was looking for, a pale-yellow postal box on a shelf full of children's toys, bits of technological devices, fitness equipment that had never been used. A muffled sorrow hung over it all, stale and persistent. I opened the box. There was a large sticky moth cocoon in the jumper, and the suede shoes looked like they were covered with mould. I was wearing both when I left the island, and wore them later, too. In the bag's inner lining, I found Speiche's glasses — when I lay ill in the Klausner, I'd stuffed them in there at some point, and had not thought of them again, not for a second.

Keeping these things could not have been anything more than an attempt to hide the fact from myself that I had used and worn out a few things that weren't mine. If Speiche ever showed up one day, then I'd be able to ... This or something along these lines must be what the person I was back then had thought for a short time, before he forgot the box all together.

Although my actions were (to a certain extent) the opposite, I felt like a graverobber when I entered the cemetery with the box under my arm. I had just put the box down when someone behind me began calling in Russian. I didn't look around, but the man came closer. He was wearing a uniform, his coat was open, and without a doubt he was drunk. I hastily assembled the remains of my schoolboy Russian (maybe twelve words, occasionally more) but didn't use them. 'Not drink, fascist!' The Russian grabbed my arm and led me across the cemetery, past the golem, and over the long, sodden paths, to the grave that belong to him. He pointed at it.

There were three of them, two women and him. The women wore coats and scarves over their heads, the older one had felt boots on her feet. They sat on a small sheet of plastic. A dishcloth was spread over the lower half of the grave on which chocolate, ham, and cigarettes had been spread out. A tin can was leaning against the headstone. 'Drink-drink, comrade, five minutes — no fascist!' He sliced his hand through the air in front of my chest, and with that it was decided. The vodka was called Parliament. They'd even brought glasses with gold rims. The soldier poured the first swallow in the grave's upper-right-hand corner, next to the headstone. Then he lit two cigarettes. He stuck one in the grave, and it slowly burned down. The women spoke to the deceased, stroking the earth and blowing on the cigarette's embers. Now and then, they whimpered softly, a kind of weeping that lasted a few seconds, then vodka again. The Russian nodded off. He looked satisfied. I stood up and said goodbye to the women — I believe I even bowed — and went back to my grave. I was happy to have been 'no fascist' and probably was drunk.

I took the things out of the box one by one and wiped them off, at least provisionally. They'd served me well, yes, back when I had really needed them. 'Really needed,' I whispered to myself, and suddenly felt boundless gratitude streaming through me beneficially. Maybe it had nothing to do with Speiche anymore. For an imponderable moment, I saw my life as a whole, as one long story tied to these items, yes, at this moment they were the most exact expression of everything that had happened leading up to this day, this hour, this place: a pair of mouldy shoes, a bundle of wool, and a pair of spectacles with just one lens.

'Forgive me, please forgive me.' At some point, I began my speech. First, I apologised to Kruso — for not standing firm. I explained it to him. I tried not to leave anything out. I tried to summarise it all: fear and a crazy revulsion (revulsion for the dead) on the one hand, grief and a crazy sympathy (sympathy for the dead) on the other. Suddenly, I could speak. Because I was drunk, I added a few sentences I hadn't planned, that I hadn't ever spoken aloud before, about things that concerned only the two of us, Losh and me, *we two*. The tears weren't planned either. Finally, I asked Kruso's permission for *the thing with Speiche*. I explained what I'd planned to do (it was closely associated — Speiche, 'the one from the home', the orphan, at some point it had become clear to me that he had no relatives, that there would be no one other than me, his successor as dishwasher in the Klausner) and why it wouldn't stain Valentina Krusowitsch's memory or Sonya's memory (that's how I formulated it), on the contrary. I could now be here regularly and *take charge* as I'd promised. This would be the right place for the Found Department. Then I apologised to Speiche himself, first for taking his sweater and shoes. Then, as representative, for the slander, the mockery (Orphan Child, flunky, loser), all the mean-spirited jokes about someone who was, as Kruso put it, 'unsuitable above and beyond that as well'.

Over the course of autumn, Wulf D. Wätjen from the church council in Copenhagen had written again. 'I am still very sorry that I was not able to help you in your search ...' his letter began, and I have to admit that I was touched by this sentence. In the Danish newspaper *Politiken*, he had read about a project initiated by the Berlin Wall Museum. It was about GDR refugees who had fled to Denmark. The Museum had commissioned Jesper Clemmensen, the author of the recently published book *Flugtrute Østersøen*, to collect objects, names, and other details. Contact with the Berlin Wall Museum, Wätjen suggested, might help me make progress. I telephoned Jesper again, and he told me that the people in Berlin first wanted to pull together the *relevant applications* to find funding for the project. I pressed the receiver more tightly to my ear and claimed I was positive there would be funding for it, no end of money, 'what else would it be for, Jesper?'

The Russian cemetery was renovated that spring. The graves shine like new. The cemetery gates have been repainted as well (the two Soviet stars are now grey), and a stronger fence built to keep out the wild boar that rule the area.

I usually just sit by the grave, and nothing much occurs to me. No *hymns*, no *psalms*. The woods are silent or they rustle with the old sentences.

'The dead are waiting for us, Ed. What do you say to that?'

or

'Think of the green light.'

or

'Wait here long enough and don't go anywhere.'

'I promise,' I murmur, and eventually Speiche and I start talking about the Klausner, work in the dishwashing station, ladles, Viola, Chef Mike, and something that could only be found there, on the island, and only at that time. And why he still had to try, why there had been no other way for him.

When I have time, I stop on my way home at a diner called Rita's, a shack on Highway 2, halfway to my house. There is a sawmill and a decommissioned railway station named Nesselgrund. And there is a turning area for lorries — actually, it's just a very large open space, nothing but sand, three kilometres outside of Potsdam.

ACKNOWLEDGEMENTS

I would like to thank my co-workers at the Klausner, Jörg Schieke, Anke Schmidt, Ramona Zynda, and Viktor Zynda for answering countless questions. For conversations and suggestions, I am grateful to Friedrich Christian Delius, Ralf Eichberg, Gerd Püschel, and Dirk Uhlig. Thank you to Friedrich Dethlefs of the West German Radio archives for providing me quickly and easily with historical recordings. Rebecca Elsäßer, Henriette Seibold, and Antje Wischmann offered valuable assistance with my research for the epilogue. I owe special thanks to Jesper Clemmensen, without whose helpfulness I would not have found the 'Missing Department'.

The books *Über die Ostsee in die Freiheit* (Freedom Lies Across the Baltic) and *Hinter dem Horizont liegt die Freiheit* (Freedom Lies over the Horizon) by Christine Vogt-Müller and Bodo Müller, as well as *Flugtrute Østersøen* (Escape Route: Baltic Sea) by Jesper Clemmensen, provided me with much useful information. László F. Földényi's thoughts on *Perspektiven der Freiheit* (Aspects of Freedom) in Europe after 1989 still gives me food for thought.

The poem 'Melopee' (Recitative) by the Flemish poet Paul

van Ostaijen was quoted in Klaus Reichert's translation. Various quotations from *Robinson Crusoe* by Daniel Defoe are in Anna Tuhten's translation in the 1950 Reclam (Leipzig) edition. Antonin Artaud is cited in Elena Kapralik's translation. Georg Trakl's poems were taken from Franz Fühmann's volume *Vor Feuerschlünden. Erfahrungen mit Georg Trakls Gedicht* (At the Burning Abyss. Experiencing the Georg Trakl Poems), Hinstorff Verlag, 1984. Lines from Edgar's verse hoard that surface in the text come from the writings of Jürgen Becker, Friedrich Nietzsche, Gottfried Benn, and Peter Huchel. Individual sentences were also taken from Fyodor Dostoevsky, Marguerite Duras, Don DeLillo, Thomas More, and the Old Testament, as well as from news and weather reports on West German radio.

Translator's note. All quotes listed in the acknowledgements are in my translations from the originals, except for the quote from Dostoevsky, which is from Constance Garnett's translation of *Crime and Punishment.* Franz Fühmann's book on Georg Trakl's poetry will appear in English in 2017, translated by Isabel Coles for Seagull Books. I would like to thank Lutz Seiler, the Europäisches Übersetzer-Kollegium in Straelen, and Dr Renate Birkenhauer for their invaluable help with this translation.